ALMOST
DOESN'T
COUNT

Also by Angela Winters

View Park

Never Enough

No More Good

A Price to Pay

Gone Too Far

Back on Top

www.angelawinters.com

Published by Dafina Books

ALMOST DOESN'T COUNT

ANGELA WINTERS

Dafina
Books

KENSINGTON BOOKS
http://www.kensingtonbooks.com

ISBN-13: 978-0-7582-5935-6
ISBN-10: 0-7582-5935-2

First printing: September 2012

10 9 8 7 6 5 4 3 2 1

Printed in the United States of America

This book is dedicated to all my faithful readers who have continued to follow me through new doors.

ALMOST DOESN'T COUNT

1

Sherise Robinson wasn't sure how long she'd been staring out the window of her Georgetown townhouse's living room onto the street, but her baby girl, Cady, was not happy at the lack of attention and pulled on her mommy's shorts.

"Mah!" she yelled.

Sherise broke from her trance and looked down at her fifteen-month-old sitting next to her on the sofa. She had that adorable little frown on her perfect chocolate brown face. Her tiny nose was turned up and her little lips pressed together. She was not pleased.

"Sorry, baby." Sherise smiled and leaned down. She kissed her on the forehead.

"Play," Cady added, handing her mother a tiny stuffed panda bear.

Sherise took the bear and did what she thought her baby wanted. She gently pressed the bear's face against Cady's and Cady made a kissing sound.

"Is this your baby?" she asked. "Do you love your panda baby?"

Cady nodded and giggled. She pressed a tiny squeeze ball in her hands. This wasn't one of her toys. It was a stress ball her mother used to use when work got to her and she needed to calm down. But Little Grabby Hands, which she called Cady, had gotten her hands on it and never let it go.

Didn't matter much, Sherise thought with a sigh. She didn't need it anymore. Except for dealing with the adorable little handful sitting next to her, life was not terribly stressful for her anymore. Six months ago, a series of near-disastrous events urged Sherise to make the hardest decision of her life. This go-getter, who was born to compete and achieve, quit her job, turned her back on a powerful promotion on the Domestic Policy Council for the White House, and became a stay-at-home mom.

She was only twenty-eight. Her life was not over. She was still married to the man she loved, Justin Robinson, a powerful lobbyist, despite making every mistake possible that could cost a woman her husband. In fact, saving her marriage was the reason she decided to give up the career that she had often put first in her life.

Known as a relentless competitor, someone who excelled in office-place politics and games, Sherise had dreams of reaching the top of the power circles in DC. Having come from one of the worst neighborhoods on the southeast side, she fought hard against the odds to make it to assistant director of communications for the Domestic Policy Council.

Sherise had also sought out the perfect husband with great connections. Justin was a recent Georgetown law grad when she met him, but she knew he was already connected and would do wonders for her career in DC. She also knew that although she was very attracted to the tall, handsome, bookish brother, he wasn't so overwhelming that she would lose her head when it came to him. He was trustworthy and controllable.

After having Cady, Sherise had reluctantly taken six months off, instead of the usual twelve weeks, to please Justin, who had actually wanted her to stop working altogether. Although she loved her daughter more than anything, it was torture for Sherise to be out of the loop and not in control. When she finally went back, Sherise was so caught up in the game and a chance to take over when her boss announced he was leaving, she wasn't careful. She made a terrible mistake and fell into the bed of a sexy and powerful man, Jonah Dolan. A man who turned out to be as vindictive and hateful as he was tantalizing and seductive.

Almost getting found out was what made Sherise decide to give everything up and refocus her life on what mattered. When her friend Erica's boyfriend, Terrell, had discovered them and threatened to expose their affair in order to extort Jonah, Sherise was reminded of how much she loved Justin and couldn't live without him. Justin never found out, but he'd known something was wrong. He'd wanted his wife back and she'd given up everything else to be a better wife to him and a mother to their baby.

Looking down at Cady as she mumbled incoherently in a conversation with a tiny plastic pink horse, she smiled from ear to ear. She loved this little girl more than anything and couldn't imagine depriving her of a life without a father. That was the life that Sherise had and she didn't want that for her baby. Justin loved Cady and Cady needed him.

Yes, it was true that Cady might not even be his. Jonah wasn't Sherise's first infidelity. She had allowed herself to get too close to Ryan Hodgkins, a successful architect. She had been trying to make her way into the black elite social circles, but had found herself unable to fight her attraction to this married man. They'd spent one night together before Sherise came to her senses and ended it. She found out she was pregnant a month later, but had always been too afraid to find out if Ryan was Cady's father.

But things were worse now. After six months of trying for a second baby, something she and Justin wanted very much, she wasn't pregnant and Sherise was beginning to wonder if Justin could even get her pregnant. It broke her heart, but with every month that passed with no pregnancy, Sherise was becoming more convinced that Cady might not be Justin's, and she was afraid of what would come out if Justin started to suspect as well.

This was all made worse by the fact that Justin was starting to get so disillusioned with the whole situation that he wasn't initiating sex the way he used to. It was as if he was losing interest in her, and that was a foreign concept to Sherise. She was an exceptionally beautiful woman by anyone's standards.

A little taller than the average woman, but not too tall, she was a stunner. She had flawless, golden caramel skin, silky dark brown hair that went a couple of inches below her shoulders, high cheekbones, full, sultry lips, and piercing green eyes. She was fit and trim, but had killer curves that made her look incredible in the expensive designer clothes she always wore. Everywhere Sherise went, women and men looked . . . more than once. Most men wanted her and most women hated her for it.

She had always been able to control Justin and he could not resist her. The problem was that after being out of the career game for so long, Sherise was losing interest in most things, except her daughter, so she wasn't sure if she was the reason their sex life was cooling down, or him.

"Dooce!" Cady yelled. She squeezed her fingers together and smiled up at her mother with those large eyes that always got her what she wanted.

"No juice," Sherise said. "Too much sugar. Water?"

Cady pouted, seeming to understand that she wasn't getting any juice. She folded her tiny arms across her chest, looking almost edible in her little pink and white polka-dot dress. But Sherise wasn't going to give in. She wanted only the best for her daughter and that didn't just mean healthy food and drinks. She wanted a life for her daughter that included a happily married mother and father.

She had to figure out how to get pregnant. Sherise had spent a lot of time in the last six months convincing herself that if she got pregnant she wouldn't miss the world of power brokers and fast-paced deal making. She would have a baby to take care of and another to plan for. Eventually, she would go back to work, but in the meantime, two babies would keep her more than busy and satisfied. At least that was what she tried to convince herself of. It wasn't really working.

"So sorry. So sorry." Jackson Snow apologized to the other two people at his lunch table at Birch & Barley restaurant on Fourteenth Street just as he got off the phone. He placed it on the table next to him and looked across the pan-roasted fish and Yukon potatoes in parmesan broth. "So where were we?"

Thirty-year-old petite and adorable Billie Carter, formerly Billie Hass, wasn't really sure how to answer that. They had barely been able to get through a conversation, with Jackson answering the phone every five minutes. It wasn't a surprise. This was a lawyer's life, and being a newly minted partner at their firm, Jackson was smart to never pass on a phone call. It was a double standard, because if either she or her fellow associate, Richard Nelson, interrupted him to take a phone call, it would not be looked upon kindly.

"You were congratulating Billie on her work on the Bosley case," Richard interjected. Richard, who went by Ricardo in his private life, was a young, handsome Hispanic man who was always impeccably dressed. His rigid professional demeanor hid the ultraliberal interior that Billie had come to appreciate so much.

He looked at Billie and winked. He knew it would have been awkward for her to remind Jackson to continue praising her, so he did it for her. She would do that for him. He was the only person at their large law firm that she could trust, although she hadn't really tried hard to give others a chance.

Reeling from a divorce that left her in a bad financial state, Billie had to leave her position at the public defender's office and her dream of fighting for the voiceless against a powerful system and transition to a big law firm where most of her clients were the people she had built a career fighting against. She needed the money, so she decided to swallow her pride and take the high-paying associate position, hoping that one day she could be in a position to go back to doing what she loved.

It hadn't been the easiest of transitions, especially considering all of the distractions she had, including her ex-husband having one of the paralegals spy on her, but Billie hunkered down and did her best. Richard, whom she shared an office with, had helped her navigate the office politics and deal with the moral ambiguity of what she had to do at times. There was a short moment when he had tried to flash those Latin charms on her, but they had both thought better of it. It was a good idea. As friends, they had both been able to help each other focus on their jobs without any distractions. It was paying off.

"Yes," Jackson said as he reached for a fork. After stuffing a bit of fish in his mouth, he pointed at Billie with a smile across his generous face. "I don't give credit just for the sake of looking like a good guy. You made me look good on this case. The client is very pleased with the settlement. We avoided all kinds of embarrassment for them."

Billie smiled even though she wasn't so sure that was a compliment. Their client's product hurt a little boy. In a previous life, their embarrassment was the least of what she would have expected. But this was the law and her job was to protect her client to the best of her ability. A settlement that included a nondisclosure agreement saved them millions of dollars and preserved their reputation with time to remove the chance that anyone else would ever get hurt was a win.

"I'm sure we've secured their business for the future," Billie said with a smile. "I'm glad I could contribute."

"Oh, you did more than that." Jackson looked around and

waved to someone in the distance. "That guy over there, he's an asshole, but his wife is cheating on him, so it's all good."

Richard laughed along with Jackson, but Billie only forced a half smile. As someone who had her marriage destroyed by infidelity, she didn't really get the joke.

"You," Jackson said, returning his attention to Billie. "You got a good mention at this morning's partner meeting."

"That is good to hear, sir," Billie said.

She had been planning for this. She felt now was the best time to ask for what she wanted, to ask for one of the reasons she chose this firm over the others she could have gone to.

"Actually, I was wondering if . . ."

"You know who else was mentioned?" Jackson asked. "Your husband, Porter."

Billie sighed. "Porter Hass is my ex-husband, Jackson. Ex."

"Oh, yeah." He nodded. "That's what I meant. He should have made partner by now, so some people were wondering if he was gonna move on."

"I wouldn't know," Billie said.

She hated talking about Porter, but he was one of the most talked about financial lawyers in DC, and more than a few people at her firm were fans of his. She always managed to cut any questions about him short, but that didn't stop them from popping back up every now and then. They were divorced for a year now and she wished that people would let it go.

The truth was, she was the reason Porter hadn't made partner this year, but it was too long and embarrassing a story to ever tell anyone. Despite their divorce, his decision to move his mistress in with him, and using his daughter as a tool to control Billie, she couldn't get him out of her life. He even threatened to ruin her career if she cut him off from her bed. But with the help of her friends, Sherise and Erica, Billie finally turned the tables on Porter and put him in his place.

With Sherise using her influence on Jonah, some powerful

strings were pulled that put Porter in a bad light at his firm. While the last soft spot Billie held for him urged her to save his career, it did push his progress back a year and gave Billie the courage to get over Porter once and for all.

But she would never tell anyone that. No one knew what had happened except her, the girls, and Jonah Dolan, and hopefully no one else ever would. Billie was still dealing with the guilt, never one to take the underhanded route, but she knew that she had to get Porter out of her life if she was ever going to have a life of her own.

Her progress since had been slow, but she was hopeful.

"I was hoping I could ask for a pro—"

"I know what you want," Jackson interrupted her. "And I think you've earned it."

"Billie is getting a pro bono case?" Richard asked, smiling proudly at her.

Jackson nodded. "It's about time, don't ya think?"

"Yes," she said. "I do. I'm—"

"No problem," he said. "I'll have Allison give you the file when we get back. Look it's . . . ."

He jumped up from his seat to greet an older man walking by in a suit that had to cost at least five thousand dollars. The older man barely acknowledged him, but Jackson, the ever-eager networker, returned to his seat with a smile of pure joy and accomplishment.

Billie smiled, thinking that Sherise would like this guy. He was a lot like her; at least how she used to be. "You were saying?"

Jackson took a moment to focus before adding, "Yes, the case is some guy who . . . I don't know . . . He runs a home-less shelter or something and got hit with some violations that he needs to fight."

Billie's eyes widened with anticipation. She was excited. Finally, she could get a taste of the life she used to have, fighting the power. At one point, she was going to ride that life to political office. Now, she wasn't so sure where she could go with it, but this news warmed her heart. She was going to do more than get paid to do her job. She was about to do some good.

Twenty-six-year-old Erica Kent was rushing like mad through the communications department of the Pentagon building. The director, whom she worked for as an assistant, had a press conference in ten minutes and had just demanded several changes to the release that would accompany the conference. The job had been slapped on her desk and she typed at her computer as fast and furiously as she could. She made sure not to make a mistake because she had made one before—a spelling error that caused the director to accidentally mispronounce a word. After being yelled at for an hour, Erica learned her lesson fast. No more mistakes.

Rushing over to the printer, she leaned over the machine, waiting for the release to print out perfectly on letterhead. She caught a glimpse of herself in the window's reflection. You could tell she'd had a hectic day. While her fair skin still looked fresh and vibrant, her large brown eyes look tired with dark circles underneath. Her natural curly, auburn hair was going in several directions. She raised her hand to smooth it out a little, but the first copy was printing and she forgot all about herself. She snatched it and read furiously as she rushed back to her desk.

"Erica!"

The familiar voice of the director's main assistant, Jo Lemmons, got on Erica's nerve, but she was ready for her.

"Is it ready?" she asked, more in the tone of a demand, as she reached Erica's desk. "Now."

"It is," Erica said confidently as she handed the press release to her. "I'll print off twenty-five copies right—"

"Fifty," Jo said. She turned to leave, before turning back. "Bring them to the conference room ASAP. And if there is a mistake . . ."

"There are no mistakes!" Erica yelled after her as she rushed down the hallway.

In less than a minute after printing, Erica had delivered the press releases and returned to her desk. Her healthy, curvy frame made a thud as she fell back in her seat, sighing. She wanted to rest, needed to rest, but knew she had to e-mail tons of copies of those releases out.

She had been in this job for almost six months and it wasn't getting easier. She knew she'd rather things be crazy than boring, but sometimes she was just so exhausted. At least she had tonight with her girls to look forward to.

Leaning forward on her desk, Erica noticed something new. Despite the madness that this department was, she always kept her desk orderly. It was essential to her staying focused and not getting tripped up. A neat desk was an error-free desk. But now there was a little off-white envelope laying in the middle of her desk with her name written on it in cursive. It hadn't been there before she left, so someone had placed it there in just the few minutes she had run to deliver the releases.

Erica looked around. No one was paying attention to her. Everyone who wasn't at the press conference was focused on their work. She had worked at the Pentagon in Arlington, Virginia, for years in different departments, and this was the most professional one she'd ever been in. Usually, the assistants would gossip and take coffee breaks to give them a rest from their demanding directors, but not this group. Everyone was all work, all the time. Erica actually preferred it this way. She didn't want to be all up in people's business and she didn't like people all up in hers. Especially considering the secrets she had.

Erica opened the envelope and noticed the handwriting looked familiar.

Jonah would like to have lunch with you in his office tomorrow.

—Jenna

Jenna was the main assistant to Jonah Dolan, the deputy assistant secretary of defense. He was also the man who, just six months ago, Erica found out was her father. It had been a disaster.

Erica had been happy with her life. She was dating Terrell Nicolli, her boyfriend of four years. He had proposed to her the same day she'd found out she was getting a new job with Dolan's office. Dolan was a powerful and influential man, one that many people thought could be president if he wanted to.

Erica never suspected Jonah was her father. She had been told by her mother that her father was an absent man in the lives of her and her brother, Nate. She had seen the man once, whom she knew now to be only Nate's father. Her mother died from cancer when Erica was only nineteen years old and Nate was twelve. She had been struggling ever since, but was making a life for herself and Nate, and eventually Terrell. The position in Jonah's office was more money and a great opportunity for her future.

Jonah was too nice to her from day one and he seemed to like her very much. At first she thought he might have some sexual interest in her, but he made it clear that was not the case early on. But his interest in her future and his disapproval of Terrell in her life still seemed a bit too personal, especially for someone like Erica, who had problems trusting others.

Terrell, angry at Jonah's attempts to cut him out of Erica's life, was the first to find out that Jonah was Erica's father. He'd found out that Jonah and Erica's mother had a brief affair the summer before Jonah left for the military. They had not kept in touch. Earlier that year, Jonah had found out about Erica and made an attempt to bring her into his life without letting on who she was to him. Only his wife, a cold woman named

Juliet, knew and she demanded that Jonah keep this relationship a secret.

Erica's heart was broken when she found out that Terrell had gone back to his old ways of hustling any chance he got when he tried to blackmail Jonah over his affair with Sherise. This led to the discovery of Jonah's real relationship with Erica. Erica was dismayed and beyond upset when she realized that Jonah wanted to keep her a secret as if she were something to be ashamed of. Not to mention, he had threatened both Terrell and Sherise with unspeakable acts if they told the truth.

She wanted nothing to do with him, but he continued to reach out to her. She quit her job immediately. Jonah had not allowed her resignation to be formally entered and had her instead transferred to another department, the communications department. Erica didn't want to accept, but because of her financial situation now that Terrell was not going half in on their rent and expenses, and the realities of the tough job market, she agreed to take the position on the condition that Jonah leave her alone and not do another thing for her ever again.

He agreed, but immediately started to try to reconnect with her. She didn't want to hear it. She had broken off her engagement with Terrell and was alone again. She had only Sherise and Billie to confide in. She threatened to tell the media that she was Jonah's daughter if he didn't leave her alone, and for a while that had worked. But lately, Jonah was trying to reach out to her again. This was the second lunch invitation she'd gotten in the last week.

"Fuck off," she said under her breath as she ripped the invitation up and tossed it in the garbage.

She was just trying to get her life back on track. She was letting Terrell back into it one step at a time, and now Nate was giving her problems. The last thing she needed or wanted was to play an active role in being Jonah's little shameful secret.

★ ★ ★

Sherise was in a good mood. She was on her way to her favorite nightclub for a drink with her girls. Most importantly, she was out of the house and she needed to be out of the house. Justin was watching Cady and she would be back soon, but having a drink with her girls made her feel like things used to be when they were all three career women discussing their jobs, their men, their lives.

She had just stepped out of the cab when she heard her name being called. Expecting to see Billie or Erica, she was surprised to see Ameena Nixon. Ameena Nixon was a member of some of the most powerful social circles of DC. Thirty years old and Ivy League educated, she was a lobbyist like Justin. A native of Oklahoma, she worked for the powerful agriculture conglomerate and had married a rich corn-oil executive, had two kids right away, promptly divorced him, and was living well off her divorce settlement. Last Sherise had heard, she had a twenty-five-year-old Cuban boy toy helping her spend her ex's money.

"Sherise Robinson?" Ameena rushed toward her. "What a surprise!"

Ameena looked attractive in a fitted dark gray midthigh dress with black lace trimmings at the neck and around the waist. Still, Sherise knew she looked better in her Rachel Zoe brown and white print dress. She looked better than most women, which was why they usually avoided her. At least they used to when she not only looked better, but was more successful. Now that she wasn't a career woman, Sherise had fallen in stature amongst the DC power set, where the rule was that if a woman wanted to be considered top tier, she had to have a family and career.

"Ameena!" Sherise could see the look of condescension on Ameena's face before she air-kissed both her cheeks. "So nice to see you."

"I had thought you'd fallen off the face of the earth," Ameena said with a saccharine smile.

Sherise kept her sweetest smile despite the obvious dig. "No, I'm just as around as I've ever been. What about you?"

"Really?" Ameena feigned confusion. "I haven't seen you at any recent events. I would have noticed you."

It was true that Sherise hadn't been to as many social events as she usually was. She had gotten tired of being asked what she did or where she'd been. She'd gotten sick of hearing of all the big projects and exciting things people were doing. Politics were like a drug, and it was no fun being the only sober person around a bunch of users.

"Life has kept me busy," Sherise said. "I've been dipping my hands in a lot of different pies."

Ameena looked as if she didn't believe it for a second. "Well, I know being a mama is taxing work. I have two and they kill me."

"I know." Sherise knew that Ameena was rubbing it in. She was letting her know that she can have the career and two kids, but Sherise could only manage one kid. But all wasn't lost. "I don't know what I'd do without my husband. Husbands are life savers, don't you . . . Oh, never mind."

Ameena's expression temporarily went flat at the dig. "They can be a great help, if you need help. Obviously you do, so it's worked out great for you."

"Everything has," Sherise said. "I'm really happy."

"You look happy," Ameena responded with a biting tone. "Well, I have to be heading out. I've got a cocktail hour at the Capital Hilton. Those foreign dignitaries don't like to be kept waiting."

"Have fun," Sherise said, ending that with "bitch" in her head.

Ameena took only a few steps before turning back. "You know, in case you're interested in staying relevant, the Breast Cancer Ball at the White House this October is probably looking for some volunteers. You do have time for charity, don't you? That's a big housewives thing, right?"

Sherise gritted her teeth. "I've already been asked about that. I don't think I'll have time. I'm so busy with other things."

"Of course you are." Ameena smiled one last time. "Enjoy your evening."

If looks could kill, Ameena Nixon would be dead from the daggers in Sherise's eyes as she watched her walk away. "Fuck that bitch."

Was this what her life in DC was going to be? Constantly running into the movers and shakers that made her feel inadequate and useless. She hated feeling old and unwanted at twenty-eight. This was wrong. It wasn't working. She had to do something.

Billie looked down at her watch. Of course both of them were late. She was the only one who was on time, and she was the one with the least amount of time available. She had already turned down two offers to dance, wondering who these fools were that wanted to dance at a club at seven P.M. Besides, none of these boys looked a day over twenty-one. As long as she looked like a single girl at the club alone, she was going to be a prime target for every loser in the place.

"Hello."

Billie sighed as she turned around, ready to turn down another poor boy. That was until she realized who was standing beside her.

"Porter, what are you doing here?"

Porter Hass looked like a handsome model one might find on the cover of a men's magazine. He was always sharply dressed, and his hair was always trimmed tightly to his head. He was six feet tall, but his deep voice gave him a presence that made him seem taller. He had milk chocolate skin and a finely shaven goatee surrounding his full lips. His most compelling feature was his black, mesmerizing eyes that, at the moment, bore into Billie, making her feel like he was looking inside of her. Billie hadn't seen him in a couple of months and she was instantly reminded of how attractive he was. Damn him.

"This is my club," he answered, helping himself to the seat next to her at the little corner table she had acquired.

"Your club?" she asked with a tilt of her head.

"I'm the one who introduced you to this place."

He looked her up and down, noticing her hair, cut short to her head, was sleek and sexy and her glowing dark chocolate skin was flattered by the peach color of her maxi dress.

"You look great, Billie."

"Porter, I'm waiting for Sherise and Erica. If you know what's good for you, you'll leave now."

"I just wanted to say hello." He softened his voice. "It would be rude not to."

"Okay," she said. "You said hello and I'm saying hello back. Now go."

He shook his head, waving away a waitress that came to take his drink order. "Damn, Billie. You're so cold. You used to be so . . ."

"Nice? Sweet? Kind? Yeah, all those things you used to take advantage of to keep me falling into your bed even though you cheated on me."

Porter frowned. "You made your own choices, Billie."

Billie couldn't completely disagree with that. When she had found out that Porter was having an affair with a twenty-three-year-old blond associate at his firm, Claire, she made the choice to end their marriage. He begged her for another chance, but she wasn't hearing it. Even though she had been ignoring it, they had been having problems for some time before that.

When they'd first met in law school, they both had the same goal. Coming from poor backgrounds, they wanted to fight power and be a voice for the voiceless. When Porter let himself get seduced by the power of money and influence, he changed teams, and he and Billie had clashed often about that. But she had always been willing to work on it because she loved him and she loved his teenaged daughter, Tara. But Claire was something she could not get past.

While Billie tried to be civil and fair, Porter used dirty-handed tricks and all the influence he had to get the advantage in the divorce. Despite all of that, even after he slapped her in the face by allowing Claire to move in with him as his official girlfriend, Billie hadn't been able to resist Porter's seductions. Their sex life had been amazing from day one, and although she tried over and over again, when he came to her, they almost always ended up in bed. He had tried to keep her in his life—have his cake and eat it, too. He even used her affection for Tara to keep her in his bed. But finally, she had broken free of his hold.

She could look at him now and find him attractive, but not want him. It was a victorious feeling even though she still regretted that their marriage hadn't worked. But she knew she'd made the right choice. Billie didn't believe a marriage could exist without trust, and she did not believe Porter would never cheat on her again.

"I miss you," he said. "I know you miss me."

"I don't," she answered bluntly.

Porter frowned again. "You know, I'm the one who should be angry here. You damn near destroyed my life last year."

Billie could only laugh. "You got what you deserved. All your threats and games led to that. It's so like you to play the victim. Just go away, Porter."

"Look, I'm not mad at you," he said. "I forgive you."

Billie rolled her eyes. This man.

"I want us to move on," he said. "It would be best for Tara if—"

Billie leaned forward so quick she startled him. She pointed her finger in his face. "What did I tell you? I told you to never, ever use her against me again. I could still harm your career, Porter. I have enough dirt on you to get you disbarred."

"I broke up with Claire."

This was unexpected enough to catch Billie off guard. This was news. Did she care? No? Yes? What should she feel? When she'd found out that Claire had moved in with him, Billie was livid. When she'd thought that he was going to marry Claire, Billie lost her head and almost got arrested after attacking Claire. But now, it was over? Was that even true?

"It doesn't matter," she said, leaning back in her chair.

She smiled, realizing this was the truth. She wouldn't lie and say she wasn't happy that Claire wasn't going to get to keep him, but, no, she didn't care.

"How can you say that?" Porter asked, seeming hurt by her reaction.

"I just did," Billie said. "It is over between us, Porter. It has nothing to do with Claire or anything else."

"I don't believe that. I can't. You aren't over me and I'm not—"

"Your arrogance is disgusting," Billie said. "Porter, I think you need to know something."

"What?" He scooted closer in his chair with an eager smile.

"I've started the process to legally change my name back to Carter." She waited as his expression changed from bewilderment to anger to hurt. "Sorry, but you need to know that I've been using Carter professionally for a while, and legally it—"

"You made a name for yourself in the legal profession as Billie Hass," he said, his frustration visibly building. "If you change it . . ."

"I haven't been a lawyer that long," she said. "I think it's important I take my name back. We weren't married very long and—"

"It's Tara's name," he interrupted. "You're her . . . You're like her mother."

This made Billie pause for a second, but she quickly composed herself. "Tara is the only reason I've kept the name this long, but I have to do this. I am doing it. You know now."

Porter looked like a little boy who had just been scolded. He looked as if he wanted to speak, but had nothing to say. This was a first.

"What in the fuck are you doing here?" Sherise asked the second she showed up. She was looking down at Porter as if she was two seconds from kicking him out of that chair.

Porter sighed and rolled his eyes. "I'm having a private conversation with—"

"No, you're not," Billie said. "Good-bye, Porter. I warned you she was coming."

"I'm not afraid of Sherise," he said, standing up.

"But I see your bitch ass is leaving, isn't it?" she asked, placing a sassy hand on her hip.

"Fuck you, Sherise." Porter's expression of disgust turned to pain as he looked from Sherise to Billie. "We need to talk later."

"No, you don't," Sherise said.

"Shut up," he snapped at her, but Sherise just laughed in response, making him angrier.

He stormed off and Billie felt herself sigh in relief.

"What was he doing here?" Sherise asked.

"It's a public place," Billie said. "Just ignore him."

Sherise sat down next to Billie and studied her face. "Are you okay?"

Billie smiled and nodded. "I told him about my name change."

"Let me guess," she said. "He tried to talk you out of it."

Billie nodded. "He even tried to use Tara, as usual."

"You shut him down?" Sherise smiled, hitting Billie in the arm. "Look at you, girl. I'm so proud. Our little girl is all grown up and busting balls."

2

Erica was just a few seconds from the front door to the club when her phone rang. Looking down at the phone, she saw that it was Terrell and, with a smile, she picked it up.

"Where you at, girl?" he asked.

"I'm on my way to meet my girls." Erica moved to the edge of the sidewalk away from the crowd. "What about you?"

"I'm doing what I'm always doing," he answered. "Making that money. I'm waiting for some clients to come down from their place. I'm taking them to the Kennedy Center."

Terrell Nicolli was Erica's ex-fiancé, a boy she had met when she was just twenty-one years old. She was working hard, trying to be a mom to her brother, Nate, so she had little time for a man in her life. But Terrell was persistent. He was a hustler from the southeast side of town nearby where Erica had grown up. When they'd first met, he was dangerous and sexy, but as Erica matured, she wanted something more stable and legit. Terrell loved her enough to go on the straight and narrow, and she responded to this life change with her devoted love.

He had moved up from cleaning cars for Destin Limousine Services to driving them. Over the four years they were together, he occasionally fell into some old habits, looking for ways to make a quick buck. Erica had forgiven him the times she'd found out, but most times he was able to keep it from her. When they got engaged, Erica thought their worst days were behind them. When she found out that he was intending to blackmail Jonah over his affair with Sherise, Erica just couldn't find it in her heart to forgive. Sherise was her best friend, more like a sister to her, and he was willing to destroy her life for an extra buck, not to mention ruin Erica's career at the Defense Department.

She believed him when he told her he was sorry, and she appreciated what he'd found out about Jonah being her father, but there was no way she could marry him. He begged her to reconsider, but she was too preoccupied with the shock of finding out Jonah was her father to try to work it out with him.

Terrell never gave up, but tried to give Erica her space. He would still text her or e-mail her from time to time. She rarely responded. Thinking of him made her think of all the bad things that were happening in her life. He would ask if he could call. At first she told him no, but after a couple of months, she agreed to let him call. When he would, they would talk, she would pick a fight, but he wouldn't get angry. He knew she was testing him and he learned how to pass every test.

When Erica finally agreed to start seeing him again, there was a part of her that knew this was inevitable. She had put a lot of years into her relationship with Terrell, and she believed he loved her. As her anger over the situation with Jonah began to subside, she found her heart wanting to forgive him. She missed him and the familiar warmth his touch gave her.

"You gonna tell them about us?" he asked.

"Is that what you called me for?" Erica asked back.

Even though they had gone out on a few dates and even kissed, Erica had not told Sherise and Billie about it. It was very rare that they kept secrets from each other, no matter what the consequences, but something told Erica her reawakening relationship with Terrell should be kept between the two of them while it was still so tenuous.

"You know what Sherise's stuck-up ass is gonna say," Terrell said.

"Considering what you almost did to her," Erica started, but caught herself. There was no need to rehash the past. "I'm thinking about it."

"You know"—there was a heavy sigh on the other end of the line—"I've wanted to try and make it up to Sherise, but you kept telling me to stay away from her."

"I know what I'm doing," Erica said. "Sherise holds grudges . . . forever. Besides, you need to focus all your energy on my forgiveness, not hers."

"I'm trying, baby." He laughed. "If you let me, I can remind you of how convincing my apologies can be."

"Slow your roll," she said as she reached the door to the club.

They'd shared their first post-breakup passionate kiss only a couple of weeks ago. Their kisses had grown even more intense since then. Terrell had been eager to take their relationship back into the bedroom, but Erica wasn't having it.

"You have to win my heart the old-fashioned way," she said.

"Baby, ain't nothing more old fashioned than a man and woman making love."

"I'm not ready yet, Terrell."

Erica didn't want good sex—or great sex, as it would be more accurately described with Terrell—clouding her mind. She was as horny as she'd ever been in her life, but she had to keep her head on straight.

"Yet?" he asked, excited. "That means it will happen and that's all I care about. I love you, baby."

"I have to go," she said, warming at the sound of his last words, but being honest with herself in knowing that they weren't enough.

"Hello, ladies," Erica said as she approached the table where Sherise and Billie were sitting, already starting on their cosmopolitans.

"What is that smile for?" Sherise asked, curious. Erica's attitude had been pretty stinky for months now so this smile was new.

"Smile?" Erica shrugged her shoulders as she sat down and tossed her purse underneath the table. "I'm just happy to see my girls after a hard day's work."

"Bullshit," Sherise said, leaning forward. "You got some?"

"Sherise." Billie hit Sherise on the arm, laughing.

"No," Erica said, even though she couldn't help but smile. "I'm not even thinking about sex right now."

"I call bullshit again." Sherise leaned back in her chair and took a sip of her drink. "Every hot-blooded woman is thinking about sex at the club. Especially Billie."

Billie, mid-sip, almost spit out her drink. "When did this come around to me? I'm minding my own business."

"I'm starting to get worried about you." Sherise analyzed her friend, looking her up and down. "I'm afraid your business is gonna heal over."

"Hymens don't reform," Billie said. "We've been over this. Also, six months is not that long to go without sex. You married people forget that."

"You haven't had sex in six months?" Erica asked.

Billie shrank in the seat. Erica had practically yelled the question to be heard over the increasingly loud club just as an attractive male waiter came to their table. He was the only person who looked more uncomfortable than her.

"Should I come back?" he asked nervously.

Sherise was laughing while Billie covered her face with her hand.

"No." Erica leaned over to him. "I'll have an amaretto sour."

"Okay." He smiled back before turning to Billie. "Six months isn't that long, even though you are about the finest woman in this club."

"Excuse me?" Sherise asked.

Billie smiled, not as embarrassed as she had been only a second ago. It wasn't often that she didn't feel overshadowed by Sherise.

"Thank you," she said politely with a flirtatious smile.

"So, are you interested in helping her out?" Sherise asked, looking the waiter up and down.

He looked at Sherise with an amused smile. "Me?"

"Sherise!" Billie warned. "She's just kidding. Don't—"

"No, I'm not," Sherise said. "She doesn't have the balls to get back in the saddle on her own, so I'm helping her out. You interested?"

"More like pimping her out," Erica said. "Leave him alone."

"I would be," he answered. "If I was into girls."

"No," Sherise said. "I have excellent gaydar and you are not gay."

"As a bird," he said. "We're not all fabulous, you know."

As he walked away, all three girls burst into laughter.

"Why are we laughing?" Sherise asked. "Men like him get women into all kinds of trouble. You could've wasted your whole night flirting with him. Needs a damn stamp on his forehead."

"I wouldn't have been flirting with him," Billie said. "He's not my type."

"He has a dick," Sherise said. "That needs to be your type right now. Seriously, Billie, this thing you have with needing a relationship to have sex with someone is ridiculous."

"Don't get us wrong," Erica said. "We are both beyond happy and proud that you aren't falling into bed with Porter anymore, but that wasn't the only step in getting on with your life. You have to actually get on with it."

"That means getting on someone else," Sherise added. "Or under them."

"You're right," Billie said.

Sherise looked shocked. "Really? No more fighting me with waste-of-time pious arguments against casual sex?"

The truth was, Billie was horny beyond words. She was lonely and frustrated, and being a thirty-year-old single black woman in DC, she wasn't going to get anywhere just waiting around for someone to show up.

"So what do I do?" she asked. She hadn't dated since meeting Porter in law school.

"I got this," Sherise said. "I know all the single, straight men in DC and—"

"Are you sure?" Erica asked, nodding toward their waiter, who was standing at the bar talking to the bartender.

"Shut up," Sherise snapped. "I will find you a man, Billie."

"Just be open," Erica said. "Make eye contact with the guys here. If one comes up and asks you to dance, say yes."

"I'm not gonna meet my next boyfriend in a club," Billie said. "No way."

"Just a dance," Erica said. "You don't want to go home with anyone here."

"She doesn't?" Sherise asked.

"No," Erica answered, "but you want to flirt. You want to get that mojo going again. You trust me, don't you?"

She did. Billie trusted Erica and Sherise more than anyone else in this world. They were more than her best friends. They were her sisters. Their life together despite being different ages, growing up on the same block, in the same neighborhood in southeast hadn't been easy, but together they made memories to last forever and formed a pact, a promise to be there for each other and make a success out of their lives even though the world was telling them they weren't meant to.

They faced a lot of challenges as children, watching other girls and boys around them get lost in a system that was setting them up to fail. They knew there was a better life and they knew they would need each other to get through it. That meant focusing on their education, no getting in trouble, no drugs, and no getting pregnant.

It was harder on some of them than others. Neither Erica nor Sherise had a father around. Billie's father had been around until he was sent to prison for a crime he didn't commit. Sherise's mother didn't care about her, but both Erica and Billie had loving mothers until they lost both women to cancer.

In the end, it was the three of them that picked each other up when setbacks knocked them down, and they kept each other focused on having a better life than the one they started with.

"I trust you." Billie pointed to Erica but turned to Sherise with a scornful stare. "But not you."

Sherise rolled her eyes to signal how little that mattered to her. "I always only do what is best for you, and getting some non-Porter booty is what is best for you right now."

"What about you?" Billie asked, eager to take the focus off her sex life.

Sherise knew what she meant, but smiled with an evil grin. "All my booty is Porter-free. Always has been and always will be."

"Amen," Erica added as she felt her cell phone vibrate in her pocket.

"You know what I'm talking about," Billie said.

Sherise hadn't always stuck to their promise to tell each other everything. While she had told them about her flirtation with Ryan Hodgkins, even going so far as to confess she had kissed him passionately, Sherise had never told them she actually slept with Ryan. Both girls encouraged her to stop seeing him immediately and she'd told them that she had. Of course, she hadn't.

When she'd found out she was pregnant, she told herself that, for Cady's sake, she was going to take her night with Ryan to the grave. After all, she could be Justin's, and even telling the girls, despite their vow to keep each other's secrets, even the slightest chance it could get out and ruin her marriage—Cady's chance to have her parents raise her together—was not worth it.

She had told them everything about her affair with Jonah Dolan because she had no choice. The affair was merging into their lives and she needed her girls to help her deal with the mess she had gotten in. Unlike Ryan, Jonah wasn't willing to let her go at first. Now, with her attempts to get pregnant not working out and her sex life with Justin losing its steam, Billie and Erica were the only two people she could talk to about it.

"Don't get me started," Sherise said.

"Isn't that the problem?" Billie asked, laughing. "He's not getting you started."

Sherise's eyes turned slits as she glared at Billie. "Ha, ha. You're so funny. You know we're only having sex like once a week now."

"That isn't bad for a lot of married couples," Erica said as she read the message from Terrell telling her how he was looking forward to their dinner tomorrow night. "That's what I hear at least."

"It's bad for us," Sherise said. "And it's bad for anyone trying to have a baby. I'll be ovulating in a few days."

"It's your anger," Billie said. "You resent him for having to quit your job and it's keeping you from really committing to having this baby."

While Sherise didn't doubt the underlying premise of Billie's words, she doubted a little resentment could prevent sperm from implanting an egg.

"I had to quit," Sherise said. "I lost sight of my priorities. Jonah was gonna fuck up everything."

"Erica made sure he's not a threat to any of us anymore," Billie said. "You need to get over all that."

"I feel like I have," Sherise argued. "I really wanted to get pregnant when we started this. I wanted to make Justin happy."

"But you're not happy," Billie said.

Sherise shook her head. "I'm trying to be, but I'm just not into it. I feel like the world is passing me by and I'm sitting around waiting to get pregnant."

"And taking care of Cady," Billie reminded her.

Sherise smiled. "If it wasn't for her, I would shrivel up and die. But, it's not just me. Justin seems to have . . . given up. He's the one who wanted another baby so bad. Things are just off."

"If you're not going to see a marriage counselor," Billie said, "you need to at least see a fertility specialist. Isn't that what Justin wants?"

"It was what he wanted." Sherise had been scared to death to go see a specialist. If they found out that Justin was shooting blanks, all hell would break loose. "He doesn't ask about it so much anymore."

Billie was about to mention how that wasn't a good sign, but was distracted by Erica's laughter. Was this funny to her? She turned to her and noticed that Erica was no longer involved in their conversation. She was texting furiously with a smile on her face.

"Who are you texting?" Sherise asked angrily.

Erica pressed send before looking up. Both Billie and Sherise had an expectant look on their faces. Well, this was as good a time as any. Erica sighed, trying to relax before the expected onslaught.

"I have something to tell you both," Erica said, zeroing in on Sherise. "And I don't want to hear shit from you."

"You'll only hear the truth from us," Billie said. "Whether you think it's shit or not is up to you."

Sherise gasped. "You've got a new boyfriend?"

"Well . . ." Erica started.

"I knew it." Sherise was getting excited. "That smile on your face. It's the kind of smile caused by a man."

"Who is he?" Billie asked, excited.

"Don't get excited yet," Erica said. "But Sherise is kind of right. I am seeing someone, but he's not new."

Sherise felt a brick in her stomach as she threw her hands in the air. "Oh, for Christ's sake!"

The waiter suddenly returned with Erica's drink.

Billie took a second before realizing what she was saying. "Wait . . . what? You're . . . what? Terrell?"

Erica nodded nervously as she grabbed the drink and quickly thanked the waiter before taking a sip. She should have ordered something stronger.

The waiter started, "Can I get you ladies any—"

"Are you out of your fucking mind?" Sherise asked.

"What a surprise," Erica said. "Sherise is judgmental instead of supportive."

"Wait!" Sherise called after the waiter, who had started walking away. "Shots. Bring shots."

"Of what?" he asked. "How many?"

"Just make them strong and bring three," she answered.

"I don't want a shot," Billie said.

"Neither do I," Erica added.

"They're all for me," Sherise said. "As fast as you can, please."

"Let's just stay calm," Billie said to Sherise before turning to Erica. "Really, girl? I thought you were done with him?"

"I was never done with him," Erica said. "I told you guys that I still loved him."

"But you promised you would get over him," Sherise said. "You promised to stay away."

"That wasn't as easy to do as I thought," Erica said.

"Things have changed and he sort of . . . he slowly worked his way back into my heart."

Erica was smiling as she spoke, but from the looks on Billie's and Sherise's face, she was alone in this. "Okay, listen. I was cautious, too, but he's really sorry. We spent a long time talking and working through our issues."

"A long time?" Billie asked. "Why are we just now hearing this?"

"Why?" Sherise asked. "Because she knew we wouldn't approve. Why else would she keep it a secret?"

"I don't need your approval," Erica said even though it wasn't true. What Billie and Sherise thought meant more than anything to her, but she wasn't going to back down. "I'm seeing him again and I just wanted to keep it between us until I knew it was what I wanted."

"Erica," Sherise whined. "You had a chance to trade up. You could have gone out with any of the guys I tried to set you up with. You could have gone out with anyone else. Why would you go back to this hood?"

"He's not a hood," Erica snapped.

"No," Sherise agreed. "You're right. He's bumped up to extortion, so what does that make him? A high-class hustler?"

"Shut up," Erica said. "He made a mistake. He realizes that he could have ruined lives."

"My life!" Sherise yelled.

"Hey." Billie held up a hand to Sherise. "You calm down. You put yourself in a position to have your life ruined, so stop looking for scapegoats."

"Exactly," Erica chimed in.

"But you." Billie turned to her. "What Terrell did was awful. Do you really think you can trust him?"

Erica wanted to say yes, completely, but she couldn't. "I'm not exactly there yet, but I'm getting there. He's trying so hard."

"They all try," Billie said.

"I love him," Erica admitted hopelessly.

Billie's concerned frown softened into a smile. "I know you do, sweetheart."

"You fucked him, didn't you?" Sherise asked, not trying to hide her disgust. "He put his little dick on you and you believe anything he says."

"You're the only one who seems to have a problem falling for the wrong dick," Erica said with a haughty roll of her head. "And his . . . is not little."

Billie could see this was getting out of hand. "Let's try to focus, girls. Erica, no one would blame you if you were . . . you know . . . dickmatized. It happens to the best of us."

"I'm not," Erica said. "We haven't even had sex yet. We've only been on a few dates and maybe kissed once or twice. Who are you to judge me, Sherise?"

"I admit my mistakes," Sherise lied, "but that doesn't change the fact that this is a mistake, your mistake. You had gotten rid of the trash, just to turn around and bring it back in. He'll find a way to fuck everything up again. It's what brothas like him do."

The waiter returned with three shots of Patrón.

"Well," Erica said, "if you keep your panties on and stop fucking the wrong people, you won't have anything to worry about from this brotha."

"Damn," the waiter added.

All three ladies looked up at him. He composed himself and walked away.

"You aren't fooling anyone," Sherise said. "You keep trying to bring up my mistakes to deflect from what you know is your own."

This incensed Erica for some reason. She wanted to jump out of the chair and slap Sherise. "Just work on your own marriage and don't worry about my relationship with Terrell. I know what—"

Erica halted as a man approached their table. He was tall, dark, and handsome in a very traditional way. He was a professional, dressed in a navy blue suit and a white button-down shirt. He looked to be in his thirties, with a close, neat cut. He clearly had a goal in mind, and that goal was Billie. He didn't have eyes for anyone else.

"Sorry to interrupt." His voice was compelling and deep. "My name is Robert. You are?"

"Billie," she answered cautiously.

"Hi, Billie." He flashed a million-watt smile. "I noticed you sitting over here and I was wondering if you would be interested in dancing with me."

Sherise made a smacking sound with her lips. What kind of man asked a woman to dance this early in the club these days? "We were actually in the middle of a—"

"Sure." Billie got up from her seat quickly, tossing her purse on Erica's lap. She looked at her. "I'm taking your advice."

The truth was, she didn't want to be at that table anymore. When Sherise and Erica got into it, it was like a world war all over again, and she was always caught in the middle. She was tired of trying to be the peacemaker. They could work this one out themselves. She was gonna dance.

When she reached the dance floor, which was more crowded than she expected for so early on a Friday night, Billie tried as best she could to let loose. She wasn't particularly interested in Robert, but he was cute and seemed harmless. Besides, out of the corner of her eye, she could see Porter standing by the bar looking at her with unabashed jealousy. Icing on the cake.

It was only ten at night when Sherise slipped back into her Georgetown townhouse. Climbing the stairs, she knew that Justin would still be up. He would likely be working, but she wasn't really thinking about him. Instead of heading to the master bedroom at the far right of house, she went straight for the door in the middle of the hallway.

Quietly opening the door, she tiptoed over to Cady's crib. She looked down at her baby sleeping peacefully and a sense of calm and warmth crept through her. She reached down and ran her finger softly along Cady's cheek. She wanted to kiss that teeny little sweet mouth, but wouldn't dare wake her up. The little demon looked like an angel when she was sleeping.

Sherise felt so blessed to be able to look at the reason she was alive, the reason her life was worth anything. There it was, sleeping in Winnie the Pooh jammies. Without her career, Cady seemed to be the only thing that Sherise really understood and knew was real. She smiled, in her heart knowing that she was lucky. How many women would be deliriously happy to be stay-at-home moms with a husband earning six figures and a healthy beautiful baby?

So why wasn't she? Was it because she couldn't get pregnant again? She had wanted to wait at least a couple of years between babies, so she could focus on her career before taking another maternity leave. But being so jarred by the horrible mistake she'd made with Jonah made Sherise think differently. Making Justin happy was what mattered. Keeping her family together was what mattered. Having another baby, bringing another person into their wonderful family, had been her goal.

Now that goal was sort of becoming a nightmare. Every month when she got her period, she felt like a failure. Every month she realized she wasn't pregnant, she felt closer to Justin finding out that Cady wasn't his. What if she wasn't? Looking down at her now, Sherise believed she saw Justin's nose on the baby, but was she just convincing herself of that in order to believe she was his?

"How drunk are you?" Justin asked as soon as she entered the bedroom.

He was looking up at her from his side of the bed, his laptop on his lap as he leaned against two big pillows.

She smiled at him as she tossed her shoes to the side of the spacious room.

"Just enough," she answered as she walked over to the bed. She leaned into him and he lifted his head up to kiss her.

He seemed happy and looked at her with affection for a few seconds more before returning his attention to his computer. Sherise looked down at him adoringly and reached out. She placed her delicate fingers under his chin, lifting his face to hers again.

"We should all go to Eastern Market in the morning," she said. "Remember how we used to love that Saturday mornings? Buy some fruit, eat some pancakes, and look at the art. It would be nice . . ."

"I can't, sweetie." He took her hand and kissed the inside of her palm before letting it go. "I have a nine A.M. tee time at the club. I told you I was playing golf with some clients."

She nodded. "I'm sorry. I forgot."

Not a word was spoken as she went to the bathroom and changed into her nightgown. She didn't wash her face, but splashed it with water and put her hair in a ponytail. She still wanted to look nice. She wanted to make love to her husband tonight.

When she slid into the bed, Justin's attention was on his computer. He was reading an article on the financial industry, his specialty, as Sherise slid up to him and began rubbing his arm.

He looked at her and laughed. "You're drunk."

"I'm not." She smiled. "Okay, maybe a little, but you should be happy. You get to take advantage of a drunken woman. When was the last time you did that?"

"When was the last time you were drunk?" He let her kiss him before returning to his article. "I need to finish reading this, baby. This is what everyone is gonna be talking about at tomorrow's golf game."

She reached over and placed her hand on top of the laptop and slowly pushed it closed. "They can all talk about this article while you talk about how you fucked your gorgeous wife."

He seemed annoyed, but let her push the laptop off his lap and onto the bed. It was comforting to Sherise to see that he didn't resist her. In the past, Justin could never resist her. No matter how awful she'd been or how preoccupied he was, he was always willing and eager to make love to her. That hadn't been the case so much recently. Their inability to conceive was affecting him just like it was her. She was going to change that tonight.

Her lips teased at his as she reached down and grabbed the bottom of his T-shirt. He lifted his arms as she pulled the shirt up and off him. He met her with a more passionate, deeper kiss as his hand went to her shoulders.

Their tongues began to explore each other's mouth as she felt his fingers gently lift the straps of her nightgown and slide them down her shoulders. He let out a soft groan as his mouth traveled down her neck to the soft flesh of her chest.

Sherise let him guide her back to where she was lying on the bed and he was moving on top of her. His mouth was kissing the space between her breasts as his hands began to caress her hips. Her hands went to his head as she ran her fingers over his hair.

Sherise was waiting for the passion to come, but it hadn't arrived yet. She felt a little spark, a little pull in her center, but she wasn't set on fire. She closed her eyes and spread her legs as Justin positioned himself in between them.

When his tongue traced her nipple, it felt warm to Sherise, but when she felt his teeth teasingly bite at her, she flinched. She usually liked a little biting, but this didn't feel good. It made it only glaringly obvious to her that none of this felt good. Or maybe it just didn't feel right.

"Justin. Justin," she repeated. "Please."

She pushed against the bed, lifting herself up.

Caught up in the foreplay, Justin looked up, expecting to continue.

"Wait," Sherise said as she pushed away.

Justin looked at her confused. "What? What did I . . . Did I hurt you?"

"No," she answered, shaking her head. What was happening to her? "I just . . . I . . . I'm sorry, Justin."

"What?"

"I . . ." She shrugged as he realized from her expression that she was telling him she didn't want to go any further.

"What is wrong with you, Sherise?" he asked angrily as he sat up.

"I don't know," she said. "I think it's the alcohol."

"Alcohol makes you not want to have sex?" Justin reached for his T-shirt and began putting it back on. "You expect me to believe you're the only person on the planet that happens to? This isn't the first time you've done this."

"I'm sorry." She sighed, reaching out to him. He leaned away. She felt awful. She regretted pushing away. She should have just gone through with it even if it wasn't what she really wanted. "I just feel sluggish. I can make it up to you in the morning."

Justin didn't respond as he got out of bed.

"What are you doing?" she asked. "I know you're mad, Justin, but shit, I'm sorry. Maybe in the morning, we can . . ."

"Don't do me any favors," Justin said as he snatched his laptop. Without looking at her, he turned and left the room. "I'm gonna be downstairs. Don't wait up for me."

"Come on," she called after him. "It's not that serious."

"You started it, Sherise!" He slammed the bedroom door behind him.

Now she really regretted not following through. What was wrong with her? She had resolved to make love to Justin before leaving Cady's room just moments earlier. She wanted him, but it just fizzled. She wasn't feeling it from herself. Or was she not feeling it from him? It couldn't be him. He was upset that they weren't making love.

"What is wrong with you, girl?" she asked herself as she reached over to Justin's side and turned off the lamp. She was in need of some serious groove therapy.

3

Billie wasn't sure what she had been expecting, but she hadn't been expecting what she got. As she entered one of the smaller conference rooms in her law firm offices where her new pro bono client was waiting for her, she stopped at the door. Standing at the other end of the room, looking out the floor-to-ceiling windows of the room overlooking Farragut Square, was Ricky Williams.

He turned to her and started walking toward her. He was a very good-looking, milk chocolate–colored man with a clean-cut, clean-shaven look. He had piercing black eyes, a strong nose, and rigid jaw. His short dark hair was cut close to his head and he looked a few inches over six feet. He was sharply dressed in casual khakis and a blue and white striped button-down neatly tucked inside.

"You must be Billie Carter," he said in a deep voice.

Billie quickly pulled herself together and met him halfway. She shook his hand as firmly as she could. He had a strong grip. "Yes, I am. And you must be Ricky Williams."

"Well," he said. "You're . . . I saw your picture on the law firm Web site and, well, it doesn't do you justice. You're very pretty."

"That's nice," she said, feeling a little uncomfortable. No, a lot uncomfortable all of the sudden. "It's very nice to meet you."

"I don't know if you're going to feel that way for long," he joked.

She gestured for him to sit down at the conference table behind him. "Are you telling me that you're a nightmare client?"

"I'm probably nothing like some of the people you've defended."

She joined him, sitting at the corner of the table, placing her file folders down. She studied him for a second. No, he wasn't at all what she'd expected. "So you've been researching me?"

"I know you used to be a public defender," he said.

"Well, this isn't a criminal case," she said, "so that—"

"Not yet," he interrupted.

Billie paused, intrigued. "You planning on breaking the law?"

"I feel like it's already been broken," he said. "Not by me, but by the government. Just don't get your hopes up. I'm not."

"I always get my hopes up," Billie said. "It's a personality flaw. I believe in my client. I fight for my client. And I get my hopes up for my client."

Ricky didn't seem to share her enthusiasm. "I don't know, Ms. Carter. I think . . ."

"Billie," she corrected him. "I doubt our ages are that far apart, so no need for formalities. I can call you Ricky?"

"You can call me anything you want," he said, suddenly flashing a flirtatious smile. "But there is some seriously shady business going on with my case. You can't fight the man."

Suddenly Billie heard music and the muffled sounds of singing.

So you got to try a little tenderness . . . a little tenderness . . . a little tenderness . . .

"Sorry," Ricky said as he reached in his back pocket and pressed a button. "That was my phone."

"Is that Otis I hear?"

"The one and only," he said, smiling. "You like Otis Redding?"

"I don't associate with anyone who doesn't."

"He was the man." He looked impressed. "I'm surprised a young woman like you even knows who he is."

"My daddy was his biggest fan," she said. "He used to play his music all the time. I don't care who you are, when you hear that man sing, you have to fall in love with his voice."

"That," he said, pointing into the air. "That is the God's truth. That man just had soul seeping from every pore. R&B these days . . . these boys just don't know."

Billie laughed, nodding in agreement. He looked at her and their eyes met for a moment that made things suddenly awkward. She should be happy that they were getting along since this wasn't always the case with a client. But something told her this was probably not a good idea and she better get back to business.

Billie looked down at the file folder on the table, flipping it open as she cleared her throat.

"I can tell you that you are wrong on one account," she said.

"Not about Otis," he answered back.

She looked back up at him, her head held high. "No, but when you said you can't fight the man. You can fight him. It's what I do. It's what I love to do and I've gotten pretty good at it."

His eyes softened as a satisfied expression came over his face. "Well, you have spirit, and I could tell from the second I read up on you that you have the brains. Not too bad to look at, either."

"Thank you," she said appreciatively. "First, I want to let you know that I appreciate you coming to our offices on a Saturday. I'm sure you're busy."

"I'm busy?" He laughed, looking around. "I walked up in here expecting half the lights to be off and see nothing but a janitor. I must have passed at least twenty people on my way to this room. This is how you guys roll here?"

"Gotta make those hours," Billie said. "This place is pretty much poppin' on Saturday and Sunday."

"That's wrong," he said. "I mean don't get me wrong. I'm glad you're here to help me, but a beautiful sister like you should be out running the streets with her man or her girls on a nice summer Saturday."

Billie agreed, but she had given up a lot of her personal life when she started working at the firm, but there was no point in going into that now.

"Let's get down to business," she said. "I'm gonna tell you what I know of your case and you fill in any blanks."

"Shoot," he said, leaning back in his chair.

"You started working at the shelter, Saturn House, ten years ago." She was looking directly at her notes. "You house immigrants who have acquired asylum from prosecution in their countries in transition. They stay with you an average of two months before moving on their own or to relatives in other parts of the DC area or the country."

"We take entire families," he said, proudly. "We can house up to thirty people at a time."

She admired the pride he took in what he was doing.

"I've looked into your past, Ricky."

He rolled his eyes. "Oh, here we go."

"I'm not judging you," Billie said. "You got into some trouble as a kid. You were also caught in possession of marijuana when you were twenty-three?"

"Who hasn't carried some weed on them every now and then?"

"I haven't," she answered. "But it looks like you've been on the straight and narrow . . . mostly. What led you to Saturn House?"

"Not easy for a black man with a record to get a job in this world," he started. "I was walking by Saturn House ten years ago and saw they needed a handyman. The woman that owned it, Della, was the only person in DC willing to give me a chance. At least it seemed like it."

"How did you go from being the handyman to owner in ten years?"

Ricky smiled as if he was in wonder at that reality himself. "Went from handyman to cook, then helped Della manage some of her papers, started making friendships with the local donors, etc. Della came to trust me and the transition made sense."

"Good for you," Billie said.

She was proud to see a brother who wanted to do something good for the community. She'd seen too many Porters, men who had the brains and potential to do great things in the community, become dazed by money and power and decide to do good things only for themselves.

Billie tried to focus on the work at hand. "About a year and a half ago, Sanders Realty approached you with an offer to buy your property."

"They approached Della at the time," he answered. "She was dead set against selling for obvious reasons. This place means everything to her. It means everything to a lot of people. She made me promise not to sell to them."

"So you claim that"—she checked her notes—"Alex Mattas from Sanders became very aggressive with you as you refused his repeated offers."

Ricky nodded. "Meanwhile, he's . . . Sanders Realty is buying up everything around me. He kept telling me that no one wanted a . . . he called it a halfway house . . . in an up-and-coming neighborhood."

Billie shook her head. "You claim that he is behind the people who call the police suggesting that they have witnessed criminal activity around the building?"

He nodded. "I know he's behind it."

"But you have no proof it's him. None of those calls could be traced back to him in any way." Billie would have to see how much more information she could get about that. "When did the notices from the DC Housing Authority start coming?"

"The first one was eight months ago." He pointed to the notice as Billie pulled her copy from her stack of papers. "That's the first one. They start telling me that they have reason to believe that my living conditions don't meet code and they have started an investigation."

"And you say no one has actually visited Saturn House?"

"Someone came for the first time last month. That was after the third notice that included a threat to contact the Feds and demand they cut the funding for the house and our tax-free status."

"But your house is in good condition." She wrote a note to have pictures taken of every inch of the home, inside and out.

"My house is immaculate," Ricky said proudly. "Honestly, Della was OCD, if you ask me. She always demanded the house be spotless. I've kept it that way. Everything is up to code."

"But you have a notice you received two weeks ago that references several code violations." Billie looked at Ricky, seeing that he was getting angry just thinking about it. She didn't blame him.

She studied the code violation notice and it looked completely legit, but she would have to investigate more. "Your argument is that this violation is based on lies."

"It's all lies, Billie. I'm telling you. I followed that guy around every inch of my house and he barely looked at anything. He kept saying everything was fine, fine, fine, and left in a real hurry. Next thing I know, I get this notice. They're trying to shut me down, the government."

"I won't let them," Billie said. "I know a guy at the firm who is an expert on federal housing law that governs DC. We're going to get behind this and find out what's going on."

"The government is all a bunch of corrupt bastards, Billie. I'm looking at you and seeing that you're smart, but are you tough enough?"

"Don't let my size fool you," she said. "I know how to fight in a courtroom. I've fought more powerful enemies than the DC Housing Authority."

He slowly smiled and leaned back in his chair. He gave Billie a look that made her feel a little uncomfortable again. He had seductive eyes, and as his anger over discussing the problem subsided, his smoother, more charming side resurfaced.

"You know," he said, "I'll bet you have taken down some big boys. I like your style, Billie. I think you and I are gonna get along real well."

Billie hoped for the same. This case wasn't going to be easy, but she had a feeling it was going to be fun. "Let's get to work."

"Damn, you look good," was the first thing Terrell said as soon as he opened the front door to his apartment and saw Erica.

She did look good. Erica spent a lot of time and effort to look good tonight. Her hair was up in a banana clip, with curly tendrils falling across her face and down her neck in a wistful, sexy manner. As usual, she wore hardly any makeup, just some gloss to add shine to her full, sexy lips and mascara to accent her long, dark eyelashes.

She was wearing a blue, red, and silver paisley-border print dress with soft ruffles down the front, stopping just a couple of inches above her knees, defining her generous curves.

"You looking pretty good yourself, boy."

He had forgone his usual sport jersey and jean shorts and was wearing a pair of nice jeans and a hunter green polo shirt.

He had to wear a suit every day when he drove his car, so he was always reluctant to dress nice on his free time. She knew this was dressy for him and she appreciated it.

Just as she stepped inside, he wrapped his arms around her and pulled her to him. He looked into her eyes before kissing her tenderly. She felt a little tug in her belly, but tried to ignore it. When his lips came down on hers again, she responded by wrapping her arms around his neck. She kissed him back for a few seconds, feeling the heat before realizing where she was.

She pushed away, looking around the small two-bedroom apartment in the Adams Morgan neighborhood. "Where is Slade?"

"He's out with his latest girl." After closing the door behind her, Terrell took Erica's hand and led her farther into the apartment.

After their breakup, Terrell moved out of the apartment they shared and moved in with his friend Slade. He'd had other friends who he could have moved in with, but he'd told Erica that he'd chosen Slade because Slade had never been a hustler and would not tolerate it. Slade was the safest of the safest, an accountant for the state department. From the beginning, Terrell had been thinking of Erica, thinking of what would impress her.

"Come on." Terrell led Erica through the living room and down the hall.

She hesitated. "What . . . What's going on?"

"I want to show you something," he answered, turning back to her. "It's in my bedroom."

"Terrell." She snatched her hand away and placed it on her hips.

"Girl, stop it. Just real quick before we go to dinner. I'll behave, I promise."

Erica continued following him even though she knew that she wasn't so worried about him being on his best behavior.

She was worried about herself. If she was being honest with herself, she'd have to admit that while she was getting ready for tonight, she was thinking about the possibility of the night ending with sex. It had been so long.

He opened the door to his bedroom and Erica cautiously stepped inside, looking around.

"Is this what you wanted to show me?" she asked. "You cleaned your room?"

"Proud of me?" he asked with a beaming smile.

"I'm a little pissed," she said. "How many times did I try to get you to clean our bedroom, and get nothing done?"

"It's all part of my transformation." Terrell went over to the dresser against the wall and grabbed a folded piece of paper.

"Check this out, baby." He handed her the folded piece of paper.

"What is it?" She looked at it, but didn't unfold it.

"Look at it." He stepped a few inches closer until he was less than a foot away from her.

His closeness made Erica a little uncomfortable, so she looked down at the paper. Tossing her purse on the bed next to her, she flipped the sheet of paper open and read it. She smiled a delighted, proud smile.

"Operations agent?" Erica said it like more of a question than a statement. "You got a promotion?"

He nodded, so excited he was biting this lower lip. "For the last couple of months, I've been helping Scott, the operations director, with managing some of his work. He really liked what I was doing and talked it over with the Jamie, the president. They agreed to give me a chance."

Erica felt awkward. She was excited for him enough to want to reach out and hug him, but the whole situation was weird. Was he her man again or not? How was she supposed to handle this?

"Congratulations." She handed the paper back to him.

Terrell was clearly disappointed with her reaction. "You know what this means? I'm not a driver anymore, baby. If I accept, I'll have my own office."

"I'm so proud of you." There was a part of Erica that was sad that they weren't officially back together because she could have enjoyed this moment even more.

"Are you?" His eyes held a pure eagerness. "Because that means everything to me, Erica. I can't tell you how much you've been on my mind at work. Like, it used to be cool out there, driving around, but this is more stability. I knew if I could move up, you would be more proud."

"It never mattered to me what you did at work," Erica said. "I just cared how you treated me. That's all that's ever mattered."

He nodded. "I know and I fucked that up, but I'll be able to do more for you now. This is opening new doors for me. I'm not just doing this for you. I'm doing it for us, for what I hope is us."

"Terrell."

Erica couldn't help herself as she reached out and touched his cheek. He wasn't free with his emotions. Terrell always thought it was weak for a man to have his heart on his sleeve. So these moments, as she watched him get a little emotional, were extremely touching to her.

Terrell placed his hand over hers and pressed it even more firmly against his cheek. "You do want an us, don't you? I'm not fooling myself, am I?"

"I want to be able to trust you again." Erica moved closer to him, wanting to kiss him, dying to kiss him. Suddenly she remembered something.

"Wait, what do you mean, if you accept? Are you basing your acceptance on me, because if you are . . ."

"I accepted verbally yesterday." He stepped away from her, letting her hand fall to her side. He placed the paper on the nightstand. "This is just the formal offer that makes it official."

"Well, don't wait," she said, relieved. She didn't want his career to hinge on her. "Call them tomorrow and let them know."

"I'll tell them Monday," he said. "I got plans tomorrow. It's my day off."

"You're taking a day off?" Erica was impressed. "Mr. Gotta Make That Money Seven Days a Week is taking a day off? When was the last time you did that? About a year ago?"

"I actually wanted to talk to you about that."

"Do you want to do something?" She suddenly got excited. She hardly ever got a free weekend day with Terrell because he worked nonstop. Now that they were seeing each other again, she thought of all the things they could do. "Eastern Market? Brunch?"

"I can't spend my day off with you," he said. "I actually called Nate and asked him to hang out with me tomorrow."

Nate and Terrell weren't necessarily great friends. Living in the same home for a few years allowed them to form sort of a bond, and Erica told Terrell as long as he kept the hoods out of his life, Nate could hang out with him. Their relationship mostly consisted of the occasionally violent movie and video games. There had been many times when Erica and Nate had gotten into it and Terrell was there, as an older man, to keep Nate in line. Erica really missed that, especially now.

Terrell returned to her. "You've been talking about him a lot lately. I can tell it's really upsetting you."

Nate had been hell on wheels lately. In the past month or so, he'd been arguing with Erica nonstop over just about anything big or small. She couldn't say a word to him without him taking it the wrong way and snapping at her. Erica had a temper and usually regretted letting it go because she only made it worse. He would go missing for days at a time and she tried not to give him a hard time about it. She knew he wasn't a boy anymore and she should mind her own business, but any inquiry was met with a verbal attack from him. Erica was very upset and was at her wit's end with him.

"You usually tell me that he's grown-ass man and I should stay out of it," she asserted.

"He is, Erica. He's twenty and he needs to be doing his own thing and making his own mistakes."

"The problem with that is, for a young man in DC, a mistake can cost you your freedom or your life."

"He's obviously going through something he's not comfortable talking to you about." He reached his hand up and rubbed her shoulder. "It's not your fault. You're kind of like a mom to him more than a sister. He'll open up to me. Maybe I can help him out, give him a little insight. I've learned a thing or two in my old age."

Erica was incredibly touched and, admittedly, a little turned on by his taking control. She was a modern girl who liked to handle her own problems, but she missed having a man who could take things over for her every now and then.

"You would do that for me?" she asked.

"I would do anything for you," he answered back quickly. "And I care about Nate, too. But most importantly, I want you happy and I know how much you love that boy. You won't be happy as long as he's troubled. I want to fix that."

There was a voice in the back of her head that told her he was using that tone of voice, the one that always worked on her. The smooth-operator tone of voice that soothed her concerns and turned her on. She didn't care. It was working. This gesture to help her with Nate made her miss him more now than ever.

She didn't hesitate before grabbing him and pulling him to her. She went straight for his lips and pressed hers against them. Just as she did, his arms wrapped around her waist and their bodies slammed against each other.

His mouth explored hers deeply, and she immediately began to feel the effect swim through her entire body. Terrell always did this to her, even after all these years, he got her motor running right away.

Feeling her passion intensify, Erica reached for his polo and tried to lift it off his head. He leaned away.

"What about dinner?" he asked.

"Are you really thinking about food right now?" she asked.

Backing away from him, she slowly sat down on the bed, inching back until her body was fully on the bed. She watched with excitement as Terrell looked down at her slowly and seductively. He was looking at her as if she were the tastiest meal he could have ever wanted.

When he joined her on the bed, he reached out for her again, this time more forcefully, more urgently. Erica felt her body begin to pulse all over as their hands furiously pulled at each other's clothes.

Their mouths were everywhere. Her body began tingling all over as his lips left a trail of fire down her chest, across her large breasts, and tickled her belly button. She felt his hands reach around her hips and caress them aggressively, stoking the fire hotter and hotter.

Erica got lost in the pounding sound in her head as her body throbbed with intense need when she felt his mouth touch her center. She was already wet when he'd gotten down there and his lack of hesitation made her feel so good she called out his name.

She heard him call her "baby" as his tongue took a short break to lick the inside of her thighs. Quickly, her body began to move back and forth with anticipation, with anguish. She wanted him badly, more than she could place in words. All she could do was let out the groan that was aching inside of her and he knew.

When he returned to her, he grabbed her hair and pulled it, making her head go back. He let out a carnal moan as he entered her, hard and ready. He filled her up quickly as she wrapped her thighs around him. She lifted her pelvis to meet him and they began that familiar, sweet movement that set it all in motion. He thrust as her body quivered. Dirty words were spoken in between promises of love. Moans of intense and purely pleasurable pain mixed together.

She came twice before he did and that was only the first session of the night.

Sherise wasn't sure how long she'd been zoned out, but the smell of the pork chops she was frying beginning to burn brought her senses back. She grabbed the pan and removed it from the heat. Placing it aside, she grabbed the spatula and turned them over. One slipped out of the spatula's grip and fell in the pan, splashing grease that landed on her hand.

"Dammit!" she yelled in pain.

This got the attention of Cady, playing in her high chair at the kitchen table. She let out an excited yip and waved her arms.

"Mommy's sorry," Sherise said to her as she reached over the sink to run the cold water over her hand.

This was just the cap to a bad weekend. She had barely spoken to Justin since he walked out on her Friday night. After returning from his golf game the next day, he tried to spark some conversation with her, but she wasn't having it. Her pride was still hurting from him walking out on her even though it was her fault. They'd both spent Saturday night doing their own thing at the house, and she pretended to be asleep when he finally came to bed.

The morning hadn't been much better. They already had a date for brunch with a coworker of Justin's and his wife at Black Market Bistro. Sherise had hoped it would break the monotony of her weekend, but it only made her feel worse. While Justin and his coworker talked about work and new clients, his coworker's wife, a young, beautiful red-haired woman named Elisa, could not say enough about her recent promotion at her public relations firm and how challenging it was going to be to manage twenty people.

Sherise felt like a loser. The few times she tried to contribute, she could talk of only her past accomplishments and it made her seem sad. She pretended to tend to Cady to avoid the conversation, but she felt sick to her stomach inside. Life was passing her by while she was feeding her baby overcooked eggs.

She hadn't intended to take her anger out on Justin, but every time he tried to talk to her after they'd gotten home, she just snapped at him in return. He didn't even tell her he was going out. She just heard the door slam. She tried to call him. He didn't answer, only texted her back, saying he was going into the office for a few hours and would be back by dinner.

And now, she'd even ruined that.

When the phone rang, she quickly turned the water off and grabbed it with her dry hand. She recognized the name on caller ID. LaKeisha Wilson was an old coworker of hers when she was a legislative assistant on Capitol Hill. She hadn't spoken to her in a few years.

"Hello?" Sherise cradled the phone in her neck as she dried her hand.

"Sherise Robinson?" LaKeisha, born and raised by a middle-class family in Texas, had a strong southern-belle accent.

"Yes," she responded flatly. Calls from the past always made Sherise suspicious.

"Sherise! Girl, it's me, LaKeisha Wilson. You remember me, don't you?"

Sherise faked the most excited voice she could, given her current mood. "LaKeisha? Of course I do. How you doing, girl? What's up?"

"Is it true, what I hear? Are you doing the real housewives gig? Stay-at-home mom and all that?"

"Actually I am. How did you hear?"

"Believe it or not, your name came up in a conversation I had last night with some women at an FCBA event."

FCBA stood for Federal Communications Bar Association, an organization for people involved in federal regulation of the communications industry.

"So you're working in regulation now?" Sherise asked.

She didn't really care what LaKeisha was up to, but thought she'd be nice before she found out which bitch was talking about her. Sherise tried to catch herself, realizing how malicious her thinking was without even knowing what had gone on.

"I was at the FCC for a year and a half," she answered. "I'm with the Northman campaign now."

Jerry Northman, former chairman of the FCC, the Federal Communications Commission, had recently quit his position at the agency and announced he was considering a run for president in the next election just under two years from now.

"How nice for you," Sherise said. "Who were you talking to?"

"What?" LaKeisha sounded disappointed that Sherise wasn't more interested in what she was doing. "Oh, well, yeah . . . it was . . . I can't remember all their names. It was just a group of women. I think her name was something Ross. Jessica or some Jacquelyn, something that started with a J."

Sherise picked her brain, thinking of all the Jessicas and Jacquelyns she knew. "What did she look like?"

"She was pretty, black, and . . . that's really all I can remember. I didn't really talk to her. I was talking to Lucy Adams, who was with her. Anyway, your name came up because I was talking about people that were really good at communications."

Sherise was at least happy to hear she was still being talked about in relation to her professional skills. So maybe she wasn't that much of a has-been after all.

"What for?"

"For the Northman campaign," LaKeisha said. "I mentioned how I'd heard a while ago that you were doing good things at the White House, and this woman . . . Jessica or whatever, said you were a stay-at-home mom now."

"It was my decision," Sherise said strongly. "They were very upset that I left, but I needed to make the right choice for myself. I'm thinking about—"

"Who are you fooling, girl?" LaKeisha asked. "I remember Sherise Lynn was all about the game."

"Well, of course, I'm planning to go back soon."

"You might want to consider a little sooner than soon," LaKeisha suggested. "Sherise, we're really looking for someone to head Northman's communications on the campaign. You know how great his chances are."

The latest poll had him leading among Democrats, but Sherise knew all these polls changed every month. He was the newest candidate, so of course he would be at the top.

"Are you asking me to join the campaign?"

"I'm giving you the opportunity to join the campaign and be in charge of all his communications. Do you know what this could mean for you, Sherise, when he wins?"

"If he wins," Sherise said, but she was already getting that pull in the pit of her stomach that came only when a great opportunity presented itself.

If Northman won the election, she could be White House press secretary.

"Even if he lost," LaKeisha said, "which he won't, you could write your ticket for what job you wanted next."

"Does Northman know about this?" Sherise asked, already imagining herself in this position.

"Yes. He's left the decision to me. He trusts me completely and he already told me he wanted a person of color in his communications role. You'll be the face of his campaign for the press. He knows that's good for him."

Just then, Cady, seeming to sense that she was being ignored, yelled out loud and threw her tiny set of plastic keys in her mother's direction. The set landed on the floor a few feet from Sherise. She looked at Cady, who was reaching her arms out to be picked up.

It hit her like a brick what she was doing and sort of amazed her at how quickly she had forgotten about her reality.

"You can meet with him next week if you—"

"Wait," Sherise said. "LaKeisha, this is a big deal. I have to talk to Justin about it and think about . . . I . . . We were planning on growing our family."

"You can't pass this up, Sherise." LaKeisha's voice sounded disappointed. "The Sherise I knew would never pass this up. We're talking about the White House here."

"I know, but . . ." Sherise no longer felt excitement. She was now anxious and upset, feeling resentment creeping in. "I just need time."

There was a pause as LaKeisha sighed before saying, "Let's at least have lunch next week, okay?"

Sherise hesitated for a second, but finally said, "Yes, let's do that. How about the Blue Duck Tavern in West End at noon on Wednesday?"

They set the date, and just as Sherise placed the phone down, it rang again. This time it was Justin. She wasn't looking forward to having this conversation with him about a possible position on Northman's campaign and didn't intend to say a word until she knew exactly what she wanted.

"When are you getting here?" she asked impatiently.

"I'm gonna be here a little while longer," he said, seeming to not notice or to be ignoring her tone. "Jason and Rhoda are here, too. We're just gonna order dinner and try and knock out these talking points."

"So when are you getting back?"

"I don't know," he said. "Baby, I don't want to leave yet. We're on a good groove."

"Fuck your groove," she said. "I'm cooking dinner for us."

"You're such a hypocrite, Sherise. Remember when you

were working on that big U Street project? You called to cancel our date nights or called me to tell me you were coming home late all the time. This project is like that for me."

Sherise was struck with a pang of guilt when he mentioned the U Street project. That project was a lie. She had used it as an excuse to spend more time with the Chains, the ladies' club she was trying to get into, and more time with Ryan Hodgkins.

It suddenly struck her. Was Justin lying to her? He was calling her from work on a Sunday saying he'd be skipping dinner. Was he at work? Had he been golfing yesterday? She thought of all the excuses she'd made when she was spending time with Ryan, including that fateful afternoon when she'd met him in a hotel and made love to him that one time. That one time that she thought might have changed her life forever.

Who was she kidding? This was Justin she was talking about. Cheaters always suspected everyone else was cheating, and that is what she was. She had cheated on her husband twice, and it was only natural that she believed he was cheating on her. But Justin wasn't a cheater and he would never cheat on her. One of main reasons she married him was because he was reliable and trustworthy.

"I'll see you when you get home," she said sweetly before hanging up.

She rushed over to her baby, and to Cady's great delight, picked her up and held her in her arms.

"Mommy is being silly," she said. "All kinds of crazy thoughts. She needs to calm down and you and I need to order Italian."

4

Billie regretted a lot about having to leave the public defender's office for big law, but things were getting better for her. With her new pro bono case, she was finding a way to love her new life. And she was finding a way to love her new shopping budget.

Running her weekend errands, she couldn't help but stop by the Bottega Veneta store. She was eyeing the Fire Opal Waxed Cervo bag and was falling in love. The little angel on her shoulder telling her she did not need an eighteen-hundred-dollar bag was on its last breath. The little devil telling her how much more fabulous she would look, and besides, she deserved it for working so hard, was clearly winning.

The battle between common sense and fashion sense was interrupted by the tiny beeping sound her phone made, telling her there was a text message. Grabbing her phone out of her Burberry purse, which suddenly seemed old and worn now, she noticed the number on top of the text was unfamiliar. She read the text.

Otis Redding tribute concert at the 9:30 Club
tonight. Remember getting your groove on?

Billie smiled, remembering the short moment she shared with Ricky during their meeting earlier that week. The 9:30 Club was a local club on U Street where mostly R&B bands performed. She wasn't sure if it was the lawyer in her or the woman in her, but her overanalyzing gene kicked in. Was he just trying to ingratiate himself with his new lawyer or was he flirting with her? Was he asking her out or was he just mentioning it for friendly purposes? He couldn't possibly be asking her out. That was silly. She would have loved to have gone though.

She pressed the button to reply, trying to think of something witty to say, but as her fingers typed the first few letters, she stopped herself. She was giggling like a schoolgirl and this was wrong. This was her client, and if it was true he was flirting with her, these were not the conversations they should be having. She knew this and wondered what had made her temporarily forget it. This was her first pro bono case and she had to be perfect. She couldn't make stupid mistakes.

She canceled the reply and put her phone back in her purse. Just as she let it go, she heard the beep again. Grabbing it again, she read the text.

Wanna meet up there?

Oh, no. Billie realized this could be dangerous. Not because he asked her out. She had defended more than a few men, and one woman, who asked her out during or after their professional relationship. The problem was, for the first time, she wanted to go. She wanted to see the concert, and she had been looking forward to meeting with him again anyway. She was telling herself it was to update him on the case, but she was lying. She liked him. They had clicked during their short meeting, and she had thought of him a few times since.

She wasn't going to reply. It wasn't his fault. He had no

idea what the rules of their professional relationship were. She would explain it to him at their next meeting at the office.

She placed the phone back in her purse and paused for a second before letting the beauty of her new bright summer purse get her back on track. After all, she deserved it.

"You better not let them see you like this."

Billie looked up at Richard sitting at his desk across from her in their shared office. "What do you mean?"

"That smile on your face," he said, laughing. "You're practically giddy. You're working on your pro bono case, aren't you?"

"Just doing a few checks." She placed her finger to her mouth in a hushing gesture. The door to their office was open. She didn't want anyone to know she was working on this right now.

"You never smile when you're working," Richard said. "If they see you smile now and find out that you only do it when you're working for free . . . well, it's not going to impress."

Billie couldn't hide her excitement. "There is something here, Richard."

"There probably isn't." He leaned back in his chair, joining his hands behind his head. His smile was charming. "You're an idealistic lawyer. You want there to be a government slash corporate conspiracy behind every little guy's bad luck."

"You mark my words," Billie said as she bit on the cap of her pen. "There is something going on. Ricky is a good brother. If he says his building is up to code, then—"

"He would have no idea," Richard interrupted. "His word means nothing. You would be wise to wait until you have the shelter professionally coded to find out the truth."

"Something is up," Billie said. "I can smell it."

"You mean you want to smell it. This is your daughterly justice syndrome. Don't let it cloud your judgment, Billie."

Billie's father died in prison, serving time for a crime he

didn't commit. He'd been in the wrong place at the wrong time after a tourist from Germany had been robbed and stabbed in an alley behind the restaurant where he worked as a cook. Tony Carter was not well educated, but he had never had trouble with the law. He was a good husband and a good father. He was caught in the alley by the police only minutes after the crime and identified by the victim.

Of course he never confessed to the crime, but an apathetic public defender and a system set up to usher him into prison without a second thought were both more than he could fight. He was making progress on an appeal when a fellow inmate stabbed him after Tony refused to help him keep some contraband in his cell. He died from his wounds. Billie, only fourteen at the time, decided then that she would become a lawyer and try to prevent what happened to her father from happening to anyone else.

There was a knock on the door and Billie looked up to see Charles Eckley. Charles was a thirtysomething man who emigrated to the U.S. from Bulgaria when he was eighteen. He was extremely kind and very bright. He was an associate in the real estate practice of the firm and had contacts in every state or federal housing division on the East Coast. Billie liked him very much. He was just one of those incredibly pleasant people who got along with everyone and had the best manners.

"Charlie!" She waved for him to enter.

"You busy?" he asked in that nervous, unsure way he always did.

He looked over to Richard for approval, but Richard reached for the ringing phone on his desk.

She shook her head. "Don't tell me you have some info for me already. I just asked you Monday morning."

He remained at the edge of the door. "You seemed to have an urgency about you."

"Sorry if you felt rushed."

"I'm not finished," he said, "but I have some news for you.

I called my contact at DC Housing and asked him about the guy who inspected the shelter. Nic Wyle has been reprimanded twice for bogus reports. He's not known for his attention to detail."

"Could you find any evidence that he was influenced into giving my client a bad report?" Billie asked.

Charlie shook his head. "No, but the issue with housing is that usually it's the homeowner that does the influencing to make the inspector overlook the bad stuff."

Billie wasn't satisfied. It was possible that Nic's report of the shelter was due to laziness on his part, but that would more likely work in Ricky's favor, not against him.

"I'll keep looking," Charlie said. "If there is more, my contact will be able to find out."

"Thanks for everything," Billie called out as Charlie waved and headed out.

"A lazy government employee," Richard said, hanging up his phone. "There's your lead."

Billie grabbed a Post-it note, crumpled it up, and threw it across the room. It hit the edge of his desk and fell to the ground. "Nine-one-one is giving me the runaround for those calls that were made about suspicious activity at the shelter, too."

As Richard shrugged his shoulders, Billie turned her attention to her ringing phone.

It was Sierra, the afternoon receptionist. "There's a Robert Frask on the line for you."

"Who?" Billie quickly tried to think of whom she knew named Robert, but before she could respond to Sierra, the line beeped and she knew Robert was on the line.

"Hello?" she asked.

"Billie?" The deep voice sounded uncertain over the line.

"This is Billie Carter."

"It's me," he said. "Robert Frask. We met at the club last week and danced."

She remembered immediately. She had agreed to dance with him only to get away from Sherise and Erica and their endless squabbling, but she actually found him cute. They spoke briefly and she didn't give him her number, but did tell him where she worked. Sherise pulled her away from him in the middle of their conversation to dance with her and Erica.

"Oh, hi," she said cautiously. "Robert. I remember you."

"I was, um . . . I enjoyed talking to you even though it was very brief."

There was a pause as she wasn't sure what she was supposed to say.

"I hope you don't think I'm stalking you," he continued. "But I was wondering . . . I know you're busy, but I scored an invite to an art event at Touchstone Gallery and I was wondering . . . Well, you mentioned that you liked art."

"I love art," she said, biting her tongue the second she spoke.

Was he about to ask her out? He was definitely about to ask her out. She wasn't really that interested. It wasn't so much that she wasn't interested, but she didn't know him. She didn't know how to date anymore.

"It's Wednesday night," he continued. "Sounds interesting. Some modern art exhibit thing. I thought we could do dinner first."

As she was trying to quickly come up with a kind way to let him down, there was a knock on the door. She looked up to see Amira. Amira was Richard's ridiculously beautiful, Italian girlfriend. She was an investment banker with long, black hair and olive-colored skin. She had piercing green eyes and was at least five-ten. She made Billie feel like a hobbit every time she stopped by.

Billie watched as she sauntered into the room to an eagerly awaiting Richard. As she watched him embrace her and kiss her passionately on the lips, Billie felt jealous. Not because she wanted Richard for herself, but because she wanted to feel that again. The joy on his face at the sight of her, the anticipation his entire body exuded as she approached. It had been so long.

"Actually," she said, returning her attention to the phone. "An art exhibit sounds like a great idea. I need a break from work."

Erica was home for only a few seconds before she started hearing the noises. They were coming from Nate's room down the hall. He was slamming things around, throwing something, and as she got closer to the room, screaming out swear words.

Erica sighed as she stood outside his bedroom door. She was reluctant to go in. She'd had a rough day at work and her body was screaming for her to sink into a hot bath and eat some ice cream. Nate's moodiness was getting worse. It was as if he was being a teenager all over again. She'd already dealt with that, raising him on her own all those years.

Erica had to admit there was a part of her that wished Nate would move out. She had tried to keep him close for so long to make sure he didn't go the same way so many young black men in DC went. She made sure he went to work and stayed away from thugs, and tried her best to instill in him the values their mother had been teaching them when she was alive. Terrell wasn't so happy that he was part of the package when he and Erica moved in together, but he grew to care about Nate, and Erica had thought he'd be a good example for him.

But Terrell had been urging Erica to cut the cord with Nate and let him go out on his own. He was all the family she'd had left so she was reluctant to do so. When she'd gotten engaged, she thought finally this might be the time for her and Terrell to be alone and begin their future together. Then all hell broke loose and she needed Nate around just to remember where she belonged. Besides, without Terrell around to pay half the rent, she needed Nate's income to help her handle the bills.

But lately, Nate was bringing down the whole house, and Erica really wasn't in the mood for it. She was happy again for the first time in a while. Making love to Terrell earlier that week filled her with hope that they had a future. Except for the odd lunch invite, Jonah hadn't been bothering her much lately. She'd been having mostly peaceful days until Nate came home and spread his attitude all over the apartment.

She knocked on the door. "What is your problem, boy?"

"Fuck off, Erica!" he yelled back.

"Oh, hell no." Erica grabbed the doorknob and swung the door open. "Who the hell do you think you're talking to?"

Nate, who had been pacing back and forth in his room, stopped and turned to her. His anger was evident on his face. He was a good-looking twenty-year-old with nut brown skin and thick black eyebrows that framed his handsome young face. He had a large nose and full lips and was sporting a short afro after a few years of going bald.

"I didn't tell you you could come in!"

"Do I look like I give a shit?"

She stepped inside, noticing the mess his room was. There was no way to tell if he had been tearing it apart. It pretty much always looked as if a bomb had recently gone off.

"It's my room," he shouted. "No one respects my fucking space. I'm sick of this shit . . . all this shit!"

"What shit are you talking about?"

He walked over to his window and looked out even though all he could see was part of an alley and the brick building right next to them. "Just go away."

"What is it, Nate?" Erica could tell something more than just a bad day was at play. The way he slumped his shoulders as he looked out the window. He was really defeated. "Tell me what happened and I'll leave you alone."

Nate kept his back to her. "I don't need to hear any more shit from you, Erica. You're not my mother."

"You better be glad I'm not," she said. "Because if you talked to your mother that way, you would be in for an ass whupping."

"I'm twenty years old!"

"No expiration date on a deserved ass whupping." She walked over to his bed and sat down. "Come on, Nate. What is it? You fight with Kelly again?"

"Fuck Kelly!" He slammed his fist against the wall so hard it made a small crack.

"There goes the security deposit," Erica said. "I hope you know you're fixing that, and what's up with this rage? Why do you have to be so violent?"

"I don't talk to that bitch no more." He leaned his head against the window, looking more like a sad puppy than a man. "I told you not to mention her name again."

Erica found that comical. Kelly had been Nate's girlfriend for almost a year now, but they had been having problems for the last month. She finally broke it off with him two weeks ago and Nate was trying his best to act as if he was fine, but he wasn't. When his boys were around, he acted as if he could barely remember her name, but when it was just him and Erica, he talked about her nonstop and acted lovesick.

"So you got into a fight with her again."

Nate turned to his sister. "She called me! This bitch calls—"

"Stop it," Erica said as she held her hand up. "You know how I feel about you calling her a bitch."

"Even if it applies?" he asked. "She called me about some shit she heard about me talking to some girl at the club."

"That's none of her business," Erica said. "But why are you talking to some girl if you just broke up—"

"I'm not!" He placed his hand against his chest as if to accentuate his earnestness. "I wasn't talking to nobody, but even if I was, like you said, it's none of her damn business."

"So what is this about, then?"

He shook his head. "We got into it on the phone and I kind of lost my temper. So some motherfucker comes up to me and is all like, you need to be quiet in the hospital and—"

"Nate, you got into a shouting match over the phone at work?"

He looked at her as if she hadn't been listening at all. "That's where I was when she called me."

"You know how frustrated you get when you talk to her. You should have made her hold on until you found—"

"I really don't need a lecture from you, Erica!"

"Fine." She placed her hands on her lap and looked up at him without another word.

"So, I get into it with this asshole," he continued, noticing Erica rolling her eyes. "I know it was stupid, Erica. I don't need your attitude, too."

"So, what happened?"

Nate shrugged and shuffled slowly over to the bed, where he sat next to his sister. He was looking down at his hands. "I had no way of knowing this, but . . . seriously, this dude was wearing jeans and a Lakers' T-shirt."

"Oh, no." Erica knew what was coming.

"Turns out he was a member of the hospital board." Nate slowly looked up at his sister with an embarrassed look on his face. "I got fired, Erica. They fired me."

"Holy shit," was all Erica could say even though she thought she probably should have said something more comforting. "Did you apologize?"

He made a dismissive gesture with his hands. "I ain't apologizing to that asshole. Fuck him. They never even gave me a chance. He was all, you're done here, you're done here. I told him to fuck off and went back to my job. Ten minutes later, I get called to the human resources office and escorted out of the fucking building."

Erica's first thought was of their mother, Achelle. She had worked at Sibley Hospital since she was twenty. They loved her so much there and tried to help her when she was sick. Erica later found out it was where she'd met Jonah Dolan as well. It was because of their mother that the hospital was happy to offer Nate a job as a maintenance worker there. He'd been there for three years. In the beginning, he hadn't appreciated the opportunity and was late showing up to work and slacked off a bit. Because of their mother, he had been forgiven and eventually he got his act together.

"You have to go back," she urged. "You have to go back and beg. You have to get on your hands and knees and—"

"I ain't doing that!" He shot up from the bed. "I ain't beggin' for nothing!"

"Just tell them you're under a lot of pressure," she continued as he began pacing the room again. "Remind them of Mom. They still have a soft spot for her there."

"Not these people," he said. "The administration has been all changed out. The old people are gone. All the people in charge are new within the last couple of years. They don't give a shit about Mom or me."

Erica wasn't sure what to do. "You need that job. We need that job."

"Fuck them and Kelly. It's her damn fault."

"Okay, then what do you plan to do?" Erica asked.

"I don't give a shit!" Nate grabbed his keys off his dresser and went to the door.

"Where are you going?" she asked, standing up.

He opened the door and, without looking back, shouted, "Anywhere!"

She went after him, calling his name a few times, but he stormed out and never looked back. Erica was left standing in the living room, feeling helpless. She didn't know what to do. The only thing she could think of was to call Terrell and that was what she did.

"What is it, baby?" he asked, sounding excited to hear her voice.

"It's a fucking mess," she said.

"Speak to me, girl. I can fix it for you."

His words were soothing and allowed Erica to calm down long enough to tell him what had happened. Terrell did what he always used to do. He agreed with her and used sympathizing and comforting words. She knew what he was doing and it was exactly what she needed. It was why she used to love just letting out all her frustrations and anger with him. He always knew how to respond. He never told her what to do or made judgments, and he always offered to help fix whatever was wrong.

"I'll talk to him," Terrell said, after listening to everything. "I'll tell him to try and get his job back. I promise, Erica, if I can coach him on the right way to go about this and keep his attitude in check, he'll get that job back."

"Terrell," she said, "I don't want this family's legacy at that hospital to end like this. My mother would be so disappointed."

"I'll take care of it, baby," he promised. "I will get Nate his job back and figure out how to set him straight. Okay?"

"Okay," she said as she felt her entire body sigh in relief.

In between Foggy Bottom and Georgetown was a DC neighborhood called West End. It was known mostly for its hotels, but there were also a few restaurants in the area. Blue Duck Tavern was one of those restaurants and one the nicest restaurants in DC. It had been a while since Sherise had been there, but she had an appointment at an area nail salon and thought it would be a good place to have lunch as well.

Sitting among movers and shakers in the area, she immediately felt right at home outside in the café area enjoying the summer day, eating her mango chicken salad. She shared little pieces of mango with Cady, who was sitting in a high chair between her and LaKeisha.

Sherise's adrenaline was high. Since her telephone conversation with LaKeisha on Sunday, she had done some research on Jerry Northman in her spare time. He was onto something.

He had a real chance of being the next president of the United States, and he was suddenly amassing a group of some of the best minds in campaigning. She had wanted to discuss it with Justin, but decided against it. If he was against it, it would just kill her mood, and besides, he was going to be out of town until Thursday, so she told herself she would just talk to LaKeisha one more time before discussing it with him. He didn't need to know anything yet.

But she was in trouble now, because after only forty-five minutes with LaKeisha telling her stories of the excitement she worked within every day, Sherise was salivating. She wouldn't let LaKeisha know, of course, but she wanted to do this. This was new ground. She had volunteered on some campaigns over the years, but she had never been in such an integral leadership role, and if Northman won, what could that mean for her?

"I can't wait until you meet Jerry," LaKeisha said, biting into her tomato salad. "He's wonderful to work for. He's not idealistic, which makes him so real, but he is inspiring."

Sherise tried to act as nonchalant as she could about this. "Well, if I do decide to look into this further, I probably should meet with him. I know you said he trusts you, but . . ."

"Jennifer!" LaKeisha yelled as she raised her finger in the air.

Sherise noticed that a few people stared at her, including Cady, who was a little perplexed.

"That was her name," LaKeisha said. "The woman who mentioned that you were a homemaker now. I couldn't think of her first name, and for some reason it was getting to me. I'm sure it's Jennifer now. Jennifer . . ."

"Well, I'm not really a homemaker," Sherise said. "I was just taking some time off to focus on other things. I'm not the homemaker type."

LaKeisha seemed happy with this. "That's why I know you'll take this opportunity."

"Jennifer who again?" Sherise asked. She wanted to know who was going around telling people she was some sad old housewife.

"Ross," LaKeisha said, frowning. "I think it was Ross. I can't remember exactly."

"Da-da!" Cady suddenly yelled as she threw her hands in the air. "Da-da!"

Sherise turned to her baby and smiled, but her mind was on Jennifer Ross. Who was this woman? She would have to do some asking around.

"Da-da!" Cady repeated.

"Daddy is out of town, baby," Sherise said as she reached for a napkin to wipe Cady's face with.

Just out of curiosity, she turned toward the street where Cady had been pointing. The street they were on had two hotels right across from each other and was busy and hectic, so there was no way to know what she was talking about, but just before she was about to turn back to Cady, something caught Sherise's eye. The cab screeching to a halt caught her attention and in the second she looked at it, she could have sworn Justin was the man who had gotten inside. She squinted, as if that would help her see better, but the way the light was glaring at her, she could not see into the car through the windows.

The car sped away as quickly as it had shown up.

"What is it?" LaKeisha asked, seeming to notice the look of curiosity on Sherise's face.

"Nothing." Sherise turned back to Cady and tried to wipe her face with the napkin, but Cady was pushing her hands away. "She saw that man across the street get in the cab and he looked like Justin."

"You said Justin was in Philadelphia, right?"

Sherise nodded. "I dropped him off at Reagan National Airport myself. It did look like him a little bit, but she's done that before. One time when we were in Neiman Marcus, she reached out and tried to grab a man who, from behind, looked a little like Justin. She screamed out 'Da-da.' You should have seen the look on her face when he turned around."

Sherise laughed along with LaKeisha, but as she finally gave in and stopped trying to wipe Cady's face, there was something in the back of her mind that wanted to tell her she had seen Justin. That was crazy. She had taken him to the airport herself. Why would he be back so early? Was he trying to surprise her?

No, she said to herself. It wasn't him. Even if Justin was back, he wouldn't be in this area. He worked and lunched around K Street and Capitol Hill. Justin was in Philadelphia and she was being silly. She dismissed it from her mind and went back to discussing a possible meeting with Jerry Northman.

Billie was trying to look at this evening from a positive standpoint. She wasn't at home eating a frozen dinner for one. She was eating with company, a free dinner at Estadio, a place she had wanted to eat at for a long time. She got to wear her nice new Alfani dress, which flattered her petite figure. Not to mention her date, Robert, was nice to look at.

Seeing him a second time, Billie was happy she agreed to have dinner and attend an art show with him. He was more attractive than she remembered. They agreed to meet instead of the formal pick-up, allowing them both to work as late as they could and change quickly before heading out to dinner. They had in common demanding jobs that required ridiculous hours.

When Billie arrived, more than a few heads turned her way, but Robert's wasn't one of them. As the hostess guided her to their table where he was seated, waiting, he was focused on his phone, typing a message furiously. When he realized she was there, he quickly placed his phone down and got up from the table. He looked pleased, but so was she. He looked very nice in an expensive charcoal gray suit and blue shirt. Seeing him in the light, his strong, traditionally handsome features were more defined and his sharp jaw line and piercing dark eyes appealed to Billie.

They got off to a quick good start, but within ten minutes of the date, Billie realized how the evening was going to go. It was all business. Robert, a financial consultant with one of the largest wealth management firms in the country, was constantly on his phone. It would vibrate for a phone call and make a ping sound when there was a text or e-mail. And they never stopped coming.

Being a lawyer, Billie's phone was always vibrating with a new e-mail or call, but she had no intention of picking it up during the date. Robert, on the other hand, was not going to pass up one message or one call. He always politely apologized before checking the phone and was as brief as he could be, but Billie was not impressed.

Even less impressive was Robert's incessant name-dropping. He was one of those DC elites who only cared about who you knew and what school you went to. He'd gone to Columbia and Brown, so he was Ivy League through and through. He seemed disappointed that she wasn't as socially active as he was or didn't seem as impressed with the names of the rich and powerful he knew. She picked up on a senator and a congressman or two, but Billie was probably one of the few people in DC who didn't worship at the altar of politics.

They were able to discuss some mutual friends. He had heard of Justin and Sherise and had met Justin at some finance events. He remembered Sherise being his beautiful wife, but hadn't known that it was Sherise at that club the evening they had met. He'd heard of them as an up-and-coming power couple. Billie would have to tell Sherise this. She would be happy to know that her name was still on the tongues of the DC elite.

Unfortunately, but not surprisingly, he also knew about her ex-husband, Porter. He was one of the most promising financial lawyers in DC, and this was Robert's world. He'd never met Porter, but had heard his name bantered about often. The one time Billie was grateful for Robert's ringing phone was when he asked her how she and Porter got along these days. Before she could nicely tell him it was none of his business and she didn't want to talk about her asshole ex-husband, his phone rang and the topic was never brought up again.

It was while he was on the phone that time that Billie realized what she was doing. She was having dinner with a near clone of her ex-husband. Robert had come from humble beginnings but had left behind everything he'd known to go after the almighty dollar and social status. She wasn't hating on him for it, but it made her question her own motives. Had she been initially attracted to him because he was similar to Porter? She knew in her heart that she was over her ex-husband. She had been for a long time, even before she'd stopped sleeping with him. But was her interest in going out with Robert a way for her subconscious to draw her back in?

It was silly, she thought. It was just a date, and as long as he kept taking his calls, returning his text messages, and name-dropping, there probably wouldn't be a second. She had done what she'd promised Erica and Sherise. She was getting back out there and she would do it again. It just wasn't likely to be with a clone of her ex-husband.

It wasn't all a loss. The meal was delicious and she was thoroughly enjoying the dessert. She was grateful to have someone to have dinner with besides Erica and Sherise for once.

Then, just when she had pretty much written Robert off, he seemed to turn a sharp corner.

"You are striking, you know," he said, as if he was suddenly realizing it.

Focused on her food, Billie's head shot up and she looked at him. He had been in the middle of a story about how he'd gotten his most recent promotion when he'd stopped midsentence to say that. Looking into his eyes, Billie couldn't help but notice that his expression seemed different.

"Thank you," she said softly.

"I have to apologize," he added. "I go on and on. It's my job to talk and talk. I schmooze people constantly. You know. You're a lawyer. You're always talking when you're with people. But you seem to know how to turn it off when you're supposed to."

"It's not easy, I know." She wiped at the edges of her mouth with her napkin.

"Can you teach me?" he asked.

His eyes held a humble expression, letting her know he was aware that he had not impressed her with all his power talk, and she had to smile. So he wasn't a complete loss.

"How would I go about doing that?" she asked.

"With patience, I hope." He leaned across the table.

"That is not my strong point," she replied. "But I can start by telling you to turn your phone off."

"It's on vibrate." He looked down at it as it sat next to his plate.

"Off," she said firmly.

She watched as he seemed to cringe, but his expression softened and he smiled as he reached down and turned off his phone.

"Put it away," she ordered kindly.

He took the phone and slid it down the table, placing it in his jacket pocket.

"Lesson one is over," she said. "That wasn't so bad, was it?"

"That was rough," he said in almost a sigh. "But I'm not dropping this class. I like you, Billie, and it's not just because you look banging in that dress. You've made a success of your life, but you still seem real."

A success? She almost wanted to laugh at that. She had been divorced at twenty-nine and had to leave her dream career to pay off debt. But it could be worse, much worse. Where she was from taught her that. Considering where many people expected her to end up, she was doing amazingly well.

"What do you define as real?" she asked.

Robert didn't seem sure how to answer that. He was silent for some time.

"I don't know," he finally said slowly. "It's not a thing that can be defined in words. It's a vibe. It's a feel. And it's something I'm starting to think you couldn't pick up from me."

"I think you could be real, Robert," she assured him. "I just need to know who you really are. Is there more to you than your job and your networking skills? What do you really enjoy?"

Robert shrugged and embarrassingly said, "Work. I love work. I'm sorry, but I love the deal, the chase . . . the close. What about you?"

Billie's first thought went to her pro bono case. It was one of the only fulfilling things in her life. She smiled, thinking of the next time she would be working on the case. Then, suddenly, out of nowhere, she realized that she was looking forward not just to working on the case, but seeing Ricky again. What was the matter with her? That was so out of the question.

"Billie?" he asked, as if noticing he was losing her.

"Hobbies," she said suddenly and nervously. Anything to make her stop thinking of Ricky.

"You love hobbies?" he asked, seeming confused.

"No." Billie giggled awkwardly, still feeling weird about thinking about Ricky. "I just mean . . . We'll talk about me later. We're starting lesson two now. You tell me your hobbies that have absolutely nothing to do with work."

Robert frowned as if this was one of the most difficult questions anyone could ask.

"I'm gonna have to think hard about this one, because I

used to have hobbies that I gave up because work didn't allow for them. If I can think of one, is that what we can do on our second date?"

Billie rolled her eyes flirtatiously. "Let's take this one question at a time."

5

"That depends," Erica said into the phone she was cradling in her neck as she typed into her computer the e-mail addresses of all the people who would receive the press release she had been asked to send out.

"Depends on what?" Billie, on the other end of the call, asked. "He reminds me of Porter. Done and done."

"Not done and done," Erica corrected. She kept her voice as low as possible even though there was no one around her desk at work at the moment.

Billie had just told her about her date last night with Robert and was trying to get some feedback.

"It depends on how he reminds you of Porter," Erica continued. "In a good way or in a he's-a-materialistic-power-whore-who-would-cheat-on-you-with-a-twenty-three-year-old-blonde way."

"He had some redeeming qualities," Billie said. "But I think it would be leading him on if I went out with him again."

"So, I take it there was no kiss?" Erica asked.

"We hugged."

Erica was about to give her opinion of that when she noticed Jenna walk into her section of the room straight toward her. She had a look of determination on her face.

"I have to call you back," she quickly said to Billie as she hung up and placed the phone on her desk.

"Hello, Jenna," she said kindly.

Jenna, Jonah Dolan's assistant and gatekeeper at the Pentagon, was a fiercely loyal taskmaster. Working under her for the short time she did pushed Erica very hard. She had nothing against Jenna, but had been grateful to get away from her.

For a while, after Erica had left Jonah's team, he would send Jenna with peace offerings in an attempt to use her as a messenger, but after Erica turned her away a few times, she hadn't seen much of Jenna.

Jenna approached her desk, looking around the place.

"You seem to be doing well here." The hefty brunette in her mid-fifties seemed neither pleased nor displeased.

Erica nodded. "What brings you over here?"

"Jonah," she said, then noticing Erica's reaction, added, "and it's not what you think. He didn't send me."

"What is it?" Erica had enough to deal with trying to figure out how to handle Nate and reuniting with Terrell. She didn't need Jonah bothering her again.

"You do know he is being considered for secretary of defense?" Jenna asked.

"Everyone knows that." Erica pointed to the press release sent around the Pentagon on her desk. Jonah was just one step closer to the White House.

When she'd read the news, she had to laugh. Her father could be president of the United States one day. What a joke.

"Is that what you came here for?"

"No," Jenna said flatly. "I came here to tell you his father died yesterday."

Erica was speechless for a second. She didn't know what to say. She was sad to hear that as she would have been had she heard anyone she'd known had lost his or her father. She understood the pain of losing a parent. Before she'd known Jonah was her father, they had briefly bonded over the loss of their mothers, whom they both loved very much. Afterward, Jonah had told Erica that she reminded him of his mother.

"He lost his battle with pancreatic cancer," she added after a few moments.

"I don't know what I'm expected to say," Erica offered finally.

"He was your grandfather," Jenna said.

Erica's eyes widened with shock at Jenna's words. "How?"

"He told me," Jenna said. "After you threatened to quit and all his efforts to find you a job elsewhere and his peace offerings, I had thought . . ."

"You'd thought he'd been sexually harassing me?"

Jenna nodded. "While you were working with us, I was a little unnerved by the gifts he gave you and his desire to get you to like him. I didn't ask questions. But then he was so upset when you threatened to quit, I demanded he tell me what was going on or I would quit."

Erica wondered how long Jonah expected to keep her a secret if people kept finding out.

"I'm not going to go more into it than that," Jenna said definitively. "I just came here to tell you that his father is dead, if you care."

"Am I supposed to?" Erica asked. "Does he even? I got the distinct impression he hated his father."

"Your father is your father," Jenna said, not trying to hide the double meaning of her words. "He still loved him. Besides, I think he's mourning more that he's an orphan now than anything."

"What does he want from me?" Erica asked.

"Nothing. I told you he didn't send me, but he's told me more than once that he wished he could see you, talk to you, in the past couple of days. I thought you might be interested in calling him."

Erica sat back in her seat. "Or maybe I should drop by his house and pay my respects. That sounds better. I'll just show up and introduce myself to everyone as his daughter and show how I've come to comfort my daddy."

Jenna knew Erica was referring to Jonah's desire to keep his relationship with Erica a secret for the sake of his career and family, but she didn't let it show.

"His wife, Juliet, would love that, don't you think?" Erica asked sarcastically.

"I'm not a part of that, so please don't try to make me," Jenna responded.

Erica straightened up, knowing she had been wrong to do that. It just made her angry.

"Well, I'm not really a part of it either," Erica said. "Jonah decided I wasn't going to be a part of it publicly and I've decided I'm not going to be a part of it privately."

Jenna looked at a small piece of paper in her hand for a second before placing it on the desk in front of her.

"This is his private cell number in case you've lost it."

"I haven't lost it," Erica said, ignoring the paper.

"The choice is yours." Jenna gave her one last emotionless glance before turning and walking away.

Erica sat there for a few minutes after Jenna had left, unsure of what to do. Of course there was a part of her that wanted to feel sorry for Jonah. All her life she had wished she'd had a father, one who cared about her, spent time with her, showed her complete devotion. She envied little girls who had been blessed with that relationship.

She believed Jonah when he'd told her that he hadn't known her mother was pregnant. They hadn't been in a real relationship. It was a summer flirtation that ended when he left for the military. He had moved on with his life, married a wealthy woman with connections, and never looked back.

It was by chance that he'd found out Erica was his daughter, but from that moment on he'd had a chance to be honest with her and he chose instead to lie to her and deceive her. That, coupled with the threats he made to Terrell and Sherise once they'd found out, set his image in stone for Erica. When she realized that he wanted to be her father, but only in secret, she knew she would never want anything to do with him. That was that.

So why was her hand reaching for that sheet of paper on the desk? Was she stupid? She quickly pulled her hand away. She didn't need this. She had enough on her plate. Jonah had done well in his life to this point without her. He could handle this without her as well.

"It's about time you got here," Sherise said as Billie finally joined her at their lunch table at Café Milano, a restaurant near Billie's office.

"I'm sorry." Billie placed her purse on the table, but before she sat down, she reached for Cady and picked her up out of her baby stroller. "How is my baby?"

Part of Sherise envied Billie's hurried state. She remembered being a busy career woman and usually being the one who showed up late. But these days, she had all the time in the world.

Billie kissed a giggly Cady on both her cheeks, just loving every bit of it.

"You love you some Auntie Billie?" Sherise asked, smiling proudly.

Billie sat down with Cady in her lap. "I haven't seen you in a few weeks, little girl. I can't believe it, but she's grown in even this short time."

"Like a weed, girl. But I love it. Gives me an excuse to buy her new clothes all the time."

"I'm sorry I'm late," Billie said. She reached out with her free hand and grabbed a menu. "Just crazy as always. Have you ordered?"

"I ordered the prosciutto di parma appetizer for both of us." Sherise watched as Billie kissed the top of Cady's head while perusing the menu. "You are such a natural."

Billie smiled. She thought she would make a great mother one day. She had been hoping to start a family just before finding out that Porter was cheating on her. Her life should be so different right now. Fuck Porter!

"Hopefully, if things go well with Robert," Sherise said. "This time next year, you could be engaged and—"

"Stop," Billie interrupted. "We haven't even had a second date."

"But you're planning to?" Sherise asked.

"We're meeting for drinks this evening. Happy?"

Sherise frowned. "Drinks? After you've had dinner? That's a backtrack. What's wrong?"

"Nothing," Billie said. "He's got a big client lunch today and I have to work late, so we decided to just have a couple of drinks and head out."

Sherise was not pleased. Despite the fiasco that was Porter, she trusted Billie's ability to identify a suitable date. Unlike Erica, Billie had good taste in men and didn't seem to have an allergy to the more aggressive, ambitious, and successful type. The second she'd known Billie was going to dinner with Robert, she made her calls and did her research. He had a lot of potential, and with Porter's hold over Billie squashed, now was the time to strike for her girl. She hoped Billie knew that. If not, Sherise was going to let her know.

"This is bullshit," Sherise said. "I know it's been a while since you dated, but you know better than that. From dinner to drinks? You're putting him right in the friend zone."

Billie laughed, bouncing Cady on her lap. "Don't push me, Sherise. I will cut you off from information on this boy."

Sherise made a smacking sound with her lips. "Please, girl. You know I'll find out anything I need to find out whether you tell me or not. My concern is only out of love."

Billie knew that was true. She never doubted Sherise's or Erica's love for her, but things had been a little rough between her and Sherise for a while. Six months ago, she'd found out that Sherise had cheated on Justin with Jonah Dolan. Still sore from the destruction of her own marriage due to infidelity, things were tense between the two of them. They put their issues aside to help Erica through the shock of finding out that Jonah was her father, but tensions remained between them for a while.

Billie appreciated that Sherise had quit her job to focus on her family, because she knew how big a deal that was for Sherise. It was a small step along the path of their relationship, but as time passed, her anger went away. In the end, she couldn't stay angry with Sherise or Erica. It was impossible. They were her girls, her sisters, and nothing between them was unforgiveable.

The waiter returned to the table with their appetizer and took their lunch order before leaving again.

"You're scared," Sherise said. "I get it. I can see it just looking at you now. You're avoiding eye contact with me just talking about it."

"I'm not scared," Billie said, making sure to look her in the face as she said it. "This is a new thing. I just don't know yet."

"And don't let that discourage you," Sherise said. "Too many sisters are single because they want to be floating in the air around fireworks and rainbows the first time they meet a guy. If I felt that way, I wouldn't have married Justin."

Sherise knew the second she met Justin he was the husband type. Before him, she had gone for the super-sexy, dangerous type. She had wanted the guy who couldn't be tamed so she could say she tamed him. She had wanted the guy that sucked all the air out of the room and made every other woman green with envy. But she knew marrying that man would be a disaster. So she gave the handsome, but not too overwhelming, reliable-type Justin a chance.

"And you wouldn't have gotten this little blessing," Billie said as she looked down at Cady.

Sherise smiled nervously. "Exactly. Although I have a feeling she might be the only blessing we ever have."

"I'm sure you'll figure out a way to have a baby," Billie said. "And what about adoption?"

"It's a possibility," Sherise said, "but we've only been at it for six months and we haven't really been at it much lately."

"Go see a psychiatrist," Billie urged. "What's your problem with that? Just go see one."

"I don't need to." Sherise grabbed a piece of prosciutto and stuffed it in her mouth. "I know what they'll say. My lack of sexual desire is because of my lack of career fulfillment. I'm just not happy without a career."

"But is your marriage gonna be strong with you having one?"

"What happened between me and Jonah didn't happen because I had a career."

Billie's expression was strained. "That isn't true and you know it. It was exactly why it happened."

This was true, but Sherise didn't want to admit it. She was used to using her beauty to get the attention of men and using that to her career advantage. She knew that getting to lead the project that partnered her department with Jonah's program was key to getting the position of director of communications, which was held by her outgoing boss.

She had some competition in the form of Toni Williams, but as with other office rivals, Sherise had done away with her hastily. However, while she jockeyed for position close to Jonah, she found herself strongly attracted to the very powerful, very demanding man. He was also very attracted to her and pursued her aggressively. His pursuit included promises and connections that would enhance not only her career but her social standing, which, in a city like DC, meant everything.

"Well, what the fuck am I supposed to do?" Sherise asked, exasperated.

Billie covered both of Cady's ears. "Just tell him. Do it tonight. Make him one of your incredible dinners and tell him that you're unhappy and you can't see any way of you all being a happy family without you having some kind of a career."

"I can't tonight," she said. "He'll be too exhausted. He hates doing anything on the nights he comes home from traveling."

"Traveling?" Billie asked.

"He's been in Philadelphia for the last three days," Sherise said.

"For what?"

"For your firm. Some lobbyist conference."

Billie frowned, a little confused. Even though the lobbyist arm of the firm had practically no interaction with the legal arm, Justin had enough influence to get her an interview when she asked. The two of them rarely ever saw each other at work because their divisions didn't interact.

After chewing that last of her food, Billie said, "Every week we get an e-mail telling us if anyone in our firm is speaking or being published anywhere. I feel like I would have remembered if Justin had been on that list."

Sherise's antenna went up. Until that very moment, she had all but forgotten about thinking she'd seen Justin outside Blue Duck Tavern the other day. "But your e-mail is just for the lawyers, right?"

"No, it's for every division." Billie shrugged. "Maybe I just skipped over it."

"But did you know about the conference?" she asked.

"I'm sure I read it," Billie said. "I just don't think I would have forgotten his name. Although obviously, I did."

Sherise pressed her lips together as she watched an oblivious Billie pretend to eat Cady's little hand as Cady screeched in delightful fear.

So now what? Was she supposed to question him as to whether or not he was at the conference or hanging out in West

End? Was she supposed to first try to find out on her own if he was in Philadelphia? Did he speak at that conference? She couldn't deny that she had some doubt, but of course Billie could be right. She'd just overlooked his name on that list. Sherise wondered if she should try to get her hand on that list. This was ridiculous, wasn't it? She was talking about Justin.

Sherise just knew she wasn't going to let this go, she just didn't know what she was supposed to do.

Billie was thinking too much. She had to stop it. As she walked down the street to her apartment building next to Robert, she tried to remember what Sherise told her. Explosions and fireworks didn't have to come right away.

She had enjoyed evening drinks with Robert. They spoke more about sports, something he'd said was his hobby on their first date. She was impressed that Robert was able to focus on something other than work even though she didn't know very much about sports.

The bar they met at was only four blocks from her apartment, so Robert offered to walk her home and catch a cab from her place. Being walked home by a handsome man was something she hadn't experienced in a while, so Billie appreciated it. But during the walk, it was nagging at her that she still wasn't sure if she really liked him. Why not? He checked most of the boxes that any single professional woman in DC could and should want, but for some reason, Billie spent most of the night thinking about getting home and relaxing in bed with a glass of red wine . . . alone.

"You have to forgive me," Robert said, "but I'm about to mention something that relates to work."

Billie laughed. "It's okay. You did very well tonight, so I'll allow it."

He paused, turning to her with an excited look on his face. "I'll allow it? That sounded like sexy lawyer talk."

"Unintentional." She flirtatiously slapped at his arm and

could feel a muscle or two under there. *Don't give up on him yet,* she urged herself.

"Okay," he continued. "Well, we have the Lyle McBride annual fund-raiser happening at the Four Seasons in a week. It's a big, big deal in the finance world."

"I know," Billie said. "He was like a banking titan and the event raises funds for prostate cancer, which he died from."

"You do know."

"Everyone who is anyone in the finance world in DC is there," Billie said, repeating the phrase she'd heard her ex say several times.

"You've been there?"

"This is my place," she said as they reached her building. "I used to go with my ex-husband all the time."

He nodded. "I remember seeing him there last year. That was my first year. But I didn't see . . ."

"No," Billie said. "You probably saw a twenty-something blonde."

Robert's expression made it obvious he wished he'd never brought it up.

Billie placed a gentle hand on his arm. "It's okay. No big deal. I'm over it."

"So," he said slowly, "you probably don't want to go this year."

"Are you asking me?" she asked.

He seemed apprehensive. "I was going to, but if you don't want to run into your ex."

"That's unavoidable." Billie opened the front door of the building with her key card. "We're both DC lawyers. We run into each other at events."

Robert held the door open for her. "Well, look, Billie, I would love for you to go with me."

Billie fought every bone in her body that told her to decline. She wasn't going to let Porter interfere with her life anymore. Robert was being considerate and sweet.

"I would love to go," she answered quickly as they reached the second floor.

"Good." Robert said it as more of a sigh than anything else.

"This is me." Billie stopped in front of her door and turned to Robert. "You seem so nervous. I thought we had a good time."

"You may not know this," he said, "but whenever your ex's name comes up, you get this look on your face like you'd rather be somewhere else."

Billie's cheeks felt hot. "I didn't notice. I'm sorry. We don't get along very well and everyone likes to talk about him."

There was an awkward moment of silence as Billie tried to get over her quick embarrassment. She had been so preoccupied with wondering whether or not she wanted Robert, she didn't think that all this time, she might be turning him off.

Without thinking, she reached out and placed her hand behind his neck. Pulling him toward her and leaning his face down, she kissed him smack on the lips. He reacted immediately and wrapped his arms around her, leaning lower so she wouldn't have to strain so much to meet him.

Billie found the kiss nice, even nicer when he started kissing her back. He was strong and his grip on her was firm, but not too tight. She wasn't feeling any fire, but it was nice to kiss someone and not feel like she was ruining her life in the process.

Crash.

Billie stopped and pulled away. Looking into Robert's eyes, she wondered if she was hearing things, but he had a frown on his face as well. He looked at the door to her apartment.

Billie swung around to her door just as she heard more sounds inside. She felt her stomach tightening as she looked down at the lock. Nothing seemed broken in. She reached for the door, but Robert pulled her back.

"Are you crazy?" he whispered. "Give me your keys. You stay here."

He turned the lock and slowly opened the door.

"Hello?" he asked. "Who's in here?"

"Who are you?" the babyish-sounding female voice asked from inside.

"For Christ's sake!" Recognizing the voice immediately, Billie walked past Robert inside her apartment.

Tara Hass, her former stepdaughter, now fifteen, was standing in the middle of the kitchen about twenty yards from the door, holding a pot in one hand and a box of macaroni and cheese in the other. She was wearing a cute purple maxi dress, and her long, jet-black hair was in a ponytail. The confused look on her face at seeing Robert turned to a smile once she saw Billie.

"Hey, girl!"

"Tara! What are you doing here?" She turned to Robert. "It's okay. I know her."

Robert closed the door behind them and with a smile said, "She doesn't look too threatening."

"Robert, this is Tara Hass, who is not supposed to be here. Tara, this is Robert Frask."

The second Tara seemed to realize she had interrupted a date, a sly little smile formed at the edges of her lips. She looked Robert up and down and raised her eyebrows as she turned to Billie.

"What have we here?" she asked, walking toward them.

"It's nice to meet you, Tara." Robert held his hand out to shake hers. "Hass? You—"

"Don't mention him," Tara said with disgust as she shook his hand. "I hate him."

"Oh, here we go," Billie said.

Porter loved his daughter immensely, and even though he had used Tara as a tool to keep Billie in his life after they separated, she didn't doubt he would do anything for his daughter. But the two didn't get along and they hadn't for a while, since Billie left.

Billie had fallen in love with Tara quickly after they met. She started dating Porter in law school at Georgetown and found his love for the daughter he'd had as a teenager inspiring. He'd come from a bad neighborhood in Detroit and gotten a girlfriend pregnant. While she spiraled into drug use, refusing his offers for help, Porter took his daughter and left. He'd been raising her by himself for a very long time.

Billie was the only real mother Tara had ever had, and Billie loved her like a daughter. The divorce put an awful strain on their relationship, especially when Porter tried to bring his former mistress-turned-girlfriend, Claire, into Tara's life and their home. Billie had never adopted Tara, so she had no rights to see her once the marriage was over, but was finally able to convince Porter to let her be a part of Tara's life. He knew he was in over his head dealing with a headstrong teenaged girl on his own.

But since their last falling out, in which Billie had to threaten to give information she had on Porter to the DC Bar, possibly ruining his career, the real love of his life, just to get him to stop interfering with her personal life, things had been difficult. She was rarely allowed to spend time with Tara, and Tara was always angry with her for it.

"What are you doing here, baby?" Billie asked. "It's nine in the evening. I know Porter isn't just letting you wander the streets."

"What would he know?" she asked. "He's probably still at work."

"He doesn't know you're here?" Billie could just hear Porter blaming her for all of this somehow. "He thinks you're at home?"

"You have to help me," Tara said. "It's an emergency."

Knowing Tara and her penchant for drama, Billie was sure whatever it was actually was not an emergency at all. Regardless, she had to deal with this. She turned to Robert, who was already backing his way to the door.

"I'm sorry," she said, even though the date really wasn't going to go any further than the kiss anyway.

"It's okay," he said. "I had a great time."

She walked him to the door and stood in the doorway as he stood outside. He really seemed like a great guy. Why wasn't she more gaga over him?

"I'll call you?" he asked.

She sensed that he was more apprehensive than before. No doubt seeing her ex-husband's daughter at her apartment sent him a message that maybe Porter was still a big part of her life and always would be.

"She's a teenager," Billie explained with a shrug. "It's not a big deal."

He shrugged as if it didn't matter before saying good night awkwardly, as if he wanted to kiss her again, but also didn't.

Closing the door behind her, Billie returned her attention to Tara, who was fervently trying to make something to eat.

"You're not blowing up my kitchen again." Billie grabbed the pot from her and pushed the box of mac and cheese farther away on the table. "Now what are you doing here? I know you still have a curfew and it's up in a half hour."

"I need someone to talk to." Tara backed up against the counter and pushed herself on top of it. Sitting on the edge, she played with her hands over her lap. "You totally ignore me, Billie."

"That's not true," she said. "You know this is complicated. I'm not in the mood to get into this with you. When you do stuff like this, you only make it more difficult."

"Is that guy your boyfriend?" she asked. "Is he why you never talk to me anymore?"

"Stop it," Billie ordered harshly. "Guilt tripping me isn't going to get you anywhere. I need to take you home now."

"Are you having sex with him?" she asked.

Billie was shocked. "What in the hell? Why would you ask me that?"

Tara suddenly looked regretful and shy. "I'm curious. Like how long did you date before you had sex with him? How long did you date my dad before you had sex with him?"

Billie's first instinct was to get on Tara for asking such an inappropriate question, but fortunately she paused before letting it go. Looking at the embarrassed expression on the girl's face, she realized what was going on.

"Are you having sex, Tara?" she asked gingerly.

Tara didn't answer, only looked down at her hands.

Billie moved over to her and placed her hand on her arm, rubbing it comfortingly. "You can talk to me, baby. We've talked about sex before."

"Don't turn into an after-school special on me, please."

"I won't." Billie wasn't sure how to handle this. She knew that Tara would have sex one day, but she was only fifteen. "But you need to tell me. Are you having sex? Are you thinking about it? Are you on the pill? Do you use condoms?"

"Stop with the twenty questions," Tara said, leaning her arm away from Billie.

"Okay," Billie said. "I won't talk. I'll just listen."

After a short pause that was killing Billie, Tara finally spoke up.

"It's Greg," she said, her voice barely above a whisper. "He's been talking about it a lot. He wants to do it."

Greg was Tara's first real boyfriend. Billie had met him only once when she'd had lunch with Tara at the National Zoo and chaperoned their date, which was the only way Porter would let her go out with him. He seemed like a nice kid. Billie liked it that he seemed like a bit of a nerd. She thought it might make him a little safer than the wannabe hustlers going around high schools these days. It looked like she was wrong.

"All that matters," she said, "is what you want to do and what you're ready for. Tara, you're only fifteen. You're too young to . . ."

"I don't want to lose him." Tara was suddenly on the verge of tears.

Billie was angry now. "Has he threatened to break up with you if you don't have sex with him?"

"No, but . . . What if I don't? I mean, what am I supposed to do? I can't talk to Dad. He doesn't even listen to me when we're in the same room together. He's always working and you're always working, and now you have a new boyfriend, so you're just gonna . . ."

"Hold on a second," Billie said. "That is not my boyfriend, but nothing could make me turn my back on you. I'm sorry I've been so hard to connect with, but I'm here now. You and I will figure this out together."

"You can't tell Dad."

Billie's heart sank. "There is no way I can keep this from him, Tara. He's your father. I'm not your stepmother anymore. Even if I was . . . he has a right to know this."

"Know what?" she asked. "What if I don't do anything?"

"Which I'm hoping you won't."

"If I don't, he doesn't need to know." She buried her face in her hands. "It's too embarrassing."

"This is about more than embarrassment, sweetie. Sex is about your health, physically and emotionally. Even if you de-cide not to do it now, it is a part of your life, and you need your dad's guidance."

"Can you just take me to a gyno?"

"I will definitely take you to a gyno," Billie said. "But not without Porter's knowledge. I just can't do it."

"So you can't help me!" Tara hopped off the counter in a huff. "I might as well be talking to him."

"No, I will help you. Tara, I will work through this whole thing with you, but—"

"Forget it." Tara brushed past her. "I gotta catch a cab."

"No, Tara." Billie realized she wasn't going to stop, so she grabbed her purse and went after her. "Tara, wait!"

6

In the middle of her ranting and raving about how difficult Nate had been these past few weeks, Erica realized that Terrell was just sitting across from her at the dining room table in her living room, leaning back in his chair with a content look on his face.

"What?" she asked.

"Nothing." He reached for a french fry from his plate and popped it in his mouth. "Go on."

She was frustrated by his nonchalant attitude. "You're not taking me seriously, Terrell. This boy is driving me crazy."

"He is not a boy," Terrell said. He wasn't going to stop reminding her of this until she kicked Nate out and made him make his own way in the world. "But that ain't the point. Go ahead with what you were saying."

"Fuck it," she said. She reached for a glass of wine and took a sip. "You don't seem to want to hear this."

"What?" He raised his hands in the air. "I'm listening."

"But you aren't sympathizing," she complained. "I love that thing you do."

"What thing I do?" he asked, smiling.

She laughed flirtatiously. "You know, that thing. How you're always like, 'yeah,' or, 'how dare they!' "

He laughed. "You know I'm always supporting you."

She threw a french fry at him. "What's so funny? You've had that smirk on your face all night."

"I might have some good news," he said between chewing the fry he caught. "But I want you to talk first. A gentleman always lets a lady come . . . I mean, go first."

"Stop being dirty." She pointed a finger at her. "Tell me your news."

Terrell looked very satisfied. "I got Nate a job."

Erica yelped and jumped up from her seat. She rushed across the table and landed in Terrell's welcoming lap. "Tell me everything."

Terrell explained to her that a friend of his, Donnell, was second lead on a construction project in the Friendship Heights neighborhood of DC. They were looking for some extra help doing general lifting and delivery. The friend owed Terrell a favor and he called it in. Terrell told Nate earlier that day.

"How did he react?" Erica asked.

"He seemed grateful. We had a long talk about how he's been acting lately. I think he's going to get better. At least this job will keep him real busy."

Erica was grateful for that. The last thing any young man in DC needed was a lot of free time, especially one who seemed to be in a constant bad mood like Nate, which just invited trouble.

Terrell held her tighter, loving the way she smelled. "Now, it's only for the summer, but it pays seventeen dollars an hour."

"That's more than he made at the hospital." Erica suddenly felt bad, thinking about the hospital.

"I know what you're thinking," Terrell said. "You still want him to go back to the hospital, but, baby, you can't make Nate some symbol for your mother."

"I know." She lowered her head, nestling it in his neck. "I just hate the way that ended. Mom wouldn't have liked that."

"I told him that you would help him write a letter of apology to the hospital. He said he would be okay with that."

She slapped him on the chest. "Bullshit."

Terrell shook his head. "It took some convincing, but I think our Nate is about to get his shit together. Who knows? Getting fired from that hospital might be the best thing that ever happened to him."

"I can't believe you did this for me, baby." She grabbed his face with both hands and pulled him to her. She kissed him on his lips passionately and tickled his ears.

He leaned away and looked into her eyes as if he was searching for something in her joy, something not for her, but for himself. "I would do anything for you, baby. I want to be with you forever."

"I love you," she said softly.

She knew that she never stopped loving him even when she was angriest.

"I love you so much, Erica." He sighed. "If it wasn't for me fucking up with Jonah, we would be just a few months from our wedding right now, and I will always regret that. But if you can really find it in your heart to forgive me, I know we can get on that path again."

She knew he wanted to talk about getting married again and this frightened Erica. She knew she wanted to be with him again in a committed relationship, but her heart told her she had to take this slow.

"Speaking of Jonah," she said, trying to change the subject.

"Please don't." He rolled his eyes.

"He wants to hear from me. His father died."

"Baby, I do not have a single fuck to give about anything that happens to that man."

"Terrell, his father is dead. It's sad."

"Are you sure he didn't kill him?"

"Okay, that's it." She tried to get up, but he grabbed her and held her down.

"Okay, I'm sorry. I'm sorry, but you aren't thinking about going to see him or anything?"

"How would I do that?" she asked with a smirk. "Agree to meet him out back by the shed so we can share a few tender moments without anyone seeing? Fuck that. No, but I was gonna send flowers."

"He doesn't deserve it," Terrell said.

"He's an orphan now," she said. "I kind of know how that feels."

"Listen to me, baby." Terrell's face held a serious stare. "That man is a manipulator. He will play on your sympathy. Men like him, that's what they do. That is how they get where they are. He'll have you supporting him while he's still treating you like a shameful secret. Give him an inch . . ."

"He'll take a mile," she said, nodding. "You're right. Forget the flowers."

"Forget all about that man," Terrell said. "And concentrate on this one holding you. This man wants you and wants the whole world to know how much he loves you and how happy he is that you're in his life."

As she kissed him tenderly, Erica was only reminded of how much she missed this man for so much more than the way he made her feel when he touched her.

Sherise wasn't sure when she started to doze off in bed, but as soon as her iPad fell into her lap, her head shot up. It was only nine P.M. and she was falling asleep? What was she becoming? Yes, she had been running errands all day and dealing with Cady. She'd made dinner and finally got Cady to bed after her bath. Still, she was way too young to be this tired this early.

And she was angry. Justin hadn't been very helpful that day. She had left him alone mostly because he was dealing with some family drama. His father was retiring and his parents were sending him all types of financial questions and it was stressing him out. She knew she should have comforted him, but there was a voice in the back of her head still curious about his trip to Philadelphia.

Listening to the shower running in the bathroom, Sherise realized that she had an opportunity to investigate in that moment. Marking her place in the book she was reading on her iPad, she placed it on the nightstand and got out of bed. Going over to their closet, she looked through the clothes set aside for the cleaners. Whenever Justin came back from a trip, he placed his clothes on the short stand next to the rack to let Sherise know they needed to go to the cleaners.

She quickly ran her hands through the pockets of his suit jacket, suit pants, and the pair of jeans on the stand. She didn't find anything. Looking over the rack, she searched for the shirt she had packed for him. It was a baby blue with navy stripes Hugo Boss shirt, but upon grabbing it, she realized it had no pockets.

Leaving the closet, she made her way to the dresser inside the bedroom. The top three drawers were hers and the bottom two, his. She knelt down and opened the drawers, riffling through his underwear and socks. She started laughing to herself, because she had no idea what she was looking for. This kind of suspicion of Justin was new ground for her.

Closing the drawer, she stood up with her hands on her hips. She was about to turn and head back to the bed when she realized what was sitting on top of the dresser right in front of her. Justin always emptied his pockets out there and the contents would stay there until Sherise removed them or nagged him enough to clean it up himself.

There was some change and little pieces of paper. The first thought that came to her mind was a taxicab receipt. Would she find one from a DC cab on Wednesday around noon?

There was nothing but a couple of ticket stubs and a receipt for coffee at Starbucks. She grabbed the coffee receipt and noticed it was for the Starbucks at the Reagan National Airport on the day she picked him up. She was about to put it down when something caught her eye.

The time on the receipt said one fifteen P.M. She checked the date again. She wasn't sure why, but for some reason she felt she needed to. This receipt was saying that he bought coffee at the airport Starbucks at one fifteen on the day she picked him up. But she didn't pick him up until four thirty P.M. Grabbing the plane ticket stubs, she checked the time. Flight 821 from Philadelphia got into Reagan National Airport at 3:55 P.M. that day.

"What in the fuck?" she whispered to herself, looking toward the bathroom.

Just then, the shower turned off and Sherise quickly put the ticket stub down and returned to the bed. It would be a few more minutes before Justin emerged from the bathroom, but that was more than enough time for her mind to wander all over the place.

"What?" he asked upon noticing the angry expression on her face.

"I didn't say anything." She was sitting up on her side of the bed, arms crossed over her chest, staring him down.

Justin rolled his eyes and he reached for his laptop sitting on the chair just outside the bathroom.

"I'm tired, Sherise. No time for twenty questions. You wanna tell me what's wrong or do we just go to bed with you angry?"

"It's not like you to lie to me, Justin."

Just about to slip into bed, Justin froze in place. He looked at her confused. "What have I lied about?"

"You tell me," she said.

"Oh, fuck this." He got into bed and reached over to the nightstand for his reading glasses. "You've been acting weird since I got back, and I'm not in the mood to try and decipher you."

Sherise turned sideways to face him. "You used to love trying to figure me out."

He looked at her as if he was feeling a little guilt. "I still do, baby. Just not tonight. I just want to get some rest."

"Speaking of since you got back, let's talk about that."

"About how you keep giving me weird looks?"

Sherise didn't really know how to play the game from this end, so she decided to just go for it.

"No," she said. "About how you were in the airport for hours before your plane supposedly landed."

He flipped open his laptop and turned to her, his dark eyebrows slanting downward. "You're not making any sense."

"I noticed your receipt from Starbucks on the counter there." She pointed to the dresser. "The receipt said you got coffee at one fifteen. Your flight hadn't even left Philadelphia then. So how are you having coffee in a DC airport when you're supposed to be in Philadelphia?"

Justin looked confused. "Is this some kind of a game? Because I'm not amused."

Sherise's lips thinned tightly to express her anger. "Do I look like I'm trying to amuse your ass?"

Justin's expression hardened. "What do you think I was doing, Sherise?"

"Don't fuck with me, Justin."

"Then don't fuck with me," he said back. "I don't know what you're getting at, but I stopped by the Starbucks after I got off the plane. I finished it just before you arrived."

"But the receipt says—"

"I don't give a shit what the receipt says. Obviously the Starbucks computers are off. What do you think I did? Did I get an earlier flight in and just hang out at the airport for three and half hours?"

"Maybe you did, or maybe you . . ."

"Did you look at my plane ticket stubs? They say the time of my flight. While I can't vouch for the coffee store's register computers, airlines sure as hell aren't going to fuck up the time on their tickets."

Sherise stared him down as he looked at her a second before making a dismissive sigh and turning his attention back to his computer.

"Billie said she didn't have any idea you were even going to a conference last week, and usually they—"

"Billy works on the legal team. She wouldn't . . ." He sighed before turning his entire body to face her. "Look, Sherise. I don't know what you're getting at, but I think I have an idea. I understand why you would think I was messing around. It's not far-fetched."

"Excuse me?" she yelled.

"After all, you barely have sex with me anymore."

"That is not all on me, and how dare you suggest that it's okay to—"

"I never said it was okay," he argued firmly. "I just said I understand why you'd be suspicious. I have reason to be suspicious, too. You sure as hell aren't interested in having sex with me, so I can wonder who you might be having it with."

"How dare you!" Sherise scoffed.

"I'm not cheating on you, Sherise." He closed his laptop and placed it under his arm as he got out of bed. "But I'm not sure how much more of this shit I can take."

" 'This shit'? What shit is that?"

He stood at the edge of the bed. "The shit where you welcome me with a freezing cold bed and then accuse me of cheating. That shit."

"It's not all me!" She yelled after him as he left the room and slammed the door behind him.

★ ★ ★

Billie looked out at the Potomac River from the little corner she had procured for herself on the massive yacht. The sun
was setting and the boat hosting the annual must-be-at charity
gala was heading out of Georgetown harbor for an evening
cruise. It was a beautiful evening somewhere in the low seven-
ties, and the light breeze moved against her, causing her flowing baby blue chiffon strapless dress to slide across her smooth
skin. It felt good. She felt sexy.

"I found you."

Billie didn't turn around. She waited for Robert to approach the rail she was leaning against before turning sideways
to face him. He looked amazing in a tuxedo as he handed her
a glass of wine.

"You trying to hide from me?" he asked, leaning against
the railing as if he were a male model doing a photo shoot.

Billie sighed. "I needed to get away from all the panicky
investors who seem to view the world in terms of the Dow
and the S&P."

"Don't forget the NASDAQ." He held up his glass and she
clinked it with her own. "You know I'm not like them."

"I didn't say you were," Billie answered.

"But you're thinking it," he said. "You're wondering if I'm
real or if I'm one of them."

"Them being power-hungry, materialistic capitalists." Billie put her hand over her mouth, surprised at her own words.
"I'm so . . . I can't believe I just said that. I'm really—"

"It's okay." Robert reached out and placed his hand on her
right shoulder. "You finally got it off your back. Feel better?"

Billie smiled and tilted her head. "Actually, it does. It feels
great."

"Maybe this will feel even better."

Billie looked into his eyes as she felt his hand move up her
neck to her face. She felt like she was floating when his lips finally met hers. The kiss started off smooth and soft just like

their last interrupted kiss. But suddenly it grew harder and Billie felt her body begin to heat up. Something was wrong. No, not wrong . . . different. Something was different.

She leaned back, opening her eyes, and gasped at what she saw. It wasn't Robert anymore. It was Porter.

He smiled a wicked smile and said, "I realized you were planning to ignore me all night, so I thought I'd come and say hi to you."

"You can't kiss me anymore." She pushed him away, but he didn't budge. "You can't kiss me at all."

"What's the difference?" he asked, seeming confused. "Me or Robert, we're both the same. Despite what you keep telling yourself, this is obviously what you want, baby."

Billie was shaking her head furiously. "I don't want another you."

"You don't know what you want," he said, annoyed. "Let me show you what you're supposed to want."

He was leaning in to kiss her, but Billie wasn't having it. She pushed against him with all the might her petite frame could manage. He didn't budge, but the force of her push made her back away. She backed into something.

Or someone.

"Evening, Billie."

Billie swung around to come face-to-face with Ricky Williams. He was smiling at her in a way that told her he knew that she was attracted to him so there was no point in pretending.

"No," she protested. "This can't happen. You're my client."

"You can't deny what you feel," he said.

"I don't even know you," she insisted. "Just because you look good doesn't mean I want you."

"Well," he said, seeming unfazed by her rejection. "Let's see if this makes you want me."

His face leaned in to her as his eyes closed.

Billie's eyes shot open as she sat up, startled, in her bed. She felt her heart beating ten million times a second. She looked at the clock on the nightstand. It was three in the morning and everything around her was pitch black. She was at home and in bed, not on a yacht in the Potomac. It took her a few seconds to get her wits about her, but once she had, things weren't any better. What was her dream . . . no, her nightmare, trying to tell her?

"To hell with all men," she said. "I just don't need this."

"Sherise!" Billie snapped her fingers in front of her friend's face twice.

Sherise snapped out of her mental vacation and came back to the present. She was sitting in the bar area of Circa in the Dupont Circle neighborhood of DC, catching an after-dinner drink with the girls, but her mind had been a million miles away.

"What?" she asked.

"What is wrong with you?" Erica asked, sitting across from her at the small table. "Billie just mentioned that she's meeting Porter . . . alone, and you have nothing to say?"

"I didn't hear that," she said. "Why would you do that?"

Billie knew her lack of reaction was too good to be true.

"Don't worry about it," she said. "He can't seduce me any longer. I am so over him. When I dropped Tara off at his place, he asked if we could talk, but I just drove off."

"I have faith in you," Erica said, her voice holding just a hint of uncertainty.

"I don't," Sherise countered. "There's nothing you have to say to that man you can't say over the phone."

"Tara considering being sexually active is not really phone conversation," Billie said.

"Please tell me you talked her out of it," Erica said. "She's just a baby."

"She isn't," Billie said. "That's the point. To us, she seems like one, but today, their hormones are crazy and their bodies are so developed, I just . . ."

"It's in a public place right?" Sherise asked. "Do you need me to come with?"

"Stop it," Billie ordered. "I'm not under his spell anymore. I've moved on."

"Have you though?" Erica asked. "I'm not getting any fireworks vibe from . . . what's his name?"

"Robert," Sherise answered for her, "and he's perfect for you. You better cultivate that shit."

Billie was suddenly uncomfortable, even though she shouldn't be with her girls. "I don't know about that."

Sherise studied her. "Don't screw this up, Billie. He's a good catch."

"Have you even kissed him?" Erica asked.

Billie nodded. "It was okay, but I think . . . I have to tell you guys something and you can't judge me, okay?"

Both girls leaned in for what they assumed would be juicy news. Billie told them about her disturbing dream.

Sherise rolled her eyes. "You just need to get over that shit right now. It doesn't mean anything."

"Dreams can tell us a lot about how we feel," Erica said.

"Look who suddenly turned into Oprah," Sherise said. "Of course you want to encourage this. You date beneath you, why not encourage Billie to do the same."

"He's not beneath her," Erica said. "And Terrell is not—"

"It doesn't matter," Billie said. "Erica is right. He isn't beneath me. He's done quite well with his life."

"He has a record, doesn't he?" Sherise asked. Upon seeing Billie's eyes diverted, she said, "For fuck's sake, Billie."

"Really?" Erica cringed. "I don't know about that, Billie."

Sherise reacted. "The only reason Terrell doesn't have a record as long as my arm is because he's just smart enough to not get caught."

"I will throw this drink in your face," Erica warned, lifting her cosmo. "Besides, this isn't about Terrell. This is about Billie and Ricky."

"There is no Billie and Ricky," Billie said. "It was just a dream. And he sort of invited me to a concert."

"He asked you out?" Sherise asked. "Fire him as a client. Or give him to someone else."

"I am not giving up my first pro bono case," Billie said. "I don't know if it was really a date."

"Did you say yes?" Erica asked.

"No. This is what I'm trying to tell you. I can't date him. It's against the rules."

"Good." Sherise finished her Americano cocktail. "Then it's settled. Back on Robert. When are you gonna sleep with him?"

"Can we not go there?" Billie asked.

"Just do it," she urged. "Take it for a test drive and see if you like it."

"Stop trying to live out your ho life through other people," Erica said before looking at Billie. "I think the dream is telling you that you don't want Robert."

"The dream isn't telling you shit." Sherise sighed impatiently. "It's just a fucking dream. If you screw up this thing with Robert, you'll have to answer to me."

"Who the fuck are you?" Erica asked. "And why are you being such a raging bitch tonight?"

"Have we met?" Sherise asked. "I'm always a raging bitch."

"You're being a bit more of one tonight," Billie said. She was eager to get the attention of the group off her. "What's going on with you?"

"Nothing." Sherise opened up her purse on her lap, pretending to be busy looking for something.

This was a lose-lose situation for her. Yes, she should be able to confide everything in her girls, but her episode with

Jonah changed the dynamic. They knew she was a cheater now, even if they thought she cheated only once. With Billie's experience as a cheated-on spouse and Erica's constant self-righteous judgment, Sherise didn't feel comfortable telling them she thought Justin was cheating, even though it was pretty much all she was thinking about. She had to think of something quick.

"I'm just nervous," she said. "I'm meeting with Jerry Northman and his team tomorrow night and I might be working for his presidential campaign."

"What?" Billie looked shocked. "What is this about? A job?"

Sherise updated them on her conversations with LaKeisha.

"What does Justin think?" Billie asked.

"He . . . um . . ." Sherise went back to her purse.

"You haven't told him, have you?" Erica asked. "Mmm."

"Stop it," Sherise scolded her. "You don't know the situation."

"That you're keeping secrets from your husband," Erica said. "Is that not the situation?"

"Erica," Billie warned.

While Sherise was the one to usually start their fights, Erica was in one of her judgmental moods and that only made things worse. Billie realized she was going to have to be the peacemaker . . . again.

"Justin knows I'm unhappy being a stay-at-home mom," Sherise said. "He knows that I might want to do something more."

"Last I heard, he knew you were trying to get pregnant," Billie said. "How does this work together?"

"Does he even know you're going to meet Northman?" Erica asked.

"I want to see how this meeting goes first," Sherise said. "Then I'll tell him, if it's even necessary."

"You two really need to go to counseling," Billie said.

"You're overreacting," Sherise said.

"What about your family plans?" Billie asked.

"Like I can't have a kid after the election is over next year? This is a once-in-a-lifetime opportunity."

"It's a mistake," Erica said. "There was a very specific reason you quit your job to focus on—"

"Don't you say another word!" Sherise pointed at her. "You don't know what the fuck you're talking about. You've never even been married. You don't know how this goes."

"Neither do you, apparently," Erica spat back.

"Okay!" Billie, sitting between the two, placed her hand on Sherise's arm when it looked like Sherise was about to stand up. "Calm down."

"Fine," Erica said. "I don't care. Go ahead and ruin your marriage for yet another job."

"My marriage is fine!" Sherise realized how loud she had yelled that when both girls' eyes widened in response.

Her stomach was tight as knots as she looked around. The couple at the next table had turned to look at her as well.

"Dammit." She leaned back in her chair, feeling herself start to get too emotional. "Fuck you, Erica."

"I'm sorry." Erica was genuinely apologetic after seeing how upset she'd made her.

The table was silent for a few moments as Sherise regained her composure.

"I know I have to tell him, and I will after tomorrow night." She grabbed her purse and stood up. "I have to go. The babysitter can only stay until eight tonight. I'll talk to you guys later."

"I said I was sorry," Erica repeated.

" 'Night," was Sherise's only response before heading off.

"What was that?" Erica asked.

"Something is seriously wrong there," Billie said. "And you were just making it worse."

"I didn't mean that," Erica said. "I do care about her marriage. I love Cady and I love her. But something is wrong with that girl. She's gonna mess it all up."

Billie didn't want to agree with Erica, but she was worried, too. She wondered if Sherise's mistakes were finally going to catch up to her. She had no doubt the girl would land on her feet no matter what, but she didn't want to see her marriage fall apart.

"We have to get to the truth," she said. "Whether she wants us to or not."

7

Billie took a deep breath before she put her hand on the door to the small conference room and opened it. She was already doubting herself. She was doing a good job on this case, and one stupid little dream shouldn't take her off her game. She was too good a lawyer for that and she knew it.

She had never been physically attracted to a client before, but she had to stay focused. This would be the first time she encountered Ricky since the concert invite. She never responded to the text, but did send him an e-mail reminder of their scheduled meeting today. He never responded, but he was here, waiting.

As soon as she entered the room, she was presented with Ricky's back to her. He was sitting at the head of the small conference table, looking down in front of him. No reaction. She closed the door behind her and still no reaction. She swallowed hard and walked toward the table.

"Hello, Mr. Williams," she said in the most polite professional way she could manage.

"Hello, Ms. Carter." His voice sounded distant, but polite enough that she couldn't tell if he was angry.

She sat down two seats from him and looked at him with a smile pasted on her face. He was barely smiling, and after making eye contact with her, he looked down at the folder on the table in front of him.

"How are you doing today?" she asked, hearing her voice seem a little high.

"I'm alright." He shrugged. "I've heard you have some news for me."

"We're making some progress." She was grateful to get down to business as she opened the folder in front of her and began discussing the case.

This wasn't working. Billie was trying to focus on the case as she shared her progress with him, but he was making it hard. He was looking at her, no, staring at her with an indescribable expression on his face. She couldn't tell if he was angry or not, and refused to look at him long enough to figure it out. She was only a few minutes into her update when he stopped her cold.

"Billie."

Looking down at her notes, she could tell from the tone of his voice that he was irritated. Then she heard him sigh and she finally looked up. His face relayed a growing impatience.

"What's going on here?" he asked.

"This is good news," Billie answered, trying to appear oblivious to what he was really referring to.

He wasn't buying it. "I'm not talking about this case and you know it. There's, like, some kind of awkward wall made of icy bricks between us all of the sudden and I think I know why."

Billie fidgeted nervously and she maintained her posture. "I'm sorry if you feel I'm being cold to you. I'm only trying to help—"

"It's about the concert, isn't it?" he asked, leaning forward.

Why was he moving closer to her? So she could get a better look at those seductive dark eyes of his?

"What concert?" she asked, adding, "Look, I think we should just talk about what our next steps are and—"

"I was asking you out for a date and that was my fault," he said. "I shouldn't have done that. Clearly you aren't interested in me that way and—"

"It's not personal," she interrupted. While it would have probably been best for Ricky to maintain his current assumption, Billie felt compelled to clarify, even though it wasn't in her best interest to do so.

"You didn't respond," he said. "I can take a hint."

"I would have loved to have gone," she said, stuttering through her words. "It's just . . . You're my client. I can't get involved with you while we're on this case."

Ricky's brows raised and he smiled a bit. "So you were interested?"

Billie smiled nervously like she was sixteen. "What I meant was that I was interested in going to the concert with you, I just . . . We have to keep this relationship professional."

"Because it's the smart thing to do or because we have to?"

"We have to," she insisted. "And it's the smart thing to do."

He leaned back in his seat, looking at her with a mischievous grin on his face. "You missed a great set, girl. The brother singing sounded more like Otis than anyone I've ever heard."

"So you've seen many Otis Redding impersonators, huh?" she asked, laughing.

"I've seen a few. I told you I'm a fan. I thought you said you were, too."

"I am. I just didn't know people were going around covering the man."

"Well, now you know." He playfully smacked his hand on the table with a laugh.

George Credin did not knock before opening the door to the conference room, and when Billie turned to him, the expression on his olive-skinned young face seemed confused as to why they were laughing. It made her uncomfortable.

"Sorry to interrupt," he said as he cautiously approached

her. He reached out his rail-thin arm and handed a piece of folded paper to her. "You wanted this as soon as I could get it."

"Thank you." Billie took the paper. "Mr. Williams, this is George, one of our paralegals. George, Mr. Williams is a client."

Billie gritted her teeth as Ricky smiled in a way that made it clear he knew she was trying to cover by being so professional. Did he think this was funny? This was her professional reputation. George worked with all the lawyers in her practice, including the partners. If he went back and told everyone that it looked to him like Billie was flirting with a client, she would have trouble.

The men greeted each other briefly before George looked at Billie, turned, and left.

"Nice save there," Ricky said.

"It wasn't a save," Billie answered back. "I'm a professional and that is how we should—"

She was stopped in her tracks by what she saw on the piece of paper George had given her.

"What is it?" Ricky asked, looking concerned. "Is it my case?"

"Yes." Billie looked up at him. "It's bad news and good news."

"Bad news first," he said.

"We tracked down the time frame for the nine-one-one calls reporting you, so we can get a step closer to finding out if Sanders Realty is behind it."

"That is . . . um, good news, right?"

"There were four calls made in the span of two weeks and three of them are missing."

"How can they be missing?"

Billie shook her head. "That they're missing is the bad news. Only someone with a lot of influence could do this. This is extremely difficult to do, Ricky. Sanders Realty couldn't do this. Someone in the DC government has to be involved."

"I knew it." He stood up from his chair and placed his hands on his hips. "I knew it. Those motherfuckers paid someone off to get rid of those calls. I bet they did it as soon as they found out your firm was working on the case."

"We don't know that yet." Billie stuffed the paper in the folder and closed it. "I have a lot of work to do, but this could work in our favor."

Ricky nodded. "I knew this was the best decision I made the second you walked in that door. I can tell from the look on your face, you're gonna get to the bottom of this."

"I'm not a detective." Billie was flattered by his confidence. "But the firm hires them to look into things like this. It might take a little while, but I'm going to get right on it. Do you mind if I cut our meeting short?"

When she stood up, he took a step forward, and Billie realized that she was only a foot away from him.

"As much as I enjoy spending time with you," he said flirtatiously, "I want you to get on this now, too."

Billie tried to ignore the little spark she felt as she took a step back. "I can show you out."

"I know the way," he said. He approached the door before her, placing his hand on the doorknob. "Wait a second."

"Yes?" She stopped.

"You said something before that I need clarified."

"Of course," she said, opening her folder to review what little notes she had shared with him.

He reached out and closed the folder back up. His hand brushed against hers and Billie felt a little jolt of electricity run up her arm. She stepped back.

"You said earlier that you can't get involved with me while you're on the case." His voice was quiet, but direct. "Does that mean that when this is over, I have a chance?"

Billie rolled her eyes flirtatiously even though she didn't mean to. She shouldn't do things to lead him on. "Can I please just get to my office so I can work on your case?"

He laughed, opening the door for her. He was halfway down the opposite end of the hallway before he said, "Imma take that as a yes."

Billie froze in place, wondering who heard him and what they thought. She rushed out of the hallway before any curious people could come out to see what was going on. She stepped in the elevator and the doors closed. The doors were floor-to-ceiling mirrors and she could clearly see herself smiling from cheek to cheek.

Domesticity was a compromise for a modern woman. This was the excuse Erica gave herself as she lifted the precooked rotisserie chicken out of the container it came in and placed it on top of the platter. Chicken from the store and mashed potatoes from a box.

"I made the salad," she exclaimed to the empty apartment.

She placed the chicken and the pot of mashed potatoes in the oven just to keep them warm. She looked up at the clock on her kitchen wall. Terrell would be there soon, after his first day in his newly promoted position, and she wanted to have dinner on the table and look sexy. She didn't have much time to change.

Just as she was about to rush down the hall to her bedroom, the doorbell rang.

"Shit," she said. Today of all days, Terrell decided to be early.

She looked down at herself. She looked okay in the black slacks and red rayon short-sleeve blouse she'd worn to work, but she sure as hell wasn't looking sexy.

"Hey, bab—" She swung the door open and was stopped in her tracks as she realized it wasn't Terrell.

"Hello, Erica," Jonah Dolan said quietly.

Jonah Dolan was a very attractive older man with a powerful presence. He looked to be in his forties even though he was a decade older. He was about six-four, with a conservative dark brown haircut with distinguished graying at the temples. His white skin had a nice warm hue to it, almost a light tan. His face was commanding and very handsome in a traditional way. He had a firm jaw line and thin lips that made him look very serious all the time.

"What are you doing here?" Her tone was more of an accusation than a question.

"Can I come in?" he asked.

"Why?"

"Erica."

Without even thinking, Erica stepped aside. The man had a way about him and a voice that made you instinctively just do what he told you to. He made Erica almost feel guilty for questioning him.

He stepped inside, looking around the apartment. "It smells great in here. What are you cooking?"

"Dinner for me and my boyfriend." She thought to close the door, but decided to leave it open. She wanted Jonah to know he wasn't staying long. "And I need to get back to it."

He turned around to face her, his expression softening. "I'll only be a minute."

"It's a minute longer than you're welcomed," Erica said.

He looked hurt for only a moment before brushing it off. "So you're back with him. Terrell."

"Yes, I am." Erica placed her hands on her hips. "It's none of your business."

He looked very disappointed. "You can forgive him, but not me?"

"Terrell owned up to his mistake," she said. "He's not the one who went around threatening people. He's not the one who wants to keep me a secret."

He sighed and nodded as if he accepted her judgment, knew he deserved it.

He pointed to the sofa. "Can we sit down?"

"You can sit," she said, "but I'll stand. I'm very busy."

"I guess we can do this standing." He walked toward her.

Erica backed up. She wasn't sure why, but she could tell it hurt Jonah's feelings.

"I'm not going to hurt you, Erica."

"How do I know?" she asked. "You threatened to hurt Terrell and Sherise. Why not me?"

"You're my daughter," he said defiantly.

Erica stood her ground, showing she was unmoved by his appeal to a meaningless genetic connection as if it meant they had a relationship.

"You know, Jonah, I was thinking about that. You don't know that for a fact. Unless there was some DNA test you did without my knowing. You said yourself that you and my mother weren't in love. Maybe she—"

"Don't," Jonah ordered, his expression darkening. "Don't disrespect your mother's honor just to hurt me."

Erica and Jonah held eyes for a moment as she wanted to say something cruel or mean, but couldn't. He was right and it hurt her to realize what she was suggesting about her own mother. Besides, Jonah had made it clear, and Erica later realized, she looked just like his mother, only a darker shade. He was her father. There was no denying that.

"What do you want?"

"I was hoping to see you last week," he said. "My father died."

"I know and I'm sorry, but that doesn't have anything to do with me."

"You're right," he said, nodding. "I was just . . . This isn't really about that. We're trying to get all his things in order so we can donate them."

"I'm not a charity case," Erica said defensively.

He seemed surprised. "I would never consider you that. Erica, any time I ever gave you anything or offered to give you anything, it was because I care about you. But that doesn't even matter."

"What does matter?" she asked. "Because I have to get back to making dinner."

Jonah reached into the pocket of his expensive coat and pulled out a silver chain. He opened his hand, offering it to Erica.

"I don't want gifts from you," she said, folding her arms across her chest.

"This isn't a gift from me," he said. "Take it, Erica. Look at it."

Erica took the chain. Looking at it, she realized it wasn't just a chain. It had a small pendant hanging from it. She brought it closer. It was a gold-lined topaz heart with the inscribed words To Achelle from Mama. Luv.

Erica gasped as her heart caught in her throat. "This is my . . ."

"It's from your grandmother, right?" he asked, smiling.

"This is Mom's pendant." Erica felt her eyes welling up with tears. "Oh my God. She was looking for this. I remember her telling me how she regretted losing this."

"I thought you'd want it."

"She gave me this." Erica reached under her shirt and pulled out her necklace with a pendant. "It's the exact same except it's morganite and not topaz."

She leaned forward so Jonah could see it.

"It's lovely," he said.

"She told me to never, ever lose this because she lost the one Nana gave her and she always regretted it."

Erica felt a tear roll down her cheek. She couldn't believe she was holding this. She had never met her grandmother, but had seen many pictures and heard stories of her from her grandfather and her mother about how amazing this woman was. She had a heart the size of the sun, a wicked sense of humor, and was whip smart despite having only a ninth grade education. She had high blood pressure her whole life and passed away too early after complications from a stroke.

"How do you have this?"

"Your mother showed that to me the summer we were together. She was at my house and . . ."

"I thought your relationship was a secret."

"It was," he said, sounding as if he wanted to seem ashamed of that point. "My parents were away. I sneaked her over. My sister was there, but she already knew about us. She took this off and showed it to me. I guess she left it there; either I put it away somewhere or the maid did. I found it going through some boxes of my old stuff in my dad's attic."

Erica walked over to the sofa and sat down, not taking her eyes off the pendant. She didn't notice when Jonah joined her, but after a while, she looked at him.

"She must have cared about you," she said. "She took this off to show you. I doubt she took it off for just anyone."

Jonah smiled warmly. "I asked to see it because she was always touching it, and when she touched it, she would smile."

"And then forgot about it."

"Well, that was my fault. We started kissing and . . . I think it just left her mind."

Erica smiled. "That must have been some kiss."

"It was."

Erica was starting to feel guilty about the way she'd treated him. "I'm sorry about your dad."

"It's okay," he said. "He was an asshole."

"Jonah, you shouldn't say that about your dad."

"It was the truth." Jonah appeared unaffected. "I loved him and I guess a part of me will miss him, but . . . well, it was what it was. I just don't want you to feel the same about me."

Erica managed a tentative smile.

"What in the fuck?"

Erica turned around to see Terrell, who had just come in the apartment, heading straight for the sofa. Then Jonah shot up from his seat and she knew something bad was about to happen.

She jumped up and rushed to Terrell just before he reached a ready and unflinching Jonah.

"Stop," she ordered. She grabbed him by the arms and pushed him back. "Just calm down."

"What the fuck are you doing here?" he asked. He wasn't charging anymore, but Erica was still holding on to his arms.

"You need to watch how you talk to me," Jonah warned.

"Really?" Terrell laughed, but with an expression that showed he didn't find anything about this the least bit funny. "You forgot to add 'boy' to the end of that sentence. I know you were itching to."

"Terrell," Erica pleaded. "He had to give me something of my mother's. That's why he's here. Don't start anything."

"He's not welcomed here," Terrell said.

"You don't live here anymore," Jonah said. "You don't speak for her. You never did."

"Okay, that's enough." Erica held her hand up to him. "You have no right to speak to him like that."

Jonah's glare left Terrell to focus on Erica. "You can't possibly be getting back together with this . . . this . . ."

"Say it," said Terrell. "Just give me a reason."

Jonah laughed. "You need a reason? You're already behind the game, then."

"Jonah!" Erica knew that if she let this go on, something horrible would happen. "You need to leave."

Jonah's posture softened, but only a bit. "I'm sorry, Erica. I didn't mean . . . I'll just go."

"You do that," Terrell added.

Erica slapped him in the chest. "Enough!"

Jonah looked at Terrell, shook his head in utter disappointment, and walked past them both out the door.

"I want an explanation for that asshole being here!" Terrell demanded.

"Who do you think you're talking to?" she asked. "I don't

owe you any explanation for anything. This is my apartment and I can let in whoever I want."

"So you defending this dick?" Terrell stepped back, looking hurt and angry.

"If I was defending him," Erica said, "I would have made you leave."

"So what was he doing here? What did he give you?"

"I don't want to talk about it." Erica looked down at the chain she had wrapped around her hand. She felt like she was holding a part of her mother that had been lost forever.

"It wasn't a big deal," she added. "Just let it go. He's gone."

Terrell just shook his head. "Ain't nothing good gonna come from letting that man in your life, Erica. Nothing good."

"I don't care what you have to do," Billie said, then caught herself. "Wait a second. I didn't mean it like that, David."

David Eklind was one of the firm's private investigators and she was working with him to get more information on the missing 911 calls for her pro bono case.

"I know," he answered in his raspy voice. "You don't mean break the law."

"And don't be unethical about it," she added.

He laughed.

"I'm serious, David."

"That's why I'm laughing," he said. "Look, I won't break the law. That's what I promise."

"You can't do anything to jeopardize my case."

"I know that. I've been working for the firm for ten years."

"Okay. Just get everything you can and update me. Don't wait until it's done. I have a feeling if we don't ruffle some feathers right now, it will get so buried that we won't have a chance."

"I will get back to you as soon as I know something."

As soon as she hung up her office phone, her cell phone,

lying on the desk, began to vibrate. She looked at the ID and saw it was Sherise.

"I'm really busy right now," she said as she picked up.

"You need to look something up for me," Sherise said.

She was going to do it. Sherise had been debating it all week, but decided she couldn't hold it in any longer. She needed to know if Justin was cheating on her, and something told her this "trip" to Philadelphia was shady. If she could have done the investigation without involving the girls, she would have, but she needed them. Besides, after finding out about her affair with Jonah, there was no point in trying to hide anything . . . well, anything more, from them.

"I'm not your personal researcher," Billie said.

"It will only take five minutes."

"Why don't you call Justin and ask—"

"It's about Justin," Sherise said quietly.

Billie paused. "What about him?"

"I think he's having an affair."

"You're crazy," Billie said. "Is this why you've been acting so weird lately?"

"I'm not sure, but I think he is."

Billie was extremely doubtful. Justin was probably the most honest, reliable man she knew. The only one left. "Why? Because he can't get you pregnant, you think he's cheating?"

Sherise was pacing the kitchen as she had been for the half hour it took her to get up the nerve to make that call.

"We would actually have to be having sex in order to get pregnant."

"You know what I think?" Billie asked. "I think you know Justin won't want you to go work for Northman and you're trying to turn him into the bad guy to justify doing it anyway. You do that, Sherise."

"What are you talking about?"

"When you know you're wrong, you try to make the other person the bad guy so you can say at least they're worse."

"Are you really attacking me now?" Sherise asked, getting angrier every second. "I come to you for help and this is your response? You're turning into Erica, blaming me for everything."

"I haven't seen him with anyone here at the firm," Billie said. "There aren't any rumors going around. Is that what you want to know?"

Sherise explained everything that she had heard and seen up to that point, including the receipt at the airport, which had added to the tension in their marriage before their argument and since; Sherise needed to know more.

"I went online and couldn't find any information on that conference, except that it happened at the Westin Philadelphia on the dates Justin says he was there."

"Lobbyists like to keep their conferences secret," Billie said, even though she didn't know that was true. It sounded better. "But he had the date right."

"But there was no hotel charge to any of our credit cards."

"The hotel and airfare would have been prepaid for on a corporate account."

"Can you find them?" Sherise asked.

"I can't go through billing and ask for someone else's receipts."

"Then what about the e-mail?"

"What e-mail?"

"The one announcing speaking engagements within the firm."

"You're being ridic—"

"Billie, just do it!"

Billie was taken aback by the desperation in Sherise's voice. She did not sound like the woman she knew. She was seriously worried.

"Hold on a second," she said calmly. "It was a while ago. I've already deleted it. I have to go back and find it."

"I just need to know if the company confirmed he was speaking at that conference or not."

"Okay," Billie said. "I really do think you're overreacting, Sherise. I think you need a weekend off or something."

"Off from what?" Sherise asked. "I don't do anything."

"Just some time away from your life."

"I can't go anywhere," Sherise said. "Jerry Northman has asked for my help with a fund-raiser."

"So you're working for him?"

"It's sort of a trial," Sherise said.

"Which, let me guess, you have not told Justin . . ."

Sherise felt her stomach tighten at the silence. "What? What is it?"

"I found it."

Billie pulled up the e-mail that was sent weekly to announce who within the firm received an award, was quoted in an article, or would be speaking on behalf of the firm around the world.

"Okay," she spoke as she read. "This week's speaking engagements. Cole Slinken and Brian Wong will be speaking on a Regulatory 101 panel at the New Finance Reform Public Affairs conference in Philadelphia at the Westin hotel."

Sherise recognized both the names as Justin's coworkers. She had met both men and their wives.

"And that's it?" she asked.

Billie sighed. "Yes, but, Sherise, they could have made a mistake. They might have missed his name or it's possible he replaced Cole or Brian, but the firm didn't update their records before—"

"He wasn't there," Sherise said solemnly. Was this really happening to her?

"Maybe he wasn't speaking," Billie said. "Maybe he was just attending. That happens all the time."

"Or maybe he's lying." Sherise felt like she was going to be sick.

She kissed a cooing Cady just to make herself feel better, but it didn't work. She felt like a brick was sinking in her stomach.

"I just don't believe it," Billie said. Maybe she was just being hopeful. Justin was nothing like Porter. "He's just not that guy."

"Every guy is that guy," Sherise said. "I guess I deserve it."

"Don't say that." Billie couldn't think of more to say about that.

She knew Sherise didn't have much moral ground to stand on if it was true, but that didn't matter. She was her friend and she was scared.

"I know that's what you're thinking," Sherise said.

"I'm thinking that you need more than this to assume Justin is cheating on you."

"What else can you get me?"

"Me?"

"You've been through this before, Billie. You know what I need to be doing. Besides, you're right there with him every day."

"I'm not with him," Billie said. "I go weeks without even seeing him in the hallway."

"I need you to spy for me. I'm gonna—"

"No, Sherise."

"I'm gonna follow him the next time he goes out for a meeting," she continued as if not hearing Billie's protests. "You can go through his office."

"I can't do that," she whispered into her phone even though she was alone in her office. "This is a law firm. There is very confidential information floating around here."

There was silence and Billie wondered if Sherise was still on the line.

"I need you, Billie."

Well, damn. Billie wasn't going to be able to turn that down. They were there for each other no matter what. Sherise would do it for her without question.

"Fine. What do you want me to do?"

Billie glanced at her watch. It was seven and Porter wasn't there yet. This was all she needed. From the second she got up that morning, she was dreading this meeting. Now Sherise was demanding she investigate Justin for cheating. She was thinking about rescheduling drinks after such a hectic day, but she knew that Tara's well-being was a priority.

Her phone vibrated on the bar next to her glass of cabernet sauvignon. She didn't recognize the number, but she wondered if it was Porter calling her to tell her he was late, so she answered it.

"Hello?"

"Is this Billie Carter?" a man asked.

"Yes," she answered, still trying to get used to that name again.

"Are you the one investigating the Saturn House code violations?"

"Who is this?" Her red flag went up.

"You should think twice about fighting for Ricky Williams. He's not who you think he is."

"If you don't tell me who you are, I'm hanging up."

"One of those nine-one-one calls was not removed from the log. Wonder why?"

"I don't know who you think—"

The static sound ended and Billie looked at her phone. The call was over. They had hung up.

"What in the hell?" she asked out loud.

"I'm only a little late. Don't get so mad."

Billie hadn't even noticed that Porter had taken a seat next to her at the bar.

"I'm not talking about you," she said.

Porter eyed her pleasingly. "You look nice, Billie."

"Look, I don't have a lot of time, so let's get right to it."

Porter frowned like a child disappointed he wasn't getting the attention he thought he deserved. "I was just complimenting you. Can we go somewhere more private? It's kind of noisy in—"

"Yeah, right." Billie laughed. "Look, Porter, this is as private as you and I are gonna get."

"Afraid of being alone with me?" he asked with a sly smile.

"More like disgusted at the thought," she answered back.

"I guess Robert Frask doesn't disgust you."

She thought for a second to ask him how he knew about her and Robert, but didn't bother. He would probably lie and just get a kick out of her showing it bothered her.

"This is about Tara," she said.

"Are you sleeping with him?" Porter asked, his expression showing some mixture of jealousy and curiosity.

"Fuck off," she said. "Can we get to the point? Your daughter is considering having sex with Greg."

Porter's expression froze. "What the fuck are you talking about? How do you know that? I'm gonna kill that mother—"

"Porter, focus please. Let's not go all caveman. She's not having sex with him yet and I don't think she wants to."

"She can't!" Porter slammed his fist on the bar. "I knew I should have never let her have a boyfriend."

"That isn't the answer," Billie said. "And, Porter, you need to understand that if she wants to have sex, she can and she will. We can try to make her understand why she's too young, but ultimately I think our job . . . your job is to make sure she is safe."

A familiar mask of stubborn insistence clouded Porter's face. Billie knew this wasn't a good thing.

"I can't do this alone, Billie. I need you. You're the only mother she's ever known."

"But I'm not her mother," Billie said. "You are her parent, and you have to take the lead on this. You can't let your anger and protectiveness get in the way."

Porter looked genuinely anguished and it touched Billie. His one redeeming quality was his love for his daughter.

"I don't want her catching something or getting pregnant and ruining her life." He ran his hand over his head before it fell forward. "Jesus, Billie. I don't know what to do."

"Here." Billie reached into her purse and pulled out some pamphlets. "This is from Planned Parenthood. Also, this is a good ob-gyn to take her to. She can probably talk you through this as well."

"I don't want any of that." He slammed the papers on the table. "I want you, Billie. I need you to help me."

Billie sighed. Why was she all of a sudden everyone's savior? "I'm more than willing to go to the doctor with you. In fact, I think she'd prefer it if I . . ."

"Billie." He reached out and placed his hand over hers. "I don't want to go to a doctor. I want to talk her out of this. I need your help. We can do this . . . together. If we—"

"Stop." She pulled her hand away. "Porter, we aren't doing anything together anymore."

"Fine." He stood up suddenly and looked at her with derision. "I'll do this on my own. I'm gonna forbid her to see Greg or any other boy. I'm enrolling her in a girl's school, and that's the end of it. She's not having sex."

"That's not the answer," Billie pleaded. "You'll make things worse. Listen to me."

"No," he said angrily. "You've cut me out of your life, Billie, so I'm cutting you out of hers. Just stay away from Tara and me. I'll handle this without you."

"Porter!" Billie called after him as he walked away, but she knew he wouldn't come back.

She ached at the thought that she had just made things worse for Tara. She was only trying to help the girl and she couldn't let Porter's anger push Tara in the wrong direction and end up causing her to ruin her chances for a good future.

8

Erica wasn't sure what was going on.

Terrell's head was between her thighs as his tongue traced the outside of her center. Usually it would have her moaning and her body moving every which way. Her hands covered his as they caressed her large breasts.

He dug his tongue inside of her and made a loud groan as his hands left her breasts and gripped her hips. He lifted her up, so he could go deeper. It felt good and she wanted more, but something was just wrong. He was trying so hard, she let out a fake moan just to make him feel better.

Then he stopped.

She looked down and he was looking up at her. Their eyes connected, and the second before she was going to try to fake it some more, she knew it was a waste.

"I'm sorry," she said as he sat up.

"What am I doing wrong?" he asked.

She sat up and waited for him to slide next to her. "You're not doing anything wrong."

"I know you, baby. I know your body." He watched as she covered herself up with her bedsheet. "You're not here with me. This is about Jonah, isn't it?"

"I'm just not feeling it," she said. "A lot of things are going on and . . ."

"I knew that fucker trying to come back into your life was gonna fuck things up."

Erica turned to him. "You can't blame it all on him, Terrell. You made the situation worse."

"It's my job to protect you, Erica." He slapped his chest. "I'm your man. Or am I wrong on that?"

"This isn't the time to test me, Terrell. You know you're my man, but you're not my father and I'm not a child."

"He's not your father either," Terrell pointed out.

"Whatever he is, that's for him and me to figure out," Erica said. "You have to stay out of it."

"I see what's happening," he said. "He plays on your sympathy with his dad's death and your mother's necklace. All of a sudden you're thinking you got a daddy."

Erica angrily wrapped the sheet around her as she slid out of bed. "If you're going to be patronizing, then you can just leave."

"It's the truth, baby."

"No, it's not." She turned to him, standing at the side of the bed. "Terrell, I've changed during those six months we were apart. Don't assume you know me like you used to."

Terrell looked hurt. "I know who you are in your core, Erica. I love that woman with all my heart. I would die and kill for that woman."

"But you won't trust that woman?"

Terrell just shook his head. "I also know that woman, just like me, wishes she had a father growing up, and I'm just afraid that wish is gonna make you fall for his shit."

"Jonah has shown his true colors." Without thinking, Erica's hand came to the pendant on her necklace, and her fingers brushed against it. "But he is my father and I don't really know if I can just ignore him completely. I don't know if Mom would have wanted that."

"Why do you think she didn't tell you about him? She obviously knew something was wrong."

"She probably didn't want to interfere in his life." She went over to the plush chair near the window and reached for her clothes. "Besides, that doesn't matter. What matters is that I'm not looking for a real relationship with him. I just think I shouldn't treat him like he's my enemy."

"Not yet at least." Terrell laid back in the bed.

She placed her hands on her hips. "What does that mean?"

"It means that man is going to be defense secretary and probably president. You're more dangerous to him now than ever."

Erica was fuming. "So what are you saying, Terrell? You saying this is all an act to get me on his good side so he can keep me under control and make sure I keep his little secret?"

"I'm saying you can't put it past him. I'm saying that you can't let anything make you forget that he threatened me, threatened Sherise, and admitted to having done horrible things to people who cross him."

"He wouldn't hurt me," Erica protested.

He looked at her as if she was a naïve child. "Bullshit. That man does not have good in him. Men like him don't get that close to that much power if they have a soft spot in their heart. Erica, I think you know I'm telling the truth. That's why you're mad. You know and I know, you cross him . . . he won't give a shit who you are."

Sherise was doing a lot of pacing these days, and once again, she was pacing her living room waiting for her husband to come home from work. She had made a decision. They were going to have it out. She had hesitated as long as she had because of her own guilt. Yes, she was being a hypocrite, but she couldn't help it. She had given up one of the most important things in her life, her career, to make him happy, and he was repaying her by having an affair.

There could be no other explanation, she told herself. She should be pregnant by now. He should be happy that he had his little stay-at-home wife. But no one was happy and there was another woman behind this. The second she found out who that woman was, Sherise was gonna make her wish she had never been born.

And as for Justin . . . well, she had to hear what he was going to say. She had to think of what was best for Cady, and if Justin wanted to work on this marriage, she would try to make it work. After all, she knew better than anyone that temptation was a bitch.

She had gone over in her head how she was going to force the subject and not let him divert the issue like he had before. When her phone rang, she rushed to it, hoping to God it wasn't Justin telling her he would be late again. She wouldn't stand for it tonight.

It wasn't Justin. It was Dr. Peña's office. Why would her ob-gyn's office be calling her?

"Can I speak to Mrs. Sherise Robinson?" the squeaky voice on the other end of the phone asked.

"This is Mrs. Robinson."

"Mrs. Robinson, this is Karen from Dr. Peña's office. How are you today?"

"What are you calling for?" she asked impatiently. She had no time for niceties.

"Oh . . . um." She cleared her throat. "Okay, well, there was a hold up on the records you requested. The woman who was supposed to process—"

"What records? I didn't request any records."

"Oh, um . . ."

There was a pause and Sherise heard some frantic hands on a computer keyboard.

"Sherise Robinson of 1783 O Street in Washington, DC?"

"That's me." Sherise felt her chest tightening. She didn't need any more bad news.

"You asked to have copies of all your records for Cady sent to your new doctor last week, but the woman who was supposed to do it just up and quit and we're—"

"Wait a second!" Sherise shrieked. Just the thought of someone curious about Cady made her nervous. "Cady? Someone asked about my baby?"

"Um . . . you did."

"Obviously I didn't, you twit. Was it my husband?"

"No, ma'am. I'm sorry, but the form here was filled out by you, signed, and includes your social security number."

Oh my God! Sherise knew it had to be Justin. Who else knew that number? Was Justin curious about Cady's paternity? She felt her heart begin to beat so fast and loud she thought she was going to have a panic attack.

"When . . . When did this happen?"

"A week ago," Karen continued. "The day you sent the form, the woman, Gillie, was supposed to process this, but she quit that afternoon. Her files got mixed up. It wasn't until you called again—"

"I called again? Who did I talk to? I want to talk to that person now!"

"Ma'am, I—"

"Now!"

Sherise felt her legs getting weak and she had to sit down on the living room sofa while she waited for someone to return to the phone. The woman who picked up introduced herself as the office manager, Thalia Adams.

"First of all," Sherise began, "I never called and asked you to send my information anywhere. I want to know exactly who called and what they said. Was it a woman?"

"Look," Thalia said in a deep, smoker's voice, "Mrs. Robinson, just let me say that I had no idea—"

"Fuck your apologies," Sherise said. "You almost sent my family's private medical information to some random stranger, and that makes you subject to a serious lawsuit, so you're going to answer every question I have, and if you hold anything back, the next call will be to my lawyer."

When Sherise finally hung up the phone, her hands were shaking. She didn't know what to do. She knew what she wanted to do and that was call Billie and Erica. She needed their help, but she couldn't do it. She would have to tell them everything.

What she knew now was that a woman, pretending to be her, faxed the office a copy of the standard records release form, including a signature and social security number. The form, which the office would be e-mailing to Sherise immediately, requested the medical information be sent to a Dr. Michael Moss's office in Dallas, Texas. Requested was any and all information on Sherise's pregnancy, birth, and the care of Cady.

Thalia, reviewing the faxed form, noted that the sending fax number had a 202 area code, so it was made from somewhere in DC. She was told the information would be processed and sent within the week. They had not known the information hadn't been sent; the office received a call from a woman claiming to be Sherise complaining that it was never received. Thalia promised to work hard to find the number that call came from.

Despite her frantic demands for more information, Sherise knew that Thalia couldn't do more for her at the moment, so she hung up and tried to figure out the tornado her life had just become.

There was still a thought in the back of her mind that Justin was behind this, but it didn't make sense. He had no clue that Cady might not be his. The only other person who could possibly know was Ryan, but she had neither seen nor heard from him since breaking it off after their night together. She was relieved to hear that he had moved to Atlanta shortly after their encounter. No one had known about their affair, and the way she had met him, fund-raising at a country club, was not well known.

Sherise had been hoping to get Ryan to contribute to a charity she was raising funds for. She hadn't want anyone to know she was wooing him because she'd felt that if she had, someone would try to usurp her. She had been trying hard to get into the inner circles of the back elite in Washington, DC, and she knew there were more than a few women who hadn't thought she belonged. Ryan was going to be her surprise contribution to the organization's major charity event of the year.

Very few people knew they even knew each other, and as soon as she'd made that awful mistake of sleeping with him, she cut of all ties with him. He didn't make much protest, having known that she was married in the first place and probably not wanting to risk destroying his marriage further. When he moved to Atlanta, Sherise was about five months pregnant and nothing could have relieved her more.

Was he back? Was he curious to find out if Cady was his?

Just when she thought Justin possibly having an affair was the biggest problem in her life, Sherise realized that things were way out of her control. She wasn't going to let anyone rip Cady from the only father she'd ever known, and no matter what Justin was doing behind her back, Sherise knew he loved Cady desperately and she would never want him to find this out. He couldn't. This just couldn't happen.

What was she going to do? Whatever it was, she couldn't do this alone. It pained her to no end, but Sherise knew that she might actually have to do it: She might have to tell Billie and Erica about Cady's possible paternity. She didn't want to. She was on the verge of losing her marriage and having her whole world fall apart. Was she going to lose her two best friends in the whole world as well?

★ ★ ★

"You've called emergency nine-one-one. Can I help you?"

"I want to report some drug activity in the alley on Charlie Street," the elderly female voice on the recorder said. "Y'all need to get over here."

"What is your name, ma'am?"

"Etta Gladstone. Y'all need to get over to the alley behind that shelter off Charlie Street. They selling drugs over there."

"Are you witnessing this now, ma'am?"

"They just started," she said just above a whisper. "It doesn't last long, so y'all better get on over here."

"Are you talking about Charlie Street in Southeast, ma'am? What is the cross street?"

"Look, y'all know where it is. It's, um . . . I don't know the girl that is buying, but it's Ricky dealing again and that boy, Randy or Ralphy or whatever the hell they call him."

"Are you witnessing a drug transaction, ma'am, or does it just look like it could be one?"

"I'm sick of you guys not doing anything." She made a loud smacking sound with her mouth. "You want to get these dealers off the streets, you get over there. If not, then don't. I'm done doing my part."

The emergency services person said hello a couple of times, but the call was dead.

Billie pressed the stop button on the recorder. This was the only 911 call that mentioned the shelter that her investigator could retrieve for her. He was still trying to track down the others.

She had been eager to get her hands on this recording ever since that mysterious phone call she had gotten the other day. Despite wanting to ignore that call, the fact that this emergency report was not removed indicated that it was separate from the case at hand. Now that she had heard it, Billie had a bad feeling in the pit of her stomach.

Reason told her that this call had nothing to do with her

case. Her case was about faulty housing code violations, and she suspected someone was trying to get Saturn House shut down so they could move Ricky out of there. She still believed this to be true, but there was an aching feeling about this call.

Ricky wasn't a drug dealer. She had defended many of them in her short career as a public defender, and she never got that vibe from Ricky. The woman sounded very elderly and Billie doubted she could see clearly in a dark alley from the comfort of her home.

She looked at the log for the call and it was three thirty in the afternoon. So it wasn't a dark alley, but still.

Billie knew she should set the call aside and focus on the other aspects of her case. This was a personal journey she had taken and shouldn't have done it. She shouldn't give a damn what Ricky did or didn't do behind the alley. The enemy here was the housing development officials in the pockets of the developers trying to push an important resource out of the way.

But she did care. She cared about Ricky and she cared about who he was and knowing that, even if she couldn't be with him, he was at least a man worth wanting to be with. She needed to know more about this call and about what went on in the alley behind the shelter for herself.

"Erica! How you doing, girl?"

"Hi, Tia." Erica smiled as she approached the receptionist desk of Destin Limo Services' small office in Silver Spring, Maryland. "It's been so long."

Tia, who in addition to being the receptionist was the daughter of the company's owner, seemed genuinely excited to see her. She was a very perky, petite girl who reminded Erica of Billie sometimes. Erica felt sorry for the girl because there were no other women working there. It must feel lonely at times.

"When was the last time you've been by here?" Tia reached over the counter to meet Erica halfway and gave her a hug.

"It's been a while."

"Well, girl, it was hard around here for a while when you and Terrell broke up. He was not the easiest person to get along with for a while."

"Well, that's over now," Erica said, hoping it was true. Despite her and Terrell's recent arguments, she still wanted him back in her life again. "Is he here?"

"Yes, let me call him and—"

"No, I want to surprise him." Erica patted the large canvas bag around her shoulders. "I have some treats in here. I want to walk in and surprise him right away."

"Okay." She pointed down the hallway to the left. "He's all the way at the end on the right now."

Outside Terrell's office, Erica heard a man's voice that wasn't Terrell. She wasn't sure what to do. She didn't want to interrupt a business meeting. She thought she might wait a moment, but wondered, if this was a meeting, why Tia hadn't said anything?

Erica jerked back a little as there was a sudden slamming sound from the room. Immediately after, she heard Terrell yell.

"I said no! Are you fucking deaf? Not him!"

The other person in the room started laughing and Erica couldn't hold off for another second.

She knocked on the door, but wasn't waiting for permission. She swung the door open to the tiny office and surveyed the scene. Terrell was leaning slightly forward behind his desk, his hands formed in fists on top of the desk in front of him. Erica didn't recognize the other man standing in front of the desk. He looked about twenty-five years old, was fair-skinned, and had a short afro. He was wearing Washington Redskins gear that was one or two sizes too big. They were both staring at her, and she could tell, despite the laughter of the one man, that she had interrupted something serious.

"Baby!" Terrell stood up and started toward her. His arms opened wide. "What are you doing here?"

"I came by to see you." She hugged him and he kissed her

quickly on the cheek. Looking into his eyes, she saw he seemed nervous and uncomfortable.

She looked at the other man, who had stepped away from the desk and was leaning against the wall now. He crossed his arms over his chest and looked at her, annoyed. Erica did not get a good vibe from this guy.

"I wanted to bring you by some lunch." She pulled the bag out of her oversized purse. "Am I interrupting something?"

"Why aren't you at work?" he asked, taking her by the hand and leading her to his desk.

"She works for the government," the other man said, his voice dark and deep. "They get any excuse for a holiday off."

Before Erica turned to the man, she noted the death-ray glare that Terrell sent him.

"You seem to know who I am," Erica said. "But I don't know who you are."

"That's your man's fault," he said. He stood up straight and headed for Erica.

It looked as if he was going to hold his hand out to shake hers, but Terrell stood in between them.

"That's Reedy," Terrell said. "He's one of my old friends from high school. He works at the car wash that we use a couple of blocks away and he has to get back there now."

Reedy laughed, nodding his head. "I get it. Okay. If my lady was this fine, I would want to be getting rid of you just as fast."

Erica feigned a smile as Reedy looked at her one last time before walking slowly to the door. She turned to watch him leave and noticed his style was just like the boys she grew up with. He thought he was hood and refused to grow up. He wasn't in high school anymore, but was virtually indistinguishable from high school boys in the way he dressed, talked, and carried himself. It was the way Terrell used to be before she came into his life.

"Who is Reedy?" she asked, turning back to Terrell.

"Nobody." He was focused on the large Tupperware box in her hand. "What did you bring me?"

"He looks shady," she said, sensing that Reedy was the last thing Terrell wanted to talk about. It made her curious.

"Every brother who ain't wearing a suit and tie looks shady to you." Terrell opened the Tupperware, looking inside. "He's okay."

"What were you arguing about?"

"We weren't arguing," he said. "You like my office?"

Why was he trying to distract her? "I heard you yell at him and he laughed."

"He laughed 'cause I was just joking around." Terrell removed a paper plate and plastic utensils. "It's all good. He's just looking for a job. He wants to leave the car wash and start driving. That's why he came over."

"Terrell, why won't you look at me?"

Terrell stopped what he was doing and looked up at her. He looked confused and a little nervous. Then he smiled and shrugged.

"I'm sorry, baby. I'm a little nervous. I was hoping to have this place looking a little better before you saw it for the first time. I wanted to impress you."

He walked over to her with an apologetic grin. "This is not a lot, but it's all I have and I want you to be proud."

"I am proud of you." She reached out and gently touched his cheek with her hand. "I don't care how big your office is, Terrell. I just felt like you were trying to hide something from me with that guy."

"I'm not," he assured her. "I wouldn't do that. I love you, Erica. I just know that you don't like me hanging with my old high school friends and I didn't want you to think we were friends or anything."

That was not what she wanted. She had come here to take a step forward in their relationship.

"Hey," he exclaimed, pointing to box. "Is that fried chicken? I know you didn't fry up some chicken just for me."

Erica smiled, proudly. "I didn't just make you some fried chicken, but I made mashed sweet potatoes and coleslaw. All your grandmother's recipes."

"What?" His eyes opened wide. "You dusted those off?"

She nodded. "I wanted to make it special for you. I was slaving over the stove all night."

His smile was ear to ear as he watched Erica place the food on the plate, and it made her so proud.

Standing behind her, Terrell wrapped his arms around her and pulled her body to his.

"I love you, baby." He kissed her on her neck softly. "I hope this is just a wonderful gesture for gesture's sake."

"It's an apology," she said. "I've been hard on you because of Jonah."

Terrell's enthusiasm disappeared as he let her go and backed away. "Can we please not talk about that man?"

"I'm trying to apologize to you."

"You don't have to apologize to me." Terrell sat down in his chair. "Just be careful about him. That's all I want. All I'm thinking about is you, baby. He's a dangerous man."

"And I know I've been trying so hard to prove to you that I can protect myself." Erica handed him a plate full of food. "But I want you to know that I love that you want to protect me. I'm not slapping you in the face."

"It feels like it." He took a bite of the potatoes.

She reached out and ran her hand over his hair. "I just need you to respect me enough to make a decision about Jonah on my own."

"You want me to stay out of it."

"No." She sat down in his lap and took the fork from his hand. She reached out and took another helping of potatoes.

"You gonna feed me?" he asked. "Best apology ever."

"I want you to support me." She playfully placed the fork

full of food in his mouth. "I want you to be there for me. I want . . . I want you to be with me like you used to."

"I'm here for you, baby. You know that."

"No, Terrell." She pointed to his heart. "I know you're here for me there. I want you here for me physically. I want you back."

Terrell's eyes widened as he realized what she was saying. "You want me . . . back?"

She nodded. "I want you in my bed and I want you to make my house a home again."

"Baby!"

He wrapped his arm around her waist and pulled her closer to him. He kissed her on the lips, shaking her until she starting laughing.

"Where in the hell is my phone?" Sherise yelled as she entered the main ballroom of The Willard Hotel in downtown DC. "Has anyone seen—"

"Here!"

Sherise was taken aback at seeing Erica there holding out her phone to her.

"What are you doing here?" she asked, retrieving the phone.

"You asked me to help you, remember?" Erica could see that Sherise had no idea what she was talking about. "Sherise, I took the afternoon off of work to come and—"

"Oh, yeah," Sherise said even though she didn't remember. "I'm sorry. I forgot. I'm glad you're here."

The event the next evening was for Northman's first official fund-raiser since announcing that he was launching an exploratory committee for a possible run for the presidency. He was giving Sherise an opportunity to help with communications and press. She was at the hotel to get video and pictures of the setup. Only her mind was anywhere but there.

She had found out that the health records request had been

faxed from the Fairmont Hotel in the West End neighborhood of DC. She had not heard back from the doctor's office on the phone call, but intended to call them again today and remind them of her threat to sue them. She had contacted the hotel but had gotten nowhere. She was going to have to hire someone, someone who would be willing to break the law if that was what it took to get the job done, to get more information.

She had pretty much ignored Justin when he'd gotten home. She was afraid he would notice she was terrified and also afraid that he still might be behind this and she would give away that she knew something. She didn't trust him. She was barely functioning at this point. She knew she should care because this was her test for Northman, but too much was at stake.

And seeing Erica standing there didn't make things better. She ached to tell her what she was going through, but she didn't. Right now, her girls were the only people in her world she could trust, and she didn't want to risk losing them.

"What do you need me to do?" Erica asked, noticing that Sherise had a frantic look in her eyes. "Hey, are you okay?"

"No, I'm not. The photographer took forever to get here. I lost my phone and . . ."

She looked down at the phone and realized that Justin had tried to call her twice, but did not leave a message. What did he want? Had he found out she was investigating who wanted her medical records? Had the doctor's office screwed up again and contacted him? What did he—

"Sherise!" Erica snapped her fingers in front of her face. "What's going on with you?"

Sherise blinked, trying to focus again. "It's just crazy around here. Look, I need you to pose for some pictures. We need to add some more diversity to the images we want to use for the Web site. So can you—"

"I'm just here to make it seem like Northman has a diverse

staff?" Erica frowned, placing her hands on her hips. "Good thing you didn't tell me beforehand. I would have said—"

"Can you just not judge for five seconds and help me out?"

"Yes," Erica responded. "And I can also turn around and walk out."

Sherise sighed. "Erica, I just need you to help me out today."

"That's what I'm here for." Erica was confused. Sherise was usually game for their back and forth, but seemed unable to keep up this time. "What can I do?"

Sherise pointed to the woman standing on the ballroom stage. "That woman in the red dress is Eden Gale. She's the event manager. She'll tell you what she needs help with. Then let me know, so I can send the photographer."

"Fine," Erica said. She turned toward the stage, but remembered something and turned back. "I have a condition."

Sherise sighed. "I'm gonna strangle you."

Erica laughed. "Terrell gets to come with me tomorrow night."

"No," Sherise protested immediately. "Absolutely not."

Erica placed her hands on her hips. "If I come, he's coming."

"Then you don't come." Sherise pointed at her. "You're not even invited. This is a fund-raiser at twenty-five hundred dollars a person. You're only coming as a friend of mine. One poor person at this party is enough."

"Fuck you, I'm not poor. I want him there with me."

"He wouldn't even enjoy it, Erica. This is not his element. Besides, there will be metal detectors outside."

"Bitch." Erica socked her in the arm. "You're not funny."

Sherise couldn't believe it, but she found a way to smile. "Seriously, Erica. This is my chance to prove myself to Northman. Don't do this to me."

"He'll be on his best behavior," Erica said. "He would

never do anything to upset me. Not now, especially since he's moving back in. He wouldn't mess that up by embarass—"

"Moving back in?" Sherise shook her head. "You are the most backwards-moving bitch I have ever met in my life. You could have moved on."

"There is no moving on," Erica said. "Not without Terrell. At least not for me. You need to face it, Sherise. Terrell is coming with me tomorrow night. He's back in my life and there is a chance that Jonah might be, too. Deal with it."

Before Sherise could protest, Erica had turned and headed off. Erica bringing up the possibility of Jonah in her life made Sherise wonder. Was the latest nightmare in her life connected to him? He had threatened her the last time they talked, when he thought she knew about his real relationship with Erica. Was this his threat, merely delayed, playing itself out?

Jonah was a powerful man, one of the most powerful in the country. If he wanted information to hurt someone, he could get it. If he wanted a social security number, he could get it. Hell, he could manufacture it if he wanted to. He could destroy lives as a hobby, if he wanted to.

She thought she was safe. They had planned the situation right. If Jonah even hinted at following through on his threats to her or Terrell, Erica would cut him out of her life. But hadn't she done that? After what Sherise had just heard her say, obviously that wasn't the case.

Whatever the truth was, Sherise could hope only that Jonah wasn't behind this, because if he was, she was outgunned. This man had the power to ruin her life.

9

Saturn House was a modest old home that resembled a bed-and-breakfast one might find in the country, but with a modern twist. The design of the home reflected the cultures of the people who had called it home for temporary periods of time. These weren't cheap pieces of clay or pottery one might find at a flea market or a museum gift shop. The rugs, the paintings, the wooden sculptures and ceramic bowls that adorned the three-floor home had been contributed by people who brought these things with them to America.

Billie loved that about this place, and as her formal tour, given to her by Ricky, was coming to a close, she got a very warm feeling about the home. She could also tell how much Ricky loved this place and how much the people who were living there now respected him.

She felt silly now, having thought of coming here to discover something about Ricky that would confirm her worries. This man was no drug dealer. He was a strong brother committed to his community. That, and he looked dangerously sexy in jeans and a black turtleneck just tight enough to define his muscular body.

The last hour had gone by quickly. Ricky showed her

around the shelter, but they had never been alone. People were coming and going out of the rooms and hanging out in the living area. Twin eight-year-old boys followed them around most of the time. It was a nice distraction. But now, the two of them stood alone in the kitchen, and Billie was suddenly aware of her attraction to him. She kept her distance, standing against the refrigerator as he leaned back against the large sink.

"What?" he asked, studying her. "What is that look?"

"What look?" Billie laughed girlishly. She didn't have the best poker face.

"You need to loosen up, Billie."

"I thought I was loosening up." She realized he was heading right for the refrigerator and quickly stepped aside. "I've enjoyed myself."

"You were enjoying yourself." He opened the refrigerator door and reached for two cans of soda. "You were real up until a minute ago. Now, you've tightened up. You're all business again."

He offered her a can of soda.

"Well, this trip was business," she said. "I'm fighting to help you save this shelter. It's essential I know what I'm fighting for."

"Is that the truth?" he asked, his expression not hiding his skepticism. "Working here, I've come to read people real well. You have to learn how to do that quickly around here."

"What are you reading from me?" She was starting to fidget.

"You wanna ask me something," he said. "You're itching to. We're alone now."

She felt her body begin to tighten up as he took a few steps toward her.

"So ask," he said, stopping only a foot from her.

She took a deep breath. "I do need to ask you about what goes on out there."

He turned to where she was pointing, out the back door.

"The alley?" he asked, smiling. "It's an alley. What goes on in every alley? What are you talking about?"

"Can we step out there for a second?"

Ricky seemed confused at first, and Billie could sense that he was somewhat offended, but he hid it quickly.

"You wanna go in the alley?" he asked. "It's pretty dirty out there."

"I'm not afraid of dirt," she said.

"That suit you have on probably cost four hundred dollars. You don't want it to get dirty."

"This one is due for the dry cleaner's anyway." She was curious as to why he seemed reluctant. It made her only want to go out there more.

"Well, then," he said. "Follow me."

She followed him to the back door. He unlocked it and opened it for her. She stepped through the door and into the alley, which was wider than most she had seen in this part of the city.

"This isn't that dirty," she said, turning to him as he stood in the doorway.

"Just be careful," he said, looking around.

"I heard this neighborhood was turning around," she said. "Isn't that why Sanders Realty is buying everything up around here?"

"It's still sketchy in parts," he answered. "But look, Billie, if you expected to see a drug deal, you're gonna be out of luck."

"Why would you ask me that?"

He laughed. "That's what you want to know about, isn't it? You've heard rumors."

"Are they just rumors?" she asked, walking closer to the corner. She could see directly across the street on Channing Street: 2812 Channing Street was in clear view of the alley. Etta Gladstone's apartment was on the second floor of 2812 Channing Street. She had a direct view.

"What are you looking at?"

Billie jumped and turned around to face Ricky, who was standing only inches behind her. She had no idea he had gotten that close. She was looking straight into his curious eyes and she felt a tingling sensation run through her. She was a little frightened and a little turned on at the same time.

"You scared me," she finally said once she found her voice.

"Sorry." His brows centered with curiosity. "You seemed particularly interested in something."

"No, I . . ." Billie took a few steps back. "I was just looking around."

"Billie I know what you're thinking," he said. "Yes, there is some drug activity around here. I've actually seen it happen in this alley. I don't want trouble for the shelter, so I don't snitch. You see, if someone gets mad at me, it's not just me I have to worry about. I have families here."

"So you just mind your own business?" she asked.

"I do my best to make sure they don't feel welcomed, but my priority is keeping the people in the shelter safe."

"I've heard rumors about a twenty-something African-American man by the name of Ralphy or Randy or something doing deals around here. Do you know this guy?"

He squinted, looking away for a second, then shook his head. "A black man named Ralphy?"

Billie smiled. "I'm being serious."

"I mean I know a few Ray Rays and a Ray Dog, but not a Ralphy."

"Stop playing."

She pushed against his chest in an unintentional move, but regretted it the second she did. Feeling his tight muscles against her hand as she failed to move him even an inch elicited a reaction from her. Before she could remove her hand, he grabbed it with his own, keeping it pressed against him.

"Ricky," she said, feeling frightened and excited. "Don't."

"Don't what?" he asked, stepping closer to her. They were

only a couple of inches away. "You smell like a fresh summer morning."

"It's the dry cleaner's scent on my clothes," she said. "Now let my hand—"

"I thought you said this suit was due for the dry cleaner's?" He kept his hand right where it was, over hers against his chest. "So you lied. This suit is perfectly clean."

"Ricky." She tried to look away, but the charming smile that formed at his lips compelled her eyes to stay on him.

"Well," he said, leaning in. "If it's going to the dry cleaner's anyway, we should try and get it a little dirty to get your money's worth."

Billie jumped with a little scream as the phone in her pants pocket began to ring. She was grateful for the scare because it allowed her the strength to move away from Ricky. She looked at him as she reached for her phone and could see the disappointment on his face. What had she almost done? She couldn't be this foolish.

"I have to take this," she said, as if she had to offer an explanation. "It's work."

It wasn't work. It was Sherise, but Billie didn't care. Sherise had probably just saved her from making one of the biggest mistakes of her life.

"Hello?"

"What have you got for me?" Sherise asked, her voice clearly agitated.

"What do you mean?"

"On Justin!"

"I . . . um . . ." Billie was trying to clear her head. "Nothing right now, but I'm working on it."

"Billie, I'm counting on you."

Sherise was relying on Billie to get her Justin's work schedule, and after a lot of begging and pleading, she had promised to try her best to let Sherise know when her husband was going to be out of the office.

"Yes," Billie continued, ignoring Sherise. "I can get on that right now. I'll be back in the office in ten minutes. Yeah . . . Okay . . . 'Bye."

She hung up and turned back to Ricky, who hadn't moved from where he'd been standing.

"I have to go," she said. She headed for the back door of the shelter, keeping a good distance between them as she walked past. "I'm sorry. I really did enjoy the tour."

"Billie!"

She turned around and he was still standing there. He had an impatient look on his face.

"You gonna just walk away from that?" he asked, his voice hinting at his disappointment.

Billie thought at first to play it off, but she knew better. "That isn't gonna happen, Ricky. You're my client. It's just . . . not gonna happen. I have to go."

She didn't wait for a response as she rushed into the house. She couldn't get out of there fast enough.

Erica was in her bedroom, still with curlers in her hair, when she heard noises in the living area. Even in just the slip she was going to wear under her dress later that night, she rushed out of her bedroom to confront Nate.

"Where the hell have you been?" she asked as she entered the room.

Nate, wearing jeans and a white T-shirt that looked like it needed to be cleaned badly, was leaning into the open refrigerator. He looked up in response to Erica's demanding question. She noticed right away that something was wrong with him. His eyes seemed . . . glossy.

"What the fuck, Erica? Put some clothes on."

"You haven't been here for three days! I was worried sick about you."

"I'm a grown-ass man." He slammed the refrigerator door

shut and reached for the box of cereal on top. "I don't need to tell you where I've been."

"Three days, Nate!"

"And the world is still spinning. Who would have thought?"

"We need to talk."

"I'm all talked out, Sis!" He grabbed a handful of cereal and stuffed it in his mouth.

"Then I'll talk," she said. "Terrell is moving back in."

He stopped chewing and looked at her. He hadn't expected this. "What?"

"He's moving back in this weekend."

"That is fucked up," Nate said.

"Why would you say that?"

"You don't want to do that, Sis."

"Why not?"

Nate just shook his head. "You gotta make your own mistakes. Imma move out soon anyway."

"Move out?" she asked. "And go where? And what's with your attitude about Terrell? After everything he's done for you. He got you this new job."

"Fuck that job."

"Are you high?" she asked, walking up to him. She grabbed him by the arm and turned him to face her. "What is wrong with your eyes?"

"Nothing," he said. "Let me go."

"I swear to God, Nate, if you've taken something, I will—"

"Do nothing," he said. "You ain't gonna do nothing to me."

Erica gasped as he pushed her away and she fell back against the kitchen counter.

"Nate! You almost pushed me down!"

"You deserve it!" he yelled. "You're not my mother, Erica. Lay off."

He stormed right past her as if she wasn't even there. It took Erica a few minutes to get herself together, but the second she did, she noticed that he had left his phone on the kitchen counter. She didn't know what else to do. She checked his calls and realized that the last ten calls he had made were to his ex-girlfriend, Kelly.

She pressed redial.

"What the fuck do you want now?" Kelly's irritated voice asked immediately.

"Kelly, it's not Nate. It's Erica."

"Oh . . . Well, hi, Erica. Why are you calling from Nate's phone? I almost didn't answer."

"Why does he keep calling you?"

"Because he's messed up, that's why. I wish you would tell him to leave me the fuck alone."

"He just called you ten times in a row. Did he mention anything? I'm desperate, Kelly. I want to help him, but I don't know what the hell is going on in his life."

"Drugs," she said. "That is what's going on with his life. He's been high on something these last two days and keeps calling me just trippin'. He's going downhill, Erica. Something has gotten worse. I'm sick of it. Just make him stop."

She hung up without saying good-bye, but Erica didn't blame her. Nate was driving her crazy stalking her. This was a mess. She thought of calling her girls. She called Billie, but got her voice mail. She didn't bother calling Sherise because she knew she was already at the hotel for tonight's fund-raiser. Besides, Sherise couldn't help her with this. Only one person could.

"Baby, I know I'm late," Terrell said as soon as he answered, "but I am on Pennsylvania. I'm gonna be there in a quick second. I promise."

"Hurry," she said. "I need your help with Nate."

"So he finally decided to come home?"

"That's not all." She quickly told him of the events that just transpired. "He's on something, Terrell."

"Shit!" There was a short pause. "Look, baby, I'll handle it."

"And when I told him about you moving in, he acted like . . . Have you two had a fight or something? He acted as if that was a bad idea."

"What the fuck did he say?"

"That it was fucked up."

"Is that all?"

"I just told you everything he said. Terrell, just get over here as soon as you can. I'm worried about him."

Sherise felt the tension in the air the second Justin entered the master bathroom. She avoided eye contact with him as she stood at the vanity trying to put her necklace on. She could see his figure standing behind her, looking at her. She looked sexy in her fire red La Perla strapless bra and panties. Was he admiring her? Was he realizing what a mistake he was making by risking losing her? Sherise knew she had a killer body. It was one that Justin used to be unable to resist.

"Do you need help?" he asked, suddenly coming up behind her.

She paused for a second before saying, "Yes, please."

He took the necklace from her, his fingers brushing slightly against hers. She felt a little flutter in the pit of stomach at his touch, but nothing like she usually felt. There was too much between them now. It was like he knew it and she knew it, and one of them had to have the balls to speak up.

For Sherise, his affair was secondary to her now, and honestly, she felt if that was all it was, it was something they could move beyond if it ended immediately. She was no saint in this area, and she knew Cady having her family together meant more than a fleeting temptation. She had bigger fish to fry.

"What are you thinking right now?" Justin asked as he placed his hands gently on her bare shoulders.

"Isn't that usually my line?" She finally made eye contact with him and could see he was reacting to her. He got that look in his eyes when he wanted her. He loved her in red.

"You're usually crazy before an event, but you've been pretty calm and silent all day."

"My role was pretty small here." She'd told Justin she was only volunteering to help a friend out, not trying to prove herself for a possible job.

"Your role is never small." He lowered his head and kissed her neck.

Without thinking, she leaned away from him. Did he really think he could have her and a mistress?

"What's wrong?" he asked. "I just wanted to kiss you."

"I'm trying to get ready." She stepped away from him, walking into the bedroom.

"I can't even kiss you anymore?" he asked, exasperated as he entered the bedroom.

"I'm trying to get—"

"More excuses," he said. "There'll be another one tomorrow."

"All of the sudden you want me again?" she asked, turning to him. "These last couple of weeks you haven't laid a hand on me."

"That's because all you do is nag and accuse me, Sherise. It's not a turn-on."

"You know what's a turn-on, Justin? Trust." She walked over to her closet. "Yeah, trust is hot. Don't you think?"

Justin's impatient expression grew darker. "I know what this is about."

"I'm sure you do," she said.

"You're trying to make excuses to avoid having another baby with me."

She turned, her eyes wide. This was unexpected. "I've given up my life to have another baby with you."

"Really?" he asked. "You seem to have been working a lot lately."

She laughed. "Is that why you think I'm not pregnant? Because I've taken on a small project for the last couple of weeks? It has to be me, right?"

"I'm trying," he said as he reached for the tie she'd laid out for him on the bed.

"Are you really?" she asked. "Or maybe you're trying, but just not with me."

"Fuck this!" He tossed the tie on the bed. "I don't need this."

"You started it! I guess it's okay to accuse me of being a bad wife, but once it goes the other way, the conversation is over."

"Conversation?" He laughed. "We haven't had a conversation in months, Sherise."

"Where are you going?" she asked as he headed for the door.

"There's a game on tonight. I'd rather watch that than deal with your passive-aggressive bullshit all night."

"Justin!" She rushed to the doorway. "You have to come tonight! I can't show up there alone!"

"The way you ignore me lately, you'd be alone even if I was with you."

He rushed down the stairway. She knew he wasn't going to come back. In the end, she probably thought it was best, considering she didn't want him knowing about her real reasons for helping out with the event.

"At least make yourself useful and get Cady from the babysitter!" she yelled after him.

Sherise wasn't sure what her problem was. She was angry with him, feeling certain he was cheating on her, but she knew she still loved him and wanted to keep her marriage together. So why wasn't she doing something about it? She was a planner. She didn't jump into the important things like other people. She was waiting for definitive proof, but she wasn't sure she would get any. She had to do something about this now or there was going to be nothing left of her family.

But first things first.

Billie, looking amazing in her cobalt blue Ralph Lauren off-the-shoulder floor-length dress, was not the least bit surprised when she saw Sherise show up at the hotel without Justin. She was surprised she was showing up as late as she was. She looked flawless in a fire red Allen Schwartz strapless cascading gown. Anyone who didn't know she was having trouble in her marriage couldn't tell.

"Where's Justin?" she asked as soon as she reached her.

Sherise was waving at LaKeisha across the room. "He's not coming. Asshole."

"It just makes this easier." Billie reached into her small clutch and pulled out a folded piece of paper. "This is all I could get."

"Thank you!" Sherise grabbed the sheet of paper and unfolded it. It was Justin's Outlook calendar schedule for the next week.

"I don't like doing this," Billie offered.

She had actually gotten lucky. His assistant had printed out a copy of his schedule and placed it on her desk for reference. It took Billie only ten seconds to grab it, copy it quickly, and replace it.

"I know this will help me get something on him." Sherise folded the paper back up and placed it in her small purse.

"He's not going to have a ten A.M. meeting with mistress on there," Billie said.

"Of course not, but—"

"Hey, girls."

Erica, wearing a brown and white striped satin sundress, joined the two of them and leaned forward for a kiss. Only Billie kissed her. Sherise was busy giving Terrell, who was standing about ten feet away, the stink eye.

"You brought him anyway," she said. "Even though I told you not to."

"We've been through this." Erica rolled her eyes. "What is this about a mistress?"

"What have you heard?" Sherise asked anxiously.

Erica noted her quick reaction. "Billie just said it."

"She thinks Justin is cheating on her," Billie offered.

"Keep your voice down!" Sherise sent her a dagger glare.

"This again?" Erica asked. "Where is he?"

"He's not here," Billie added.

"Why not?"

"Never mind that!" Sherise said. "Why did you bring that thug to a presidential political fund-raiser?"

"At least I can trust that thug," Erica said in a biting tone. "Can you say as much about your man? Or better yet, can he say that about you?"

"Erica," Billie warned.

"You're such a bitch." Erica waved a dismissive hand and headed back for Terrell. "Whatever. I'm done here."

"What did I say?" Sherise asked.

Billie looked at her like she was crazy, astounded that she really didn't get it. "Let me go talk to her."

"I don't have time for this," Sherise said.

Just then she felt someone behind her and noticed a familiar, unique cologne. She slowly turned around.

"Hello, Sherise," Jonah said in his textbook deep, commanding voice.

Jonah looked amazing as usual in a tailored black suit.

"I didn't know you were going to be here," she finally said, hoping that her voice would not betray the unease she felt.

More than seven months go by with no word from this man, then suddenly . . . She was suspicious to say the least.

"I've been a supporter of Northman since his days as a state congressman." He looked her up and down, his expression not so much pleased as remembering. "You look lovely as usual."

"What do you want?"

"I just wanted to say hello," he said. "Is that forbidden?"

"Considering our last conversation, I didn't expect another word to be spoken between us."

He nodded hello to a man who called his name while passing by. "That's all in the past, don't you think?"

"You've said hello," she said, "so I guess this conversation is over."

She turned to leave.

"Sherise, wait."

She didn't turn around because she wanted to. She couldn't resist. There was something about a man like Jonah that made people do whatever he told you to.

"Erica and I are on the verge of turning over a new leaf," he said. "I think you and I making peace would go a long way in helping her."

"Helping her?" Sherise laughed. "Yes, I'm sure that's your main concern."

His expression stilled and grew very serious. "I care about Erica and I know you're important to her."

"Which is why I'm still here, right?"

"The things I said to you were just angry knee-jerk reactions to being rejected. It's something that doesn't happen to me. I'm not angry at you anymore."

"Really? And I'm not supposed to believe there's some coincidence in you showing up now to make a point of telling me you harbor no ill will toward me."

He frowned, seeming unable to comprehend what she was insinuating.

"Just remember," Sherise warned, leaning in. "No matter how close you can get to that daughter you're too ashamed of to tell anyone about, she will always love me more than she loves you. If you fuck with me, I can turn her against you."

Sherise knew that Jonah was not used to getting threats, and from the expression on his face, he was about to let her know it. She didn't care. If somehow he was behind this, he had to know who he was dealing with.

He smiled kindly in that way a man does when he thinks the woman he is talking to is crazy and Sherise considered that a good thing.

"We'll see," he said softly before turning and heading for Erica only steps away.

"I thought you had left me," Robert said as he reached Billie.

Standing at the rail overlooking the lobby of the hotel, Billie turned and smiled at him. She didn't have the heart to tell him that she was kind of leaving him. She liked Robert enough, but he was such a schmoozer that she needed a break from watching him. He liked power and there was a lot of it in the ballroom. She, on the other hand, was thinking of only one thing. How she almost kissed Ricky and put her case in jeopardy.

"Just need a break from all that hot air," she said.

He looked nice in an ordinary gray suit and white shirt. It impressed her that he chose to go a little off-color, out of the ordinary.

"You're not enjoying yourself," he said, joining her as he leaned against the rail. "I think it's great in there. I've already gotten seven business cards. A lot of wealth-management opportunities."

"Enough," she said. Mostly because she wanted him to shut up, but also because she wanted to think about someone other than Ricky, Billie reached out and grabbed him by his expensive tie. She pulled him toward her and leaned up. She planted a kiss on his lips.

"This is nice."

She separated from Robert and turned toward the familiar voice. Could he have worse timing?

"I'm surprised to see you, Porter." She pasted on a saccharine smile that doubled as a get-the-hell-away-from-me signal. "You must be a plus one, because I know Sherise would have never let you get on this invitation list."

Porter was ignoring her. He had eyes for only Robert as he approached.

"I was wondering when I'd meet you," he said.

"There's no reason for you to meet him," Billie added, resenting the possessiveness of that statement.

Porter offered him a tepid smile before turning to Billie. "So, what have you been bugging me about?"

"Now is not the time," Billie said.

"You've left me three messages," he answered back. "Now is your chance."

She had been trying to talk to him about Tara, hoping he would reconsider what she felt was punishment for being a teenaged girl.

"Can we meet at another time?" she asked.

"I guess Tara is only important enough to not interfere with your love life."

"You know that's not true." Billie could see Robert's growing discomfort.

"Then talk to me." He smiled as if he was proud of his disruptive presence.

"Stop being a child," Billie demanded. "Wearing your jealousy on your sleeve is not a good look."

Porter's grin vanished. "I was just giving you a chance, but I can see that your little date is more—"

"You can't see anything," Billie said. "You can't see anything beyond your ego and pride. I'm on a date. Grow up and deal with it. If you can't do that, then go away and show out somewhere else."

"Classy, Billie." He tried to hide behind a disappointed glare, but it wasn't working. He seemed to know it and, after giving Robert one last disapproving glare, turned and walked away.

Billie turned to Robert, who was the poster boy for awkward. "I'm sorry about that."

"I like you, Billie," he said after a short hesitation.

She recognized that tone. "But?"

"But I'm not a fool," he added. "There is still something between the two of you."

Billie laughed, but stopped when she realized he wasn't laughing along with her. "You're serious, aren't you? Jesus, Robert. No, there is nothing between us."

"Are you sure about that?" he asked.

"Not that it's any of your business," she answered, "but I'm sure."

"Trying to keep a man in your life through his kids is textbook," he said.

Billie was frozen in place, her jaw almost dropping to the floor.

"I beg your pardon?"

"I'm sorry," he stammered. "I didn't mean to offend you, but it's the truth."

"Well, you did offend me and it's not the truth. I care about Tara like a daughter, and the only reason I'm trying to . . . Why am I even saying this? I don't have to explain myself to you."

"You're right," he said. "I'm sorry, I just . . ."

"You're just like him," she said, looking him over. "You and Porter should date each other."

"I think you're out of line," he suggested firmly.

"I'm out of line?" She laughed. "At least with you I know straight up who you are. Porter used to be different. He turned into you. I'm not about to make the same damn mistake again. Enjoy your night of networking, Robert."

He didn't call her name at all as she walked away. It wouldn't have made a difference if he had, but that fact that he hadn't only told Billie she'd done the right thing. This man was not what she wanted.

10

"Take this," Erica shoved a glass of wine in Sherise's face. "You look like you need it."

Sherise took the glass even though she knew she needed something much stronger. "You've been ignoring me all night."

"Um . . . maybe because you're being a bitch."

"I'm dealing with a crisis here."

"Justin is not cheating on you, Sherise. Stop it."

"Not that." Sherise stopped herself before she went further.

"Then what?"

"No, I mean . . ." She didn't know how much longer she could keep this up. "Just try and have some compassion."

"I was trying," Erica said. "But you fuck it up insulting my boyfriend."

"From boyfriend to fiancé to boyfriend." Sherise made a mocking gesture. "That sounds healthy."

"See, there you go again." Erica threw her hands in the air. "I'm done with you for the night."

Just as she was about to leave, Billie showed up in a huff.

"Why didn't you tell me Porter was going to be here?"

Sherise shrugged. "I'm in charge of press. If I had something to do with the guest list, I wouldn't have let Porter, Jonah, or Terrell past that door."

"Bitch," Erica said under her breath.

"Well, he's here." Billie snatched the glass of wine out of Sherise's hand and took a sip. "And he's being a dick as usual. Not to mention Robert. He's done. You understand me? His expiration date was today, five minutes ago."

"What did he do?" Erica asked.

"He had the nerve to accuse me of using Tara to stay in Porter's life!"

Waiting for incredulous stares from both Sherise and Erica, Billie was infuriated by their hesitation.

"Ugh!" She slammed the glass on the closest table. "I'm going home."

"Stop it." Erica grabbed her before she could leave. "He was way out of line. Wasn't he, Sherise?"

They both looked at Sherise, but she was looking suspiciously around the room.

"What are you doing?" Billie asked.

"Nothing." Sherise shook her head. "What are we talking about? How you use Tara to keep Porter around."

"How I don't!" Billie insisted. "I'm the only woman in that girl's life. I'm trying to help her."

"Excuse me, Mrs. Robinson."

The women turned to a member of the hotel catering staff, a middle-aged Asian man, who offered a glass of a dark mixed drink to Sherise.

"This your drink," he said, although it was more of a question than a statement.

"I didn't order a drink," Sherise said, even though she took it. She hoped it was stronger than a glass of wine.

"I was told by a lady you ordered this and I should give to you."

"What lady?" Erica asked, looking around. "LaKeisha?"

"No name," he said. "Red dress."

Sherise took a quick scan of the room. "There are about twenty red dresses just in my line of sight. Was she black or white?"

"Yes," he said before turning and walking away.

Erica laughed. "Yes? Maybe she's biracial."

"So you got ladies hitting on you now, too?" Billie asked.

"This isn't the first time," Erica said. "Remember when we were at that bar above Marvin's? That blonde chick came hard at Sherise. She was all like—"

"Shit!"

Sherise was loud enough to get some stares from people nearby. Her head shot up and she looked around. She wanted to panic, but she knew she had to get control of herself. She took a deep breath and scanned the room.

"What is it?" Billie asked.

Sherise handed her the napkin that she was served with the drink. The words, written in blue pen, were a little blurry from the glass, but the words could not be mistaken.

What goes around comes around!

"What the hell?" Billie asked, showing the napkin to Erica.

Sherise eyed the room like a hawk. Her stomach was fluttering like crazy, but she looked like steel. She wanted whoever it was to know she was not going to be some sitting duck. She was studying every woman she could see in a red dress, but none of them were familiar and none of them seemed at all interested in her right now.

The only person in the room at that moment who seemed to have eyes only for her was Jonah. He stood several yards away in a circle of people chatting away. He wasn't chatting. He was looking at her. She caught his eyes and glared.

"Jonah," she said. "It's him."

"Bullshit," Erica said.

"The waiter said it was a woman," Billie interjected.

"He sent a woman to do it," Sherise said. "Of course, the man would easily point him out in a crowd."

"That doesn't make any sense," Erica said. "Jonah is having an affair with Justin?"

Sherise realized that the girls still thought she was thinking about Justin's affair. She snatched the napkin from Erica and looked at it again. The threat didn't really fit the doctor's records situation, but it did fit an affair.

"Where is that waiter?" Sherise turned around to see if she could spot him. "I'm gonna drag him around until—"

"She's probably left, whoever she is," Billie offered. "Besides—"

"Sherise! Where have you been?"

LaKeisha sauntered over to the trio of women, looking as if she'd had more than a few drinks . . . wearing a cocktail dress that seemed a size too big and reached an awkward two inches below her knees . . . and was red.

Sherise, Erica, and Billie all shared a glance, thinking the same thing.

"No," Billie said.

"No, what?" LaKeisha looked as if she knew she'd interrupted something.

"Nothing," Sherise said. "What is it, LaKeisha?"

"Northman wants to talk to you." She smiled, but it faded as she did not receive the excited reaction to her news from Sherise as expected. "What's wrong?"

"Nothing," Sherise answered suspiciously. "That sounds great. I'll talk to him soon."

"He wants to tell you how much he loved the job you did tonight." LaKeisha, even a little tipsy, seemed to realize that Erica and Billie were staring at her oddly as she looked at both of them with a little trepidation. "I know he wants you to come on board."

No one said anything.

"Permanently," LaKeisha added as if she thought it would have a different effect.

"That's great news," Sherise said, still eyeing her with subtle suspicion. "Is there anything else you want to tell me?"

LaKeisha looked around, clearly having no clue. "Um . . . no. Well, of course, there will be the background check and all that, but we know you."

"You mean like with my social security number?" Sherise asked.

Billie slightly jabbed Sherise with her elbow. She was acting very weird. "She's just playing with you, LaKeisha."

"Of course!" LaKeisha didn't do a good job of pretending she wasn't a little weirded out by the scene.

"Has anyone been asking about Sherise?" Erica asked.

"What do you mean?"

"Tonight," Erica clarified. "Do you know anyone who's been asking about her?"

"That woman!" Sherise yelled out.

Without thinking, she grabbed LaKeisha by the arm.

"Sherise!" Billie yelled and tried to pull Sherise off her.

"What's going on?" LaKeisha looked terrified.

"You said a woman was talking about me," Sherise said. "A few weeks ago. That was what made you remember me! Who was that woman?"

LaKeisha was looking at Sherise as if she was crazy, but Sherise didn't care.

Billie grabbed Sherise's hand and loosened her grip on LaKeisha. "Take it easy, girl."

Sherise tried to take a deep breath so she could calm down. The thought had suddenly occurred to her and something clicked. This was the key.

"Do you remember?" Sherise asked. "You told me her name."

Nothing.

"Think!" Sherise wanted to strangle her.

"Oh!" LaKeisha almost jumped up and down. She laughed. "That is so funny. I was like, what the hell is she—"

"Who?" Sherise demanded.

"Jennifer Ross," LaKeisha said. "Do you remember her now?"

Sherise looked at Billie and Erica. Both women shook their heads. They had no clue.

"Have you seen her here tonight?" Billie asked.

LaKeisha shook her head. "I don't . . . No, I haven't, but she's in DC all the time, so she could be here. She is a supporter of Northman, but—"

"What do you mean 'in DC'?" Sherise asked. "She doesn't live here? She lives in Maryland or Virginia?"

"No," LaKeisha said. "She lives in Texas. I think . . ."

"Dallas," Sherise finished for her.

"How do you know that?" Billie asked.

Sherise looked at her, not sure of what she should tell her. Her mind was spinning. There was no way this was a coincidence. It was true. This woman, Jennifer, was after her and she was after Cady. Why?

"I'll Google her," Erica said, reaching for her phone in her purse.

"You do that," Sherise said. "LaKeisha, you're gonna help me find that woman here tonight."

"I don't think she's here," LaKeisha said.

"She's here," Sherise responded. "And I'm gonna find this bitch."

Standing in the half-circle driveway entrance to the hotel, Erica looked up from her phone just long enough to see Jonah walk outside. He looked like an older male model, his hands stuck in the pockets of his crisply tailored suit.

What did he want from her? She had already said hello and engaged in small talk for a few minutes with him. That was really the best she could do. It was weird. He made her feel like she was doing something wrong by talking to him and she resented him for that. Still, she was curious about him.

"It's a little early to call it a night." He stopped as he reached her.

"Some of us have to be at work in the morning." She smiled awkwardly.

"Where is your date?"

"Terrell is getting the car."

He frowned. "He didn't do valet?"

Not liking the tone of his voice, she gave him a stern look.

"Sorry," he offered with a humble lowering of his head. When he looked back up, he said, "You look lovely, Erica. You're very—"

"Don't," she softly pleaded.

He frowned, looking somewhat sad. "I was just—"

"I know what you were doing," she said, "and I don't want you to do that. I don't know you, Jonah. I don't know if I want to. You're used to being in charge of everything, including every relationship you have. Not with me."

"I just wanted to say good night," he said. "I apologize if you felt I was being too familiar."

"I need time," she said.

His expression softened as he looked into her eyes. His hand reached up and gently touched her shoulder. "I'm just grateful you're giving me this chance."

"Someone will see you," she said as she looked at his hand.

He sighed before slowly removing his hand

"Sherise is being harassed by someone," she said. "If you're—"

"I would never do that," he interrupted. "I feel like we've had a breakthrough, Erica."

"Don't assume that much." This rare, tender side of him touched her, but she knew enough about him to know he usually did this when he wanted something or was up to something.

"I'll tell you what I won't assume," he said. "I won't assume you'd forgive me if I went after one of your friends."

"She's more than my friend."

He smiled. "She's made that clear to me."

"I didn't think you had anything to do with it," Erica said, "but I had to ask."

"I deserved that." He paused. "Erica, I want us to have a—"

The honk of Terrell's horn was deep and bellowing, and it made Erica jump. She turned to the car, which was on the other side of the driveway. Terrell was looking through the passenger-side window with a menacing glare directed at Jonah.

She turned to Jonah. "I have to go."

"We should talk soon."

She shrugged. "I'll see. Good night, Jonah."

"Good night, Erica."

She took a few steps forward before looking back at him. He was still looking at her and she saw a tenderness in his eyes that she wished didn't reach her. She had to be careful. Terrell was right. Every girl wants a daddy and she was no exception. This man was her father and she had to consider that some relationship, any kind, was better than none. Wasn't it?

Playing with Cady in the backseat of her car while it was parked on Eighteenth and M Streets in DC still wasn't enough of a distraction from the insanity of what Sherise was doing. This was her life now? It wasn't acceptable for her. She didn't know how it could be for any woman.

She looked out across the street at the office building her husband had gone in for his two P.M. meeting with a client. She had been following him since that morning, but nothing much had happened. At least not from this end.

Sherise felt like she was in some kind of daze, a nightmare that she might wake up from. She imagined that was the only reason why she hadn't gone insane after last night's revelations. Neither LaKeisha nor the waiter, whom Sherise found and dragged around the ballroom in search of Jennifer, could find her. She had gone. Sherise ignored LaKeisha's request she meet with Northman. Instead, she grabbed a cab home immediately.

Jennifer Ross was not on Google. At least not the one she was looking for. When found, Jennifer was either some elderly woman, white, too young, or from out of the country. LaKeisha didn't have much information for her, but Jennifer was a very attractive black woman in her early thirties. She had long, auburn hair and hazel eyes. LaKeisha knew her only through a friend that Sherise did not know, but knew her to be part of the society set in the Dallas area who used to live in the Maryland suburbs of DC for a few years.

Who was this woman and why did she have it out for her? Was she someone Sherise had stepped on to get to the top? She was a coldhearted warrior when it came to her own interests and had made more than a few enemies, but she remembered her enemies for the sole purpose of being on the lookout for revenge. How many times had someone she'd just screwed over for a promotion or stolen credit from told her she was going to get what was coming to her or karma was a bitch? Or maybe this woman had no idea who she was but was out to get her based solely on the fact that she wanted her husband. That, however, would not explain the message on the napkin. It was so confusing, it made Sherise's head want to split open.

Putting all of these elements together, nothing led her to this woman online. This amazed Sherise. In a day like today, how could someone not be traceable online? It was probably just a coincidence but it made her more paranoid. It seemed like the only way for someone to be this hard to find online was because they were purposefully trying to stay hidden. So who was she dealing with?

And, after nearly tearing her bedroom and the home office apart that morning, Sherise was getting desperate. If she was going to find out what was going on, she would have to follow Justin.

She had thought herself insane to suspect that Justin was behind the records request from the doctor's office, but she felt almost certain that the two were connected. The day she received the fax that had been sent to her doctor's office, she hadn't put the two together, but she had last night. The fax number showed the fax had been sent from the Fairmont Hotel. What she'd forgotten was that first day, the one when her suspicions began while sitting in the courtyard of the Blue Duck Tavern; the man she'd thought resembled her husband jumping into a cab had been doing that a few steps from the Fairmont Hotel.

Her mind raced, wondering why Justin and his lover would do this? Was it because she wasn't getting pregnant that he began to suspect something was up with Cady? Medical records alone wouldn't prove anything. There had never been a paternity test. If he wanted to know, all he'd have to do is get a sample himself.

She had checked Cady from head to toe that morning to see if there had been a prick anywhere someone might have taken a blood sample, but there wasn't. There was no way that could happen to her baby and she wouldn't know it. So what did they want with the records for and what were they going to—

"Oh, shit," she said as she leaped into the front seat of her Lexus SUV.

Justin had just stepped out of the building and was heading to the corner to catch a cab.

Just then, the phone rang. It was Billie. She put on the headset so she could talk and drive, and then started her car.

"What did you find out?" Sherise asked as soon as she answered.

"Nothing," Billie said. "I spent all morning on this, Sherise. That woman has no connection to this firm. I can ask around, but . . ."

"No," Sherise said. "Too many people will know someone

is asking about her. It'll get back to her. I need to catch her off guard. Justin just left his meeting."

Billie suddenly had flashbacks of driving around DC in her car in search of her cheating husband and his girlfriend, the perky, cheerleader stereotype Claire. It was sickening to think of another woman going through that.

"Just confront him, Sherise," she said. "This is ridiculous. Demand answers."

"I can't do that yet, Billie. I have to know more."

Sherise was at the end of her rope. She needed to let it all out, but couldn't bear the thought of revealing her sins, even to her best friend. She was too ashamed, too afraid.

Justin finally caught a cab and Sherise picked up the pace to follow.

"What's wrong with you?" Billie asked. "You're holding out on me. Don't deny it, Sherise. I know you better than you know yourself."

No, you don't, she thought. *If you did, you wouldn't want to be my friend anymore.*

"No, I'm not. I just don't like going in blind."

The truth was, this was about more than an affair. This was about someone with an agenda for revenge. Most importantly, this was about her baby, and there wasn't a chance in hell Sherise was going to make her fight public without knowing what was up.

"Look, honey," Sherise said. "I appreciate all of this. Call me if you know more. He's due back at the office, but he's headed in the wrong direction. I think I have something here. I'll talk to you later."

Sherise was a seasoned DC driver, so she maintained a good distance behind the cab. It took only a few minutes for her to get a feeling in the pit of stomach that it was about to go off. She knew the streets of northwest DC well, and not only was Justin going in a direction away from his office, he was going toward the Foggy Bottom area. After Foggy Bottom was the West End neighborhood. West End and the Fairmont Hotel.

By the time the cab reached the Fairmont, with Sherise only two cars behind, she was gripping the steering wheel so hard she was losing all the color in her hands.

"You son of a bitch!" she yelled.

She quickly passed the hotel as the cab went into its driveway. She reached the alley between the hotel and another building. She was about to pull out so she could find a place to park facing the hotel, but she realized that Justin stopped as soon as he got out of the car.

He looked around and she panicked. Did he see her? She suddenly realized that she was stupidly driving her own car, which he could recognize in a second.

"Well," she said, putting the car in park. "If it's about to go off, then so be it."

She waited for him to notice her. She wasn't that far away. He wasn't moving, so she stayed where she was. An employee of the hotel, standing near the side employee entrance to get a smoke on his break, looked at her like she was crazy. Yes, she knew she couldn't park there and she knew she was blocking the alley, but just try to ask her to move.

Sherise grabbed her phone to take pictures. Just then, whatever Justin was looking for, he saw. He cautiously put his hand up for a tepid hello and smiled. Following his line of sight, Sherise saw a blue BMW slow down in front of the hotel. She could tell the driver was a woman from the long hair, but the reflection from the windshield was preventing her from getting a good look at her.

Sherise felt her heart stop and time move at a snail's pace as the woman stopped in the entrance to the driveway. Justin started walking toward the car. He grabbed the door handle and opened the door. He was blocking her view of the woman as he got in.

He's my husband, she was saying to herself. *He is my hus-*

band! She felt enraged and defeated at the same time. It wasn't until the woman started backing out of the driveway that she realized she hadn't taken any pictures. It was too late. She tossed the phone in the passenger seat as she put her SUV back in drive.

"Dammit!" she yelled as a taxi drove by at turtle speed just as she was trying back out of the alley.

The woman had already cleared the driveway and was heading back down Twenty-fourth Street.

"Move!" Sherise honked her horn.

Finally the taxi cleared the alley, so she backed up. Still, this same car was traveling at a snail's speed toward the hotel.

Sherise slammed on her horn as the woman's car turned right on M Street and picked up pace.

When the taxi slowed into the driveway of the hotel, Sherise swerved around him and slammed on the gas. The light turned red just as she reached it, but she didn't care. She turned a hard right and headed down M.

She searched for the blue BMW and spotted it making a left on Twenty-fifth. She sped up and did the same.

There was only one car between them when the next light turned yellow. The BMW sped through the light and right down Pennsylvania, but Sherise was trapped. The car in front of her, a van, stepped on the brakes.

"Mother—" Sherise realized she couldn't drive on the sidewalk to her right and there was traffic in the lane to her left going the opposite way. She had her baby in her car. She couldn't be reckless. Not even Justin was worth that.

"I failed," she whispered to herself as her head lowered and she hugged the steering wheel.

She thought she'd meant that because she had been unable to keep up with them, but she realized she didn't. She had failed in so many ways, and even though she wanted to hate Justin, she couldn't blame him. She had been an awful wife, a liar, and a cheat. She had regretted her choices before, but suddenly it all came at her like a brick to the face at fifty miles an hour. Regret was crippling and she could feel her knees getting weak.

She was willing to take the punishment for all of this, but no matter what, she wouldn't let anyone hurt her baby.

She took a deep breath and lifted her head. The light turned green, and after taking one quick glance back at her baby, Sherise faced forward and stepped on the gas. She was living the consequences of her own choice and she had to face this head-on. But she wasn't alone. She was never alone. It was time to lay it all on the table, and maybe if she was lucky, really lucky, she could save her marriage and keep Cady's family together.

"Look at yooouuu!" Mabel Peterson opened her arms wide as she rushed out from behind her desk toward Erica.

"Hi, Mrs. Peterson." Erica smiled and braced for the hug.

Mabel Peterson was a very large woman, and Erica had endured her very warm and tight embraces for as long as she could remember. She usually let go when you told her you couldn't breathe anymore.

"Stop that." Mabel released her to look her over. "You're a big girl now, you can call me Mabel."

"My mother wouldn't like that," Erica said.

"Bless her heart." Mabel, a devout catholic woman, made the symbol of the cross across her chest. "I miss her so much, but I'm so glad to see you. You never come by here anymore."

Here was Sibley Hospital. This was the place that Erica's mother, Achelle, Mabel, and one other woman were the only black nurses working there a few years before Erica was born. Mabel had come from a nursing school in Atlanta and knew no one. Erica's mother and her became fast friends. Thirty years later, a widowed mother of three, Mabel had gone from a first-level registered nurse to the head of the entire hospital's nursing department and a member of the hospital's board.

"I'm sorry about that," Erica said. "Things have been crazy

for me. I haven't been by since your twenty-five-year anniversary party."

"Wasn't that fun?" Mabel did a dancing move with her hips as she sauntered over to the sofa in her spacious office. "We were dancing and carrying on girl."

Erica obeyed Mabel's instruction to sit next to her on the leather sofa.

"You have to come to my retirement party," Mabel said.

"You're retiring?"

"Mmm-hmm." Mabel snapped her fingers. "Fifty-five. Ms. Mabel got her money straight and is ready to retire early back to Atlanta and spend her winters in the Bahamas."

"Good for you." Erica wished she could be so lucky. "I hope your family is doing well."

"Wonderful. I'm about to have my second grandbaby, and . . ." Mabel looked at Erica's expression and sighed. "Baby, what's wrong. You sounded very upset when you called. I know you're upset about Nate, but there wasn't anything I could do."

"I know, Mabel." Erica sighed.

"It's a shame because you know I would do anything for you and your mama."

Erica nodded. "I know you were the one that covered for him when he started working here and needed time to get his act together."

"He's a good kid," Mabel said. "Don't forget that. None of this means he's a bad person."

She appreciatively rubbed Mabel's arm. "I'm just so worried about him. I've recently found out some information that . . . I'm just gonna be straight and honest about it."

"I know what you're going to say," Mabel said.

Erica could see the expression on Mabel's face and it hurt her badly.

"Nate told me he'd been fired because he got into an argument with an important person here, but that's not true, is it?"

Mabel pointed a noting finger. "Now, that is true. That did

happen, but wasn't why he was fired. There were suspicions about him and another young man who worked here, but that morning we had conclusive evidence."

"I talked to his ex-girlfriend, Kelly, the other day, and she told me she thinks Nate is on drugs." Erica swallowed hard. "Are you telling me you have proof?"

"I can't tell you what I think you're here for. He's entitled to his privacy." Mabel lowered her head. "What I can tell you is that we drug test every year, honey. People here have access to a lot of medications and we need to be careful."

Erica fell back on the sofa feeling as if she wanted to cry. She had tried so hard after her mother died to continue what her mother had started. She tried to raise her brother, even though she was only nineteen herself when the burden was placed on her, as best she could. She hadn't been good enough.

"This isn't your fault," Mabel said as if sensing what Erica was thinking. "Nate is a wonderful young man. He's slipped up. It happens to the best of our young men these days. We should have never hired Reedy. He was bad news. He's been a bad influence on Nate since he showed up last year."

"Reedy?" Erica looked up, wondering why that name sounded familiar. "Is he the other . . ."

"I can't tell you more than that." Mabel was getting upset. "Look, the only thing that matters is that you're there for Nate. You have to get him in shape. Tough love is called for."

"I've been trying." Erica sighed. "Terrell and I have . . ."

"You and Terrell are back together?" Mabel asked in a hopeful tone. "Nate had told me you weren't engaged anymore."

Erica smiled and nodded, grateful for something to smile about. "He's really been trying to help me out with Nate, but I don't think it's working."

"Good," Mabel said. "No offense to you, Erica, but he needs a grown man to be on him. Let me give you something."

Erica stood up as Mabel rushed over to her desk. She riffled through the drawers for something. When she found it, she pulled it out and brought it over to her. They were brochures on dealing with a family member on drugs. It sickened Erica to look at these because she never expected to be a person that needed them.

"Come here, baby." Mabel opened her arms again.

This time, Erica was the one that squeezed hard.

Walking toward her car in the parking lot of the hospital moments later, Erica got a call from Terrell and he sensed something was wrong right away.

"It's drugs, Terrell."

There was a silence on the phone, and she thought she'd lost the signal.

"Are you there?"

"I'm here," he said quietly. "Well, we kind of knew that, didn't we?"

"Nate was fired because he failed a drug test, not because he got into a fight." Erica suddenly started crying. "I don't know what I'm gonna do. I can't lose my brother to drugs. I just don't know . . . Mama would . . ."

"Calm down, baby. Calm down."

"No," she said defiantly. "I'm gonna confront him. We have to do an intervention. I'm gonna find out who this Reedy is and make sure he stays away—"

"Erica! Listen to me!"

"Terrell, we have to work together on this!"

"I will handle this," he said.

"You keep saying that, but nothing is working," she said. "Don't get me wrong. I'm grateful for what you're doing, but it's just not working."

"I've been through this before," he said. "Remember my cousin, Nick?"

"Yes." Erica remembered his cousin who dropped out of premed and got lost in drugs. He almost died. The family intervened and forced him to a clinic.

"It's not as bad as Nick," Terrell said. "And we saved him. Let me find out what's going on and I'll take care of it. It's just taking longer than expected."

"Okay." Erica slowly began to calm down. "I love you, Terrell."

She honestly didn't know what she would do without him.

"I love you, too, baby."

11

Billie was trying to focus on her work when the call came in that Ricky Williams was there to see her. She was already incredibly upset and frustrated after talking to Sherise. That ordeal was the only thing that made her stop thinking about almost kissing Ricky in the alley. Now that he was dropping by for an unexpected visit, it was back on her mind.

"Can you show him down?" she asked, reluctantly.

Billie scrambled to find her file on the case, which was coming along well but was the last thing on her mind right now. She had a meeting on another case in fifteen minutes, so this would have to be brief.

She grabbed her pocket mirror and checked herself quickly, telling herself this is what she did before she met with any client. That was true, but for some reason she needed to remind herself of that this time.

Her door was open when the receptionist ushered him in before leaving right away. Billie noticed that he was wearing a suit, looking even more handsome than usual. Damn him!

Billie got up and walked briskly around her desk. "Mr. Williams, this is unexpected. We didn't have an appointment."

"I was in the area," he said, looking at her with confusion.

She closed the door behind him and ushered him to the chair on the other side of her desk. "What are you doing in these parts?"

"Um . . ." He watched as she walked back to the other side of the desk. "I knew this was going to happen."

"I don't have much news on the case," she continued as she sat down. "But I plan to have some great news in a bit. What we've been doing has ruffled feathers and—"

"Billie, please." He held up a hand as he stood at the desk. "I didn't come by for an update on the case. I came to talk to you about your visit."

Billie sighed. She wasn't in the mood for this for a variety of reasons, but most importantly, this was her office. "Mr. Williams, I—"

"Ricky," he said, laughing. "Come on, now."

"Ricky," she said firmly. "I don't think we need to talk about that at all."

"It seemed to bother you." He leaned forward, placing his hands firmly at the edge of the desk. "I think we should talk about it."

"This is a professional setting," she argued. "It's not the time or the place to—"

"I think it's important to this case," he said.

Billie wasn't sure how to address that. It was true in a way. "I agree that the fact that we almost kissed is important to the case in the sense that going any further could have put this case in jeopardy and I'm not willing to—"

"What?" He stood up straight, his brows centered in confusion. "What are you talking about?"

"What?" She was starting to stutter. "Y-You were . . . I was. Oh my God. You're not talking about that are you?"

He smiled an accomplished smile, but it only turned her immense embarrassment into anger.

"This is funny to you?" she asked.

"I'm sorry." He took a moment to compose himself. "I

came here to talk about what you think is drug activity behind my shelter."

Billie couldn't remember the last time she felt like such a fool.

"And here I was thinking," he continued, "that was what had been on your mind these last couple of days."

Billie seethed at his arrogant grin. "The only reason I was thinking about it was because it was extremely unprofessional and won't happen again."

"Too bad." He shrugged. "I actually thought it was very nice."

"What did you come here for?" she asked impatiently.

Ricky studied her for a moment. "What's wrong with you?"

Billie sighed. "Look, Ricky. Actual suspected drug activity in the area aside, if those calls were legit, no one would have tried to get them removed."

"Tried?" he asked. "Does that mean you've located them?"

"We've issued subpoenas and we're on our way. People are nervous. That's a good thing."

"A very good thing." He made a victorious fist pump. "I knew you could do it."

"We haven't done it yet," she said, "but we will. Now if there's anything else . . ."

"So we aren't going to talk about your suspicions?"

"It doesn't matter," she said. "I'm here to try this case."

"It does matter," he answered back. "To me. Billie, I'm not a perfect guy, but . . ."

Without thought, Billie made a huffing sound and rolled her eyes. She hadn't even realized she'd done it until Ricky's quick reaction. She immediately wished she could take it back.

"What was that for?" he asked, seeming offended.

"Nothing," she said. "Go on."

"No," he said. "You clearly have a problem with me. I know it's a woman's way to make the guy figure it out, but—"

"What are you talking about?" She shot up from her chair. "The woman's way? The guy? We aren't in a relationship, Mr. Williams. You don't have to—"

"Ricky," he corrected.

"Mr. Williams," she repeated. "You don't have to figure anything out. That was a sexist comment."

"How was it sexist?"

"I've had it," she said under her breath.

"I heard that," Ricky said.

She tilted her head and squinted her eyes. "If that was all you came for, you can rest assured, it's not a problem. Now if you'll excuse me, I have to get back to work."

He watched as she walked around her desk, headed for the door.

"At first I thought this was about you being embarrassed," he said, "but it's more than that."

"Embarrassed?" She faked a laugh. "Don't worry about me."

"Some dude pissed you off, didn't he?"

He wasn't wrong. Billie had just had enough of men. Porter and Robert. Now even Justin wasn't trustworthy. Then this man came over and tried to judge her? He was right, but that made her only angrier.

"This is inappropriate," she said, standing at the door.

She reached for the door, but in that second, Ricky was there. He reached out and took a firm yet gentle hold of her face, bringing her to him. His lips descended down on hers in a quick but possessive motion.

Billie's immediate shock at the act was replaced with the explosion of desire that shot through her entire body. His lips were demanding and she gave in immediately, so fast that it frightened her. It frightened her enough to make her realize what was happening. She ignored the part of her body that told her she was enjoying this and wanted more and listened to her head.

She pushed him away from her, trying to show the angriest face she could think of, but he just smiled.

"That," he said, taking a step back, "was inappropriate."

Billie was breathless and couldn't speak or move for the next few seconds. Finally, she mustered the strength.

"How dare you do that?" she asked.

Ricky's eyes were smoldering. He was clearly turned on and this frightened her.

"I work here," she said. "How could you put me at such a risk?"

"I wanted to get it out of the way," he said. "It's hanging there between us. I'm attracted to you and you're—"

"Your lawyer," she interrupted. "That's what I am. Your lawyer, and this shouldn't have happened. You have to leave."

"Look, Billie, I—"

"Now!" She pointed to the door, taking a few extra steps back to be safe. She still felt her heart beating so fast.

"No one has to know this happened," he offered.

"I'll know," she responded, turning her back to him. "Just please leave."

She heard him sigh for a moment before opening the door, leaving, and closing it behind him. When he had left, Billie fell back against the wall with her hand to her chest. She wanted to make excuses. He had done it so unexpectedly, what was she supposed to have done? But she knew. While he had kissed her by surprise, she had kissed him back and it felt good. She felt a passion she hadn't since Porter, and her body wanted that.

But she couldn't have it. Not with him. She had to figure out a way to get that through her head and Ricky's.

When Sherise heard footsteps coming down the hallway, she sat up in bed and tried to pull herself together. After her failed pursuit of Justin and the other woman, she had gone home and tried to face her demons. She had tried to call Billie and Erica, but neither of them were picking up. She had to face the fact that up until today, there was a part of her that really believed she could be wrong. There was this little lying voice that said this was all a series of misunderstandings. It was stupid, she knew, especially after hearing from the doctor's office and receiving the napkin, but she had.

"Hey," Justin said flatly as soon as he entered the bedroom.

"Hi." Her voice sounded weaker than she'd expected it to.

He tossed his already discarded tie on the bed as he approached it. He looked at her, but she kept her head down, pretending to focus on the magazine on her lap.

"Honey?"

She looked up in response to that. He hadn't called her "honey" in a long, long time, and it touched her. When their eyes caught, she could see that her obvious pain affected him. She had been crying and her eyes were red. She must have looked awful, but it pleased her to see him at least a little upset by it.

"What's wrong?" He hurried around the bed to her side.

"Nothing." She tried to smile, but it didn't work. "I'm sorry. I didn't make anything for dinner."

"Is Cady okay?"

She nodded. "She's napping."

"What happened, then?"

Was she kidding herself or did she see real concern in his eyes? He was still her husband. He hadn't left her for that whore, whoever she was. There was still something left.

"I love you," she said, reaching out and touching his cheek gently.

She noticed a spark, just a spark, of guilt in his eyes. Sherise thought that should please her, but it didn't.

"I love you, too," he said after a moment.

He slid close to her and wrapped his arms around her. He

kissed her gently on the cheek as tears started streaming down her face again.

"Don't cry," he whispered. "Baby, please don't cry."

"I wish I was a better wife," Sherise said. "I wish I could be everything you want, everything you need."

"Don't say that," was his only response.

"Why do we fight all the time now?" she asked. "We hardly ever fought before."

"Because I always let you have your way," he said, smiling.

"I'm serious, Justin."

"I know." Justin shook his head. "We're just going through a rough patch, Sherise. It happens to all married couples."

"And it leads to divorce," she said.

"No," he countered. "Not always. That doesn't have to be us."

"Cady confused why you're gone and spending weekends with you." Sherise ran her hand over her face in sheer exhaustion. "I can't stand to think of her life like that."

"It won't be," Justin assured her. "We won't do that to her."

"It used to be easy with us," she said.

"It's always easy in the beginning, Sherise."

"Why is it so hard now? We were supposed to be on the same page."

He looked down, shaking his head. "Things happen. We're just a little lost. I think we're both frustrated about the pregnancy and . . ."

"And what?" she asked.

He looked back up, and Sherise could see from his expression that this was hurting him deeply. This made her happy. His internal pain told her that he didn't think he had a right to do this to her, that it hurt him to do this. He did love her. She knew it.

"It's my fault," she said. "I know I . . ."

"No, Sherise." He gently placed his hand over her mouth. "Don't say that. We both have to take blame."

She took his hand from her mouth, but still held it in hers. "I can get my shit together, Justin. I promise I can. We can work this out, can't we? For Cady?"

"Not just for Cady," he said. "For us. We'll work this out for us. I love you, Sherise."

He brought her hand to his mouth and gently kissed the back of it. With her free hand, she ran her fingers through his hair as their eyes held each other's. When his lips came down on hers, she met him with tender passion. She could feel in his kiss, as he pulled her body close to his tighter than he had in a long time, that he wanted her, still wanted her.

She loved him and she knew he loved her. Justin wasn't her enemy. She wasn't her own enemy. It was that woman, Jennifer. Sherise knew if she could get her out of the way, there would be a second chance for her and Justin, a second chance for Cady's family.

"Make love to me, Justin," she whispered as his lips traveled down her chin and to her neck.

Erica didn't see Jonah walking toward her area in the office, but she knew he was coming. She heard all of the greeters, formal and informal. Jonah Dolan was a god at the Pentagon.

Erica wasn't really in the mood to deal with him. She was stressing out over Nate, and dealing with Jonah's paternal needs—limited by his political ambition—was just not on her priority list. The fact that Nate hadn't come home last night again wasn't helping either.

"Good morning, Erica," he said as he approached.

"Jonah." She quickly reached for the drug brochures Mabel had given her yesterday and slipped them under the folder in front of her. "What brings you over here today?"

"What's wrong?" he asked, standing at her desk.

"Nothing." She fidgeted with items on her desk. "Just trying to get started. I'm a little behind on my work, and—"

"What's wrong?" he asked more sternly this time.

She looked up at him and could see he intended to persist.

"Nothing I want to talk to you about," she answered.

"Why not?" He walked around the side of her desk. "You've been crying, haven't you?"

"Jonah." Erica looked around. "Denise sits right across from me. She'll be back any second. I think she only went to the bathroom."

"I'll leave if she comes back."

"She's perceptive and nosy. She'll want to know what was going on."

"Stop it, Erica. Tell me what's the matter."

"It's none of your business." She fiddled with her hands on her lap, feeling like a child who had been caught and had no choice but to confess. "We discussed this. I don't like it when you try to play father."

"I am your father," he said. "You can't expect me not to care."

"Back off, Jonah."

He reached over her and pushed the folder aside.

"Stop it!" She quickly tried to grab the brochures, but he snatched them at the same time. She pulled, trying to tear them away from him. "Give those back."

"What were you hoping I wouldn't see?" he asked.

"It's none of your business."

"Helping a family member on drugs?" He looked at the brochure for one last second before letting go.

"Dammit, Jonah."

"Let me guess," he said, his voice deepening in anger. "It's Terrell. He's on something, isn't he?"

"No." She shoved the brochures in a drawer. "You'd like that, wouldn't you?"

"I would hate it," he said. "I wouldn't be surprised, but I would hate anything that hurt you."

"Just stay out of it." She shooed him away from her desk.

He didn't move. "It's Nate, isn't it?"

Erica hadn't expected it, but just at the mention of his name, she began to get emotional. "I can't do this, Jonah. I'm at work, for Christ's sake."

"Nate is a good kid, Erica."

"How would you know?"

"Achelle raised him," he said. "And so did you."

"Obviously I screwed up somewhere."

"How can I help?"

"No," she said. "Terrell and I are dealing with this. Please, Jonah, don't tell anyone."

"I would never do that."

"Look," she said, "thanks for offering, but I've got it under control."

"I don't think you do."

"Either way," she insisted, "it's none of your business."

"If he's in trouble, I can help him. Are you gonna turn that down?"

"Your favors have strings attached."

He shook his head. "Not this time. Drugs are serious business, Erica. I wouldn't play games with that, and you shouldn't turn down a helping hand when you could lose a loved one to drugs."

"Terrell would kill me if—"

"He doesn't have to know."

"What, do you expect me to lie to him? I'm not like that. We're not like that." She noticed the skeptical look on his face. "Not anymore."

"Fine," he said. "Tell him, then. It's time he gets used to me being a part of your life."

She let out a sarcastic smirk. "Easier said than done."

"I don't want to come between you two."

"Bull," she added flatly. "You would love to have that chance again."

"Terrell broke you two up all on his own."

Erica couldn't really deny that, but Jonah had to know she was going to pick Terrell's side over his.

"I can't convince you that I mean well," he continued, "but you don't doubt my influence. If you need help with something, finding something out, getting someone away from Nate that you think is hurting him, you know I'm the one who can do it. Not Terrell."

"I know you have a lot of power, Jonah. That's what scares me. I don't want you wielding it and destroying someone's life in my name."

"Even if it means saving your brother?" he asked.

Unable to come up with a retort, she looked at him for a moment longer, something inside of her urging her to tell him more, to see what he could do. This was Nate after all. He was the only family, real family, she had left, and wouldn't anything be worth saving him from drugs?

"I have a lot of work to do," she finally said. "Can I please get back to it?"

"If you insist." He turned and started around her desk. "I will tell you that the first thing you'd want to know is who his newest friends are. They're going to be the key."

"We're working on that," she said.

He turned back to her. "I could do background checks. I could find out anything about anyone. And if it turns out you need this person to stop having access to your brother, I'm the one that can do that."

He started walking away again, but he was walking slowly. It was as if he knew she was going to call his name. She did and when she did, he turned right around and returned to her desk with an eager smile.

"I just need a name," he said.

Billie was pacing her office, trying to figure out what she should do. She'd made progress. She wasn't completely freaking out anymore, but things still weren't good.

Despite playing the kiss she shared with Ricky in her mind over and over again, she still couldn't believe she'd done it. She had made mistakes in her professional career, but couldn't remember being so irresponsible. Even worse, while she should have been trying to figure out how to deal with it professionally, her mind kept going back to how much she enjoyed it.

She wanted to believe that it was because it was wrong—a forbidden fruit—but the more she thought about it, the more Billie realized that she was genuinely attracted to Ricky and there was no getting around that. That kiss had crossed more than a professional line. It had crossed a sexual line. She wanted him and that was an untenable situation.

How does one back out of a pro bono case? Handing the case over to someone else was not the biggest problem. There was no official case, so they hadn't met with any opposing side. They had requested the emergency calls, filed complaints, issued a subpoena with the DC Housing Authority, and done their own investigation. They hadn't gotten so far that getting someone else up to speed on the case would be detrimental to the case or the client.

No, that wasn't the real problem. *How does one back out of a pro bono case that they begged for, that they told the partners of the firm during their interview they couldn't wait to get?* Most importantly, what reason could she give?

"Thank you for putting all your faith in me," she said, "but I've fallen for the client. Yeah, we've kissed. I screwed up royally, so . . . Yeah, I'll just get my stuff and go."

Billie jumped when the door to her office opened without a knock. It was Richard, her officemate, who had a bad habit of not knocking. Billie knew it was his office, too, but had asked him several times to knock.

"Are you on the phone?" he asked, as he entered.

"No," Billie said, noticing that he wasn't alone.

Behind him walked James Fisk and Jackson Snow, the two men running the firm's white-collar criminal defense practice.

"Hi," was all she said, and Billie felt like a stupid girl.

These men already made her nervous. They were brilliant, extremely confident, and commanding. It intimidated her. And they were the men she would have to tell she needed to pass on Ricky's case.

"Nice to see you, Billie," Jackson said as he leaned against the wall near the door.

James walked in farther. "Hard at work, pacing?"

She smiled nervously. "Just thinking."

"If you're not talking to anyone on the phone," Richard said, walking over to his desk on the other side of the office, "then who were you talking to? I heard your voice."

"No one." She gave him a quick stern look.

He got the point and shut up.

"We ran into Richard in the hallway," Jackson said, "but we were on our way to you."

"What for?" Billie realized how awful that sounded as soon as it came out.

She was panicking now. Something made her believe they knew about the kiss even though it had happened only a few hours ago. Did they have cameras in the offices? There was a rumor they did, just to make sure the associates were working all day and night.

James frowned. "You seem on edge. Have you taken a break today?"

"I . . . um . . ." Why was the first thing that popped into her head, *Yes, I took a break today and made out a little bit with my client?*

"They want to congratulate you," Richard said as he sat down in his chair. He spoke slowly as if he realized that Billie was anxious and he wanted to calm her down.

It worked.

"Really?" she asked, taking a breath and then managing a generous smile.

"I just got a call from William Ricker," James said.

Billie's jaw dropped. "The head of the DC Housing Authority? Why is he calling you?"

"To complain about you." He smiled proudly.

"You've rattled some chains over there," Jackson joined in. "James told him that you had the firm's backing and we were going to pursue this wrongful report case to the end."

"He even admitted there might be some problem," James added, "and wanted us to give them a few days to figure out what was going on."

Billie was genuinely pleased. So the day wasn't a complete disaster. "You don't think they'll admit to fraud or bribery?"

"Of course not," James said. "And we would have never been able to prove it. The point is that we could prove enough to create a huge problem in the media."

"And with the upcoming elections," Jackson said, "that isn't what they want."

Billie tried to seem self-assured even though she wasn't feeling that so much. "I think this is a good time for me to amend my complaint and request—"

"No," James said. "Just hold on a second. We offered them a few days. We'll give them that."

"Time to make sure their cover-up is clean," Billie said skeptically.

"We're in this to win the case, Billie." Jackson pointed his finger at her. "We aren't fighting a war here. Just a battle, and you're about to win it."

"We're very proud of you," James added, as he stepped back into the doorway.

"We'll keep in touch on this, Billie." Jackson joined him.

"Okay," Billie said enthusiastically.

She rushed to the door and watched as the men, engrossed in a new conversation with each other, began walking away.

"What's wrong with you?" Richard asked.

She quietly closed the door behind her, turning to him. "I can't talk about it."

"You should be happy," he said. "You're getting recognition for doing what you love. You can make a name for yourself and start getting more big pro bono cases. That's pretty prestig—"

"You need to knock, Ricardo!"

He looked perplexed. "Seriously? You mad? You must be mad 'cause you just got ethnic on me."

"You never knock." She hurried over to her desk to make notes on the new status of the case.

"I'll try to remember, little miss petite moody."

She ignored his teasing as she pulled the case up in the internal database. He was right. She should be happy and she would try to be. With this turn of events, it would be foolish and selfish for her to drop the case. She could see that now. She was going to win, not just for Ricky, but also for the firm. She could probably get some additional cases on the same matter and put an end to this bullying. There was a lot to gain from her sticking with this case and winning it.

She just had to figure out a way to keep her hands off her client.

This was all a little too seedy for Sherise's taste, but one couldn't be cautious enough when it came to hiring a private investigator to find out exactly who was fucking your husband. So here she was in the dark end of a grocery store parking garage, getting into the passenger side of a Toyota belonging to a woman she had never met before.

"That was quick," Sherise said as she settled in and closed the door.

Beth Martin was a woman in her thirties of Asian and Irish descent. She underplayed her attractiveness, possibly in an attempt to be taken seriously in a male-dominated field, Sherise thought. She was known among some of the social elite in DC as someone you could rely on to be discreet.

Sherise had gotten her card from a friend almost two years

ago who had used her to find dirt on her husband's political opponent for Maryland state congress. Sherise had the card in her hand just above the garbage before she thought twice about it. You never knew when a girl could use an anonymous friend.

After making love to her husband again, Sherise had renewed faith that she could save her marriage and believed honestly that getting this woman out of the picture was what was needed. Justin loved her and he felt guilty about what he was doing. That seemed clear to her. She wasn't going to nitpick, considering her own past. She was going to be a better wife to him, but none of that meant anything if this woman was still in the picture. This woman who was sleeping with her husband as part of a vendetta against her. She was no longer interested in car chases around DC or fruitless Internet searches. She wanted to find out who her target was so she could plan a quick, efficient, and effective attack and get back to the business of her family.

"This will be quick, too," Beth said, her voice held a biting tone.

She handed Sherise a manila envelope.

"My bill is on top," she said. "I usually require an advance, but since you were in such a hurry."

"I'll write a check when I get home today," Sherise said.

She opened the folder. Under the bill, she saw a report that started with the woman's name and her address in Texas.

"I just want to know who she is," Sherise said.

"It was easy, actually," Beth reported. "Jennifer Ross is a Democratic campaign consultant in Dallas. She's divorced, no kids, and thirty-four years old. When she comes to DC, she stays at the Fairmont, but she used to have an apartment in Bethesda."

It bothered Sherise that she had no idea who this woman was. "What else? Tell me more about Bethesda."

"She worked for Senator Mason's and Congresswoman Turner's campaigns. She wasn't extremely social, but she ran with a pretty elite set. You'll see her picture was taken in *Capitol File* and *Washington Life*."

Sherise flipped through the small number of pages in the folder. "But I searched for her name and . . ."

"You searched for Jennifer Ross," Beth said. "She was going by Jen Hodgkins."

Sherise felt the shock hit her like a ton of bricks. Just as Beth spoke, Sherise uncovered a photo from *Capitol File* of Jennifer and her husband dressed in high-end formal wear. The caption read, JENNIFER AND RYAN HODGKINS ATTEND THE DC HEALTHY FAMILIES GALA.

Sherise knew that Beth was still talking, but it didn't matter. She didn't hear anything else. The pounding in her head was too strong. She felt like she was about to explode. She was heating up, and that itch of panic that she had been feeling since she stepped into the car blossomed into full-blown insanity. Of all the things in the world this could have been, she never suspected this. There was a slight suspicion that this was not a mere coincidence, especially after the note on the napkin, but not once had she thought a forgotten ghost like this might jump up and bite her in the ass. And this bite was big. The ex-wife of her ex-lover was now having an affair with her husband and trying to find out about the baby she'd had nine months after that initial affair with her then husband.

"Fuck me," was all Sherise could think of to say.

She had no plan for this.

12

"Hold on!" Sherise yelled as she rushed from the kitchen to the front door of her apartment with her crying baby in her arms.

She looked through the peephole to see a harried looking Billie and Erica standing at her door. Was she ready for this? She knew that she needed to talk to them, but this talk could change their entire relationship. She was in a panic right now, and as much as she needed her girls, she didn't want to risk losing them when they found out the truth.

"It's do-or-die time," she said to Cady, who responded by smacking her mother in the chin.

The second she opened the door, both girls sighed.

"Where the hell have you been?" Erica asked.

"I know," Sherise said as she stepped aside to let them enter. "I know."

"You haven't been returning any of our calls or texts," Billie said.

"Come here, sweetie." Erica held her hands out to Cady, but the baby shook her head and leaned farther into her mama.

"She's in an awful mood," Sherise said, closing the door behind them.

She knew that was her fault, too. Her baby fed off her

mood and emotions and Sherise knew her panic was sending a bad vibe to her baby.

"You can't just go chasing after some bitch with your husband and then not return calls," Billie said.

After trying to reach Sherise, Billie got worried and contacted Erica. She'd told Erica about her last conversation with Sherise and what she'd been doing. Both women were worried, and after not getting any responses after eight P.M., decided to come over and check on her.

"Is he here?" Erica asked.

"No," Sherise said with a smack of her lips. "He had to work late . . . again."

"Sherise," Billie said, "I want to pop you. You had me worried that you had some kind of confrontation and shit popped off."

"She wanted to call the hospital," Erica said.

"I wouldn't be at the hospital," Sherise said. "That bitch would have been though."

"I just can't believe this." Erica sat down on the sofa in the living room. "Justin. Are you sure there's no other explanation?"

"What happened?" Billie offered to take Cady.

"Let me put her down first," Sherise said as she headed for the playpen in the corner.

"I want proof," Erica said. "He's supposed to be one of the good ones."

"There is no such man," Billie said bitterly.

"Terrell would never cheat on me," Erica insisted.

Billie sat down next to her, looking at her with a disbelieving expression. "Didn't you just say that about Justin? They cheat. They're assholes."

Erica shook her head. "I want proof."

"We have it," Billie said. "And I have a feeling we're about to learn more."

"I can't stay long," Erica said loudly to Sherise, who was talking to a very unhappy Cady as she sat her in the pen. "Terrell is moving a lot of his stuff in right now. I can't leave him alone all night."

"He can manage," Billie said.

"I need to talk to him about something serious."

"What?" Billie asked. "I thought you two were doing well."

"Well, you know I told you about Nate's drug issue." Erica had poured her heart out to Billie on the drive over to Sherise's house. "Jonah has offered to help me out with this."

She noticed Billie's expression contort into some form of dread and disappointment.

"Look," Erica said. "I know you guys don't like him, but I'm desperate. I need to know what's going on."

"What's he gonna do?" Billie asked.

"He has connections," she said. "He can find things out about people."

Billie didn't like the sound of this. Whatever favor Jonah was offering, she felt certain some strings would be attached. "I can do that, too."

"But you're busy," Erica said. "You have work and Robert, and—"

"There is no Robert anymore," Billie interrupted.

She hadn't returned any of his calls or e-mails since the fund-raiser. He was the last thing on her mind.

"Okay," Erica said, "but you have that thing. You know, that thing with the guy that you like. That case."

"I don't like him," Billie said defensively. "He's my client."

"But you had a dream about him kissing you," Erica said. She could tell she struck a nerve with her.

"It was a stupid dream." Billie was reacting nervously. "Look, it doesn't matter. We're talking about you and you're better off with me than Jonah."

"I think he genuinely wants to help me," Erica said.

"I don't doubt it, but . . ."

"Let me handle it, okay?"

Billie could see that Erica was conflicted despite the conviction in her tone.

"We'll talk about it later," she said. "Right now, Sherise, what the fuck are you doing? Get over here."

Having finally calmed Cady down, Sherise quickly went into the kitchen to retrieve the folder Beth had given her. She was getting more and more nervous with every second.

"This is her." She handed the folder to Billie and sat down on the coffee table across from the girls as they looked through the folder. "Jennifer Ross."

"The woman LaKeisha mentioned at the fund-raiser?" Billie asked.

Sherise told them everything that Beth had told her. Everything except Jennifer's marital history. As her girls looked over the information, she could see the look of dissatisfaction on their faces. This didn't make sense. Of course it didn't. She was holding out on them.

"This is proof?" Erica asked skeptically.

"Seriously, Sherise," Billie added. "This is it? Are you sure this is her?"

"It's her," Sherise said flatly.

"And you can't think of any way that you know her?" Billie asked. "Not a work project, a social event . . . nothing?"

"So you got to see her?" Erica asked. "The woman in this picture was the woman you saw with Justin?"

"I didn't really . . ." Sherise sighed. "Trust me, it's her."

"Well," Erica concluded, "if you don't know her, then we have to assume that the note on the napkin is unrelated to this."

"It's related," Sherise said, her head tilted somberly to the side.

Billie really observed Sherise for the first time since coming over. Her eyes were red and had dark circles around them. She looked a mess. She looked . . . afraid.

"What's going on?" Billie asked.

"I just found out the name of the woman who is fucking my husband," Sherise said.

"What are you not telling us?" she asked.

Erica looked up from the photo and realized she had been missing something. Billie wasn't buying this.

"What's going on?" she asked.

"What comes around goes around," Billie said. "Why, Sherise?"

Before she could utter a word, Sherise broke down and began crying. Her face fell into her hands and she sobbed as both girls hurried to her side and wrapped their arms around her.

"It's okay." Billie ran her fingers through Sherise's hair with comforting strokes. "We'll figure this out, sweetie."

"Just talk to us," Erica added. "We've gotten through everything together. The three of us together can fix any problem, even this one. You know that, Sherise."

It was true and Erica's words allowed Sherise the strength to lift her head.

"When Jennifer was living in DC," she started, feeling sick for having to reveal this, "she was married to . . . She was married to Ryan Hodgkins."

"Who's that?" Erica asked.

"Oh, no," Billie said. "Don't you remember him? The guy that she kissed."

"Oh, shit," Erica said, suddenly recalling. "That was forever ago. She's coming after you now? He must have just told her he kissed you."

"No," Sherise said with a shaky voice. "He must have told her . . . he slept with me."

"What the fuck?" Billie asked. "Why would he say that? Do you think he knew she'd come after you if he lied?"

Erica found this incredible. "So you think she's sleeping

with Justin to get back at you for thinking you slept with Ryan? How fucking vindictive. We're gonna get this bitch."

"I did," Sherise said. She looked at Billie and then Erica before turning and facing forward as she added, "He didn't lie to her. I slept with him."

She couldn't bear to look at them as they took it in.

"Wait," Billie said. "What?"

"I slept with him," she repeated just above a whisper.

Erica leaned away, thinking she'd heard wrong. "You just kissed him."

"I told you I slept with him!" she yelled this time.

"You lied to us," Billie finally said.

"You cheated on Justin twice?" Erica couldn't believe this.

"I was too ashamed to tell you guys," Sherise said, looking down at her lap. "I was so . . ."

Billie was fuming. "So when we told you, warned you to stay away from him, you didn't do it, did you?"

"I tried," Sherise said. "I swear to God I tried, but I don't know. I just . . ."

"Jesus Christ, Sherise!" Erica shot up from the table and stepped a few feet away. She looked down at Sherise. "How many men have you slept with since you've been married?"

Sherise looked up at her and was stung by the look of disgust on Erica's face. "I swear it's just him and Jonah. I promise you."

"And what the hell does that promise mean?" Erica asked, shaking her head.

"I swear," Sherise repeated a few times as she started crying again.

"So she has every right to do this," Erica said.

"Erica!" Billie looked up at her, expressing her anger. "What the fuck is the matter with you?"

"How can you think this is okay?" Erica asked. "You were cheated on and she's a serial cheater."

"She's your best friend," Billie said. "She's your sister and she needs us."

Sherise turned to Billie. "I need you both, so bad. I want to save my marriage."

"You mean you want to keep your marriage together so you can cheat in peace?" Erica asked.

"Fuck you," Sherise spat at her. "I'm dying here, Erica. I'm dying. You just don't understand."

Erica felt a pang of compassion and guilt fight through her anger and disappointment. She sat down on the sofa and sighed. "I just can't believe you thought it was okay for you to do this, but not him."

"I'm not judging him," Sherise said. "I'm not being a hypocrite. I'm just trying to save my marriage. I'm trying to save my daughter's family."

"And we'll help you," Billie said. "Won't we?"

Erica reached out and placed her hand on Sherise's knee. "Of course we will. It's what we do for each other. It's what we've always done and always will. This bitch is history."

Sherise placed her hand over Erica's and squeezed as she leaned her head into Billie's chest. She was already starting to feel better.

Erica was physically and emotionally exhausted when she finally got home. By the time she'd left Sherise's house, they'd agreed to get together Saturday, tomorrow, and figure out how they would confront Jennifer and let her know that she was going to stay away from Justin from that moment on.

Erica wasn't happy with the decision. She wasn't used to being in these situations. While Terrell had hurt her feelings in other ways, she had never been worried about him cheating on her. In the past, if a boyfriend messed around, she'd just dropped him. No questions asked, no apologies accepted.

She knew that marriage, especially marriage with a child,

was different. Erica suggested that Sherise confront Justin first. After all, this woman, whoever she was, had not made a vow to Sherise. And what was the point of telling the woman to stay away if the man wouldn't do the same?

It was all very confusing to Erica, but she was the only one who had never been married, so she gave up arguing. As much as she worried for Sherise that her marriage could be ending, Erica was happy to get out of there. Too much heartache and fear and she was already dealing with enough of that with Nate. She wanted to get home to the one good thing in her life now, the one thing that was moving forward. Terrell.

The second she got home, he grabbed her and kissed her passionately. They sat on the only part of the sofa that wasn't covered in boxes, with her comfortably on his lap.

"I'm afraid to ask what happened over there," he said. "Just from looking at you, I know the drama was off the hook."

Erica shook her head. "Boy, you don't even know."

"Wanna talk about it?"

Erica smiled. She had forgotten how great it felt to come home to a sympathizing ear and a warm body. It hadn't been that long, but now that she had it again, it seemed like it had been forever.

"You don't want to know," she answered.

"I see. I see." He nodded. "You three and your little secrets."

"It's not my business to share," she said.

"You tell them all the shit that goes on between us, don't you?"

She tilted her head, studying him. "We're like sisters. But don't worry. There are certain things that stay just between me and my man."

"Your man." He leaned forward and kissed the exposed part of her chest just above her breast. "I like the sound of that."

She ran her hand over his head and looked into his eyes lovingly. "Me, too."

He squinted. "You don't tell them about sex with me, do you?"

"Um." She playfully pushed his face back. "Of course not. I would never."

"Girl!" He slapped her thigh. "You better tell them I'm hurting that. You better."

He grabbed her and started pulling her back as he buried his face in her chest. She was laughing as she grabbed his head. It felt nice to be happy and not think about . . .

"Is Nate here?" she asked, sitting up.

Terrell's shoulders slumped and he sighed. "Can we not talk about him right now?"

"Have you seen him?" She stood up, heading for his room.

"Stop," he said. "Don't bother. He's not there. He was here, but he left."

She turned back to him. "When?"

"After you left. He stopped by to pick up some clothes."

"Clothes? Is he moving out?"

He shook his head. "There wasn't enough for that. Just a shirt and some jeans."

"Well," she said. "What did he say?"

"He didn't want to . . ." Terrell motioned for her to return to him. "Don't worry about it, baby. I told you I got this."

Erica suddenly remembered what she had to tell him and it made her sad. She knew she would ruin the mood, but after spending the last two hours with Sherise, listening to the details of the breakdown of her marriage, Erica didn't want to keep something this important from Terrell.

"I know this isn't gonna make you happy," she said, standing in front of him. "But I asked Jonah for help. He offered and I—"

"You what?" Terrell shot up from the sofa. "Help with what?"

"With Nate." She held up her hand to calm him down. "Before you get all upset, he's just going to look into some of his new friends and—"

"Why did you do that?" Terrell was getting angrier every second. "You don't want that man's dirty hands on this."

"I wanted help."

He slapped his chest. "I'm helping you!"

"This isn't a reflection on you," Erica said.

"The hell it isn't," Terrell said. "That man wants me to look impotent to you. He knows I'm trying to help you, so he's gonna show how my help ain't shit compared to what he can do for you."

"Don't look at it that way, baby."

She reached out to console him, but he moved away. Erica was consumed with regret after looking at him. He really hated Jonah this much? More than he wanted to help Nate?

"Terrell, you have to make some peace with the fact that he's my father and he's going to be some part of my life."

"Not this," he insisted. "Not this, Erica. Call him off."

"I'm not going to hold off on getting to the bottom of what's wrong with Nate. I'm going to do what I can and I'm going to let you help, Jonah help, and Billie, if—"

"Billie?" He threw his hands in the air. "You got her involved, too? What does Billie have to do with it?"

"She offered to help, too."

"Help with what?" he asked. "What did you tell her?"

Erica was completely perplexed by his behavior and attitude. "Everything I told you. Terrell, what's wrong with you? Don't you want to help Nate?"

"I'm trying to!" he yelled. "But I can't do it if you have everyone in the fucking city interfering. Look, I gotta go."

"What?" She watched as he grabbed his phone from the kitchen counter and headed for the door. "Terrell, what are you . . . Where are you going?"

"Call off your dogs, Erica." He opened the door. "Before you do more harm to Nate than has already been done."

He slammed the door behind him, leaving Erica standing alone in her apartment in disbelief. What had just happened?

She knew she had a paranoid nature, but even taking that into consideration, there had to be more to this than Terrell was telling her. Something was wrong. Something was worse than she suspected, and considering what she suspected, that her brother had fallen into the drug crowd and was using and even possibly dealing, she shuddered at what this could be.

Her cell phone rang a few times before Erica thought to answer it. She grabbed it and looked at the ID. It was Billie. She sighed before answering.

"What now?" she asked.

"This is a mess!" Billie's voice was panicked.

"What happened?" Erica imagined a scenario in which Justin came home, a fight ensued, and all hell broke out. Sherise was not the model of restraint.

"She's going to confront that bitch," Billie said. "Get in your car and come over here."

"Wait . . . What?"

"I went to the bathroom and when I came out she was gone and left a note for me to stay and watch Cady. She's going to confront the woman at the hotel."

"What about the agreement to wait?"

"Obviously, she changed her mind."

"Where's Cady now?"

"I have her," Billie said. "You're gonna watch her and I'm gonna go get Sherise."

At first, Erica thought to ask why she shouldn't go get Sherise, but she knew why. This was a critical-mass situation, and fireworks usually happened between her and Sherise in normally stressful situations. Billie was the peacemaker, and Erica imagined, whatever was going to go down at that hotel, peacemaking was needed.

"I'm on my way," she said.

She would have to figure out what Terrell's problem was tomorrow. Tonight she had to help keep Sherise from making a terrible mistake.

★ ★ ★

Maybe that second martini was a mistake. Sherise wasn't sure and she really didn't care. She just wanted that bitch to get here. Try as she might, she was unable to get a hotel room number for Jennifer Ross. She was able to get the male attendant to ring her room, but there was no answer. That was the best she was going to get, so Sherise decided to wait. Meanwhile, she had a drink, maybe two, to try to calm her down.

This was not wise, a voice told her. Of course it wasn't. Had any woman yet invented the wisest way to confront her husband's mistress, the whore tearing her family apart? Billie and Erica had tried to help her. They had agreed to let the reality of this situation sink in for another day and then figure out how to confront this woman and make sure she stayed out of Justin's life forever. The girls were going to back her up to avoid anything getting out of hand or be her backup if anything went down.

But they didn't know about Cady, and Sherise knew she couldn't wait any longer. She imagined a scenario where she would kick through the door and find her with Justin and . . . Well, the truth was, she didn't know what she was going to do. She hadn't had a plan coming over, but she wasn't going to wait another second. Justin didn't know about Cady yet. She could tell that much. While she believed her marriage could survive an affair . . . or two, she wasn't sure it could survive the truth about Cady, especially if that truth came from someone other than her.

No, this couldn't wait another moment. This situation was going to be handled now, before it got worse. Before it got irreversible.

Sherise was feeling calmer, so maybe the drinks were a good idea. She wasn't sure. All she knew was that she could very possibly see her husband walk into this hotel with another woman and she needed a few drinks to prepare herself for that. A half hour later, she was beginning to wonder. Maybe they were in the room and no one answered the call because they were making love. In which case, Sherise would have to deal with seeing her husband step out of the elevators. What would she do then? She didn't want to confront Justin yet. She wanted to know what Jennifer had told him and what her plans were first so she could figure out how to best play it with Justin to keep him on her side. But could she resist confronting him if she saw him there? She didn't think so. She only hoped she was right in believing that Jennifer was not at the hotel and would be returning soon.

"I'll have another cosmo," she told the waiter who approached her. She was sitting in a soft set of circular chairs at a small table facing the lobby of the hotel.

She wasn't looking at the lobby at that time, but the sound of expensive heels clicking against the hard floor got her attention. Sherise looked toward the lobby in time to see Jennifer walk briskly through. In her mid-thirties, she was a very attractive, held-together woman. She walked with her head held high in a peach and gold wrap dress. She was thin, but had generous curves. Her skin was a dark caramel and her hair was a shiny auburn and went in curls down her back.

"That's her," Sherise said to herself as she shot up from the chair.

She grabbed the waiter, who was on his way back to the bar.

"Never mind," she told him. "I'm good."

Sherise didn't say a word until she'd caught up with her in the elevator lobby.

"Hey, bitch."

Jennifer, who was waiting for an elevator, quickly turned around, her hair swinging with her.

Sherise smiled at the look of astonishment on her face.

"Surprise," Sherise said as she walked closer to her. "Didn't expect to see me here, did you?"

It was clear Jennifer wasn't sure what to do at first. She opened her mouth, but no words came out.

"What's the matter?" Sherise asked. "Can't speak? Do you need another napkin?"

The elevator opened and Jennifer looked at it.

"You can run," Sherise said. "I'll follow. You're not getting away from me, Jennifer."

"So you do know who I am," the woman finally said, turning to face her. She seemed to have a little more confidence now.

"You're the whore I'm gonna beat the shit out of if you don't—"

"I'm the whore?" She laughed. "You fucking hypocrite. This is funny because you didn't know who the fuck I was when you were fucking my husband."

"I don't give a shit about you or your husband," Sherise said. "Justin is my husband, and if you don't stay away from him, you're going to regret it."

"It doesn't work that way," she said, shaking her head. "You don't get to say 'fuck you' to my marriage, but then I have to respect yours. Nothing works that way."

"You don't have to respect shit," Sherise answered back. This bitch was not going to tell her how anything worked. "You just have to stay the fuck away from my husband."

"You don't get to tell me what to do. You're the fucking home wrecker. Like I said, what goes around comes around."

"You don't even want him," Sherise said. "This is all about Ryan."

She shrugged with an evil grin. "He's not the same type of man Ryan was, but he's clearly the best you could get to marry you, so it was what I had to work with."

"This was all about me." Sherise laughed, shaking her head. "Aren't you the most pitiful bitch on the planet? How long have you been planning this? How long have you been obsessed with me?"

Jennifer's expression showed she didn't like what she was hearing. "Not long. I just recently found out about you and Ryan during our divorce. And don't be flattered. You weren't the first or the last."

"But I was the best," Sherise said. "I always am."

"I'm sure there are thousands of men who can verify that."

Sherise started for her, but was stopped in her tracks as a two young women, dressed in cocktail dresses and very drunk, entered the elevator lobby. The girls struggled to press the button.

Sherise moved away from them, almost circling Jennifer, who was staring at her with an evil smile. While she appeared completely off guard at first, Jennifer seemed to be enjoying this now. She was ready for more and Sherise was going to give it to her.

"What do you want?" Sherise asked, just above a whisper. "And trust me when I tell you, this is the last time you will be asked that."

"Isn't it obvious?" she asked. "You get to experience what it feels like to be betrayed. This is revenge, Sherise. Pure and simple. Revenge and then some."

"So you got it," Sherise said. "You took advantage of my husband to feed some sick envy you have of me."

The two drunk girls got on the elevator and the door closed.

"There was no advantage to be taken," Jennifer said. "Your husband is an unfulfilled man and was eager for my attention. It took very little."

Sherise placed her hands on her hips. "Did Ryan tell you how he pursued me? I know you'd probably love to think I seduced him, but it was the other way around. He chased me relentlessly."

"Bullshit," she said. "You wanted to trade up to a richer,

more socially connected man and you didn't care that he was married."

"Didn't care?" Sherise huffed. "Didn't know, bitch. He never mentioned you. Never wore a ring. Nothing, ho. Not a thing."

Sherise could tell this hit Jennifer hard and it excited her that she had struck a nerve. She imagined Jennifer had spent her entire marriage trying to hold on to her husband. She had probably made him her life, and nothing hurt a woman like that more than to know the disregard her husband showed her.

"But I know Justin talks about me," Sherise said. "Because he loves me. Even if you hadn't gone after him over this sick, twisted, empty revenge quest, you would know all about me. Because, Jennifer, like you said, I wasn't the first or last in your husband's infidelity tour, but you are the first and will be the last in mine."

"That you know of." Jennifer was fuming now. "You act very confident for a woman whose husband has rejected her."

"Justin hasn't rejected me. He still lives in my home and sleeps in my bed every night. Obviously, you plotted and planned this. This was your little game and I'm ending it."

"You don't have any say over what I do!"

"When it comes to my husband, I do!" Sherise came to only inches from her. "You go anywhere near my husband again, and I will—"

"While he's your husband," she said, backing a few inches away. "Which we both know won't be for long."

"You think you could take my husband away?" Sherise poked her in the chest with her index finger. "You overestimate yourself. You're a tired, old hag who took advantage of a man—"

"Who doesn't know his wife has cheated on him!" Jennifer smiled. "You see, Sherise. I have nothing to lose. My marriage is over."

"It never began," Sherise interjected.

"It was a marriage!" she insisted. "It wasn't perfect, and bitches like you messed it up!"

"You are so delusional."

"Am I?" Jennifer asked. "Am I imagining what Justin would say when he finds out about Ryan?"

"What he'll say," Sherise answered, "is that we've both cheated on each other and he won't get on his high horse about it. He won't leave me for doing something he's done to me. I guess I should thank you. You've evened this out for me. Justin is a lot of things, but he's not a hypocrite."

"Maybe you're right." Jennifer was undaunted.

"I always am."

"But what about Cady?" she asked. "Will he be as understanding about her? What about that precious little girl that was born only—"

Sherise lunged for her with a yell that came from somewhere deep inside of her. "Don't you ever mention my baby!"

Sherise grabbed her by the shoulders and pushed her to the ground. Sherise fell on top of her and tried to avoid Jennifer's swinging arms and slapping hands. She pressed her hands against her shoulders to hold Jennifer down.

"Get off me, you bitch!" Jennifer was kicking and struggling.

"You don't know who you are fucking with!" Sherise yelled. "You say one more word about Cady and I'll kill you!"

"Sherise!"

Sherise felt someone behind her, grabbing her right arm and starting to pull her back. She looked back and saw Billie struggling to pull her off Jennifer.

Jennifer took this distraction as an opportunity and pushed Sherise off her. Sherise fell on the floor beside her and Jennifer smacked her in the face.

"Stop it!" Billie tried to stand between the two of them, but Sherise pushed her out of the way.

Sherise, halfway turned around, lifted her arm and swung. Her elbow connected with Jennifer's cheek and sent her flying back, screaming out in pain. Sherise reached again and grabbed a handful of hair and pulled it with a grunt.

"Hey!"

A large man Sherise recognized as one of the doormen to the hotel reached down and grabbed each of them. His grip on Sherise was so hard that she had to let go of Jennifer's hair. Still, the women were trying to reach for each other, but he had them too far apart.

"You fucking bitch!" Jennifer yelled.

He lifted them both so they were standing up.

Sherise tried to jerk out of his grip, but he was like a stone statue. "You better get the fuck out of DC and never come back if you know what's good for you!"

Jennifer started laughing like a crazy person. "You're so stupid. You just confirmed everything I suspected about that baby but couldn't verify."

"You're dead!" Sherise pointed to her.

"Sherise!" Billie rushed in front of Sherise and grabbed her by the chin. She turned her face to her. "Shut up! Don't say that! Don't say another word."

Sherise looked at her, feeling frantic and crazy. She could see the concern in Billie's eyes, but knew she was being a lawyer right now and not a friend.

"I know you're a guest," the man said to Jennifer, who was still laughing, but was holding the cheek that had gotten the brunt of Sherise's elbows. "So you need to go to your room."

"Let me go and I will," she said.

"If you mess around again, I'm calling the police," he warned, pointing to the elevator. "Now go!"

He let Jennifer go and she backed away. She looked at Sherise with a smile and opened her mouth to say something.

"Go!" he ordered. "I'm calling the police in five seconds. Do you want to get kicked out of this hotel?"

She looked at him, rolled her eyes, and turned toward the elevator.

"Can you let me go?" Sherise asked, looking up at him.

"Do you stay here?" he asked.

"No," Billie answered for her. "She's leaving with me. You can let her go."

"I'll let her go as soon as this other lady is in the elevator," he said.

"What are you doing here?" Sherise asked Billie. "Where's Cady?"

"Erica came over to watch her. She just called and said that Justin was home, so she left. He was asking a lot of questions."

"Who the fuck is he to ask questions?" Sherise asked.

The man finally let her go after the elevator door closed behind Jennifer. "Now both of you, get out of this hotel, now."

Sherise glared coldly at him, but said nothing as Billie grabbed her by the arm and started leading her toward the lobby.

"What questions?" Sherise asked.

Billie shrugged. "I don't know. Let's just get out of here first."

Once out in front of the hotel, Billie finally let go of Sherise. She looked a mess.

"What the fuck is wrong with you?" she asked. "Threatening to kill someone? In public? In front of witnesses?"

"Stop fucking lawyering me!" Sherise took a deep breath of air. Her head was still pounding, her heart still racing. "I didn't mean it."

She did mean it. Just hearing that woman mention Cady filled her with so much rage Sherise could barely stand it.

"This was a horrible idea," Billie said. "You made things worse. You know that."

"You don't have to tell me," Sherise said. "That bitch! I was right. It's all about revenge. She doesn't give a shit about Justin."

Billie stood in front of Sherise, looking into her eyes. "What's going on, Sherise?"

Sherise looked at her confused. "What the . . . Where have you been all day?"

"I was watching you," Billie said. "When she mentioned Cady, you lost it."

"Can you blame me? It's bad enough that woman is sleeping with my husband. She doesn't get to put my baby's name on her lips. She doesn't!"

"What will Justin find out about her?" Billie asked, emphasizing her calm in order to keep Sherise from losing it again.

Sherise swallowed hard, diverting her eyes from Billie's.

"What did you hear?" she asked.

Billie sighed. "Oh my God."

She had thought about it for a second when Sherise told them she had actually slept with Ryan. She knew what was going on at the time. For just a second, she thought about it, but then erased it from her mind.

"I remember when you told us you were pregnant," Billie said, speaking slowly as her mind processed it all. "We were so happy for you."

"Billie." Sherise began crying as she reached out and touched Billie's shoulder. "Please."

"And I thought for a second," Billie continued, "that thank God you never went any further with Ryan because . . . How could you, Sherise?"

"Justin is Cady's father," Sherise insisted. The look of disgust on Billie's face broke her heart. "He's her father."

"Do you know that?"

"I know it," Sherise said, nodding. "I know it. He loves her. She loves him."

"Do you know?" Billie demanded. "Stop fucking around, Sherise. Do you know?"

Sherise lowered her head, her tears dropping to the ground. "No. No, I don't."

"Jesus Christ. This is completely fucked up." Billie shoved Sherise's hand from her shoulder and turned away. "You had a chance to come clean with us earlier tonight. I thought you had. But you were still holding out. You were holding out the most important part."

"No, I wasn't," she insisted. "Who Cady's father is is between me and Justin."

"Stop it," Billie said. "Stop making excuses. That's not how we work. That's not our relationship and you know it. If you didn't want to tell us everything, you shouldn't have asked for our help."

"Fine." Sherise lifted her head defiantly. "Fine, I'll just deal with this on my own. I got into this on my own. I'll solve it on my own."

As she wiped her tears away from her cheeks, Billie turned back to her.

"No, you won't," Billie said. "That's not how we work either. Dammit, Sherise. You really fucked up, but we'll figure it out."

"How?"

"First," Billie said, "we need to find out the truth about Cady."

"No," Sherise said, shaking her head. "If it's true that she's Ryan's and not . . ."

"You don't have the luxury of hoping or wishing for the results anymore," Billie said. "We need to find the truth and tell Justin before she does."

Sherise bent over and clutched her stomach as she threw up.

13

Billie was anxious and tired. Since Sherise's revelation about Cady last night, she hadn't been able to sleep. After driving Sherise home, Billie called Erica and gave her the news. She had to deal with that fallout. She and Erica had actually gotten into an argument over supporting Sherise and keeping yet another secret from her husband for her.

After finally getting Erica reluctantly on her side, she listened as Erica told her about Terrell storming out of the house over the news that she and Jonah were both trying to help him figure out what was going on with Nate. Billie found this suspicious as well and offered to back away, but Erica begged her for her help. Yet another thing on her to-do list.

She finally got home, her heart completely heavy from the implications of all this. She loved Cady and was afraid that the poor baby's family was going to fall apart. Billie knew Sherise was a fighter and would be okay even if her marriage to Justin fell apart. She would recover and move on. But what about Cady?

She shuddered at the thought that she had been trying to get pregnant when she found out about Porter's affair. This current nightmare was bringing back Billie's worst memories of her divorce, and she was aching over contemplations of what she might have done differently. What would she have done if she'd been pregnant when she'd found out her husband had betrayed her. Would she have divorced him anyway? Would she have tried to make it work? In her heart, she knew there was no making it work with him, but a baby was always worth another try.

At the time, she considered trying to make it work for Tara. She was the only mother the girl had ever known and it ripped Billie apart to know that she would have to leave the home she shared with Tara by leaving the home she shared with Porter. Holding that girl as she cried and begged Billie not to leave was the most painful experience Billie had ever had. The fact that she had no legal rights to the girl made it worse.

This fact was glaringly so at times like this. Billie glanced at her phone to check the time. Tara should have been here fifteen minutes ago. They had planned to meet a week ago during her lunch hour after Billie's last disastrous meeting with Porter. Billie didn't want to do it this way, but she couldn't just walk away from Tara. The girl was at a critical moment in her life—a moment where she needed her mother—and Billie couldn't let Porter's conditions and threats keep them apart.

She was starting to get worried. Even in all the chaos of her life and Sherise's, Billie remembered to text Tara last night to remind her of their meeting. She hadn't gotten a response. She had tried again this morning and received only an "I'll be there," which was an unusually short and cold response for Tara. Billie worried that things were worse than she'd imagined for the girl. She wasn't sure what she could do because of Porter's insistence that she stay out of it, but she was willing to help Tara in every way she could, even if it meant in a capacity as a lawyer acting against Porter's wishes. Tara was what was important here, not keeping peace with Porter.

She also wasn't sure what she could do because she was so

emotionally drained and exhausted. She'd wanted to tell Erica and Sherise about kissing Ricky, but she didn't feel like she could. Erica was at her wit's end with Nate and she had to deal with telling Terrell that she had involved Jonah. And Sherise . . . well, she had her hands full. Billie realized that she had taken it upon herself to take the burden of both of these problems, going beyond just mere support. She was already at the end of her rope with her own problems. Now both Erica's and especially Sherise's problems were draining her, too.

Just as she tried to convince herself it couldn't get worse, her lunch companion arrived.

"Hello, Billie."

Billie swallowed as she watched Porter, dressed in his country club gear, take a seat across from her. Their eyes met, and while she imagined hers held fear, his clearly held rage.

"Look, Porter," she started.

"No, you look." His eyes were slits and his lips were pressed together in anger as he glared at her. "Being a lawyer, you should understand the implications of you having secret meetings with my minor child behind my back and against my wishes."

She nodded. "You need to understand why I've done this."

"I understand." He waved away the waiter that attempted to approach their table. "You think you have more say in my daughter's life than I do."

"I don't," she said, "but I love your daughter as much as you do."

"Bullshit," he said. "If you loved her, you would have never left her."

"I didn't leave her," Billie exclaimed. "I left you. You're the one that keeps us apart."

"And for good reason." He slammed his fist on the table. "You're trying to get her to go against my direct wishes."

"How am I doing that?"

"This birth control shit."

"This birth control is not shit," she said. "You were fifteen once. You weren't a virgin. As a matter of fact, you were about her age when you became a teenaged father."

"This isn't about me," Porter argued. "This is about my daughter and she's not having sex."

"I'm not trying to get her to have sex, Porter. I'm trying desperately to discourage her from doing it, but you're stepping in my way."

This had him fuming. "Stepping in your way? How dare you? She's my daughter!"

"She needs me, Porter."

"She needs me and that's all she needs."

"You just told me how much you needed me to help you with her," Billie reminded him. "I guess that came with strings attached. You want me in your bed, too."

"I don't want you in my bed anymore," Porter said. "I don't want you in anything that has to do with me. If you try and contact my daughter again via text, e-mail, phone, or any other way, I'll call the police on you. I've taken away her phone and removed you from all her social networking lists."

"Porter." She leaned back in her chair and folded her arms across her chest. "You're being ridiculous. I just want to talk to her."

"She's gone," he added calmly.

"Gone where?"

"She's in Michigan. I've enrolled her in a private all-girls school in Bloomfield Hills."

"She's all alone?" Billie was horrified. "How could you do that? How could you banish her from everyone she loves? Her friends, her life, her school, me?"

"My mother is there," Porter said.

"You've punished her for having feelings. You've punished her for trying to reach out to her parents about her body. Do you know the damage this will do to her?"

"It's none of your business." Porter stood up, pointing his finger in her face. "Go near her, Billie, and you'll regret it."

He turned to leave and Billie rushed after him. She pulled at his arm, but he jerked away.

"Don't touch me," he said, his tone full of disgust. "You had a chance to be a part of our lives again, Billie. You didn't want it."

"Please, Porter. For Tara's sake, just think about what you're doing. You're her father. You just rejected her."

"I didn't reject her," he said as they reached outside. He rushed to the curb to hail a cab.

"Yes, you did," Billie urged. "That's what it will feel like. Where do you think she's going to turn for male approval?"

He turned back to her. "Greg can't reach her anymore."

"It doesn't matter. She'll be desperate for friends, for some kind of male affirmation. You've made her feel dirty for having hormones. You're playing with fire. You're playing with her life."

The cab pulled up to the curb. Porter reached out and grabbed the door. Looking at her, he said, "This is your fault, Billie. You're the one who encouraged her to get birth control. You're the one that made her think it was okay to have sex. I'm just undoing your damage."

"Porter!" she yelled as he shut the door behind him.

Watching the cab drive off, Billie was overcome with a sense of helplessness. She felt like she was going to cry. This was devastating. What had she done to the girl?

She felt like something had been ripped from her. It was hard enough seeing Tara only on rare occasions. Even under those circumstances when she couldn't see her, she knew the girl was safe and nearby with a father who loved her. Now, she was hundreds of miles away and going through an emotional and hormonal hell. Porter only made things worse, but Billie did feel responsible. She could have handled this better, but she never thought Porter would punish Tara. He lashed out at her out of fear, helplessness, and anger toward Billie. Now Tara was paying the price.

She had to fix this, but how? She needed to get to Tara. She needed to make sure that Tara understood that this wasn't her fault.

"Ma'am?" A man who had just come out of the restaurant approached Billie and touched her arm. "Ma'am, are you alright?"

Billie realized that she had been wandering around the entrance to the restaurant, probably looking as crazed and overwhelmed as she felt.

"You don't look so good, ma'am," he said. "Are you okay?"

"It's too much," she said. "It's just too much!"

She freed her arm and ran off in the direction of nowhere in particular. He called after her, but Billie wasn't listening. It was all just too much.

Terrell was happy to finally get out of work even though it was starting to rain. He was still adjusting to the white-collar side of the business. He liked the money, but he missed being able to just go home when that clock struck a certain number and not have to worry about it anymore. This was especially so now because of all the issues he was dealing with.

Everything was turning into a disaster. Actually, it was a disaster a while ago. It was now a monumental apocalypse. He had to figure out how to get Nate back in line before everything exploded and all he had worked for to get Erica back went to waste.

Or maybe it was too late.

That was the first thought that came to Terrell's mind as he started across the street to the parking lot. Blocking his way was a limousine, but it wasn't one of his. He recognized it though because he had driven one just like it. That was during his short stint as a driver for the Pentagon. A job that he didn't lose after a failed blackmail attempt, but did lose after Erica had dumped him.

The door to the sleek, black car opened, but no one stepped out.

"Fuck," Terrell muttered under his breath. This was what he'd feared since his argument with Erica Friday night.

He looked around before cautiously stepping toward the car. Once inside, he slid into the seat.

"Close the door," Jonah ordered coldly.

Terrell reluctantly reached out and closed the door. He kept his eyes on Jonah, who was looking at him intently.

"They give you guys breaks?" he asked. "I'll bet you need them. Waging war on poor countries is hard work, right?"

"You're not funny," he said flatly.

"What the fuck do you want?"

Jonah smiled. "You know. Otherwise you wouldn't have gotten in this car."

"This shit is none of your business."

Jonah's smile faded and his expression grew still and very dark. "Erica is my business. She's my daughter."

"The one you're too ashamed to tell anyone about."

"You're the link between Reedy and Nate." Jonah leaned back. "It was very easy to find out you were the one who got him a job at the hospital and then at your car wash after he was fired from the hospital. Did you introduce the two of them?"

"Go fuck yourself." Terrell felt a tightening in his stomach.

He came here only to find out what Jonah knew. He sure as hell wasn't going to give him more information. He'd been lucky when Erica had not connected meeting Reedy in his office. He knew the connection might come soon, but he would deal with that when it got to it. He figured if he could get Nate turned around, he would be Erica's hero and all else would be forgiven.

Jonah sighed as if disappointed. "Terrell, you're going to have to work with me here."

"I don't have to do shit."

"That's where you are wrong," Jonah corrected him. "Because when Erica finds this out, you're out on your ass. You'd be out on your ass for dealing with drugs in the first place, but for getting Nate involved and ruining his life? Six months of flowers and candy won't get you back in her heart after that."

"I didn't get him involved," Terrell said. "He asked Reedy himself. I didn't even want . . ."

He realized what he was doing in response to the panicked feeling Jonah's words gave him.

"It won't matter," Jonah said calmly. "This is your fault and I think you know that. I'll give you credit for that much."

"I don't need credit or anything else from you."

"What you need is for me to keep my mouth shut about your involvement in this."

Terrell laughed even though he didn't find any of this the least bit funny. "Please, man. You and I both know you can't wait for Erica to get rid of me."

"I would love her to kick you out of her life," Jonah said, "and you've given me more than enough reason. She'll dump you eventually, but if she finds this out, she'll hate you, too."

Terrell had no response. He couldn't take the idea of Erica hating him. "Look, man. You don't know how this went down. After Erica and I broke up, I was really down. I met Reedy and he—"

"Save your sob story for someone who gives a shit," Jonah said. "I'm making you an offer."

"An offer?" Terrell asked, suspiciously. "For what?"

"Right now, Erica relies on you. As misguided as that is, it's the truth."

"She loves me," Terrell said.

Jonah pressed his lips together and his brows centered in

frustration. "Whatever the case, she listens to you and I know you bad-mouth me."

"Like you do with me."

"You're going to stop doing that." Jonah leaned forward. "You're going to stop bad-mouthing me and start encouraging her to get closer to me. You're the barrier between us and now you're going to be the catalyst to our newfound relationship."

"Bullshit," Terrell said. "Your shadiness is the barrier between you and Erica."

"You're going to do what I say," Jonah ordered. "Or I tell Erica everything."

"How do I know you won't tell her anyway?" Terrell asked.

"I'll be invested in your little lie," he said. "If she finds out I knew and lied to her about what Nate was involved in, she'd cut me out of her life, too. Mutually assured destruction. Of course, yours would be worse because you're the one who got him into this while I was the one trying to help him out."

"I'm trying to help him out," Terrell said.

"Well, you suck at it." Jonah held his hand out to him. "Do we have a deal?"

Terrell looked at his hand as if it held the Ebola virus.

"I'll be calling Erica tomorrow," Jonah warned. "Will what I tell her include you or not?"

"I fucking hate you man," Terrell said with a growl.

Jonah smiled an accomplished smile. "I get that a lot."

"Billie? What are you—"

Billie rushed past Ricky into Saturn House's foyer, water dripping everywhere.

"Why are you so wet?" he asked as he closed the door.

She heard music, maybe a television, but looking around, she saw no one.

"I walked eight blocks," she said, turning to him.

"In this weather?" He looked completely confused. "Why?"

"I don't know why."

That was the truth at least. After leaving the restaurant, Billie just went walking with no destination or objective in mind. She was trying to think, but couldn't. She felt overwhelmed. She was getting calls from Sherise and Erica, but she couldn't answer. She couldn't help them. She was thinking of Tara, blaming herself, hating Porter, feeling helpless, and it was all too much.

"Come on." He took her by the arm and started leading her down the hallway toward the kitchen. "Let me get some towels. You're gonna get sick."

They passed the kitchen and continued to the back of the house. Billie didn't say a word as he led her through a bedroom, closing the door behind them, and then into a small bathroom.

"Sit here," he said.

He placed her on the toilet seat as he went to the closet next to the shower.

"Let me wrap these around you." He placed one towel over her shoulders and another on her lap.

When he went back for more, Billie suddenly felt extremely cold and started to shiver all over. He noticed it when he came back to her.

"What's wrong with you?" His voice sounded on edge. "Did something happen? Did someone hurt you?"

She shook her head.

"Well, something is wrong." He knelt down on the floor in front of her. With the remaining towel, he started wiping her bare arms. "You have to talk to me."

She looked around. "Where are we?"

"This is my private bathroom," he said. "No one will come in here. Don't worry. Do you want me to call the police?"

"They can't help me," she said.

"Help you with what? Can I help you?"

She shook her head. "I didn't come here for help."

"Well, what did you come here for?"

She could tell he really wanted to know. He looked confused, concerned, and frustrated.

"I don't know," she replied. "I just came."

He leaned forward, lifting up a bit so he could put the towel on her head to dry her hair. His body pressed against her knees and his face was very close. She liked the way he smelled and liked having him close to her, pressed against her. Feeling his hands massage her head, Billie closed her eyes.

"That feels good," she said.

Sensing that he had stopped, she opened her eyes. He was looking at her intensely and the concern had been replaced with desire. She felt powerful. She felt in control.

"Why are you here?" he asked. "I thought you said . . ."

"Shut up."

Feeling suddenly overcome with arousal, she grabbed his face and pulled him to her. She kissed him hard, her hungry lips pressing against his unexpecting lips. He quickly responded, kissing her back with a sensual urgency. Billie was starting to feel her senses spinning like a whirlwind when his lips left hers and he pulled away.

"Do you know what you're doing?" he asked, his voice breathless and his eyes intent and pleading.

Her body was already on fire as she nodded and wrapped her arms around him. There was no hesitation on his part as he pressed his body against hers and claimed her lips again. Their mouths explored each other, their tongues searching to satiate the growing desire that threatened to consume both of them.

When he lifted her up and carried her into the bedroom, she felt weightless in his arms. He was still kissing her as he gently laid her on his bed, but the second he joined her, their lovemaking became more desperate, more frantic as their need grew. Their kisses became more and more aggressive in between grabbing and pulling at each other's clothes.

Billie didn't think. She didn't care. She just wanted and ached. She couldn't have Ricky inside of her soon enough. She moaned softly as his lips explored every inch of her flesh. He left satisfying but brief kisses on her chest, his tongue tasting her breasts, caressing her hardened nipples. She let out a tormented groan as his fingers traced her body, making their own mark on her, her skin tingling everywhere in response.

He took her with an aggressive vitality that made her want to surrender everything to him. His movements were slow and tender at first, but quickly built up, urged on by Billie's assertive movements. She wrapped her legs around him and ran her nails down his back. She called out his name as the fire inside of her grew out of control.

He let out a tortured groan as he reached up and pulled her hair back and she yelled out his name. She felt waves of pleasure slamming against her, drowning her in ecstasy as her entire body shook underneath him.

Erica wasn't sure how long she had been shaking her head, but as soon as she caught herself, she stopped. She slipped the flank steak out of the marinating bag on her kitchen table and placed it in the pan. She was having a hard time concentrating on making dinner, considering all that had happened in the last twenty-four hours. Terrell running out on her and making her wonder what the hell was wrong with him was hard enough. Hearing that Cady might not even be Justin's was what really floored her.

"What the fuck is wrong with you, girl?" she asked herself as she moved over to the sink.

As she heard the door opening, Erica sped up washing her hands. It was either Nate or Terrell. Either way, someone was getting an earful.

"Hi," Terrell said as he entered and closed the door behind him.

"Don't hi me," Erica said. "Where were you?"

"Can I apologize?" he asked, walking over to the kitchen, but staying on the other side of the counter.

"Not before you tell me where you've been?"

"I slept at Slade's last night. Look, Erica, I know I was wrong to walk out on you."

"You make me question the decision to have you move in with me again," she said. "Terrell, how can you just walk out? That tells me I can't rely on you."

"That's why I left, baby." He leaned against the counter opposite from her. "I just felt so . . . I know I shouldn't have, but you made me feel impotent."

"How?"

Terrell looked around. "Is Nate here?"

She placed her hands on her hips. "What do you think?"

"Look." He walked around the counter toward her. He stopped just inches from her. "Baby, I love you and I want you to rely on me. I thought you'd put your faith in me when it came to Nate. You asked me for help in dealing with him, and I know how much you love him."

"You didn't expect me to?"

"I did," he said. "What I didn't expect was for you to ask everyone else. It made me feel useless. It made me feel like a failure."

Erica felt awful. "You're not useless, Terrell. You're the one who got him the construction job. You're the one talking to his friends to find out what's going on with him."

"So why did you get Jonah and Billie in on it?"

"They're helping in a different way," she said. "I'm sorry, baby. I was desperate. I should have just been patient, but I can't. It's Nate. He's my responsibility."

"He's not," Terrell said. "But we don't need to go into that again. It was wrong for me to leave, baby."

"Don't ever walk out on me again." She leaned into him and kissed him on the cheek. "That just makes a bad situation worse."

"What kind of make-up kiss is that?" he asked. He leaned in and kissed her deep on the lips. "I love you so much, Erica."

"I love you, too, baby." She sighed. "I'm so sorry for making things hard on you."

"I want to be your shoulder to lean on," he said. "I want to be your everything."

"You should know," Erica said, wincing. "Jonah is probably gonna call me tomorrow with some news. I don't want to turn him away."

"I don't want you to."

Erica's eyes widened in pleasant surprise. "I expected some protest and a little name-calling."

Terrell cleared his throat as he stepped away. He walked over to the refrigerator and opened it, looking for a can of soda.

"You won't get it from me," he said. "As a matter of fact, I'm glad he's helping you."

"This is insane," Erica said. "You're really trying to make up with me."

He grabbed the can and lifted up, closing the door. Turning to her, he managed a wide smile. "No, I'm serious. Look, I'm not gonna pretend like he's my boy or nothing, but he's trying to help you and that's a good thing."

Erica eyed him curiously, searching for a smirk or a sarcastic grin as he passed her and headed into the living room. Nothing. She followed him.

"You know, baby, it's not going to just be this. We're kind of . . . We might try and have some kind of relationship."

Terrell pretended to be more focused on starting up his Xbox system than their conversation. "That's okay, baby. Look, we got a new beginning. Who am I to deny that to anyone else?"

Erica felt like she was in *The Twilight Zone*. She watched Terrell as he nonchalantly started up one of his games, waiting for him to say he was kidding, but nothing happened. She shrugged, thinking she should be happy as she returned to the kitchen. Why wasn't she?

There was that suspicious nature of hers again. She could use some peace in her life, but the second it was offered to her, she didn't accept it.

14

"Dammit." Sherise hated this.

This was the third time she'd called Billie and gotten her voice mail.

"Billie, where are those damn test results?" she asked before hanging up.

She didn't want voice mail. She wanted some answers. Where were the results of the DNA test? This wait was killing her. She was grateful to Billie for using her connections to speed this test up, but it had been two days already.

Once they agreed that finding Cady's heritage was the priority, Sherise did what she had to do. She got the physical evidence and gave it to Billie the very next morning. Billie told her she could get it done ASAP.

Sherise couldn't stand waiting. This was her life. This was everything. In her heart, she knew that Justin was Cady's father in every way possible that mattered, but no matter how many times she said that to herself, it didn't work. Justin would be devastated.

"Baby?"

Sherise, having been lost in her thoughts, hadn't even realized that Justin had arrived in the living room. She smiled ner-

vously at him. He had called her baby again. Since making love
the other night, Sherise felt like she was getting him back, bit
by bit.

"You're going to work?" she asked, pouting.

He smiled. "I have to go in at some point. I can't stay home
all day. You're looking better."

"I still feel awful," she lied.

Sherise felt fine, but she had to keep Justin believing she
was feeling bad because it kept him close to home. While she
was waiting for the test results and putting together her plan of
attack against Jennifer, she needed to do her best to keep him
from her. Yes, things had been a little better between them in
the last few days, but ultimately Jennifer would try to get to
him, especially now that she had been exposed. The jig was up
and telling Justin about Cady was the last weapon in Jennifer's
arsenal. Sherise needed to keep him home, and playing sick
usually did the trick. She needed him to look after her and
help watch Cady.

He looked at her, his eyes squinting in some disbelief. "You
look okay."

"Of course I look okay." She smiled, tilting her head flirtatiously. "I always look fabulous no matter what."

"That you do." He walked over to the sofa, tightening his
tie. He looked down at her. "Seriously, I have two meetings."

"You can't teleconference?"

"When the client bothers to come in," he said, "I have to
come in."

She made another sad face and could tell it was working.
He softened.

"The meetings are from twelve to two," he said. "I'll be
home by three."

"Promise?"

"I promise." He knelt down and kissed her on the forehead. "By three."

She touched his cheek gently before he stood back up and headed for the door. She would be calling him to make sure he didn't make a little pit stop at the Fairmont to see that whore. No, she couldn't prevent Jennifer from communicating with him via e-mail, text, or phone, but she had a feeling that this was news Jennifer would want to tell him to his face, and if Sherise could prevent that from happening, she had a chance.

Her phone rang the second after he was gone. Hoping to see Billie, she was disappointed to see LaKeisha's name before remembering that this was exactly the woman she wanted to talk to.

"LaKeisha," she said. "How are you?"

"I'm fine," the other woman answered. "I was . . . Sherise, is something wrong?"

"Nothing. Why?"

There was an awkward silence before, "We were supposed to meet this morning."

"Shit." Sherise suddenly remembered that she had agreed to meet with LaKeisha this morning to make up for running out on her and Northman after the fund-raiser.

"I am so, so sorry, LaKeisha," she said. "I just completely forgot. My life is insane right now. I never do this, but I just forgot."

She heard an annoyed sigh on the other end of the phone. "Do you want this opportunity or not? Sherise, I'm the one who recommended you."

"About that," Sherise said. "Jennifer. Who else knows her?"

"What?"

"Jennifer Ross! You don't know her very well, but you've spoken to her a couple of times. Who knows her well? Who else has been around her when you've met her?"

"Sherise, do you understand what I'm calling you about? I'm telling you that Northman is upset that you've been MIA since the fund-raiser. He doesn't feel you're committed to—"

"LaKeisha!" Sherise stopped herself and took a deep breath. "I'm dealing with an emergency right now."

"What is your obsession with Jennifer? She's really not that relevant in our game these days."

"I'll explain later," Sherise said even though she had no intention of ever telling this woman anything. "Who is she still friends with up here?"

LaKeisha sighed. "I don't know. They were very benign encounters and . . . I know she knows Teresa Sampson pretty well."

That name didn't ring a bell for Sherise. She hadn't been out of the game that long? She usually had some idea who everyone worth mentioning was.

"She belongs to the Chains," LaKeisha continued, "So there is a ninety-nine percent chance she's friends with Lindsey Jackson."

"Lindsey!" Sherise couldn't believe she had forgotten her.

Lindsey was one of the most famous women in DC black high society, and Justin had done business with her husband. Lindsey was the woman who allowed Sherise the chance to participate in a fund-raiser for Chains.

"Yeah, you probably know her," LaKeisha said. "Now, what about the matter at hand?"

"Look, LaKeisha." Sherise wasn't usually in a position where her career meant nothing to her at the moment, so she wasn't sure how to word her feelings correctly. "I want to work for Northman, but the honest truth is that I haven't even told my husband yet."

"Still? What the hell, Sherise?"

"I have a lot going on, and if I can get this taken care of, which I can and will, I would love to sit down with Northman and tell him how I can help him win the White House. Right now, I have bigger fish to fry."

"Bigger than a White House run?" LaKeisha asked. "Northman doesn't wait, Sherise."

"He will if he wants the best," Sherise answered. "I'm sorry about missing our meeting. I'll talk to you soon. Thanks!"

Sherise had to work fast. She had to give Lindsey a reason to help her and get the information she needed to have some leverage on Jennifer. She had to cover all her bases if she was going to save her marriage to Justin and make Jennifer pay for having the nerve to try to go after her.

Billie had been pacing the office bathroom, but as soon as she heard someone near the entrance, she ducked into a stall and closed the door behind her. She couldn't show her face to anyone. First of all, they could tell she'd been crying and that was a no-no. You do not cry at work. Her first female mentor warned her that this was the death knell for a woman's career.

Even besides the red in her eyes, Billie imagined she looked terrible, considering all the stress she was under, most of it self-induced. Richard had noticed it the second he came in that morning and pressed her for an explanation. He was just trying to be nice, but Billie snapped at him to mind his own business and left. She hadn't been able to return yet. She couldn't face him. She couldn't face anyone. She felt so ashamed.

She had slept with her client. Worse, she had slept with him twice. Even worse, she wanted to sleep with him again.

Ricky had been amazing the other day. So amazing that he made Billie forget about all her problems, all her worries, and that what she was doing was highly unethical. It felt too good to stop. She wanted only more and more. He'd taken her and taken her away, and she loved every second of it.

When it was over, Billie came crashing back to the earth. Not only had all her other worries come back to her, but the huge mistake she'd just made crushed them with its weight and made her panic. It was lucky for her that a kitchen emergency called Ricky away. Shortly after they finished making love, someone came knocking on the door asking for help. Ricky told Billie he'd be right back, but she took that chance to grab her clothes and sneak out. It was horrible, she knew, but she imagined it would be much worse if she had to face him.

He'd been calling and texting her ever since, asking if she would call and if she was okay. She hadn't replied to any of them. What was she going to say? She had come there unannounced and within five minutes she was all over him. She went to the bathroom to try to figure out what she was going to do. She wanted to call him. She knew she would have to talk to him eventually.

Just as the woman who had come into the bathroom left, Billie's phone rang again. She had been holding it in her hand the whole time, waiting to gain the courage to call. It was Ricky again and she felt her stomach clenching again. It was crazy. She was consumed with regret, but just seeing his name on her phone made her want him again.

"Shit," she said out loud as she clicked on the answer button. She was just going to do it. She had to get on with her day. "Hello, Ricky."

"Billie? What the fuck?"

"I'm sorry," she said. "I know you're pissed."

"I'm pissed," he said, "and I'm worried about you. Why would you leave? We made love. I thought it was great. Was I wrong?"

"That's not important," she said.

"In what universe?" he asked. "Seriously, you're horrible for a guy's ego. I thought I did a good job . . . both times. Then I come back and you're gone. I think I deserve an explanation."

"Of course you do," she said. "I just don't really have one, except what I've told you before."

"Fuck that," he said. "You can't tell me we're the first two people to get together under this . . . situation."

"It's against the rules," she said.

"I told you that no one has to know, Billie."

"Someone could find out," she said. "Besides, I'll know. My professional integrity means everything to me. This mistake is—"

"This was not a mistake," he insisted. "What happened between us may have been against the rules, but it was not a mistake."

She sighed. "You don't understand, Ricky. These rules are in place for a very good reason."

"When am I going to see you again?"

"I can't work on this case anymore," she said. "I have to—"

"I'm not talking about the damn case, Billie. When can I see you again?"

"You can't," she said. "I'll have the firm contact you. Please, Ricky, don't talk to anyone about—"

"Billie, I'm not going to let you hide behind your job. I want to be with you. You want to be with me and I know it. This is not over."

He hung up and Billie felt a sense of dread. It was true. She wanted him, and that fact made this all so much worse. Billie felt like she was drowning. If there was ever a time she needed her girls, it was now.

When Erica entered Jonah's office, he was standing near the bookcase behind his desk. When he turned to her, he smiled wide and started walking toward her. There was an awkward moment when Erica thought he was going to try to hug her. She didn't know what she was going to do and she just froze in place. Fortunately, he stopped about a foot away from her.

"It's nice to see you," he said with the calm, controlled voice that he was so known for. "Let's sit down."

He walked over to the sofa against the far wall, but Erica didn't follow him. When he realized that, he turned to her. She pointed to the two leather chairs facing his desk.

"Here is fine," she said, taking a seat.

"Okay." His voice held a little trepidation. "Have you been able to get ahold of Nate since we last talked?"

She shook her head. "He came by, but I wasn't there. I don't even know where he is."

"He's staying at the place of a guy named Raneed Peters," Jonah said. "He goes by the name Reedy and he lives over on Alabama."

"He's the guy, isn't he?" she asked. "He got Nate into all this."

"He's pretty much been a crook his whole life," Jonah offered. "He has a juvenile record for dealing. He spent a short time in jail for illegal gun possession. The police suspect he deals drugs all around his neighborhood, but they haven't been able to get him yet. They'd like to figure it out."

"Why is a drug dealer working as a handyman around a hospital?" she asked.

"Health benefits?" Jonah smiled, but only for a second as soon as he realized Erica was not in the mood for jokes. "I suppose it's because he's not a big fish. Just a daily dealer."

"But he has been arrested before."

"More than once, and while I can see how he got a job at a car wash, I'm not sure how he got that job at the hospital. I would have hoped—"

"Car wash!" Erica yelled, suddenly remembering. "How could I forget? I met him. I met him when I went to go see . . ."

Erica stopped talking as it all came to her. She was confused.

"You're thinking right," Jonah said. "Terrell got Nate the job at the construction company and Reedy the job at the car wash."

"He's friends with him?" Erica said it as more of a question.

"I wouldn't say that." Jonah leaned back in the chair.

"Well, obviously he is," Erica said. "He got him the job at the car wash. He was in his office the day I came over."

"I didn't know that." Jonah frowned.

"Well, why would you?" she asked, not sure why this fact bothered him.

Jonah brushed it off. "But look, Erica. I checked into that. He's not friends with Terrell. You know I wouldn't be angry to find that out."

"You'd love a reason to dog Terrell further."

He nodded. "Of course I would."

"You'd be surprised," she said. "He's actually in support of you helping me."

"I sincerely doubt that."

"It's true." Erica leaned back and crossed her legs. "He's trying to understand you and me. So maybe you can try to understand me and Terrell."

Jonah looked away for a second, managing a slight smile. He turned back to Erica.

"The local police know who Reedy hangs with, and Terrell is not one of them. He only seems to know Reedy because of Nate."

Erica felt relieved. "Terrell wouldn't have anything to do with him if he knew he was involved in drugs."

"Of course not," Jonah said unconvincingly. "If you want to keep Nate away from Reedy and his boys, I can use my connections to put some pressure on local police to really dig into the operation."

Erica was trying to think about what was the best path. "Those sources who seem to know Terrell isn't friends with Reedy do know that Nate is."

Jonah nodded.

"Well, I don't want them pressing down on Reedy if it will get Nate caught in something. Nate has never been arrested or gotten in trouble with the law. Maybe you can wait until I make sure Nate is out of this for sure."

"I think it's best if we move quickly on this," Jonah said.

"And don't worry about Nate. I promise you. I will make sure no matter how this goes down, Nate will not be implicated. I will protect him for you."

"Can you really do that?"

He flashed her a knowing smile. "I can do anything you need me to, Erica."

She didn't doubt that and it scared her. It was that power that threatened Terrell and Sherise at one time. It was the kind of power that she always thought could lead to only bad things. But now, that same power could save her brother and keep him from ruining his future.

Erica smiled. "Thank you."

"Billie!"

Billie snapped out of her daze at the sound of Sherise yelling her name.

"What?" she asked.

"Fine, I'll get it." Sherise rolled her eyes and made a smacking sound with her lips as she headed for the door.

"Is someone at the door?" Billie asked.

Sherise looked back at her as if she was crazy. "That's usually what a ringing doorbell means."

Sherise opened the door to Erica. There was an awkward moment as the two faced each other for the first time since Erica had found out that there was a question about Cady's paternity. Sherise felt like she should say something, but she didn't know what.

"Are you gonna let me in or what?" Erica asked.

Sherise smiled and reached out to hug Erica, tight.

"Oh, stop it." Erica pushed her out of the way and kissed her on the cheek before walking inside. "So any news yet?"

"We're still waiting," Sherise said, back to biting her fingernails. "It's killing me."

What they were waiting for were the test results, which the

lab Billie used promised would come in today. To keep Justin
at home, Sherise left Cady with him and came over to Billie's
for what she told him was a girls' night out.

"Where have you been?" Sherise asked.

"You don't want to know." Erica tossed her purse on the
sofa and headed over to the dining area where Billie was standing, staring out the window. "What's up with you?"

"I didn't think you were coming," Sherise said nervously.
"I thought you were gonna bail on me."

Erica turned to her and saw how vulnerable Sherise was at
this moment. This was such a rare sight. She almost seemed
like a girl, not even a woman anymore, just scared and waiting.

"I'm here," she said. "I told you we would figure this out. I
just don't understand why you didn't tell us about Cady the
same night you told us you slept with Ryan."

"I had one tiny shred of dignity left," Sherise answered. "I
was hoping to keep it. Do you know how disastrous this could
be?"

Sherise walked over to the table and sat down. Erica turned
her attention back to Billie, who hadn't even acknowledged her.

"Billie," she said loudly. "What's wrong with you?"

Billie turned to her and shrugged. "Nothing. I'm just nervous waiting for them to call."

Suddenly, Billie's phone, which was laying in the middle of
the dining room table, began to vibrate. Sherise let out a
scream as her hands came to her cheeks. Billie looked down at
the phone, but didn't move.

Erica, realizing that neither of them was going to move,
grabbed the phone. She checked the ID.

"It's R. Williams." Without answering, she offered the phone
to Billie.

Billie waved her hand and shook her head furiously. "No.
No. No. Don't answer it."

"Isn't that your client?" Sherise asked. "The one you want
to sleep with?"

"Just let it ring," Billie said.

"Pick it up," Sherise ordered, "and then hang up. I don't want him clogging up the line."

"I'm sure she has call waiting." Erica placed the phone, which had stopped vibrating, back on the table. "Why don't you want to answer it?"

"Because she wants to sleep with him," Sherise said.

"Stop it!" Billie yelled.

Both women jumped with a start at her response.

Billie sighed apologetically. "I just can't deal with this. Not now."

"What happened?" Seeing how upset she was, Erica rushed over to her. "Billie, talk to me."

Billie lowered her head as Erica placed her hands comfortingly on her shoulders. She felt ready to fall apart.

"I slept with him," she whispered.

"What?" Erica asked. "What did you just say?"

"She slept with him," Sherise answered for her.

Erica blinked, unsure of what to say for a second.

"I did," Billie said. "I slept with him. Two days ago at his place. I was upset and I . . ."

"Wow." Erica was taken back. "I thought you weren't supposed to sleep with him. I mean, you weren't allowed to."

"I'm not, okay?" Billie was full-out crying now. "I know that. I've made a terrible mistake. It was awful."

"That's too bad," Sherise said, not taking her eyes off the phone on the table. "Broke all the rules and the sex wasn't even good."

"That's not what I meant," Billie said. "The sex was . . . it was great. It's just . . . it was an awful thing to do."

"Have you told anyone?" Erica asked.

Billie shook her head. "I don't know what I'm gonna do. I could get in so much trouble for this. I could destroy my career."

"Oh, sweetie." Erica wrapped her arms around Billie and squeezed her tight.

"You have got to be fucking kidding me!" Sherise looked at them in awe.

"What?" Erica asked.

"She breaks all the rules and you trip over yourself to comfort her, but when I do it, I get your judgment and criticism?"

"Stop it," Billie interjected. "You guys don't start over me. I don't—"

"Don't act like it's the same thing," Erica argued. "You cheated on your husband twice and lied about—"

The vibration started again and everyone immediately shut up.

"Answer it!" Sherise gripped the edges of the table as tightly as she could. This was it. She just knew it.

Erica reached for the phone. "It's Lab Corp."

Sherise let out a small yelp.

Billie's eyes widened as she looked at Sherise. She turned back to Erica and gestured for her to give her the phone.

"Hello?" she asked. "This is Billie Carter."

While Erica was trying to read Billie's expression as she listened, Sherise stared straight ahead, her lips pressed together, her fingers gripping at the table as if it would make a difference.

"Thank you," Billie said quietly. "Yes, please send a copy of those sealed results to me. Thank you again."

"So?" Erica asked the second she hung up.

Billie reached over to Sherise and placed her hand over her head and caressed her hair. She smiled.

"She's Justin's, Sherise."

Upon hearing this, Erica let out a celebratory yell and jumped in the air, but Sherise just sighed and her head fell to the table.

Sherise felt like all the air in the world had been let out of her. She was crying now as she felt Billie rub her back. She couldn't describe how she felt. All this time, she had hoped and knew in her mind that Cady was Justin's, but she was scared. She didn't want to even deal with the possibility that she wasn't. This was real. Wasn't it?

"Are they sure?" Sherise asked, her face still flat on the table.

"They are ninety-nine point nine percent positive that the male sample is the father of the female sample," Billie said happily.

"Jesus." Erica had to sit down. She felt exhausted. "Thank you, Jesus."

Sherise finally sat up, tears still flowing down her cheeks.

"Every time I looked at her," she said, speaking slowly and full of emotion, "I told myself that I saw Justin's nose or his eyes. She was his skin tone, not mine. When she smiled, it reminded me of him. But I was forcing it. I made it so that everything she did reminded me of Justin so I could believe that she had to be his. She had to be."

"She is," Billie said.

"She's always favored him," Erica said. "You weren't making that up."

"What are we going to do now?" Billie asked.

Sherise wiped the tears from her cheeks as she took a deep breath. She looked up at Billie with the determination of a woman who had just been given a second chance at life, at love, at happiness.

"Oh, no," Erica said. She recognized that expression.

"That bitch is gonna pay for this," Sherise said. "She's gonna—"

"Wait." Billie held up her hand to stop her. "Jennifer is not your priority right now. You just got a reprieve. Don't make your situation worse."

"My situation is fine," Sherise said. "Her situation is the one that's about to get worse."

"We have to think this through." Billie sat down at the table.

"You should just go to Justin," Erica said. "You have the news you wanted. Tell him the truth about who Jennifer is, why she's sleeping with him. Once he knows you know he's been cheating, he won't be as judgmental when you tell him about Ryan."

"That's a good idea," Billie said. "You have the power back. Go to Justin. It's between you and your husband now."

Sherise shook her head. "I appreciate what you two are doing and I fully intend to tell Justin what's going on, but there is no way that bitch is getting away with this."

"Sherise," Erica warned.

"She didn't just sleep with my husband," Sherise argued. "She tried to take Cady's daddy away from her. She tried to hurt my baby."

"We can deal with her later," Billie said. "First you deal with Justin and get that shit straightened out, then—"

"It's too late," Erica said. "She's already got a plan. It's probably already in the works, isn't it?"

Sherise smiled. *Hell yeah, it was.*

Walking up to her apartment building, Billie was scrolling through her e-mails on her smartphone and did not notice the person sitting on the steps leading up to the door until coming right up on him.

"Ricky," she said.

He stood up with a hurt expression on his face. "I didn't expect you to be happy to see me, but this is a little insulting."

She wasn't sure what expression she offered him, but Billie didn't have the energy to try to fake it. "I didn't expect to see you at all. How did you get my address?"

"Does it matter?" he asked.

"Of course it matters," she said. "You're my client. You're not supposed to—"

"I'm not just your client anymore," he said. "How long are you planning on running from me?"

"I'm not running." She tried to walk past him, but he blocked her way. "This is a difficult situation and I'm trying to make the best of it."

"This can't be the best of it." He reached out and touched her arm. "Us not seeing each other at all can't be making the best of it."

"Please stop," she said, already feeling a tingling sensation at his touch.

"I want to see you," he said. "I want to be with you again."

"That isn't going to—"

Before she could react, his lips were on hers, pressing against them. She could feel his desperation in the way his hand gripped her arm, trying to pull her to him.

"God dammit, Billie!"

She tore herself away from Ricky to see Porter walking toward the both of them. She could tell he was furious from the fire in his eyes.

"How many guys are you sleeping with?" he asked, looking at Ricky. "First Robert, then this guy. Who the fuck is this?"

Ricky stepped closer to him. "You might want to watch who you refer to, boy."

"Boy?" Porter looked him up and down and laughed. "Please."

"Who the fuck are you?" Ricky asked.

Billie held up a hand to stop Ricky, whose agitation was growing. "Porter, what do you want?"

"Who is this?"

"None of your business," she said. The last thing she needed was for Porter to find out that the man he saw her kissing was her client. "What do you want?"

After another hateful stare in Ricky's direction, Porter

turned to her. "I know what you did. You've already crossed the line. You can't stop can you?"

"Porter, please—"

"You called my mother to find out where Tara is!"

"Why don't you watch your tone?" Ricky assertively suggested.

"Hey, man, I don't know who the fuck you think you are," Porter said, "but this is my wife and I can—"

"Ex!" Billie yelled. "Porter, don't ever say that again."

Porter blinked, seeming very frustrated. "Look, I didn't mean to say that. My point is . . . how dare you do that?"

Billie hadn't thought it through well. She was upset and crying and wanted to reach Tara. She should have thought better about it, but it was too late now.

"Let's talk about this later," she pleaded. She just wanted Porter away from Ricky.

"No," Porter said. "Not later. You act like I have no say in what happens to my daughter, but I'm gonna show you that I do."

"Are you threatening her?" Ricky asked.

Porter's lips formed a threatening smile at the man. "What did you say your name was again?"

Billie jumped in between the two men. "Porter, just leave, okay? I promise I won't try to contact Tara again."

"I don't believe you," he said. "I'm gonna take legal action against you, Billie. You haven't given me any choice."

"I promise." She pushed Porter back to create a bigger distance between them. "Just go away."

Porter looked down at her, his brows centering as if he was trying to figure out what was going on. "This isn't over, Billie. I promise you."

He gave Ricky one last look before turning and walking away.

"He needs to be taught a lesson," Ricky said angrily.

"Just let it go," she said. "Really, Ricky, it's none of your business."

"Are you okay?" he asked, attempting to wrap his arm around her.

She pushed his arm away. She had just promised to never see the girl she thought of as a daughter ever again just to keep Porter from finding out she had slept with her client.

"No," she said. "And you're making it worse. Please go away."

"I'm not going to let you pretend like there's nothing between us, Billie. Look, if you want me to hold off until after this case is over, then I can try to do that, but I want us to be together."

"Did you see what just happened here?" She pointed toward the street. "Porter isn't going to let that happen. He's watching me. He'll find out about us. He'll hurt me. He's already taken my daughter from me. Now he's gonna take my career."

"You can't let that man control your life."

Billie laughed. "I don't have a life as long as he's in it. You just don't understand and I'm not going to explain it to you. You and I are never gonna happen."

She ignored him calling her name as she ran up the stairs and into her building.

15

Erica heard the yelling from outside the door to her apartment. She rushed to open the door and got inside in just enough time to see Terrell pin Nate up against the wall. They were yelling threats at each other. She screamed for them to stop and rushed over to them. When Terrell turned to look at her, Nate took the opportunity to push him away.

Terrell fell back, almost falling into Erica, who jumped back.

"What the fuck is wrong with you?" Terrell asked. "You almost made me knock your sister down, you stupid fuck."

"What's going on?" she asked.

"I'm trying to get this boy's head straight," Terrell said.

"I don't need my fucking head straightened!" Nate yelled, stepping away.

Erica could see from the look on Nate's face that he was a little afraid of Terrell. Terrell was stronger, bigger, and could be intimidating when he wanted to. He'd been in Nate's life for a long time now, and while he had never really taken on a fatherly role, because Nate was too old for that, Nate did see him as the man in charge when they all lived together.

"Obviously you do," Erica said. "I know all about Reedy and his dealing, Nate. How could you do this?"

Nate looked at her as if he didn't believe her for a second. Then he shrugged as if he didn't care.

"Ask your boy, here," he said.

"You better watch your fucking mouth, boy," Terrell warned.

"I'm asking you," Erica said. "What do you think Mom would say if—"

"Mom is dead!" he yelled. "Stop bringing her up. She's not here!"

"Yes, she is." Erica pushed him back against the wall. "She's with us all the time. We've talked about this, Nate. You believe that."

"I was a kid then," he argued, seeming unable to look his sister in the face.

"Bullshit," she said. "Nate, she's watching us. She's looking down on us. How do you think we've made it this far? She's been looking out for us. She loves you. You're her baby."

"Stop it." He was clearly getting upset.

"What would this do to her?" she asked.

"It's not a big deal." Nate slid past her and walked over to the kitchen. "I didn't deal or anything."

"Then what did you do?" She followed him.

"I just made some deliveries for him. Just made a few extra bucks."

"And you used," Terrell added.

Nate shot Terrell a vengeful glance and Erica observed the look between them. Something was going on here.

Nate finally looked away, rolling his eyes. "I smoked some weed. Everyone does that. You fucking do it."

"I don't," Erica said. "And you worked at a hospital, Nate. You know that's not a job where you can even do that."

"It's not a big—"

"If you say it's not a big deal one more time, boy!" Terrell warned.

"Fuck you," Nate spat back at him. "If I . . ."

"You lost your girlfriend," Erica said. "You lost your job. You're about to get your ass kicked out of this apartment."

"Why?" His expression was pure shock.

"I can't believe you just asked that," Terrell said.

"Why would you do this?" Erica asked. "Honestly, Nate. You know how I feel about drugs. All those talks we've had about those boys who are strung out, in and out of jail or dead. The common denominator of all of them is drugs. I tried so hard to keep you away from those boys."

Nate laughed. "Did you?"

"This is funny to you?" she asked, fuming at his attitude. "Well, the cops are about to crack down on that whole operation. Is that funny, too?"

"What do you mean?" Nate asked.

She nodded. "I know for a fact that DCPD is coming down on Reedy and everyone he works with and for."

"How do you know that?" Terrell asked. "And what do you mean by everyone?"

"Do you mean me?" Nate asked, his rising concern obvious. " 'Cause I only moved a few bags for him. I didn't do any—"

"Is this Jonah?" Terrell asked. "Is this his solution?"

"I told you I would make sure you were okay," she said. "Jonah is gonna make sure . . ."

"What the fuck is he gonna do?" Nate asked. "And why does he care about you? You don't even work for him anymore."

Erica had not told Nate that Jonah was her father and she didn't plan to.

"He's gonna do whatever he wants," Erica said. "I told him everything. He's the one who found out about Reedy for me. Now, Nate, it's time for you decide where you want to be?"

"What do you mean, where?" he asked, backing up as if he needed to run somewhere but didn't know where. "I'm not involved in this."

"Are you with me or are you with Reedy?" she asked.

"Fuck this," he said. "Fuck all this."

"Hey!" Terrell yelled after him as Nate rushed down the hallway to his bedroom.

"I'll get him," Terrell said, starting down the hallway.

"No," Erica ordered. "You stay here and tell me what's going on. What were you two talking about when I came in? What's this back and forth?"

"What do you mean, back and forth?" he asked. "I'm trying to help him. Don't question how I do it, Erica."

"Why did you give Reedy a job at the car wash?" she asked. "How well do you know him? What were you and him talking about when I came over to your office that day?"

"Whoa." He held his hand up. "Am I on trial here?"

"Answer the question," she ordered.

"Reedy is not my friend," he said. "Did you get a friend vibe between us when you were over there? No, I didn't think so. I gave him that job because Nate asked me to. He said they'd been fired together, and if I wanted to help him with that construction job, I needed to help Reedy, too. They only needed Nate, so I got Reedy a job at the car wash."

Erica just wasn't buying this. "Weren't you curious that this guy got fired with Nate when Nate told us he was fired because of an argument he got in with another person? Did you ask questions?"

He shook his head. "No, I was just focused on trying to help Nate. I just thought they were both fired for different reasons."

"You hired someone without asking questions?" She placed her hands on her hips.

"I didn't hire him," Terrell said impatiently.

Erica looked down, noticing that he was tapping his fingers onto his palms at his sides. After years together, she knew what that meant. He was lying.

"I recommended him," Terrell said after a while. "My boss

actually . . . Look, Erica, that doesn't matter now. What matters is what Jonah is planning on doing. Is Nate in jeopardy?"

"Fuck you, Terrell," she said.

He was taken off guard. "What? What did I—"

"When I was outside your office," she said, speaking slowly as it all came to her. "You yelled at him. You said, 'Not him.' You were talking about Nate."

"I don't think so," he said nervously.

As she slowly seethed, her anger sliding into every crevice of her being, she stared Terrell down. If he wanted to play games, so could she.

"Jonah told me, you know," she said. "He told me everything. I didn't want to believe him, but now I know it's the truth."

Terrell just started shaking his head. "Fuck him! Dammit!"

Her heart sank. She had held on to the hope that this wouldn't work. If Terrell had denied it, she would have tried to believe him. But his reaction told her everything.

"You did know who he was, didn't you?" The look of guilt on his face made her heart break. "How could you? How could you know who this person was and let him anywhere near my brother?"

"I don't control who your brother hangs with," Terrell said. "Besides, they would have probably met after Reedy started working at the hospital anyway."

"But you introduced them, didn't you?" she asked. "It was your relationship with Reedy that made Nate think it was okay to hang out with him in the first place."

"Baby, please understand." He started toward her. "I told Reedy that he better not—"

He didn't have time to react before she attacked him. She lunged at him and started hitting his chest with her fist as she called him name after name.

Terrell grabbed her arms and pushed her back, holding her out from him.

"Calm down, Erica!"

"How could you do this to me!" She was enraged, unable to even think of what she was doing. "And you were going to keep lying to me while my brother just fell into this shit?"

"I wouldn't let that happen," he argued.

She jerked herself free of him. "It has happened, you asshole!"

"Listen to me." Terrell's voice held the emotion of a frightened, desperate man. "Baby, I swear to you, this is not as simple as it seems. You have to hear my side."

"Fuck your side," she snapped. "And fuck you, too. Get out of here! Get out of here before I call the police on you."

"You're gonna listen to me," he said adamantly.

He reached out to her, but she slapped his hand away. She rushed to the sofa, where she grabbed her phone out of her purse.

"I'm dialing now," she said. "And when the cops ask why I'm kicking you out, I'll tell them because you're involved with drugs. How does that sound?"

"I'm not involved in any drugs," he said. "You have to understand what the situation was."

She dialed 911 and lifted the phone to her ear. Terrell rushed over to her and grabbed the phone from her hands. He canceled the call.

"Erica," he said, "I love you."

"Go to hell," she said and rushed past him toward her bedroom.

He called her name as he followed her, but she locked the door behind her before he reached it. She hurried to the bathroom, where she locked that door as well. Erica fell onto the toilet seat, her face in her hands as she sobbed.

Sherise had been patient. She didn't want to get into trouble at the Fairmont again, so she waited for Jennifer to leave and followed her to a café. Sherise checked to make sure she was alone, even though she wouldn't have minded giving Jennifer what was coming to her in front of friends. She was dressed very professionally as if she was waiting for a business lunch, so in a way this would have been perfect. It was just that Sherise still had some secrets of her own to deal with, so catching her alone was best.

After parking her car, she reached the café and walked along the inverted walls of the entrance to avoid being seen by Jennifer. She wanted to catch her by surprise, and when she finally showed up, she could tell from the expression on Jennifer's face that she had.

Jennifer's mouth opened, her eyes widened, and she shot up from her seat at a table in the corner.

"How polite," Sherise said sweetly, "but there's no need to stand up for me."

"What are you doing here?" she asked, looking around nervously.

"As a matter of fact"—Sherise placed her hands gently on the back of the chair facing Jennifer—"you'll probably want to be sitting down for this."

"I don't think you know what you're doing," Jennifer warned. "This isn't going to go the way you—"

"I know," Sherise said.

Jennifer placed her hands on her hips. "You know what?"

"Why you got divorced," she answered. "You pitiful thing."

She rolled her eyes. "I already told you that, bitch."

Sherise laughed, shaking her head. "No, you didn't. You little liar. It was cute how you tried to front, but I can always find out the truth. You see, I asked around and . . . well, you know how good gossip knows no boundaries."

"Do you think there's something you can say that will keep me from telling Justin the truth?" She looked at her watch. "In a few min—"

"Fuck that." Sherise waved a dismissive hand. "I'm talking about you. You want to make it seem like you're a strong sista who dropped Ryan after finding out he cheated on you. You didn't. You stayed with his ass. He was the one who dumped you."

"You don't know my marriage."

"But I do." Sherise calmly placed her purse on the table. "And I know your divorce. And tomorrow morning, so will everyone who reads the *Washington Post*."

"What the fuck are you talking about?" She walked toward Sherise with a manic look in her eyes.

"I feel for you," Sherise said. "What kind of an asshole expects his wife to accept his cheating, and then the second she dips a little, dumps her? The nerve."

"What do you mean, the *Washington Post*?" Jennifer asked. "What have you done?"

"It's funny." Sherise walked around the table on the other side. She wore no earrings and her hair was up. She was ready to fight if it came to that, but she had some more to say. "Because when I leaked it to the press this morning, they were like who the fuck is Jennifer Ross and who in the hell is Ryan Hodgkins?"

"Call them back," she ordered. "Retract it!"

"Too late for that, bitch," Sherise continued. "But then when I told them the person you creeped with was now a congressman you used to work for, they seemed a little bit more interested."

"How did you . . . ?"

"You see," Sherise said, pointing her finger at the increasingly unstable woman. "I was thinking of trying to blackmail you, but then I thought, no, I need to reserve my blackmail for someone who can help me destroy you. Blackmail is to prevent damage. You've already done—"

"You bitch!"

Sherise could see the absolute panic that had taken the woman over as she started for her. Her entire body was shaking. Sherise realized, that by walking around the table to save herself some time, she had basically placed herself in a corner. This was not good.

She tried to hop out of Jennifer's way so she could swing around, get behind, and push her into the sofa-lined seats behind her, but Jennifer was too quick. She jumped on Sherise and pushed her down. They both fell onto the leather seats lining the wall.

Jennifer was screaming, but Sherise was quiet because she was trying to focus. She grabbed Jennifer's arms at the elbow to keep the woman's hands from reaching her face. Her hands were stretched out wide, and Sherise knew the woman intended to scratch the hell out of her. With all her strength, she kept holding Jennifer's arms down while trying to kick her in the leg.

"I won't let you!" Jennifer screamed.

"I've already done it," Sherise said back, struggling with every word. "You made your bed the second you picked my husband."

"I'm gonna kill you!"

"Hey!"

Sherise jerked the second she heard that voice that she knew too well: Justin's voice. What was he doing here? She had checked his office and his assistant told her that Justin had a lunch meeting at the firm and would be unavailable until two in the afternoon. She should have assumed he'd told the girl to lie.

Justin pulled a reluctant but somewhat obedient Jennifer off Sherise and pushed her aside. He stared down at Sherise, his expression full of bewilderment and, to her pleasure, a little fear.

After staring at her in disbelief for a few seconds, he held out a hand to help her up, but she slapped it away.

"What are you . . . ?"

Sherise got herself up. "Wondering why I'm here with your mistress?"

Justin pressed his lips together as if he was going to express some anger and then stopped himself, realizing he had no right to.

"Sherise," he said calmly, "we need to talk about this."

"When?" she asked. "Because I can see that you're busy about to have lunch with your whore!"

Justin squinted and Sherise enjoyed this. She didn't want to hate him, but having him standing there just brought her anger out of her. He was lunching with his mistress. How could she not lash out at him?

"Please," he said softly.

"Do you plan to ignore me?" Jennifer asked, standing just a few feet behind.

They both turned to her, but Justin stood in between the women.

"Don't talk," he said. "You'll just make this worse. We're leaving."

"What's the matter?" Sherise asked. "You aren't going to try and lie? I'm disappointed in you, Justin. You could at least try and tell me it's not what I think."

He looked at her with sheer embarrassment written all over his face. "I don't think that's necessary."

This hurt her. Sherise wasn't sure why, but the fact that he lacked the desire to even try to make her think he wasn't cheating on her almost broke her heart.

"Justin," Jennifer said, "I need to talk to her alone. Just leave us alone."

"Don't talk to him!" Sherise yelled, pointing her finger at the woman. Something about this woman giving her husband an order made Sherise livid.

"Calm down," Justin ordered. "People are staring at us. Just come outside, now."

"You're giving me orders?" Sherise asked. "That's how you think this is going to go?"

"I want to explain this to you," he said.

He grabbed her arm, but she jerked away and brushed past him. He rushed to reach her just before she came face-to-face with Jennifer, who looked ready to resume their fight.

"Good luck finding a job after tomorrow morning," she said with a wicked smile. "You're finished."

Justin pulled Sherise away from her and ushered her toward the door.

The second they were outside, Justin began trying to explain.

"Save it," she said. "I know how this got started."

"How do you know?" he asked. "Did you ask her? Don't listen to her."

"I know more than you do, you idiot. She played you, you know that?"

"What?"

"You probably thought you were being a player, sneaking around." She laughed. "You were just a pawn, Justin. She targeted you."

He opened his mouth as if he wanted to say something but just didn't know what.

"She slept with you to get back at me," Sherise said. "She knows me."

"That's ridiculous," he said. "I'm not sure what she told you, but . . ."

"She's right."

Jennifer took a few steps closer to them on the sidewalk beside the restaurant. Justin held his hand up to her.

"Just go away," he said. "I can handle this."

"I doubt that," Sherise said.

"She's not lying, Justin." Jennifer stood her ground like a woman who still believed she had a card to play. "I'm sorry, but she's right."

He looked at her as if he was both confused and at the same time supremely disappointed because he understood.

"Now the next question," Jennifer added with a smile, "is why? Sherise, you want to do the honors?"

"Bitch, if you don't get away from me and my husband!"

"A tit for a tat, Justin," she taunted. "Your whore of a wife slept with my husband first—"

"Get away from here!" Sherise started for her again as Justin struggled to restrain her.

"What are you two talking about?" Justin grabbed Sherise by the arm and turned her to him. "What is she talking about?"

Sherise stopped struggling and looked him in the eyes. Her own were tearing up already, and she felt herself begin to tremble in fear. This was not how she wanted this to go, but she was a survivor, and adapting was the key to survival.

"Justin," she said. "You're right. Let's just go. Let's go home and we'll talk about this."

The expression on Justin's face as he went from astonished confusion to realization tore at the inside of Sherise. She said his name as he turned to look at Jennifer. He was starting to shake his head and she said his name again.

"This is . . ." He was searching for words. "This is . . ."

"It's fucked up," Jennifer said. "I know. But it gets worse."

Sherise felt weak all over as she lowered her head. She was looking at the ground as she pleaded with him.

"Please, Justin, let's leave. Let's just go. Not like this."

"Just leave us alone, Jenny," he ordered.

"Make her go away," Sherise pleaded.

"You need to know this," she said.

"It's not true!" Sherise yelled. "It's not true!"

He let go of her and his arms dropped to his sides. One hand raised up and cupped her chin. He lifted her face until their eyes met. She could see his pain and fear through her tears.

"What is she gonna say to me?" he asked. "What are you so afraid of?"

"I love you," she said. "Cady is your daughter. She is yours, I swear to God."

He blinked, inhaling sharply as he took one step backward, then another.

"She is yours," Sherise repeated. "I swear, Justin."

"I have proof," Jennifer said. "She had that baby nine months after she slept with my husband."

Sherise turned to her in a rage. "That baby's name is Cady, and Justin is her father."

"Are you so sure?" Jennifer asked. "Because you didn't seem so sure the last time we spoke. I think you're full of shit."

"Actually," Sherise said, "I'm the one who has the proof now and there is no question. You have nothing."

"Well," she said, placing her arms across her chest. She nodded behind Sherise. "That appears to be something you and I have in common."

Sherise swung around expecting to see Justin, but he was gone.

"Justin!" she screamed, panicking as she found him just as he closed the cab door behind him. "Justin!"

"It's only fair," Jennifer said.

Sherise turned back to her. "You just remember that starting tomorrow morning, you will not only be out of a job, but you will be known around the country as yet another failed politician's worthless whore."

Despite a quick flinch, Jennifer appeared unfazed. "I have a great divorce lawyer I can recommend to—"

Sherise slapped her across the face so quick she even surprised herself.

Erica rushed into Sherise's home, yelling her name.

"I'm here!" Sherise waved to her from the kitchen at the back of the house.

Erica sighed in relief. "You scared me. Your door was open."

"I opened it for you."

"I thought something bad had happened." Erica entered the kitchen, looking around. She saw Cady sitting in her booster seat trying her best to eat a plate of corn. "No word from Justin?"

Sherise shook her head. She was leaning against the sink, biting her nail furiously.

"Have you been able to reach Billie?" she asked.

"No," Erica answered. "I don't know what the hell is going on with her. I'll keep trying."

After trying desperately to track Justin down at home, at work, and anywhere else he could be, Sherise called Billie and Erica for help. Billie had been unreachable, but once finding Erica, she told her everything. Erica left work early to come and help her.

"This is exactly why we wanted you to tell Justin first," Erica said. "Dammit, Sherise. You let your need for revenge mean more than saving your marriage."

"Really?" Sherise asked in disbelief. "You're going to do an I told you so right now? Is that what you came over for?"

Erica looked over at Cady, who had started making an excited fuss as she opened her arms wide. She was practically hopping out of her seat as Erica came over and kissed her on both cheeks before picking her up out of the chair.

"You told him that she's his, right?" she asked.

"I tried to," Sherise answered. "He wasn't listening. He was in shock. That was why I wanted Billie to get the test results over here."

"I don't know if she has them yet," Erica said, "but I'm not sure looking on a piece of paper is going to make him feel better."

"You know he can't be walking around acting all high and mighty," she said angrily. "He cheated on me, too."

"Sherise," Erica warned, "this is not the time to get on a

high horse or point fingers. Honey, you beg for forgiveness and patience."

Sherise knew how hard this would be. She wasn't good at apologies, but she had never been in this position before. All she could think of was the look on Justin's face when he realized that Cady might not be his. It made her shudder.

"You should have seen him, Erica." She walked over to them and handed Erica a napkin to wipe Cady's face. "He looked so . . . so lost. He looked so hurt and . . ."

"Betrayed."

Sherise's head shot up as she heard Justin's voice. He was standing in the doorway and she hadn't heard him walk up. Neither had Erica, who'd had her back to the door, holding Cady in her arms.

Sherise and Justin's eyes met and she could see how much pain he was in. She felt her knees get weak. She wanted to run to him, to hold him, to kiss him and hug him. She loved him and this was all her fault. Why hadn't she realized how much she loved him when it mattered? When it could have kept her from making the myriads mistakes she'd made?

"Justin," she said. "Where have you been?"

Justin looked at her with a stony, emotionless expression for a moment before turning to Erica. He walked over to her, focusing his attention on Cady now. She leaned forward and opened her arms as he reached out for her.

Sherise's eyes filled up with tears as she watched him look at Cady in his arms. He was so full of love for her and looked as if he wanted to cry. She felt sick just thinking of all the damage she had done. Yes, it would have been better if she'd left Jennifer for later and not piled the shock on top of shock, but the damage would have still been done. He loved Cady more than anything in this world.

"Justin," Sherise said quietly. "She's—"

"Stop it," he said without looking at her.

He gently cradled Cady's head as he leaned down and kissed her on her crown. He closed his eyes.

"Erica," he said. "You need to leave."

Erica looked at Sherise before agreeing. "Yeah, I . . . Of course. I was just—"

"Now," he added.

She snatched her purse from the kitchen table. "Do you want me to take Cady with me?"

"No," Sherise said quickly. "She's fine here."

"Take her." Justin reluctantly handed the baby over to her. "Sherise will only try to use her to soften me."

"I wouldn't do that," Sherise said.

"And she doesn't need to see us . . . discuss this." He looked at Sherise, his expression darkening. "She doesn't need to be here now. Sherise will call you when she wants to get her back."

Holding Cady as she reached the doorway, Erica turned to Sherise one last time. She looked like a nervous, scared child, but Erica knew there were limits to what she and Billie could do for her. This was their marriage and she had to step away.

"Call me," she said.

Sherise nodded before turning away. Erica felt for her. No matter what her faults, and there were many of them, Erica loved Sherise like a sister, and she didn't want to see her in pain like this. She didn't want to see her friend cornered, even if it was a corner of her own making.

There wasn't anything she could do. She had her own nightmare of a life to deal with. She could only love and care for Cady while she had her, and be there for Sherise, no questions asked, when this was all over.

Billie walked past the hallway that led to her partner's office for the third time. She was trying to get control of her emotions and go over what she was going to say. She had to get off the case. She couldn't represent Ricky anymore. She had to tell the truth, so she could be ahead of this instead of waiting to get caught and watching it all to blow up in her face.

She turned again to head down the hallway to her partner's office when her cell phone's vibrator went off . . . again. She had been getting a few calls from Sherise and Erica in the last hour, but couldn't handle it. She had too much to deal with. She couldn't be their problem solver yet again. Their disasters would have to wait until she handled her own disaster. In a few minutes, she figured she'd probably be out of a job anyway, so she would have plenty of time to help them out.

Jackson Snow's assistant was not at her desk, so Billie headed straight for his door. Just outside the door, she got a beep from her text messages. She knew if she didn't turn it off, it would keep beeping until she answered it, so she reached down to turn it off. That was until she read the message from Erica.

JUSTIN KNOWS EVERYTHING! IT'S GOING DOWN NOW!

"Oh, for fuck's sake," Billie said.

Her words came just as the front door to Jackson's office opened, and from the look on his face, he'd heard every word.

There was an awkward moment of silence before she spoke again.

"I'm sorry, Jackson. That wasn't meant for you. It was . . ."

"I should hope not," he said, smiling. "Although it wouldn't be the first time. I think I know why you're here."

Billie's eyes shot open and she felt her chest begin to cave in. "You do?"

He nodded. "This was your first pro bono case. You wanted this."

"I know, sir, and if you only listen—"

"We couldn't be more proud."

Billie blinked, wondering if she was hearing things. She

paused for a second, trying to figure out what was going on. He was smiling. He looked proud.

"Okay," she said cautiously, still unsure. "Th-thank you?"

"We just got a call from William Ricker. He's promised to delete the code report on our client and issue a new inspection supervised by an agent of our choice."

Billie was floored. "Are you serious? This happened today?"

"I was trying to reach you in your office, but I'm only getting voice mail."

That was because she'd spent the last half hour pacing the hallways trying to work up the nerve to tell him that she'd destroyed her career.

"So I was just going to come over," he said. "Good news like this is better in person."

Billie was trying to stay focused. This changed everything. Didn't it?

"This was too easy," she said. "Something is going on here."

"We were told to just back off in return for our client being left alone."

The advocate in Billie couldn't let this rest. Her mind wandered from her own problems to her case. "But for them to react this way to the little we've done means that there is something there. They're afraid of what we'd find."

"Of course they are," he added. "And they knew we had the quality lawyers that were willing to take the time and effort to find it out for our client, a person they thought didn't matter."

"Ricky isn't . . ." She caught herself. "Mr. Williams isn't the only person they're doing this to. We need to find out who in the Housing Authority is working with Sanders Realty. An investigation needs to be launched, and we need to find out who else turned down Sanders and got threatened as a result."

"I mentioned that an internal investigation would be a good idea," he said with a voice that held a lot less enthusiasm than just a few seconds ago. "But what's important is that you've succeeded in helping our Mr. Williams."

"This isn't over," Billie said.

"It is," he said. "Thanks to you."

"What are we going to do about that?"

"Nothing, Billie. We've done our part."

"But . . ."

"Billie." He held up a hand to stop her. "I know what you're thinking and that's not what we do. We aren't trying to save the world."

"Speak for yourself," she said, with a smile.

He didn't smile. "I'm speaking for the firm. Your heart is in the right place, but we win selective pro bono cases that come to us. We don't start crusades to go out and find them. Well, at least in this case we get them dismissed, but the point is to get what your client wants, and you did that. Mr. Williams will be eternally grateful to you. Don't you think?"

She swallowed nervously. "Are you going to . . . um . . . contact him?"

He frowned as if he found her comments extremely odd. "Hell no. You're going to call him. What's the matter? You don't like him or something?"

She tried to force a smile as Jackson laughed. This was painful. She wanted to look at it as best she could. She was happy this was resolved. She was able to serve her client, that was true. But she knew she didn't deserve any congratulations and it wasn't because she'd barely done anything. It was because she'd almost ruined everything.

She was facing an internal battle now. There was a little voice that told her it was all good now. *No need to spill your guts and put your career on the line. No one was hurt.* She knew better though. This wasn't who she was. She wanted to tell Jackson everything, not knowing whether or not telling him after the fact of a victory would be better or worse.

"Jackson," she said, pulling on all the nerve she had. "I have to tell you something."

"I know what you're going to ask," he said. "And, no, you can't have another case yet. You need to focus one hundred percent back on—"

"It's not about that," she said. "I made a mistake and—"

"Oh my God, there you are!"

One of the receptionists, Sierra, had just rushed around the corner out of breath. She had a terrified look on a face that looked flawless without a speck of makeup.

"I've been trying to find you Ms. Haa—I mean, Ms. Carter."

"What's wrong?" she asked. From the look on Sierra's face, Billie wondered if Sherise had called the office frantically trying to reach her.

"It's your husband," she said.

"My ex-husband," she corrected. "What does he want?"

"The hospital called," she said. "He's been hurt."

16

"First," Sherise said after a short moment, "Cady is your daughter."

Standing only a few feet across the kitchen from her, he was just shaking his head, looking at her with disdain.

"I've had the tests done," she added. "I . . . Billie has the proof, but—"

"Let me guess," he said. "She knew, too. Both those girls knew while I'm walking around like an idiot thinking my wife loved me and my daughter was—"

"Is," she said. "Is yours. They just found out last week. I wanted to know before Jennifer had a chance to tell you."

"But it's true," he said. "You had an affair with her husband before you got pregnant. You thought Cady was his."

"Justin." Sherise used the calmest voice she could find even though she was panicky inside. "I'm not making excuses for my behavior, but let's not pretend I didn't have a fight with your mistress today."

"Answer my fucking question!"

She jumped at the tone of his voice. He rarely yelled that angrily at her.

"Yes," she answered quickly. "I thought she might be. I knew she wasn't, but I thought she might be."

"That doesn't make any fucking sense!" He slammed his fist on the kitchen counter behind him. "None of this makes any fucking sense!"

"It was just once," she explained. "I got caught up in something and I'm not making excuses, but . . ."

"I've been trying to think about what was going on between us just before we found out you were pregnant." He started pacing the around the kitchen table. "But I can't think of anything. We were fine, as far as I knew."

"I know what you're doing," Sherise said. "You're trying to excuse your affair by suggesting that we were having problems. That isn't fair."

"This is different, Sherise."

"I was just a selfish whore," she said, "but you had a reason. Is that what you're going to say?"

He lowered his head, his frustration clearly growing. "We aren't going to get anywhere this way."

"No," she said. "This is only going to work if I'm the bad guy. If I keep bringing up your cheating, well, that just isn't fair. You want to play the victim."

"Fuck you, Sherise!" He rushed over to her, pointing his finger in her face. "What I did was just as wrong as you. I'm not denying that. But, shit, you kept the truth about Cady from me. That's fucking worse!"

"And I can't tell you how sorry I am for that." She reached out to touch the finger he had pointed at her, but he slapped her hand away. "Can we just not talk about Ryan or Jennifer right now and focus on—"

"But it's all connected!" He stepped away. "Isn't it? You fucked him and she targets me to get back at you."

"You can't blame me for that," she said. "You never had to sleep with her. You made that choice. You decided I wasn't interesting enough for you anymore."

"You fucking women and your games." He pressed a hand

against his forehead and looked up at the ceiling. "Cady . . . What if she wasn't . . . Oh my God."

"She is," Sherise said. "That's all that matters."

He looked at her with a disgusted expression. "That's what you'd like to think, isn't it? That's what you want this to be about. Well, Sherise, for once in your whole fucking selfish life, you don't get to decide how things go."

"Justin." She rushed over to him, pressing her hands against his chest. "Please, you have to forgive me. I am so sorry. I know I started this horrible lie, but I am begging you . . ."

"Don't bother." He pushed her hands away and turned toward the door. "I'm leaving."

"You can't leave me!" She started after him. "Justin!"

She followed him through the living room.

"Justin, stop!" Her voice held only half the desperation she was feeling right now.

Was he really going to walk out on her, on their marriage?

"Think about what you're doing," she pleaded. "I know you hate me right now, but you love me, too. I know you do. That's why I wanted to fight for you!"

"No, Sherise!" He reached the door and opened it.

She couldn't let this happen. She couldn't just let him leave and walk out like this. Something told her if she did, she would never see him again.

"What about Cady?" she yelled. "What do I tell her? That both her parents were unfaithful to each other, but she's the one that has to pay?"

She watched as he started to step outside, but stopped in the doorway. Her hand came to her heart as she waited anxiously. What was his next move? Was this over or was there a chance?

"For her," Sherise said. "For her family, I wanted to fight. I was willing to do anything. Why aren't you?"

He lowered his head, never turning around, and said, "I need time."

He slammed the door behind him and Sherise smiled with a relieved sigh. That hesitation, that one moment he stopped and paused and thought, was all he gave her. It was all she had. It would be all she needed.

"Hello, Erica," Jonah said as soon as he answered his phone. "Are you okay? Where did you go yesterday?"

"I don't like this, Jonah."

Not wanting to go to his office, Erica found a quiet, private corner of the break room to contact him as soon as she got into work that morning.

"You don't like what?" he asked.

"You know every move I make," she said. "You're having someone spy on me and report back to you."

"Actually," he said, "I came looking for you yesterday afternoon and Denise told me you mentioned an emergency and left. I just wanted to make sure you were okay."

"I'm fine," she said, even though she was far from it.

"So, what can I help you with?"

"You can tell me why you lied to me about Terrell's friendship with Reedy."

There was a long silence over the phone.

"I know he didn't tell you," Jonah said. "So I assume you figured this out yourself. You're a smart girl, Erica."

"Woman," she corrected. "And you didn't answer my question."

"I was trying to protect you."

"You were getting something out of it," she said. "You hate Terrell and you—"

"I don't hate him," Jonah said. "I just don't think he's right for you. You can see that now, can't you?"

"What were you getting out of it, Jonah?"

"I made a deal with him."

She couldn't believe this. "Terrell agreed to something, anything with you?"

"I keep his relationship with Reedy out of anything I report to you and he agrees to encourage you to have a relationship with me."

She was disgusted. Was there one man on this earth worth trusting? "This is how you operate with everything in life, isn't it?"

"I'm a man that does what he has to," Jonah answered. "I don't apologize for that."

"But you were willing to let me stay with Terrell, knowing what he'd done even though you've never wanted me with him?"

"I knew that you would come to your senses eventually," he said. "And after our relationship was stronger, I'm certain I would have steered you away from him. Either that, or he'd fuck up again. It's who he is."

"He was on the straight and narrow for a while," she argued.

"Remember who you're talking to?" Jonah asked. "I'm the man he wanted to blackmail less than a year ago."

"He's not doing anything with Reedy anymore," Erica said, as if it meant something. "It was just a slipup. He was upset over our breakup."

"Erica." Jonah's tone was condescending. "Still making excuses for him? Well, tell me, then. What is his excuse for introducing Reedy to Nate, knowing who Nate was? What is his excuse for bringing Reedy into the car wash so he would practically be working for him?"

"Stop," she said. "You don't have to do this. I kicked him out. I'll never forgive him for connecting Nate to that guy."

"He can be properly punished for that," Jonah said. "Along with Reedy."

"I told you," she insisted. "He's not involved with Reedy anymore."

"He is," Jonah said slowly, "if I say he is."

"No," Erica said. "Jonah, please. Don't ruin his life over this. There's been enough damage."

"You disappoint me, Erica."

"I disappoint you?" She laughed. "You're willing to frame him and ruin his life and I'm the disappointing one?"

"I'll make a deal with you."

"Jonah, please."

"Hear me out, okay? I will leave Terrell out of this, just like I'm leaving Nate out of it. I will do it for you, but you have to promise me you will never see him again."

"I told you I've already broken up with him."

"You've said that before, Erica. Six months later . . . I don't want a repeat of that. I think it's a fair deal."

"Only you would say that not framing someone made you fair."

She waited for a response, but heard nothing. She knew that Jonah was not a man to take lightly.

"You'll stay away from him, too?" she asked. "I mean it, Jonah. You won't bother him at all."

"You stay away from him," Jonah offered, "and so will I. We'll do it together. Forever. No matter what."

Erica closed her eyes, feeling her heart ache. How had this become her life? She had cut Terrell out of her life and her heart, her brother's life had fallen apart right under her nose, and she was making deals with the devil. Oh, and that devil was her father.

"Fine," she said softly before hanging up the phone.

When Billie entered Porter's hospital room, she saw him sitting up in his bed talking to a female doctor, predictably asking when he was going to get out of the hospital so he could go back to work. He had a hand in a cast just past his wrist, a bruise on his lips, and a gauze covering the left side of his forehead.

When he saw Billie, he immediately got angry.

"Where in the hell have you been?" he asked.

She approached the bed. "I came as soon as I could. Are you okay?"

"Hello," the doctor said. "I'm Dr. Banks. You're the wife?"

"Ex-wife," she corrected. "What happened here?"

"I thought we were waiting for your wife?" Dr. Banks asked Porter.

Porter looked at her, seeming a little embarrassed. "I might have called her that. I was upset at the time. Someone tried to kill me."

"What happened?" Billie asked again.

Porter looked at the doctor. "Can you give us some privacy?"

She nodded and left.

"You happened," Porter finally said.

"What do you mean, Porter? And fuck off with the games. Tell me."

He cringed as he shifted in his bed a little bit. "I'm leaving my building to catch the metro when some guy hits me from behind and knocks me to the ground."

"You were mugged?"

"That's what I thought," he answered. "So I offer the guy my wallet. He doesn't want my fucking wallet. He kicks me in my ribs and tells me to stay the fuck away from you."

"What?" Billie gasped. "Me? Who was this?"

"That's what I wanted to ask you, Billie." He held his hand up. "That asshole stomped on my hand. He broke it."

It took Billie a second to register this, but she realized suddenly that it had to be Ricky. Who else would be telling Porter to stay away from her? Robert? No, he hadn't put up much protest when she'd told him that she didn't want to see him again. But in her last encounter with Ricky, she'd made it clear to him that Porter was a problem for her. But she never thought he would do this.

"Was it the same guy you saw me with outside my apartment?"

He shook his head. "No, it was another guy. The cops got him. I got lucky. One was driving by only seconds after he ran away. They sped after him."

"Porter, I don't know who would do this," she said. "I've never asked anyone."

"You know a guy named Reedy?" he asked.

Billie immediately knew where she'd heard that name last. "That's . . . That's the name of the guy I was trying to find out about . . . but that was for Erica. He's gotten Nate involved with drugs."

"So why is he telling me to stay away from you?" Porter asked. "What do I have to do with this?"

"Oh my God." Billie realized what was going on. "It's not related, Porter. He's . . ."

It was a small world, Billie thought. This was just too small. If Reedy was connected to Ricky, then that meant that Ricky was somehow involved in drugs, which answered so many lingering questions that she'd had but pretended to forget because she had feelings for him.

"What's going on, Billie?" Porter asked. "Why are you shaking your head?"

"I have to go," she said quickly. "I'm sorry, Porter. I'm glad they've caught him. You look like you'll be fine."

"Billie!" Porter yelled after her as she started out.

Billie swung around to look at him. She was distracted by her thoughts, but the look on Porter's face got her attention. He was scared.

"They got him," she said. "He won't hurt you again."

"That's not it." He gestured for her to come back to the bed. "You don't understand."

She rushed back to his bed. "What don't I understand?"

"Tara," he said. "He said that if I didn't leave you alone, my daughter would be next."

★　★　★

Without knocking or ringing a doorbell, Billie stormed into Saturn House like a tornado of rage that belied her tiny frame.

"Ricky!" she yelled throughout the house, heading straight through the foyer into the living room.

She saw a few people sitting in the living room. One man was reading a book while a woman was on the floor playing a board game with a child.

"Where is he?" she asked in a demanding voice. "Where is Ricky?"

None of them said a word. They all looked too scared of her. The man, an elderly man of about seventy-five, pointed toward the formal dining room.

"Ricky!"

Ricky stepped out of the dining room just as Billie reached it. He was wearing a blue polo shirt and jeans, and wiping his hands in a kitchen towel. He looked utterly confused.

"Billie, what the—"

"How dare you?" She walked right up to him and pressed her index finger into his chest. "How dare you threaten my daughter!"

"What are you . . . ?" Suddenly seeming to realize what she was talking about, he looked behind her at the people in the living room, all of them paying rapt attention.

"Come with me," he said, grabbing her by the arm.

She jerked free of him. "Don't touch me. I can walk on my own."

She followed him through the kitchen, into the hallway. He moved into a cramped spot underneath the stairs where the door to the basement was.

"Keep your voice down," he said.

"Why?" she asked. "Don't the people living here have a right to know who you are and what you do?"

"Before you say something you'll regret . . ."

"I regret all of this, Ricky. I regret ever meeting you, ever being put on your case. And, oh my God, do I regret caring about you for even a second."

"I would never hurt that girl," he said. "I don't even know who she is."

"Then why did Reedy threaten her?" she asked. "He did that for you, attacking Porter. What were you thinking?"

He stopped, looking at her for a moment as if to assess where she was emotionally. "I was doing this for us. You said he was the reason we can't be together. He was making you miserable. It was just a little street justice."

"It was a crime," she said. "And that lowlife drug dealer you sent to commit it confirms everything I thought about you."

"That I care about you?" he asked. "That's why I did this. I just want us to be together."

"And because you're a lowlife, this is the only way you know how to make that happen. Attack an innocent man and threaten a little girl."

He was shaking his head, clearly disappointed. "I can't believe you don't appreciate the lengths I've gone to for you."

"You're a drug dealer, too, aren't you?"

His blinked, seeming offended for a second. "You're my lawyer, Billie. You can't tell anyone what I tell you."

"You think that's going to protect you?"

"I do what's necessary to keep my shelter safe," he said. "I don't sell drugs, but I pay Reedy to keep drug dealers away from me."

"And to do odd jobs for you," she said. "Like beating up lawyers."

"I won't admit to anything," he said. "Dammit, Billie. I thought you were down."

"I'm down," she said, "but not that low."

"You're still on my case," he said. "I don't want this to interfere with you—"

"I'm not on your case anymore," she said. "It's over. You've won that one, but you've got bigger legal problems to worry about."

He smiled. "You can't say anything about this."

"I don't have to," she said. "Reedy is gonna say everything for me. He was caught, Ricky. I don't know if you know that."

From the expression on his face, he hadn't. His concern was growing.

"I still have strong connections with the district attorney's office," she added. "Many of them still owe me a favor from old cases. I didn't have to give them a reason why. All I had to do was call in a favor and ask them to offer Reedy a great deal if he talked. And from what I hear, he talked."

Just then the basement door burst open and hit Ricky in the head. He fell back against the wall as two small children ran out of the basement, laughing, in a world by themselves.

"Dammit!" Ricky yelled as his hand went to his forehead.

When he looked up again, Billie was gone.

When Justin opened the door to his hotel room at The Mayflower, his expression was predictably annoyed.

"Sherise," he said. "I told you I needed time. What are you doing here?"

She stood at the door, smiling kindly. "Why would you tell me you were here if you didn't want me to come over?"

"I told you," he said. "It was only if something happened with Cady. An emergency. You never listen."

"Why aren't you at work?" she asked. "Are you gonna let me in?"

"No," he said. "I'm not going to let you in. I'm working from home today."

"You're not at home, baby." She lifted up to look behind him into the room. "You're in a cold hotel room and maybe not alone, which is why you don't want me here."

"I'm alone." He moved to block her view. "I don't want anything to do with Jennifer."

"Now that you know she was using you," Sherise said. "Before you—"

The door to the room to the right of Justin's opened and a woman dressed in a sharp red business suit stepped out. She made eye contact with Sherise and smiled.

Sherise turned to Justin. "Shouldn't we do this inside?"

Justin looked at the woman, who gave them another glance as she passed by. He sighed, stepping aside as Sherise stepped in.

"I brought you this." She offered him a duffel bag with a few of his things.

He took the bag as he closed the door behind her.

"Sherise, what part of 'I need time' do you not understand?"

Realizing that he intended to keep her in the foyer, she walked past him into the room. Looking around, she could see he'd been working. Papers were everywhere. They'd better not be separation papers.

"The part where I don't get to see my husband so we can work out our problems."

She sat down on the edge of the bed as he placed the bag next to her.

"Please get off of there," he said.

Ignoring him, she unzipped the bag and reached in. She pulled out his iPad and turned it on.

"I wanted to show you something," she said, going straight to the app she was looking for. Pictures.

She turned the iPad around so he could see one picture of their wedding, then another.

"Stop it," he said. "You think showing me a wedding slideshow is going to—"

The next picture was of Cady. He was holding her and she

was looking up at him with an adoring worshipping expression on her face. The next was of her smiling into the camera showing her only two teeth. There was drool running down her chin as she was trying to reach for the camera to snatch it away.

Justin smiled.

"I see your nose there," she said.

The next one was of Cady sleeping on her back in her crib.

"Remember how your mother said you used to always slip one hand under your back like that when you slept?"

"Stop it." He grabbed the iPad from her and tossed it on the bed. "This is underhanded of you, Sherise."

"I'm just trying to tell you, I didn't spend all this time wondering if Cady was yours and just hoping for the best."

"It doesn't change what you did," he said.

"Nothing will change what I did," she said. "Or what you did. But I'm willing to move past it and try to work this out. Why aren't you?"

"I didn't say I wasn't." His voice was low and deep as if he was trying very hard to control his temper. "I just said I need time. Do you understand what the fuck happened here?"

"I do," she said. "I cheated on you because I was an insecure woman who thought she was stronger than she actually was. I never thought I needed to fight temptation because I knew I loved my husband. I think you did the same.

"I know what I did was worse," Sherise continued. "If that's what you're looking for me to say. I wasn't part of a targeted seduction, and when I cheated, you weren't denying me sex. We weren't having problems."

"I don't want to compare whose cheating was worse." Justin sat down on the bed next to her. "Sherise, I just . . . Fuck, I don't know. I'm so fucking angry at you and myself, and every time I think that Cady could have not been mine, I just can't even think straight."

She reached over and placed her hand gently on his shoulder as he lowered his head.

"So much has gone wrong, baby." Her voice was tender, soft, and seductive. She hadn't come here to go home empty-handed. "I lost my fire because I wasn't working. You lost interest in me because I lost my fire."

"Trying to have this baby," he added. "We've been forcing this. Going about it all wrong. I don't know how this happened. I never went looking for her."

"She was looking for you." Her hand went to his head. "Baby, I understand that you were weak. Can you understand that I was, too? I'm weaker than you."

He leaned away, but Sherise didn't stop running her fingers gently over his head. He didn't resist anymore.

"This is fucked up," he said. "You want to act like we just had a bad fight, but that's not what this is. This is our marriage and it's completely fucked up."

"That's not true." She slid closer to him on the bed. "Baby, I—"

"Stop calling me that," he said quickly.

She paused for a second. "It's going to take a lot of work and time to get us right again, but we are not fucked up. You, Cady, and me are a family. We all love each other. We all need each other."

He nodded and she leaned in to gently kiss his neck.

"Can you think of a life without me in it?" she whispered. "Can you think of a life seeing Cady every other weekend? Can you think of sleeping in a bed I will never be in with you? Because I can't, Justin. I refuse to believe that's even possible."

She leaned in and kissed his neck again.

"Stop," he said quietly, even though he made no physical protest.

Her free hand went to his thigh and rubbed it gently as her lips left searing kisses on his neck.

"Sex won't fix this," he said.

"But it will hold things together while we fix it," she responded as she bit gently at his ear. "I need you, Justin. You're my husband. I'm your wife. I know you need me."

She let out a quick gasp as his hand grabbed her wrist. His grip hurt, and when she looked into his eyes, she could see that was what he intended.

He grabbed her by the back of her head, pulling her hair. Her head fell back and Sherise felt her entire body ignite like an inferno. No, she hadn't intended to leave this hotel room empty-handed and she wasn't going to.

Erica was cautious as she entered her apartment that evening. She didn't expect to see Terrell there, but she wouldn't have been surprised. It broke her heart to come home to him not being there. She had gotten used to it for the six months they were apart, but even a few days of him being back there had warmed her heart to the idea that they were together again. Now she would have to go back to being heartbroken, to feeling alone.

Passing through the living room, she saw the television was on, but no one was in there. She glanced down the hallway and saw a light coming out from under Nate's door, but decided she needed to get her thoughts together before going to talk to him.

When she opened her bedroom door, she saw a figure sitting on her bed. She gasped in surprise, but couldn't figure out who it was because it was dark. She reached for the light and was at first relieved to find that it wasn't Terrell.

"What are you doing in here?" she asked. "In the dark."

Nate's head was lowered as he focused on his hands, which were placed in his lap as he sat on the edge of her bed, facing the bathroom.

"I was waiting for you . . . I guess."

Erica dropped her bag on the bed and walked over to him. She reached down, and with her index finger to his chin, lifted his face up to her. His expression struck her with a force. He was scared to death.

"What happened?" she asked.

"You were right," he said. "Everything went down, Sis. It was fucked up."

"What went down?"

"We were just hanging out and the cops just busted in."

"Did they hurt you?" she asked quickly. "Did anyone touch you?"

"That's just it," he said with a shrug. "Like they came in and—"

"You were at Reedy's place, weren't you?"

He nodded. "They came in and just jumped on everyone. I was on the sofa and one cop pulled a fucking gun on me."

Erica was getting angry but didn't show it. "Well you're hanging out with drug dealers, Nate. They get guns pulled on them a lot."

"Then the dude grabs me and drags me out of the place," Nate continued. "I was like, 'Get off me, man, get off me.' Then, he just . . . he let me go."

"What did he say?"

"Nothing at first." Nate was shaking his head as if he didn't even really believe what he was saying. "So I turned around and another cop came up to me and told me to get the fuck out of there."

"I hope you listened."

"Hell yeah, I listened." He lowered his face into his hands. "That was so fucking scary."

Erica dropped down on the bed next to him. She placed her hand on his back and rubbed.

"I'm glad you realize how serious this is."

"I was like, shit, my life is over. You warned me and I didn't believe you."

"Do you believe me now?" she asked.

He nodded, lifting his head up to look at her. "Are they gonna come for me later?"

"No," she said. "Not if you do what I say."

"I'll do fucking anything, Erica."

"Then," she said, "it's going to be okay."

After Nate had gotten up and left, Erica grabbed her phone and called Jonah.

"Did you know he would be there?" she asked.

"I knew he might be there," he answered.

"They scared the shit out of him."

"That's a good thing," Jonah said. "First, he needed to have the shit scared out of him for effect. Second, you don't want the other guys knowing he got off scot-free."

"I guess you're right," she said, thinking further of it. She hesitated before asking her next question. "Was that . . . was that raid . . . all that happened?"

"You're asking me if Terrell got in trouble. Erica, I always keep my end of the deals I make. I hope I can trust that you do as well."

"I intend to," she said.

"I want you to do better than intend," he said. "I want you—"

"I'll stay away from him," she said. "For good."

There was a short silence before Jonah spoke again. "We should have lunch soon. Would that be okay?"

"I'll think about it," she answered slowly.

Erica stepped out of the cab in front of the restaurant. She saw Sherise and Billie sitting at a table in the outside cafe. They waved to her. She started to walk toward them when she heard a man call her name. She knew that voice as well as she knew her own.

Her heart stung when she saw Terrell rush over to her. He looked a mess in a gray Howard University T-shirt and jeans. It appeared as if he hadn't been sleeping at all. He looked the way she felt every time she thought of him.

"Can I talk to you?" he asked, his eyes pleading. "Please, baby, just for a minute."

"I'm not your baby," she said coldly. She wanted to have compassion for him, but all she felt was anger. He ruined their dreams again. "And how did you find me here?"

"Nate told me you were gonna be here."

She pointed her finger in his face angrily. "You stay the fuck away from him, Terrell. You've already done enough damage. Just stay away from him."

"I just want to talk to you." He swallowed, seeming afraid to utter a word in case it would make her run away. "I can't tell you how sorry I am about this."

"You should just be grateful," she said.

"For what?"

"Jonah wanted to implicate you in all this," she said. "You could be behind bars right now if he had his way."

Terrell shook his head with a knowing smile. "That son of a bitch. He's the most underhanded motherfucker. This is his fault. This is all his fault."

"How can you say that?" Erica couldn't believe what she was hearing. "You really don't want to take the blame for this, do you?"

"He's the one who broke us up!"

"No, Terrell, you broke us up!" She shook her head, waving her hand. "I won't do this. Just go, and I hope for your next girlfriend's sake you figure out a way to take responsibility for your own actions."

He blocked her way into the restaurant. "I know I need to get my act together. I know I have a lot of work to do, but I—"

"What the fuck do you want?" Sherise asked as she quickly wedged herself in between the two of them.

"I'm talking to Erica." Terrell rolled his eyes. "This ain't none of your business."

"It's her business," Billie said, joining them. "Erica is our business, and it was clear to us that she was trying to get away from you before you blocked her."

"Fuck—" Terrell caught himself before he said more.

"Terrell," Erica said. "Just go."

"Erica." He tried looking around Sherise to make eye contact with Erica, but it wasn't working. "Please. I'm begging you. You and I need to talk alone."

"Here's the thing." Erica took Sherise by the arm and pushed her aside so she was facing Terrell again.

She looked into his eyes and mustered her strength.

"You can get your act together," she said. "I believe that you will. But nothing will change the fact that you let me down again. Nothing will change the fact that you let Nate get involved with someone like Reedy, knowing who he was. I will never forgive you for that. Even if you never make the same mistakes again, you've made enough with me to last a lifetime."

"Baby," he pleaded.

"Our time is over. It's not coming back. I'm moving on. I've moved on. I wish you luck, but this"—she gestured to the space between the two of them—"this is done."

She didn't wait for a response before turning and heading into the restaurant with Sherise and Billie right behind her.

"Aren't we an impressive group of sisters," Sherise said as all three women sat down at their table.

Despite tears that had begun to fall down her cheeks, Erica found it in herself to smile.

"We are pitiful, aren't we?" Billie asked. She rubbed Erica's back comfortingly.

"We're single again," Erica said to Billie and then turned to Sherise. "You're . . . I don't know what you are."

"I'm married, bitch." Sherise smiled even though it wasn't entirely funny. "It's a fucking mess, but I'm married."

"She seduced him a couple of days ago," Billie said.

"With what?" Erica asked.

"Excuse me?" Sherise asked. "With all this right in front of you. No man can resist."

"Isn't that the problem?" Erica asked, laughing.

"She used pictures of Cady," Billie added.

With a smacking sound of her lips, Erica shook her head. "Did it work?"

Sherise shrugged. "It's a step forward. He's not moving back home yet. I don't think he will for a while, but he's still my husband. He knows that."

"Sex is one thing," Billie said. "Trust me, it doesn't make a relationship."

"We aren't gonna be a repeat of you and Porter," Sherise said. "Besides, he came over this morning to spend some time with Cady."

"And you let him leave?" Erica asked. "I would have thought you'd lock all the windows and doors."

"Honestly," Sherise said, "I even surprised myself with how subtle I was. I gave him all the space he needed. He even kissed me on the cheek before he left."

"You're really going to give him the time he asked for?" Erica asked in disbelief.

"Are you planning to tell him about Jonah?" Billie asked.

"Fuck that," Sherise said. "We've had enough honesty for a lifetime."

Sherise was perfectly fine with where she was. She felt confident she and Justin would work this out. Cady's paternity was no longer a question. Jennifer's face was all over the papers and the Internet, her reputation and political career ruined forever. She had survived a disaster. She wasn't going to compound it with another one. Justin would trade her one affair for his, but two affairs? No, there would be no mention of any other indiscretions.

"That's not right," Erica said.

Sherise looked her up and down. "We can't always do the right thing. Besides, what does it get you? Look at you."

"Like I said," Billie added, "we're all pitiful right now."

Sherise pointed at Erica. "You just make sure that Jonah stays out of our lives."

"I can't promise that," Erica said. "Things are different between us. He's done me a lot of favors."

"That's what he wants you to think," Sherise warned. "They are not real favors."

"We'll see." Erica shrugged.

"If he's hooking people up for you," Billie said, "I might need him for a job soon."

"You're not gonna get fired or disbarred," Erica said, even though she had no idea what she was talking about. She was just trying to be a supportive friend.

"I can't believe you told them," Sherise said. "That indiscretion could have gone to jail with Ricky. No one would have believed his good-for-nothing ass."

"That's not the point," Billie said even though she had thought of that a million times before deciding to come clean about the situation to her bosses.

She was still waiting to hear what their decision was, and she didn't know if she'd have a job come Monday, but she had searched her soul and knew that she had to tell the truth. She had some integrity left, and getting the rest back started with her telling the truth. She was already feeling better.

"But what about Tara?" Erica asked.

Billie rolled her eyes. She was still trying to figure out a solution to this, but one problem at a time.

Porter was glad she'd been able to help connect Reedy to Ricky, which would allow the district attorney to add conspiracy to their charges. She was able to convince him to let her talk to Tara. She would have to be satisfied with that for now.

"Small steps," she said. "Small steps. Just like you."

Erica felt sad. "I'm trying to look at it this way. I'm still young and I have a lot of life ahead of me. I believe in my heart I'll meet someone else. I just don't . . . I just don't see myself ever getting over him."

"You will," Billie said as she placed her hand over Erica's.

"We'll see to it that you do." Reaching across the table, Sherise placed her hand over Billie's.

"We'll all be fine," Billie said. "Together, we got this."

"I say we make another pact," Sherise said. "It's been, what . . . fifteen years since our last one?"

"That long?" Erica asked. "Damn."

"How much time are we giving ourselves?" Billie asked.

"Six months," Sherise said. "In six months, all three of us will have our shit together, be in love, and happy."

"Oooh," Erica said. "That is one damn tight schedule."

"Compared with everything else we've done?" Billie asked. "Sounds doable."

"Deal?" Sherise asked.

"Deal," Erica said.

"Deal," Billie added.

"Now." Sherise removed her hand and raised it in the air. "Let's get that waiter over here so we can get some drinks! We're gonna need 'em."

ALMOST DOESN'T COUNT

Angela Winters

www.angelawinters.com

About this Guide

The following questions are intended
to enhance your group's
reading of this book.

DISCUSSION QUESTIONS

1. Do you think Billie was right to get herself involved in Tara's life despite Porter's insisting she stay out? How would you have handled the situation differently?

2. Do you think it was better that Sherise not tell Justin about her affair with Jonah, or should she have spilled the beans when they were putting it all out on the table?

3. Was Erica too harsh on Terrell for Nate's drug issues? Is Terrell to blame or should Nate be the only one to answer for his choices?

4. Was Billie correct in thinking that she will have to cut Tara out of her life completely if she ever wants to be rid of Porter?

5. Was it okay for Justin to walk out on Sherise after finding out about Cady even though he had been cheating on her?

6. Should Erica ever take Terrell back or should she just move on?

7. Why do you think Billie made the decision to sleep with Ricky even though she knew it could get her disbarred?

8. Sherise slept with Jennifer's husband and Jennifer slept with Sherise's husband. Was Sherise right in going after Jennifer and ruining her life, even after she was out of Justin's life, or should she have just left it alone and focused on fixing things between her and Justin?

9. Do you think it's a good idea that Erica let Jonah more and more into her life or should she heed Terrell's and Sherise's warning and stay as far away as possible?

10. If it had turned out that Ryan was Cady's father, instead of Justin, do you think things would have ended differently for Sherise and Justin?

11. In the end, Billie decided to tell her bosses about her indiscretion with Ricky. Was she right to do that even though it could cost her her job or should she have kept it to herself?

12. Do you think Sherise and Justin will make it? Should they?

Want more? Don't miss Angela Winters's

Back on Top

Available now wherever books are sold

1

Sherise Robinson couldn't believe she had let herself run behind today of all days. Her first day back at work from maternity leave and she was going to show up late if she didn't speed things up. That was not the message she wanted to send.

As she rushed around the master bedroom of her elegant Georgetown town house in Washington DC's Northwest side, Sherise felt panic start to set in. A lot was riding on how today went, no matter how much her husband, Justin, tried to tell her otherwise. The power-hungry, manipulative bitch, as her coworkers had secretly named her, was coming back, and if she showed any signs of softening, weakening, she was dead. The barracuda was now a mama and she could just imagine what they were all thinking: She's vulnerable.

As she stopped to look in the full-length mirror that covered her walk-in closet door, her confidence was lifted. She was going to show them they were wrong. Finally she found her missing Missoni stacked pumps and her outfit was complete. She looked sharp and sexy, and at twenty-seven, Sherise felt certain she showed no signs of having given birth six months ago. That was thanks to very expensive underwear that tucked everything in, but also to the fact that she made sure not to gain more than the twenty-five pounds her doctor told her was the minimum amount to be healthy during her pregnancy. While there was still a stubborn pound or two hanging around, everything was tightening up nicely.

From head to toe, Sherise checked every inch. Her shoulder-length hair, just done yesterday, was styled nicely in a sharp "don't fuck with me" bun with just a few "I might be flirting with you" dark brown tendrils falling down. She liked to keep the men confused. It gave her an advantage and Sherise was all about getting the advantage. Her makeup was flawless, highlighting her high cheekbones and dark green eyes. It was spring, so her lipstick was a soft, flirtatious pink. Her golden caramel skin was glowing and it would wow when she took off the jacket of her black and white striped Nipon wide-legged pantsuit to reveal her white sleeveless Marc Jacobs business shirt. No one who saw her at the Executive Office Building today would forget.

"I'm back," she said in that sexy, raspy voice of hers. "Bitches better step aside."

"You're late," were the first words Justin Robinson said to his wife only seconds later as she entered the contemporary European-style kitchen.

"I'm fine," Sherise answered as she rushed for the refrigerator. "I'm taking a cab."

"Ah! Ah!"

Sherise quickly closed the refrigerator door and rushed over to the little monster emitting those sounds. Her six-month-old baby girl, Cady, was the love of her life. She sat in her baby chair, her hands reaching out for her mommy with evidence of her breakfast all over her face, not to mention her bib. She was an adorable baby with soft, chocolate skin, nice and chunky with fat cheeks that Sherise couldn't get enough of.

"Sorry, baby!" Sherise leaned in for a quick kiss, but didn't trust herself for more. She knew leaving Cady today would be hard enough. "Mama has to go."

"You should eat something." Justin put down the baby spoon and leaned back in his chair. He was looking at his wife with concern. "You don't want to go in there without your fuel."

"I'm grabbing something on the way." Sherise appreciated her husband's concern, but there was a part of her that was still a little angry with him for trying to pressure her to stay home for good.

Justin, thirty, was old fashioned and his upbringing had been very different from hers. Because Sherise grew up poor as dirt on the hard streets in Southeast DC with no father to be found and a mother who couldn't give a damn, she only knew how to fight. Justin was a lover, not a fighter. From Chicago, he grew up in a traditional middle-class black family with a stay-at-home mother, a doctor for a father, and all the safety cushions that came with such an upbringing. He was stable and reliable and represented what Sherise wanted to be, which was why she decided the night she met him four years ago, when he was just a recent Georgetown Law grad, that she wanted to marry him. A reliable wage earner who was hot enough to be attractive, but not so hot that every other woman would want him too. He was the kind of guy who would come home every night. Most of all, Justin, a six-figure lobbyist on Capitol Hill, had the connections that Sherise's never-ending ambition could use to get ahead.

But Justin put a wrench in her ambitious game when he suggested Sherise be a stay-at-home mom after Cady was born. They had at first agreed to a regular twelve-week maternity leave, knowing that Sherise had plans of moving beyond her position as assistant director of communications for the White House's Domestic Policy Council. She was hungry for power

and her ultimate dream was to make it from the Executive Office Building across the street to the West Wing of the White
House. After endless fighting, Sherise went the route that had
always served her well—refusing affection until she got her
way. While she loved Justin, he did not overwhelm her, which
made him a good husband candidate for her. She could control
the way her body reacted to him, thus control the power he
had over her.

It wasn't as if he wasn't attractive. He was six feet tall and,
while he had an extra ten pounds, he wore it well. He was a
sexy dark brown with beautiful light brown eyes and a sturdy
face. He wore preppie boardroom glasses that made him look
distinguished and was always looking sharp in his expensive
business suits. The point was, while she found him perfect husband and father material, Justin had never gotten Sherise to
lose control of herself. She could resist him, but he couldn't resist her. She played her games and made certain he couldn't resist, which resulted in a quick marriage proposal. This control
over him was why her compromise of a six-month leave was
quickly accepted and rewarded with access to affection again.

Sherise felt a pull in her gut as Cady called for her again,
but she fought it and went to check her briefcase. It made her
want to cry, but she wasn't a stay-at-home mom type. She was
too ambitious, too greedy. Did that make her a bad mother?
She didn't know. She only knew that she would be miserable
without the challenge of a career. It made her feel strong, safe,
and allowed her to do what she did best—power play and win.

"I filled up her bag." Sherise's back was to her husband and
child as she organized the items in her briefcase on the French-
villa style dining room table. "So all you have to do is grab it and
walk her over to the day-care center."

Sherise almost jumped when she felt Justin's hand on her
shoulder. She turned to face him and was comforted by the
compassion in his eyes.

"I know this is hard for you, baby." He leaned forward and kissed her on her forehead. "You don't have to pretend."

"Please," she begged. "Don't do that. You'll make me cry. I can't walk in there with red eyes."

"You know that you'll be back in the swing of things before noon," he said. "Don't sweat it, baby. Cady will be fine at day care. I'll drop her off on my way to work and you can pick her up on your way home."

"And you don't hate me?" she asked.

Justin smiled his usual charming smile. "I couldn't if I tried."

She knew that. She could always rely on Justin to be a supportive husband and a fully involved father. Which made her feel all the worse knowing that Cady might not even be his child.

Billie Hass felt her stomach getting tighter and tighter as every second passed. Her petite fingers gripped the coffee cup in her hand as she stood at the counter and looked out the window facing the street. The building where she was starting her new job on K Street was right in front of her. She didn't look much different than any of the expensively suited lawyers who walked inside, but she knew she was different.

Growing up in Southeast DC, Billie had witnessed the injustices against the poor firsthand. Having a father she watched accused of a crime he didn't commit and railroaded by the legal system, and a mother who died trying to fight the corruption of health insurance companies, had molded her opinion of power. Billie knew two things. She had to get out of poverty and she had to fight for those who couldn't fight for themselves. This motivated her to get through law school, always with the objective of fighting for justice.

She graduated four years ago, at age twenty-five, and began

her career as a public defender in DC. She was chided for not shooting for Big Law and six-figure salaries, but was planning for something better. Billie intended to run for office one day and use her power to fight for legislation that spoke for the voiceless. The young men who were guilty until proven guilty and poor women who the system shepherded toward dependency. She had met with a lot of obstacles but was winning more than losing. That was until Porter Hass happened.

Billie met Porter at Georgetown Law School. He was four years older than her, having spent time in the navy before going to school, so she found him a bit more knowledgeable than the average brother she dealt with every day. They had so much in common. While Billie had grown up on the tough streets of Southeast DC, Porter had struggled to survive in the dangerous Highland Park neighborhood of Detroit. Seeing cops shoot and kill his brother at the age of ten and get away with it, Porter had many of the same plans to fight injustice when he started law school.

But something changed. Another thing Porter and Billie had in common was a desire to live a better life than they had known as kids, to escape the ghetto mentality of "bad is good and there is no way to succeed so why bother." They wanted to escape always being on the wrong end of . . . well, everything. But unlike Billie, who only wanted to get rid of the bad, Porter began to desire an escape from all of it. Billie didn't want to forget everything about the hood, but Porter did, and at some point during law school, he decided he wanted to *be* the power that they were supposed to want to fight.

Despite their differences, she married him because she loved him and he had a lot of good qualities. He was smart and sexy and he was a great father to his now fourteen-year-old daughter, Tara. While he was still in law school, Porter fought for custody of Tara when her mother, Shawn, got too deep into drugs to care for her. Porter and Shawn were teenagers when she got pregnant and, while Porter fought his way out of it all, Shawn never bothered. He never turned his back on Tara, and for that Billie loved him. That, and the fact that he set her body on fire every time he touched her. She had never felt the passion for a man that she had for Porter. Their sexual chemistry blew her mind.

But while it blew her mind, it wasn't enough to save their marriage. Billie could handle Porter's negative comments about the people she defended and even his digs at what he called her "ghetto tendencies," but if it wasn't clear they were moving in different directions, his affair with the blond, perky twenty-three-year-old clerk at his law firm, Claire Flannigan, was as clear as rain. The heartbreak was followed by a divorce in which Porter's expertise and connections gave him the upper hand over Billie. It all put her in a position where, financially, she could no longer afford to work for a pittance. She had six-figure student loans, new bills, and Porter had taken everything in the divorce.

Now, here she was on the corner of K Street and Eighteenth in Northwest DC, barely visible above the morning crowd with her petite five-foot-three frame. She had the skills to get a high-paying job in Big Law white-collar criminal defense. Her money problems were taken care of, but starting her life over, divorced and single at twenty-nine, was not what she had imagined.

Feeling her phone vibrate in her pants pocket gave Billie an excuse to wait just a few more minutes before entering the building and leaving the career she loved behind. The fact that it was Tara was just icing on the cake.

"Hey, sweetheart," Billie said, holding her finger to her free ear to drown out the crowd noise. "What's up?"

"I hate that bitch!"

"Whoa, Tara. What is going on?" Billie knew her stepdaughter had a short temper just like her father; she angered easily. "What's wrong?"

"Claire," Tara said with a voice that sounded a lot younger than fourteen. "Billie, you just don't know what I deal with."

"What did she do now?" While Claire was the last person Billie wanted to talk about, she would never turn Tara away. Porter was making it hard enough for her to spend time with the girl now that they were divorced. She loved Tara and missed her terribly, which Porter knew.

"She's moving in," Tara answered.

Billie felt her chest tighten at the words. She tried to control her emotions. Their divorce had only been final three months. "Well, she is your father's girlfriend."

"She's his jump-off," Tara corrected. "You don't marry the side piece."

"He's not marrying her." Billie shuddered at the thought. "At least not yet."

"He married you after you moved in," she countered. "Only I liked you. This stuck-up Barbie is not going to be my new stepmother."

Billie sighed. "Tara, I can't really tell you how to be with her. You know I'm compromised on this."

"You hate her," Tara said. "Just like me. She's selfish and stupid and had the nerve to try and tell me what to do this morning."

"You really need to talk to your father about this." Billie's instinct was to advise Tara to tell Claire to go fuck herself, but she knew that wasn't right. Tara didn't need to be put in the middle of this more than she already was. "You're gonna have to sit down and . . ."

"Billie?"

Billie didn't even need a second to recognize the voice of her ex-husband. Porter had a deep, mesmerizing voice that pulled at something inside her even when he was mad, like now.

"Billie," he repeated. "Is that you?"

"Yes it is." Billie could hear Tara complaining in the background. "Look, Porter, I was just—"

"You're not allowed to talk to my daughter without my permission!"

"Since when?" Billie asked.

"Since I said." His voice was cold and short. "You're not her stepmother anymore."

"But you know I love her and she loves me," Billie said. "We were just talking."

"You're trying to turn her against Claire," Porter accused. "And I'm not gonna let you do it."

He hung up before Billie could defend herself. Not that it would have made a difference. While he had promised to give Claire up once Billie found out, she knew he never had. And when she made it clear a divorce was what she wanted, he made it clear that Claire was what he wanted. Ever since, Billie saw only the ugly side of the man she used to love. He had humiliated her and betrayed her and now he was going to try to keep her from Tara, the closest thing she'd ever had to a child of her own.

Which made it all the more insane to Billie that she was still sleeping with him.

Perfect timing!

Erica Kent had both hands on her curvy hips and a "don't-even-try-lying-to-me" look on her face as the front door to her Adams Morgan apartment slowly opened. In walked her boyfriend of four years, Terrell Nicolli, looking guilty as hell. She wasn't about to fall for that puppy-dog look in his dark eyes as he came toward her. He was looking good in blue jeans and a short-sleeve T-shirt that fit tight enough to show off the muscles under his light brown skin. He always looked good, but Erica was so mad, nothing was going to distract her.

"Baby." Terrell held his arms out as he approached but was stopped in his tracks as she held her hand up.

"Don't try that shit with me, Terrell." Erica could deceive many with her girl-next-door cuteness but she was not one to be trifled with. "It's eight in the morning. Where in the hell have you been?"

"You know I'm working the night shift," Terrell said as he bypassed her and went for the kitchen of their tiny two-bedroom apartment. He had hoped she would have left for work by now. "You leave me some breakfast or did that asshole brother of yours eat it all?"

"Your shift ended at six," Erica said, following him to the kitchen. "Why are you walking up in here two hours later?"

Terrell took a gulp of orange juice right out of the container before answering. "Why don't you just ask me what you want to ask me?"

"I already did!" Erica knew what he was talking about and she wasn't going to let him take it there. Yes, there was a part of her that suspected he was out hustling, but he had promised that was no longer a part of his life and she chose to believe him.

"I was making some extra money," Terrell said before adding, "and not hustling. It was honest money."

"Doing what?"

"One of my clients needed me to take him all the way to his house in Bethesda and then out to Dulles airport." Terrell approached Erica and leaned in to kiss her, but she backed away. That line wasn't exactly true, but baby girl didn't need to hear that it was his client's mistress instead of him. "He paid me two hundred fifty dollars, baby. Under the table."

Erica rolled her eyes at him, not sure what to say. She was supposed to believe him. She knew Terrell loved her, but she also knew Terrell lied to her. When they met, they were both only twenty-one, and while Terrell was hustling to get by, Erica had to work two jobs to support herself and her younger brother, Nate. Their father had never been in the picture and when their mother died of cancer, Erica was only nineteen and Nate was twelve. Erica was young and easily impressed by the money Terrell flashed in front of her. He was cute and charming and treated her better than any man ever had.

But like a lot of women, as you mature, you can grow less impressed by what used to turn you on. It wasn't okay anymore that he was hustling. She needed Terrell to get his life together and that meant an honest job and helping her look after Nate. Terrell loved her enough to make that change, but he slipped up now and then. However, for a few years he'd had a job as a driver for Destin, a local limo company, and looked to be on the straight and narrow. With her secretarial position at the Defense Department, they were making a respectable living. She shouldn't complain.

"Why you gotta be so suspicious all the time?" Terrell asked. "I just paid our cable and electric bill in less than two hours."

"Is that the truth?" Erica asked. She couldn't help herself.

"Baby." Terrell slid close, this time wrapping his arms around her. He leaned in and kissed her on her full lips. "You know I would never do anything to lose you."

Erica felt herself soften and heat up at the same time. Even after all these years, she loved how it felt to have her body pressed against his. He was strong and powerful and when he kissed her, he could really get her going. She had to be more trusting in him. He was her man, the only man for her. Even though her friends disapproved and said he was too "street," Erica knew that Terrell was good and, more important, he was good to her.

"I'm taking you out tonight," Terrell said as his mouth

lowered to her neck, kissing her softly, loving the taste of her and the smell of her, so sweet and soft.

Erica's eyes closed as she soaked it in. "You have to work."

"My shift don't start till ten." He tugged at her shirt until it was out of her skirt. His strong hands slid up her waist. He was already getting hard. "I'm taking you somewhere nice."

"We can't afford . . ."

He covered her mouth with his as his hands cupped her large breast. Erica had real curves and that was what he loved about her. She never showed it off, but her body was crazy and Terrell couldn't get enough of it.

"Where is Nate?" he asked in a whisper.

"I have to go to work." Erica didn't even know why she said that. She knew she was going to make love to Terrell. They hardly ever saw each other, both of them working so hard. With only a few minutes alone, she knew what was about to happen and she couldn't wait.

He was caressing her breast aggressively now because he knew she liked it like that. Sometimes Erica wanted the soft romantic stuff, but most of the time she liked it a little rough and that was just another one of the things he loved about her. They could break some furniture if given half a chance.

"Where is he?" he asked.

"He spent the night at his girlfriend's place." Erica was tugging at Terrell's shirt, pulling him toward the sofa. "I . . . We should . . ."

His mouth took over hers again, and as their bodies fell to the sofa, they were furiously pulling at each other's clothes. Removing her bra, he was calling her baby as his mouth trailed from her neck down to her full breasts. He kissed them, licked them, and opened his mouth softly to take one in. Her body was wriggling beneath his as he tasted her and his tongue played with her belly button.

Her nails dug into his shoulders as he went lower. He

tugged at her panties with his teeth, pulling them down as she lifted her hips up. He finished pulling her panties off and positioned himself between her legs. Their lips connected again and Erica could feel how hard he was against the inside of her thighs. She reached down and took hold of him, stroking him gently at first, but harder and faster as she went along while he continued to kiss her face, lick her neck, and tug at her earlobe.

"You good, baby?" he whispered into her hair.

"Yes, baby."

She let out a moan as he entered her slowly and she took him all in. He was large and her body had to adjust to his size every time, but the pain was sweet and enticing. She loved him and wanted every piece of him.

The Executive Office Building, the famous French Empire–styled building located next to the White House, was occupied by most of the employees of the West Wing, the executive offices of the president. Sherise had worked there as assistant director of communications for the Domestic Policy Council for a year before taking her maternity leave. Her journey leading to this position was untraditional and defied most logic. Positions at this level were rare, sought by people with long-held connections and ties.

Sherise had been working her way toward the West Wing as long as she could remember. As a young girl, the only time she would see powerful people in suits anywhere near her neighborhood was when Capitol Hill, White House, or other government-related executives would venture in groups in search of some good soul food. She wanted to know where they'd come from. Her mother told her "Northwest" was where they came from. It was the other side of town and from the looks of those people, Sherise thought it was where she was supposed to be.

Always with her focus on getting to the other side of town, Sherise used her shrewd skills and smarts to spend as much time as possible over there. In high school, she found out about internship opportunities for Southeast kids and got herself one making copies at the Department of Agriculture. Making sure she outshined all the other students, even when she had to secretly sabotage them, she got a scholarship at the University of Maryland, interning every summer on Capitol Hill, referred to as The Hill. By the time she graduated from college, Sherise had made an impression on more than a few powerful people on both sides of the political spectrum so her fate wouldn't change even when administrations did. She had to sleep with one or two and blackmail was always a last resort, but she was well on her way.

Justin was the icing on the cake. As a former legislative assistant to two senators, Justin transitioned into lobbying and made a living by knowing everyone with decision-making power on The Hill. Sherise was always sure to make it seem as if she wasn't using him to get access, but he was smart and knew better. With every door that opened, Sherise was looking for the next door. Now at twenty-seven, she had maneuvered into a good position, in charge of a small team of people and making sure that her boss gave her credit for everything that went well, even if it wasn't her work.

But the power game of politics was brutal and while it was sort of a revolving door, if you stepped away, you might have a hard time coming back. That was if you weren't Sherise Robinson. She'd only been back at the office for a few hours but was already feeling her groove. She was barking orders to her staff, the women were looking envious, and the men were intrigued and intimidated—just as she liked it.

She was positioning pictures of Cady on her desk, just about ready to dig in to the new project file her boss had given her, when she heard a knock on the door.

"Come in." Sherise made sure to sound annoyed. That way anyone she didn't want to stay would already feel pressured to leave even before walking in.

Jessica Colvin, administrative assistant to the director of communications, and Sherise's boss, Walter Nappano, stepped inside. Jessica was one of the people Sherise walked a fine line with. She was the boss's admin, so she had to get in good with her, but she also had to assert her authority when it came to getting access to Walter, which was not easy considering Walter spent most of his time out of the office.

"A warning." Jessica helped herself to the seat across from Sherise's desk. She was a fifty-something plump woman with fiery red hair who wore a dress or a skirt every day because of her religion. She was easy to manipulate. Sherise had figured out that by just asking about Jessica's favorite grandchild, a girl named Peppa, she could get anything she needed out of Jessica.

"A warning for what?" Sherise sat up straight. Warnings were not what she wanted on her first day back.

"Your welcome back party was postponed till Wednesday."

"I didn't even know there was one," Sherise lied. She was not happy to hear this.

"Yeah, right." Jessica wasn't buying. "It was supposed to be today—a surprise. But Walter has news."

Sherise leaned forward with a wicked grin. "That you're going to tell me before he tells everyone else . . . ?"

"Consider it my welcome back present." Jessica smiled with accomplishment. "He's about to announce he's retiring."

Sherise gasped before managing to ask, "What for?" even though she didn't really care. She was already thinking about what this meant for her.

"He's taking a position with a private company," Jessica answered. "Money and all that. I'm going with him."

"Are you now?" Sherise asked, wondering why Walter had

never even hinted at a new job during their conversations while she was on leave. "How nice for you."

"He's not going to be leaving for three months," Jessica said. "So you'll have that much time."

"I'm sorry?" Sherise feigned confusion.

"I know you, Sherise. You've been eyeing his position since the first day you started your job."

Actually it was before that, but Sherise didn't need to share that bit. "Well, I *am* next in line."

"Technically."

Sherise knew what she was talking about. "I know this Toni person has been interloping in the department, but there is no way she—"

"There is a way for everything," Jessica interrupted. "And Toni Williams has been working Walter like crazy since you left. It's been six months, Sherise."

"I told you to let me know who was sidling up to him."

Sherise's staff had handled most of her work and Walter had taken on what was above their levels. Sherise wasn't at all worried about anyone on her staff outperforming her. But she had found out that, less than a month after she left, another department had half its budget cut and was loaning out its people who had a lot of time on their hands. Toni Williams, deputy communications director for that department, had stepped in, but Sherise had made sure to find out if she was doing too good a job. No one seemed particularly impressed. Sherise felt her job was safe.

"And I did," Jessica said, "but things have kind of changed."

"Like how?" Sherise asked. "Is she sleeping with him?"

"Oh God, no," Jessica said. "But in the last month, he seems to think the world of her. All I know is that same file Walter put on your desk this morning is also on hers."

Sherise had to admit that she hadn't been on top of things in the last month. She was dealing with weaning Cady off breast milk and the emotional strain of accepting she would be separated from her baby for most of the day. She took her eye off the ball.

"What has changed?"

"That I can't say," Jessica added. "He's not giving any reasons. I've tried to hint at it and it's not happening. He never takes the bait."

"Well, I'll get it out of him." Sherise could play Walter pretty well. He was a sucker for a pretty face and based on his reaction today, he was very happy to see her back. She would stroke his ego a bit and play the awed protégée and he would tell her anything she wanted to know.

This was an unexpected turn and Sherise was not happy about it. Her glee at an opportunity to take a step up was dampened by the surprise of some real competition. She'd been gone for six months and in a what-have-you-done-for-me-lately industry, Sherise could see where she had a disadvantage. However, her advantages were abundant and as soon as she could get little Miss Toni Williams out of her way, Sherise was going to be one step closer to an office in the West Wing.

"You gonna be okay?" Justin asked.

Billie turned to him with a smile. "This is my office?" Looking around the small, dark, cherrywood office with badly decorated shelves and dark rose red furniture, she noted that the only light seemed to be the single small window that offered a view of the back of another building.

After spending the morning with paperwork and other administrative annoyances, Justin had made his way from the lobbying division just one floor below within the same firm, retrieved Billie, and walked her to her office.

"*Your* office?" Justin laughed. "Used to be three to an office. You're actually lucky. You only share it with one other associate. Layoffs and all."

Billie shrugged. "I only had half a desk at the public defender's office. So I guess it's a step up."

"Hey, Billie." Justin stood in the doorway. "Give it a chance. You'd be surprised at how much you could like this."

"I intend to give it the best chance I can." Billie smiled appreciatively. "I know you put yourself out there to get me this job."

"It wasn't that hard," he said. "You're good. Besides, Sherise would've divorced me if I didn't help you out. She loves you like a sister."

"She is my sister," Billie said, meaning every word of it.

Justin sighed heavily. "Billie, can I just give you a warning?"

"Why do I feel like I'm gonna get a lot of those today?"

He smiled. "Porter."

"What about him?"

"They love him here."

Billie let out a sarcastic laugh. "Yes, I figured as much when they kept asking me about him during the interview process."

"He just got named one of the up-and-coming in commercial transaction law."

"But he works for the competition," Billie said. "I thought that made him evil."

Justin nodded. "Yes, but it also makes him a . . . possibility."

Billie felt ill in her stomach. "Porter would never consider coming here if I was here."

"And I'm sure they'd never try to hire him now that you're here," Justin said. "But you should know that you'll probably get questions about him even though everyone knows you're separated."

"Divorced," she corrected.

"You're here!"

Justin quickly stepped aside as a young brunette woman with large eyes, a friendly smile, who was dressed in a sharp gray suit shot into the office with her hand held out.

"I'm Callie Brewer," she said. "I'm the head paralegal on your team."

"Yes." Billie shook her hand. "I was told you would show me the ropes today."

"We have a pretty tight schedule," Callie said, turning to Justin. "So if you don't mind, Mr. Robinson."

"I'm way ahead of you," Justin said. "I've got to get back to my side of the house."

"Okay." Callie waved for Billie to follow her on her way out of the office.

Callie was already reading off the day's schedule when Billie, after waving good-bye to Justin, caught up with her. She named off all the people Billie was going to have to meet and the work they would be assigning to her. About seven people into the list, Billie had to cut her off.

"Wait a second," she said. "I'm meeting all these people today?"

"Absolutely," Callie answered.

"I'm meeting everyone at the firm on day one?"

Callie laughed. "You're so silly. Those are just the people in the White Collar Crime practice you didn't meet with during the interview process."

"This place is huge," Billie said. "It's easy to be intimidated."

Billie was surprised when Callie swung around to face her with a very serious, almost warning look on her face.

"But never, ever show it."

"What?" Billie asked.

"I'm gonna give you some advice," Callie said. "You didn't earn your ropes here, so the natives are gonna be watching you, waiting to pounce on any weakness. You're an outsider. They usually don't last long here."

"Is there anyone in particular out to get me?"

"They all are," Callie said nonchalantly all of sudden. "They think you're easy prey 'cause you came from a bleeding heart liberal public defender's office. This is cut-throat and they eat softies alive. Just so you know."

"Duly warned," Billie said. As disheartening as that news was, she had heard worse things about Big Law. She decided to see it as a challenge. As a black woman in the legal industry, she was already rare and knew that there were odds stacked against her, but there were plenty of people here who believed in her and she would pull on their support. As for those who didn't believe in her, they didn't know where she came from. She'd fought worse demons before the age of twelve.